RESURRECTION ENGINES

JIM MORTIMORE, JONATHAN GREEN,
ALAN K. BAKER, RACHEL E. POLLOCK,
ALISON LITTLEWOOD, SIMON BUCHER-JONES,
CAVAN SCOTT, KIM LAKIN-SMITH, ROLAND MOORE,
PAUL MAGRS, JULIET E. MCKENNA,
ADAM ROBERTS, PHILIP PALMER,
BRUCE TAYLOR, BRIAN HERBERT,
SCOTT HARRISON

EDITED BY SCOTT HARRISON

Proudly published by Snowbooks

Snowbooks Ltd
www.snowbooks.com

British Library Cataloguing in Publication Data.
A catalogue record for this book is available from the British Library.
Hardback ISBN13 9781907777684
First published 2012
Paperback / Softback ISBN13 9781907777844

CONTENTS

THE SOUL-EATERS OF RAVELOE

Alison Littlewood

It was the last day of the last month of the century, and the young were out New Yearing. Silas could hear them from his place by the boiler, where he sat soaking up the glow from its pulsing sides. He scowled, pulled down the hatch and scooped in coal. He had plenty of coal, rough and shining like black jewels; he didn't need more, certainly not the crumbs provided by the New Year bearers. Still, as if in defiance of his thoughts, he heard the sharp *tang* of metal against his door.

His frown deepened. He lived a distance outside Raveloe, on the rough land by the clinker pits: the New Yearers never came this far, and anyway, he didn't let them in, never let them in. He didn't like the young, their sharp high voices, their bright ways. His own face had settled to a dull patina, layered with micro-fine scratches. It had begun to stiffen, his fingers too, though he still worked the forge, still shaped his creations, so much more agile and flexible than the hands which formed them.

Tang. Tang. And then a shout: *Silas, you old devil. It's the century's end: show some spirit.*

He knew the voice, and he knew who it belonged to: Gadric of Red Forge, the walled edifice that occupied prime land at the heart of Raveloe, its earth so rich with minerals Silas could smell them as he passed by. He let a sour puff of steam escape his lips and rose to his feet, hearing his joints creak.

There were five of them, young and wealthy; he didn't know their names or their families, but he could see it in the clear jewels of their eyes, the opals and rubies set into their cheeks. Gadric stood behind them, half shadowed. *Old year out*, they said.

Old year out, New Year in
Please will you let
The little birds in.

Silas scowled. What did they mean by calling themselves birds? He had created his own birds often enough, bending over them, ruining his eyes and his hands, forming each feather from platinum, finishing them with gold, setting the combs and levers that would make them sing; yes, sing, so much finer than these privileged pups.

"Open the door, Silas," said Gadric. His tone was jovial, but the message was clear: *or else.*

Silas shoved the door wide with his foot. He needed the approval of Gadric, or at least his tolerance. Who else had the money to buy his creations? Not that it mattered now, not any more. All the same he edged aside and the young moved in, eyes agleam, heads turning this way then that, setting up a sharp high whine of excitement, spreading across the floor as though sectioning it between them.

"Tell them," said Gadric.

"Come in," said Silas needlessly, swivelling his head to stare at their backs. As one, they turned and looked at him, their eyes blank. One of them held out a small piece of coal; and something in Silas seized, making a sharp *clink* of discomfort.

The youngster turned and set down the coal by the boiler.

Silas' eyes shot to the hole in the wall. No one knew about the hole in the wall, though he supposed they must know it existed, or something like it, hidden deep in his home. Now he would have to find another hiding place.

The youngsters whirred their disapproval.

Silas moved to the wall and pressed on the panel to open it, tried to block their view as he reached in. When his hand withdrew it was holding a single perfect pearl: far too much, but there were other things inside more precious yet, and they were drawing closer; he didn't want them to see, and so he closed the panel, which blended seamlessly with the wall. He turned and thrust the pearl into their grasping hands.

"A fine gift," said Gadric. "You are to be thanked. You must have heard it to be my wedding day."

Silas gawped.

"I bound myself to Miss Nansee of Lanterton this very morning. I'm surprised you haven't heard." Gadric paused. "Or perhaps I shouldn't be."

"I live a quiet life."

"So you do. Well, I thank you for your good wishes."

"G – good wishes. I'm surprised you—" Silas peered down at the young. Really, his eyes were fading: he should do something about it, but there were other things to do, other calls on his time.

"But of course, I'm partaking in the New Year ceremonies – it is expected, is it not? It is a blessing on a new binding. Nansee and I can expect good fortune." He waved his hands over the youngster's heads. "We can expect many children."

Silas nodded. He went on nodding as he closed the door behind them, his neck setting up a soft *ee-ee-ee* sound. He thought of the space behind the panel in his wall and sighed. He thought of the youngster's bright blank eyes, staring at him without recognition or warmth, and he shuddered.

§

There was one bird left. Silas knew it as he worked, pressing fine filaments of living metal into its heart. There. It was finished: the metal began to pulse under his fingers, slow at first and then faster. Something that would live longer than he would, that would sing better than he ever had; something that would *live,* and take joy in living, and be as Silas had never been. He pored over the creature, breathing his life and spirit into it along with his heated breath.

After this, there would be no other. He was failing and he knew it: after this, there would be nothing left to give.

There were only the feathers still to add, and the adornments, and the jewels for its eyes. Silas had chosen them already; two clear emeralds without flaw or impurity to impede the passing of light through their substance.

§

The bird was finished. It flittered about his head, thrusting high trilling music into the air, forcing out the sound through its wide-open beak. Silas turned to watch it. The bird was his finest yet, its wings finely articulated, its feathers a bright flash. He looked down at the table spread with what remained of his jewels. He had earned them from the sale of his creations and he smiled over them. He felt their light on his face. They warmed it.

E – eee.

Silas frowned and looked at the bird. Its song continued, bright rills as clear as molten heart-metal. So where had that flat note come from?

E – eee.

It was coming from outside, from the clinker pits. Silas went to the door and looked out. At first he couldn't see anything at all; there was a blow today, and the air was filled with fine dead flakes of ash. He started to close the door when he heard it again, that same empty sound: *e – eee*, a sound with a catch in the middle like de-toothed cogs.

He looked back at the table, at the jewels. He remembered the youngsters looking around the room. No: he would not leave them, would not venture outside.

In the next moment the bird had flown past him with a flash of platinum and gold, into the burnt air.

Silas let out a hoot of rage and fear. He started after it, his feet loud against the loose powdery rock. Everything was colourless. He couldn't see the bird anywhere, but he heard it; its song was muffled, as though ash was getting into its voicebox, filling the mechanism. He hurried after, feeling his joints sticking.

There, amidst the grey, swathed in its shadows, was something else: something dark and slick and oozing. The bird was there too, the only bright thing he could see.

Silas went to it and, with much creaking, knelt. The thing on the ground was a child. Its form was crushed and broken, its metal darkened, flecked with rust-coloured ague. Thin red-black oil leaked from it, darkening the small round stones on which it lay.

Silas recognised it.

He had made it, Silas knew: Gadric of the Red Forge, but not with his precious Nansee of Lanterton, oh no: he had made this child with another, one too poor, with a grain too coarse to stand at his side. He had heard it spoken of in the village, and now here it was: something half-made and then abandoned. Gadric would have new young now. He didn't need this any longer.

Silas looked up, into the greyness. A short distance away was another wasted form: it was the child's mother.

Her body was broken. Clear heart-metal dampened the ground. Silas shook his head. Had she thrown herself into the pit, or been thrown? There was no way of telling. It was too late.

E – eee.

The sound was low and dull but it cut the air easily and Silas turned and looked at the child. He made a moue of revulsion. It was alive, but no life remained for it: there was nowhere it could go, no purpose: waste.

A moment later he had caught hold of the bird, spun on his heel and was heading back to his hearth.

§

The table was bare. Silas blinked over it, each flexing of his eyelids making an audible *ee –ee*, a little like the sound he'd heard earlier. He rested one hand on the surface, scraped it across the smooth metal. It was his eyes that were at fault, that were always at fault. He would feel them there, the living jewels, sense their heat on his skin.

They were not there.

Silas felt the pressure building inside him. He burst into motion, crossed the room and put his head inside the hiding place in the wall. It was empty. His jewels, the fruit of the work of his hands, were gone.

He tipped back his head and opened his mouth and vented his horror and his loss.

§

Silas dropped into the seat by the boiler, leaning against it, taking in its heat and its comforting murmur and rattle. He had been to the village to appeal to the citizens of Raveloe, but none had seen the thief, none heard who it might have been. They had shaken their heads in his face, one after the next, the monotonous motions so infuriating Silas could hardly bear it.

Now he turned to look at the thing he had brought from the pits, leaning dark and ugly against his silvery walls. He didn't know why he had done it, only that he had reached out for something to appease his loss, to fill the empty space. His jewels had gone, and this had come, so he had taken it for his own, this ruined, needless thing. He didn't want it. He didn't want to see it in his home, but couldn't muster the energy to put it out again.

At least he had the bird. It perched high on the piping that led from the boiler, up near the ceiling, as if it knew that Silas too was broken and wanted to distance itself from him.

Silas looked again at the ruin of a child. Its head hung loose, the metal creased and misshapen and powered with clinker. As he watched, it opened its blank eye sockets.

E – eee, it said.

§

Silas oiled the metal. He worked furiously, a creature in a dream, over and over, until he began to see a dull shine beneath the ague and the powdered rock. The detritus flaked over his hands: he didn't care, wasn't really thinking about anything at all. While he worked, the ache went away; while he stared at darkened metal, the vision of his jewels shining just beyond sight ceased to haunt him.

The sound came more quickly now and more often, those two syllables, *e – eee, e – eee*, the squeak and stop of a voice already worn out. When he thought of that, Silas felt a stab of excitement. No one made finer voices than him; he knew that from the bird which flew constantly around his head. He had been offered good money for the bird, but he could not sell it; the jewels it brought would not replace what he had lost, and anyway, it was the last beautiful thing he had made, something finer and nobler and purer than himself. The bird was his child. This other thing that had come to him – he did not know what it was. He only knew that it filled his days, his hours, his minutes, and made them bearable.

E – eee, it said.

"Eppie," Silas replied. He did not know if Gadric had ever given it a name, or the thing that had been its mother. Now it had a name: Silas had named it. *Eppie.*

§

The thing wheezed, sending pulses of warm moist heat into the air. Silas didn't help, just watched as it flexed its legs, stretched out its arms. It flailed, and its flails were like death throes. It grasped at the floor, fingers closing on nothing. *Wheeze. Clank.*

He heard metal crumbling. Perhaps it had been too late after all, his efforts wasted. And yet—

It set its curled fists against the floor, pushed itself to its knees. Then it paused, tilted its head, as though seeking for vision with its blind eye sockets. It sucked in air and pulsed out steam. It clicked and whirred. Slowly, it rose to its feet.

Silas stared, hardly daring to believe.

It stood. It was quite steady until it tried to take a step, then it wavered. The metal was too stiff; it needed to soften. Silas didn't want it to break, so he stepped forward and caught it as it fell. He laid it down in the corner and left it there. Still, pride pulsed through him. It was a broken thing and he had fixed it; *begun* to fix it. Next time it would do better.

§

Eppie walked ahead of Silas. At first she had grasped hold of everything she passed – the table, the cylinder, the sturdy side of the boiler. After a time she no longer needed to; she had found her balance. She felt her way, hands stretched out so that she didn't walk into things. After a while she had memorised the layout of the room.

The bird sang and Eppie chirruped back. Silas hadn't yet fixed her voice but she croaked her delight.

Now she found the door and felt around and turned the handle. Before Silas could stop her she was on the threshold. His joints were thickened by the work he had carried out and Eppie was growing more nimble by the day, more flexible from the silk-oil with which he treated her skin. When he reached her she was waving her hands in front of her face, feeling for the barrier that suddenly wasn't there any more. She stepped onto the path, coated with a fine layer of fallen ash. She shuffled her foot, tilted her head to one side, made a gurgling sound.

Silas froze in the aspect of reaching for her. Why not? She would need to go outside eventually, and anyway, he wanted to see what she would do.

He followed her along the path. He was so intent on her progress that at first he didn't notice where she was going; it was only when she led him to the very edge of the clinker pit that he realised. He wondered if she remembered – if she knew how Silas had found her. She made no sound, gave no indication. Instead she turned and began to walk, quite steadily, towards Raveloe.

The sounds of industry reached them as they passed the outer forges. There was the pulse of steam, the shunt and push of the engines, the bang and clash of iron presses. Everywhere was sound, and Eppie greeted it with silence, reaching out her hands as if she could catch it.

She walked on to the mines. There were figures gathered outside, squat and blackened from their work. She turned her face towards their hisses. The nearest creased his features into a grimace. Another spat thick black oil onto the ground. And Silas saw what they saw: an ageing, squint-eyed recluse, fit only for the scrapheap, and a small misshapen thing, teetering from one step to the next. He saw their disgust, their revulsion, their pity, and he knew that they were right; they *were* pitiful, but he did not care. He looked on Eppie and felt his heart would burst. He was filled with wild, uncontrollable pressure: these people did not *see*. Eppie had been ruined and now she walked. And he recognised this thing he felt as pride: pride in the skill of the work of his hands.

§

Silas was ready to give Eppie her voice. It had been ready a while, but it had almost been a year since he took her in, and it had seemed fitting to wait. The mechanism, he was sure, was perfect. The metal was not new – he had taken some of it from a panel on his own leg, which now wept and oozed. But the workmanship – despite his shortcomings, he had made each filament as fine as spun gold, each strand perfectly placed and pitched. He opened her throat and set it in position, trembling over the delicate work. Then he closed her up again. He could not tell what she was thinking: her dark eye sockets showed nothing.

She opened her mouth, made a dry wheeze. Again. Silas could hear the mechanism becoming lubricated, loosening. *Ahh,* she said, a high, airy sound.

The bird, sitting in the corner of the room, lifted its head.

Ahh-ah, she tried again. This time the bird answered with a sweet note. Eppie paused for the longest time, and then she began to sing.

Silas had heard the tune before, many times. It was the song the bird had sung over and over while he worked. *All the time*, he thought. *All the time, she was listening.*

The bird lifted into the air and swooped around her head, its notes blending and soaring, a virtuoso dancing around a rock. Eppie's voice failed and she reached out with her hands.

The bird flew into them.

"Eppie, no." Silas's voice was sharp. But she took no notice: her hands closed over the golden feathers.

"Eppie, bad. Let it go." Silas reached out, but it was too late: if he tried to grasp her fingers he would only close them tighter. "Eppie."

She bent her head over the thing she held. She made a gear-sound in the back of her throat. Silas realised she was crooning to the creature, speaking to it in a language Silas didn't know and couldn't understand. She loosed her fingers, released the bird's head: he saw, for a moment, its brilliant eyes.

Then it was free, and it flew up, sparking away from her. Eppie tipped back her head as if she could see it, gurgling louder, and she began once more to sing: this time a new song, her own song. Silas didn't know what it meant. He could only watch as Eppie blindly moved her head, following the movements of the bird around the room.

§

Silas groaned, a deep sound that rose from deep within, that shivered each part and made his limbs tremble. He tightened his grip on the spike, rested it against his knee. In his other hand he took up the hammer and struck hard, without hesitation, opening the joint.

Dark fluid spilled out, more viscous and paler in colour than it had been when he was young. He opened his mouth and spat out the taste of burnt gases.

The jewel was in the heart of the socket, still alive and pulsing, feeding his body with warmth. He eased tweezers into the space and grasped it. When he drew it out, it was easier; the joint quickly went cold. He sealed the wound and bent his leg and straightened it again. It didn't creak any longer; it clanked.

He had two of them now, matching diamonds, a little cloudy. He held one up to the light, saw the occlusions and the flaws. They were never meant for eyes, but they would have to do.

He called Eppie to him and she came. She had been singing, her own peculiar blend of musical tones and other sounds that were almost words. She stopped when he held the diamonds against her dark sockets. The jewels were too small, but he sealed them anyway, setting them firm.

Around their heads, the bird flashed and sang.

§

Eppie danced down the path, gurgling her pleasure. She often accompanied Silas into the village now, to gather supplies, or simply to enjoy the rich mineral air. Her limbs were looser, and the villagers did not laugh; none save the young, who stood in their finery and mocked her. Today there seemed to be none such around. It was a fine day, the pale grey sky deepening to a rich crimson on the horizon. The scent of smelting was on the air and Silas took it in deep, felt it fanning the heat inside him.

"Morning, Master Silas. Eppie." It was Mother Hopper, her face cheery and bright as hearthfire. Eppie waved and danced around her. She liked Mother Hopper. She had been one of the first to show her kindness.

Silas stopped and smiled too, opened his mouth to speak, when something darted out of the air, sending out snips of silvery sound almost on the edge of hearing.

Eppie squealed with delight and hastened after it.

"No, Eppie." Silas recognised the thing at once: he should, he had made it with his own hands.

"Now, Silas, it's all right. They often let it fly about. It amuses—"

But Silas pulled away, hurrying after Eppie. The thing she was following was a bird. He had made it some years ago, and he had sold it. The price had been two fine emeralds.

He was too late. She was ahead of him, heading past hearths and homes into the centre of Raveloe, but Silas already knew the place it would lead her: the place he was careful never to go. Up to the gate of the Red Forge she went, and then he saw the bird lead her away, around the side of the building. Silas followed, and he heard new sounds: shouts and whoops, different voices, but all with the same flat dead tone.

When he caught up with her, Eppie was standing quite still, her back to him. She was staring over the wall, into the rich garden at the back of the forge. Silas went to her side, started to pull her away, then he saw the things she saw.

They had eyes, looking back. Fine, expensive eyes. But their faces—

Eppie pulled away with a cry.

"Eppie, come away now." Silas's voice caught. He couldn't stop himself from looking at them. There were seven. They were well grown, younger and yet taller than Eppie, and finely formed. But the stench. The air was full of their rank odour, bitter and sweet, clinging to the tubes of Silas's throat.

"Come away." It was Mother Hopper. "They don't like you to look. They don't like people to see." She pulled on Silas's arm, but he didn't budge.

The children had flesh for faces. It was repulsive. They had their right bodies too, their true bodies, clean and gleaming; but they stank. Each released steam from their throats and Silas could hear the sizzle as it scorched the misplaced flesh, saw their skin shrink from the heat.

"Corpse-flesh," he whispered.

There were pieces of it on the ground, charred and broiled, fallen away. Silas thought of having to follow them, pick up such aberrant matter, and choked.

"They're all like that," said Mother Hopper. "The master and his wife – they tried so many times, but they come out wrong – some say it's because they're cursed, a cursed match that wouldn't burn." She tugged on Silas's arm and this time he moved, bringing Eppie with him.

"That – *stuff*," he said.

"They keep growing it. Dead stuff, coming out. I know, it's horrid. Come along, Eppie, that's a dear."

But Eppie pulled away. She had seen the bird flying in among the twisted shapes in the garden. She reached out, even though it had passed out of her reach. Not so the children. They moved together, closing in, and one of them let out a fat, wet sound as it caught it.

In the next moment, it had crammed the bird into its mouth. It chewed, crushing the thin feathers, the subtle mesh.

Eppie cried out.

"They're soul-eaters," said Mother Hopper. "They'll take anything bright and beautiful and whole and alive. They'll eat and eat, if they're able. They try to sustain themselves, but of course it doesn't work, doesn't take. They're never satisfied. They always crave what they can never truly possess: life. A soul."

Silas looked back over his shoulder as he guided Eppie away. Those blasphemous things – those *children* – were watching them, their faces without expression, their eyes a row of rich jewels trained on Silas, each one perfect and cold as a stone. And another, taller figure, who had emerged from a doorway at the back of the house: tall and keen-eyed, watching him leave along with the rest.

§

Later, Eppie sang to him. She sang in a low, sweet, sad voice, and he touched her head. He saw the back of his hand, veined and cracking, and he didn't care. Eppie glowed. She was supple, without adornment, her eyes a little cloudy, but still they shone with her own plain beauty. He remembered those monstrosities he had seen at the forge and shuddered.

Her voice, despite his efforts, was not as beautiful as the bird's, but her song had words in it that soothed him. He listened, and his heart swelled; then came a clanging at the door that made it jump painfully.

"I'll get it, father," Eppie said, and leapt to her feet. Silas gawped. *What* had she called him? The word was strange. He could not think how she had learnt it.

He turned to see her standing at the open door, looking at him. Behind her stood Gadric; next to him, a woman Silas didn't know. Gadric reached out and rested his hand on Eppie's shoulder. He smiled.

§

"She's mine, Silas," Gadric said. His voice was soft, so unlike the way Silas had last heard it he could hardly be sure it was the same man. "You know she is."

"I made her," Silas said. "I shaped her."

Eppie watched from the corner.

"You did, and you are to be applauded. You will be paid, Silas. You lost your money once." Gadric pulled a bag from his side and opened its mouth. Light spilled from it. "You will be paid well, with our thanks. But she belongs with us."

"With those – *things*?"

Gadric looked away. "They are all my children, Silas." He glanced at Eppie. "All of them."

Silas closed his eyes. When he felt a hand on his arm, he opened them again. It was Nansee, Gadric's wife. She looked at him with two clear sapphires. They were full of sympathy. "You may visit," she said in a soft voice, "Whenever you wish. But you are old, Silas. You are failing."

The words ate into him. Silas knew that she was right: he had been failing for many years.

"She is young, Silas. She needs us."

Silas felt the heat sapping from his body. It was true: he would fail and Eppie would be left alone. Slowly he nodded.

Nansee crossed the room to Eppie. She bent at her side. Silas looked at them together, Nansee's golden head next to

Eppie's plain steel. Nansee's skin was studded with living rubies and emeralds, far finer than Silas could ever afford.

"Come, child," Nansee said.

Eppie opened her mouth and let out an ear-bursting shriek.

§

Later they sat by the hearth together, sharing its warmth. Silas kept nodding, then opening his eyes wide to look at her: she would smile back again, as if to say that yes, she was still here.

Gadric and Nansee had been forced to leave by her shrieking. Silas thought of it now and his heart glowed. And yet – she could have had anything. *Everything.*

"Wait here," he said.

The golden bird was sitting on the table, its wingtips just touching the surface. It didn't make a sound when Silas picked it up.

"What is it, father?"

"It's time," he said. "I know now – just wait, Eppie."

He went to the corner and picked something up. It shone in the half-light. The bird was silent. Silas handled it carefully. There was no need for it to be ruined. He held its body, his fingers gripping around the neck. He held the spike tightly in his other hand and set it to the place.

"Father, no."

Silas merely nodded.

"Please don't."

Silas looked at her face. Her eyes were at once shining and dull. No matter how brightly her spirit shone through them, they would always be clouded. The diamonds were poor next to the bird's clear emerald. He took aim once more, the spike screeching against metal. The bird let out a pitiful sound.

Silas remembered making the bird, the hours he had spent forming each filament of every feather, setting the stones in place, so many of them. He had wanted it to be perfect. It *had* been perfect. And then his jewels had gone and she had come to him, and how he had worked: so long, so hard. He remembered the way she first stood, balancing on those ruined legs. The time he had spent scraping and shaping, adjusting and mending, until she had become beautiful. Beautiful, yes. But not *perfect*.

Now he was ready. He slipped the tool into the groove he had made; and he felt her pulling on his arm. He slipped, scoring a nasty scratch across his hand. He opened his fingers and in the next instant the bird had flown, crying out in panic.

Eppie ran after it, but couldn't reach it. And then she was standing by the door, her eyes flashing. "It's not enough," she said. "Is it?" And she turned the handle.

§

The bird was gone, and Eppie with it. Silas followed, huffing and clanking, but could not keep up. She was following the bird, her arms still outstretched to catch it, but its flight was fast and erratic, panicked and riddled with shrill, unpleasant sounds.

It headed away, through the village, swooping and soaring. Silas was barely conscious of where it led, but he saw the mines, the surprised faces of the workers. He didn't care. *Eppie*, he tried to say, but he couldn't catch his breath: it came out wrong. *E – eee.*

She went on, and at last, Silas recognised the place. He tried to straighten, let out a low groan. Then he followed. There was nothing else to do.

The bird sat on the wall that ran around the edge of a fine garden. In the garden, children were gathered. They didn't move. There was something wrong with them.

Eppie reached out her hands, calling for the bird. The children, as one, turned their heads towards her. Silas saw them. He saw the bird cock its head on one side, listening to them, watching with its beautiful eyes.

"Eppie," he mouthed.

She was motionless. Then, smoothly, she edged towards his creation, reaching for the golden feathers. Silas realised he was still carrying the spike in his hand; he let it fall. The bird started at the sound then rose, rapidly flapping its wings, setting up a high *whirr – whirr – whirr*. It rose beyond Eppie, out of reach: over the wall and into the garden.

Silas heard a pulse of excitement rising from seven throats. He could smell them now, sense their ruin. Surely the bird would not go into such a dying stink: and yet it did. It swooped in amongst them, and they opened their arms and welcomed it in.

Eppie let out a piercing sound. In the next moment she had scrambled onto the wall, was on the other side. She strode towards them, Gadric's cruel children, swiping at their hands, trying to release the bird. It let out a single futile note.

Silas's mouth moved. She would be safe, he thought. What had Mother Hopper said? *They're soul-eaters. They'll take anything bright and beautiful and whole and alive.* They would crave golden feathers, platinum wire, pulsing green eyes: Eppie would be safe. They could never desire her base dull metal.

One monstrous child stepped forward. It had golden feathers clutched between its fingers, dripping with the flesh that was melting from its hand. It looked at Eppie and smiled. Then its hand opened and the bird flew up, catching the light from the sun.

The child's eyes snapped back to Eppie.

No, mouthed Silas. He scrambled at the wall, but couldn't pull himself up: Nansee had been right, his old limbs were failing, and he *had* failed. At the last, he had failed.

The children closed in around Eppie, their hands grasping, pulling her down, pulling her under, and the abominations closed over her head. There was one bright scream, sharp and pure, and then there was nothing.

§

When Silas came to himself he was sitting on the ground by the wall and the bird was next to his hand. He twitched one finger and the bird stepped onto his palm. It wasn't looking at him. Its feathers looked whole, not crushed or malformed by its ordeal. The work of his hands, the finest he had ever produced: beautiful. Whole. Alive.

His throat hitched. It was perfect, but it was not enough.

In the next moment he had closed his fingers and crushed it, feeling its structure crack, the bellows that were its lungs crumpling in his hand, the tiny furnace of its heart searing his skin before fading into the clear air.

He let what remained fall to the ground. He closed his eyes. He could see Eppie. She was standing by the door, the dull diamonds of her eyes flashing, her fingers wrapped around the handle.

It's not enough. Is it?

Silas didn't move. He could hear the children on the other side of the wall, the dead sounds of their monstrous games. He found he was listening for a familiar voice, but it did not come. He felt the cold ground aching into his joints. After a time he tried to flex his fingers and found he could not. It didn't matter.

He did not open his eyes but he sensed the light draining from the sky as night fell. Still he did not move, was no longer sure he *could* move. All of his joints felt frozen. Now there was silence on the other side of the wall. Cold air began to move across his skin. He opened his eyes and saw that soft flakes of ash were floating out of the dark, drifting this way and that, covering the world with their greyness. He let them fall, let them settle on his face. He opened his mouth, their burnt taste on his tongue, and slowly, slowly, tilted his head back: closed his eyes once more as he allowed them to fill his throat.

A Journey to the Centre of the Moon

Alan K. Baker

1

THE IMPOSSIBLE METEORITE

I suppose I should have realised that something was wrong the moment I entered my uncle Otto Lidenbrock's house in Königstrasse. My darling wife Gräuben and I had received an invitation to lunch at his snug little home in the middle of Hamburg's old quarter, which until recently she and I had shared with him. Since we had no particular plans for that Sunday, we readily accepted.

In the six months following our return from the fantastic expedition to the centre of the earth, Professor Lidenbrock had become world famous, the toast of a scientific community that made ceaseless requests for his time as a speaker and contributor to all manner of projects and journals. It was therefore rare that we had a chance to meet, and both Gräuben and I never missed an opportunity to spend some time with him.

The front door was opened for us by Martha, Uncle Otto's faithful old housekeeper. The frightened expression on her face took us both by surprise.

'Why, Martha!' I exclaimed. 'Whatever is the matter? You look like you've seen a ghost!'

'Oh no, Mr Axel,' she replied as she took my hat and cane, 'It's the Professor! He's...'

She was interrupted by a shout from within the house. 'Martha! Is that my nephew? Show him into my study at once!'

With a glance at Gräuben, who seemed a little hurt at having been so completely unacknowledged by her godfather, I shrugged, took Martha's hand and gave it a reassuring pat. 'Don't worry, I'll see myself to the study.' And then, turning to Gräuben, I added: 'Why don't you wait for us in the dining room, my dear? I'm sure we won't be long.'

Gräuben sighed and shook her head, but did as I suggested. She was well acquainted with Professor Lidenbrock's tendency to disregard anything and anyone not directly connected to whichever matter was claiming his interest at any given moment. She went towards the dining room while Martha hurried back to the kitchen, doubtless to finish preparing our lunch.

I found Uncle Otto pacing back and forth in his study, his hands clasped behind his back, his face set in a frown of intense concentration. Tall and thin, with a blade-like nose and piercing eyes, he looked like some curious flightless bird examining the floor in the hope of finding a tasty morsel. He stopped when he saw me enter. 'Axel, my boy, I had considered myself blessed to make one monumental discovery in my life, but it appears I have now made two!'

'I'm very glad to hear it, Uncle,' I replied, 'but why has it got Martha in such a panic?'

He waved aside the question with a snort. 'Never mind Martha; she's always in a panic about something. Come and look at this.'

He beckoned me over to his desk, which as usual was strewn with papers and all manner of mineralogical samples. Nestling amongst the clutter on his desk was a large, irregularly-shaped block of stone, whose pockmarked surface was tinged with pale olive-green, and which he indicated with his outstretched hands in the manner of a stage magician revealing some clever trick.

'What do you think this is?' he asked.

I shrugged, and replied: 'It looks like basalt.'

'Very good ... and where do you think it came from?'

I glanced at my uncle, and noted the keenness of his expression, the glint of excitement in his eyes, which were magnified by his huge spectacles, and I felt the sudden conviction that whatever answer I gave him would be incorrect.

'It could have come from anywhere in the world,' I replied.

'Ha!' he exclaimed loudly and triumphantly. 'There you are wrong: this sample is most definitely *not* terrestrial. I have analysed it and found the iron content to be far higher than in any terrestrial basalt. It also contains a higher proportion of titanium-iron oxide than any basalt found on earth.'

I shrugged again, feeling somewhat at a loss. 'Well then, in that case where *did* it come from?'

My uncle gave me a broad smile. 'I believe, my dear Axel, that it came from the Moon.'

I looked at him blankly. 'From the Moon?'

Uncle Otto gave a vigorous nod.

'How did it get here?'

'Don't be obtuse, boy!' he said in an exasperated tone. 'Lunar meteorites are pieces of the Moon which have been launched from it by impacts from space. Most are flung off into the depths of the Solar System, but some are captured by the Earth's gravitation and fall to the surface. This sample is part of a meteorite which fell to Earth some time ago and which was recently discovered in the desert wastes of the Rub' al Khali in Arabia. It's part of a collection which I purchased not long ago – although I had no idea that it included such an inestimable treasure as this.'

'What do you mean you had no idea? Surely this piece was listed in the catalogue...'

'Ah! You misunderstand, although that's not your fault, since I have yet to make you aware of the exact *nature* of the treasure.'

'Uncle Otto,' I sighed. 'You're speaking in riddles. I'm hungry and Gräuben is waiting for us in the dining room. Would you mind awfully if we continued this conversation over lunch?'

'Lunch? Pah! Who can think of lunch at a time like this?'

'I thought that was why you invited us,' I said.

'*This* is why I invited you, Axel,' Uncle Otto declared.

'To look at a lump of rock from the Moon?'

He grinned at me. 'Not quite. It isn't the *exterior* of the sample that's of such paramount interest to us ... it's the *interior*.' As he bent over the rock fragment, he continued: 'When I first took it from its packing case, it broke in two. Initially, I assumed it had split along a natural fracture line ... but how wrong I was! Look...'

He took hold of the meteorite, which was about fifteen centimetres across, and gently prized it apart along a line of separation, which I confess I had not noticed until then. He then laid the two halves side by side and stepped back.

I leaned forward to examine the interior of the meteorite and took a single gasp.

The interior was almost perfectly flat and smooth, and contained what could only be described as a meticulously carved inscription.

'This is impossible!' I stammered. 'Either this is not what it appears to be, or this rock sample is not, in fact, a meteorite.'

'Do you think I don't know my business, boy?' growled Uncle Otto.

I sighed and offered him an apology. Professor Otto Lidenbrock was, after all, one of the most highly respected mineralogists in the world. There was precious little he didn't know about the geology of the Earth, and I believe it would be fair to say that what he didn't know, no one else did either.

I leaned forward and examined the interior surface of the meteorite. Uncle Otto pressed a magnifying glass into my hand, which I passed slowly over the inscription. It was composed of ten lines of characters, each about a centimetre high, which appeared to have been deeply and expertly incised into the rock. They were not in any language or alphabet known to me, and I shuddered slightly as I took in the strange angles and bizarre curves of which they were composed.

'I suppose it would be foolish to ask if you recognise the language,' I said.

'Yes, it would,' Uncle Otto replied laconically.

'Astounding!' I said in barely more than a whisper. 'But what can it *mean*?'

'The inscription, or the fact that it comes from the Moon?' said Uncle Otto.

'Both,' I replied, handing the magnifying glass back to him.

Uncle Otto chuckled. 'I think you already suspect the answer to the latter question. It means that the Moon was – and perhaps still is – home to intelligent life. As to the former, the meaning of the inscription itself ... well, it would appear that there is only one way to find out.'

'And what is that? I mean ... this isn't like the Saknussemm parchment, which at least was composed in a known language. I can see no conceivable way in which it might be translated.'

Uncle Otto grinned at me in a way that made my heart sink. He leaned forward and placed a hand on my shoulder as he replied: 'Not unless we seek out those who carved it.'

2
The Castle of Ortenberg

Two days later, I was sitting beside Uncle Otto in a four-wheeled carriage clattering along a road that wound through the Kinzig Valley near Offenburg in the midst of the Black Forest. On each side of us vast swathes of conifers spread to the horizon, covering the mountainous landscape in a thick carpet of silent green spires. The sinister beauty of the forest had always held a powerful fascination for me and I recalled how the Romans had so named it because even bright sunlight failed to penetrate its depths.

We had travelled by train from Hamburg to Offenburg, changing at Frankfurt, and for the entirety of the journey I had thought only of Gräuben and the troubled and incredulous expression that had spread upon her face when Uncle Otto insisted that I accompany him on this bizarre journey. I had taken her aside, and confided to her what I believed to be the truth: that Uncle Otto was suffering some strange delusion. A piece of rock containing an inscription born of intelligent minds could not possibly have come from the Moon, and my uncle's unshakable confidence in his outlandish hypothesis caused me no small concern. I had managed to coax an agreement from Gräuben that I would accompany him to the Castle of Ortenberg, which was, he claimed, the home of a brilliant inventor who had contrived a means of flying to the Moon. I did not believe it for one moment, of course, but I owed it to my uncle to be with him while his strange fantasy played itself out. Then, once the edifice of delusion had come crashing down, I would take him back to Hamburg, where I would make arrangements for him to see an alienist who might discover the cause of his mental malaise. Personally, I believed that the likeliest explanation was overwork, but we would leave the diagnosis to the professionals.

Gräuben had seen the logic in what I proposed, and had agreed, albeit with some reluctance, to my accompanying Uncle Otto to the Castle of Ortenberg, where we were to be the guests of the owner, Baron Cornelius von Schellenberg.

During our journey from Hamburg, Uncle Otto described to me how he had struck up a correspondence with the Baron following our return from the inner realms of the earth. Our expedition had made us famous throughout the world, and von Schellenberg was one of the many men of science who had sought to make the acquaintance of the great Professor Lidenbrock and discuss the fantastic discoveries we had made. For his part, Uncle Otto had happily obliged and had exchanged a great deal of correspondence with the Baron, who, apparently, was also a quite brilliant chemist.

My first view of the Castle of Ortenberg came as some surprise, for its outline did not call to mind German architecture at all, but rather that of England or France. I was reminded somewhat of the Château de Vincennes near Paris, although Ortenberg was altogether darker in aspect, being constructed of rich, red-ochre stone. The central keep rose from the top of a low hill and was bounded at its corners by four elegant but sturdy towers. It was an impressive sight, and I confess that, in spite of my trepidation regarding my uncle's mental state, I found myself looking forward to visiting the castle and making the acquaintance of its owner, if only briefly.

We were admitted by an ageing but immaculately liveried manservant, who led us through the grand entrance hall to a large and sumptuously appointed drawing room, where Baron Cornelius von Schellenberg was waiting for us. Our host certainly cut an impressive figure. He was tall and of a slim but evidently athletic build; his bearded jaw was firm and square and his blue eyes shone with intelligence and vitality.

'Professor Lidenbrock,' he said in a rich, melodious voice, 'it's a great pleasure finally to meet you in person.'

Uncle Otto stepped forward and took his outstretched hand in a firm grip. 'And for me also, Baron.' With a flick of his head, he added: 'This is my nephew, Axel.'

'Ah! The gentleman who accompanied you on your astonishing expedition to the centre of the earth. I am delighted to meet you both and I welcome you to my home. Please, have a seat.' Von Schellenberg indicated three exquisitely carved and beautifully upholstered armchairs, which had been placed before the hearth.

'I must thank you for agreeing to receive us, Baron,' said the Professor as he took a seat and placed the leather valise which he had been carrying on the floor beside him.

Von Schellenberg gave a smile and a shrug. 'Your letter was intriguing to say the least, Professor Lidenbrock. "A discovery which may well change the course of human history" – that was how you described whatever it is you've found I must admit, though, that I was rather perplexed at your reluctance to go into details.'

'I believe you will understand the need for discretion when you see it for yourself.' My uncle replied.

'Then you have brought it with you?' The Baron's gaze fell upon the valise at Uncle Otto's feet.

At that moment, the elderly manservant entered bearing a tray containing three glasses and a decanter of wine, which he placed on a table nearby.

'Thank you, Friedrich,' said von Schellenberg.

The manservant bowed and tottered out of the room, while von Schellenberg poured each of us a glass of quite excellent dry white wine.

'Yes, I have it.' The Professor opened the valise and carefully withdrew the meteorite.

'Bring it to the table here,' said the Baron, pushing aside the tray of wine.

The Professor briefly described how he had come upon the meteorite, as well as his belief regarding its origin, and then pulled apart the two halves, just as he had done for me.

Baron von Schellenberg examined the inscription in silence for a full minute. Presently, he said in a low voice: 'Now I understand why you think discretion is of such importance.'

'I am fortunate to have many admirers in the world of science,' Professor Lidenbrock replied, 'but I also have many envious rivals who would like nothing more than to exploit this discovery in my stead.'

The Baron turned to face him. 'Exploit?'

My uncle returned von Schellenberg's questioning gaze. 'It is my intention,' he said, 'to travel to the Moon and seek out the beings who created this artefact.'

'But astronomers have pronounced the Moon to be a dead world,' the Baron rejoined. 'Do you really think it is home to intelligent creatures?'

The Professor pointed to the inscription on the rock. 'This proves that it was once so, and perhaps still is. This is the reason why I have come to you, Baron von Schellenberg, for you are the only man in the world who is capable of travelling there.'

Our host smiled and nodded. 'You are referring, of course, to my Æther Ship.'

'Have you tested the craft?' asked Uncle Otto.

'Yes, once, and it performed perfectly. Would you believe me if I told you that I have flown around the world at an altitude of two hundred kilometres in a little over one hour?'

'One hour?' I echoed, aghast. 'Two hundred kilometres up?'

'It sounds utterly fantastic, doesn't it?' said the Baron. 'But I assure you it's quite true.'

'So the æther-resistant coating on the propellers works,' said the Professor.

'It has taken more than ten years to arrive at the correct formula, the correct proportion of elements,' replied von Schellenberg, 'but yes, finally I have succeeded in producing a substance which is capable of direct physical interaction with the rarefied substance of the Luminiferous Æther which fills interplanetary space. When applied to the airfoils of a propeller, this substance, which I have taken the liberty of naming "Schellenite", allows the device to perform the same function as within the dense atmosphere of earth, by which I mean that the rotation of the propeller creates a pressure difference between the forward and rear surfaces of the airfoils. My æther propeller therefore creates propulsive thrust in outer space.'

'Astonishing!' marvelled Professor Lidenbrock.

I, too, was impressed with the Baron's claims for his invention, but in a most fearful way. I had hoped and believed that von Schellenberg was a mere fantasist whose reputation was undeserved and whose claims far outran reality.

'Would you like to see the *Hermes*?' asked von Schellenberg.

'The what?' I stammered.

'It is the name I have given to my Æther Ship.'

'We should be honoured and delighted, Baron,' enthused Uncle Otto.

Our host gave us a broad smile. 'In that case, if you will follow me...'

We followed von Schellenberg out of the castle and into the grounds where, we discovered, he kept his laboratory and workshop in a quite enormous and solidly built wooden building, which stood about a hundred metres from the outer curtain wall.

The sight, which greeted us as we entered the vast space was stunning to behold. Standing (or perhaps I should say *floating*) at the centre of the workshop, tethered to the floor by several thick ropes, was an immense dirigible balloon. It was perhaps thirty metres in length, and upon its side was painted a beautiful crest, which I assumed to be that of the Schellenberg family. The gasbag appeared to have been heavily reinforced with steel rings and braces and from its stern two thick metal stanchions extended, at the ends of which were two large and powerful propeller engines.

'Magnificent!' said my uncle in a breathless whisper. 'Utterly magnificent!'

Baron von Schellenberg gave a brief bow.

'And with this stupendous vehicle,' continued the Professor, 'I take it you are planning to explore the Solar System?'

'Correct,' replied the Baron. 'Beginning, of course, with the Moon.'

The Professor turned to face him. 'You intend to go there first?'

'Of course. It is, after all, the closest celestial body to the earth; it's the logical choice for a proper test flight.'

My uncle sighed and said: 'In that case, Baron von Schellenberg, the time has come for me to ask the question I have travelled here to ask.' He hesitated, and then continued: 'Do you have room on the *Hermes* for two extra passengers?'

Two? I thought. *Oh dear Lord, no!*

Von Schellenberg stepped forward and offered Professor Lidenbrock his hand. 'It would be an honour, sir! I have no doubt that we are about to make history. The names Otto Lidenbrock and Cornelius von Schellenberg will live forever in the annals of human exploration!'

'Uncle Otto,' I said. 'I wonder if I might have a word with you in private.'

Von Schellenberg glanced at me, and with a smile of understanding walked away towards a large workbench.

'What is it, Axel?' asked my uncle with more than a trace of irritation.

'What is it?' I echoed incredulously. 'You are actually going through with this insane plan? Flying to the Moon in search of a hidden civilisation? What's more you intend that I should accompany you?'

'Why, certainly! It's the only chance we will ever have of proving that the Moon was once home to intelligent life – and perhaps still is. To turn away from this marvellous opportunity would be to set ourselves against every principle by which we have lived our lives; it would be a betrayal of science itself!'

I was about to tell my uncle that I would have no part in this madness. If he wanted to fly off into the great unknown of interplanetary space on this outlandish contraption that was his business and I would wish him the best of luck while fully expecting never to see him again.

But then my mind flew back to Hamburg and the days before Uncle Otto and I had departed on our expedition to the centre of the earth. I recalled Gräuben's reaction when I had met her on the Altona road and told her of his plans. My sweet Virlandaise had been filled with excitement and admiration for the great undertaking upon which we were about to embark. I recalled her words as clearly as if she had spoken them a minute ago: 'It is a good thing for a man to distinguish himself by some great enterprise.'

What would she say if I returned to her now, having abandoned my uncle to the strange journey upon which he had set every ounce of his resolution? I had no doubt that she would think me a coward, and a callous one at that, for a voyage into interplanetary space would be every bit as dangerous as the journey to the centre of the earth which we had undertaken. Probably a great deal more so.

My heart shuddered as I thought of the expression that would cloud Gräuben's face when I told her that Uncle Otto had embarked upon a voyage to the Moon, while I had decided to return to the safety of Hamburg! I sighed and shook my head, my misery complete. The undeniable fact was that I had no choice but to embark once again with Professor Otto Lidenbrock on an insane journey into the unknown. To prevent an estrangement from my adored wife, I would have to become estranged from the very earth itself!

3
OUR VOYAGE BEGINS

We left the following morning, departing from the world without fanfare – without the knowledge of any human soul other than Baron von Schellenberg's faithful old manservant, Friedrich. I questioned the Baron on this, since I had assumed that the launch of the *Hermes* would be attended by all manner of dignitaries, not to mention half of Europe's journalists.

The morning sky into which the *Hermes* lifted her graceful bulk was bright and cloudless. It was the beginning of another summer day for the rest of Germany – indeed for the rest of the world and every man, woman and child upon it. As I sat in a chair by one of the starboard portholes of the large gondola slung beneath the balloon, I thought of all their unknown lives, and how they were preparing to meet the mundane mystery of the new day's as yet unknown events. With a deep sigh of trepidation I reflected that no one on the entire planet could be feeling what I was feeling just then. The mystery, which Uncle Otto, Baron von Schellenberg and I were about to face, was of an entirely different order.

My uncle broke into my thoughts, the excitement in his voice only increasing my fear and misery. 'What do you think, Axel? Isn't it a magnificent sight? See how the world falls away, like a Christmas bauble dropped by a careless child! Offenburg is now no more than a blemish upon a great field of green. Look, we can see the Black Forest in its entirety!'

I nodded and forced a smile, and looked once again through the porthole. I began to regret partaking of the large and delicious breakfast of rye bread, cheese, ham and fruit which the Baron had prepared for us. Von Schellenberg had warned us against eating too much, but I had been hungry and had ignored his advice.

As the earth fell away from us completely and I regarded, with a mixture of horror and fascination, the coastal outline of Europe, I experienced a dreadful sensation, as if some ghostly hand were reaching into my body and wrenching my stomach upwards.

'We are leaving the gravitational field of earth!' called von Schellenberg over his shoulder. He was sitting in the pilot's seat at the front of the gondola, manipulating the vessel's bafflingly complex controls with the skill and finesse of a surgeon. 'Make certain that your magnetic boots are always in contact with the deck, otherwise you will embark on a little flight of your own!'

I reflected despairingly that my stomach had already done so, and I was immensely grateful for the waxed paper bag which Uncle Otto suddenly pressed into my hands, and which I used loudly and comprehensively.

Von Schellenberg glanced back at me and laughed. 'Poor Axel! I warned you about eating too much breakfast!'

Uncle Otto laughed also as he took the bag from my trembling hands and placed it in the waste receptacle which the Baron had shown us earlier. In abject misery, I wiped my mouth with my handkerchief and looked through the porthole once again. In the meantime, von Schellenberg had altered the attitude of the *Hermes*, so that I could see the earth's horizon – although it was like no horizon I had ever seen before. It was curved to a fantastic degree and beyond it the sky was blacker than any terrestrial night.

Good God! I thought. *We have left the earth as completely as if we were in our coffins!*

I turned away from the terrifying profundity of that black sky and looked around the passenger cabin instead. The *Hermes* had already been equipped for her Lunar voyage when Uncle Otto and I arrived at the castle, and so there had been no reason to delay our departure. The interior of the gondola had been designed with both comfort and practicality in mind. Although the floor was of bare metal, to allow unimpeded contact with the crew's magnetic boots, the rest of the cabin was as sumptuously furnished as any drawing room in Europe. The chairs on which we sat were upholstered in the finest Moroccan leather of a rich burgundy colour, and the instruments and gauges which were attached to the walls and bulkheads were fashioned from rich dark wood and polished brass.

The most unusual features of the cabin were undoubtedly the walls and ceiling, which were heavily padded and covered with velvet of the same hue as the chairs. Von Schellenberg had explained to us that this was to prevent concussive injury, should contact be lost with the metal floor. For my part, I considered it highly appropriate that this journey should be undertaken in what was, for all intents and purposes, a padded cell.

The rear of the cabin had been carefully and intelligently packed with all manner of equipment, most of which would have been instantly recognisable to anyone familiar with the practice of rock climbing and mountaineering. In fact, much of it was similar to that which Uncle Otto and I had used on our expedition to the centre of the earth.

Our equipment included an Eigel Centigrade thermometer; a manometer of compressed air to indicate the pressure of the Lunar atmosphere (if such even existed); a rather handsome-looking Vacheron & Constantin chronometer; two compasses, one for inclination, the other for declination (in case the Moon possessed a magnetic field); a night glass; and several electric-powered Ruhmkorff lanterns of the type the Professor and I had used on our subterranean journey.

Our provisions consisted of meat extract, biscuits, and an assortment of citrus fruits to offset the effects of our restricted diet, along with a large quantity of water sealed within airtight containers.

We also carried a comprehensively stocked medicine chest containing scissors, splints, linen, bandages and compresses, lint, dextrin, medical alcohol, liquid acetate of lead, ether and ammonia.

As I regarded this assemblage of equipment and supplies, I found myself in the paradoxical position of bemoaning their necessity while feeling profoundly glad of their presence.

Von Schellenberg assumed that its small size relative to the earth meant that the Moon possessed little or no atmosphere. He also had come to the conclusion that the atmospheric conditions (that is, pressure and composition) on the other planets of the Solar System were radically different to those on earth; and for this reason he had designed a suit which would protect the wearer from their environments.

In fact, he had made four of them: a primary suit and three backups, in case of malfunction. Since Uncle Otto and I were of a similar build to the Baron, he anticipated no difficulty in our using two of the spares. The suits were strapped to the rear bulkhead of the passenger cabin, and looked rather like deep-sea divers' suits, although of a far sturdier construction, and with bulky air tanks attached to their backs.

Once again my thoughts were interrupted by the Professor, who beckoned me across the cabin to the porthole at which he was sitting. 'Axel! Come and look at this.'

'I don't think I can, Uncle,' I replied.

'Nonsense! It will do you good to move around – it'll help you to get your space legs.'

I stood up and, with all the steadiness of a deep-sea diver staggering across an ocean floor in the midst of an underwater earthquake, tottered across the cabin to his seat.

'Look here,' said Uncle Otto. 'What a magnificent sight!'

Gazing through the porthole, I saw the earth now as no human being had ever seen it before. The sight of that gentle orb, luminous in the reflected light of the sun, of its sapphire oceans, its emerald forests and grasslands, its ochre deserts and snow-frosted mountains, of the clouds that partially veiled it ... all this made me want to weep with terror and joy.

All sense of my physical discomfort was swept from my mind as I watched the orb slowly diminish in the blackness. Glancing at my uncle, I saw that he, too, was profoundly affected, for the expression of wild excitement had gone from his face. He simply sat and watched, and thought...

For my part, I felt privileged to have been afforded this miraculous view of our planet; but my gratitude towards Baron von Schellenberg was tempered by the question that echoed through my mind:

Would we ever set foot on our world again?

WHAT WE SAW ON THE LUNAR SURFACE

For day after day, we sailed across the interplanetary void between our verdant home world and the mottled grey orb of the Moon. The twin engines of the *Hermes* performed admirably. Their Schellenite-coated propellers scythed the rarefied substance of the Luminiferous Æther, pushing us through the darkness at an astonishing speed while generating a sonorous hum, which gave the impression of strange life, as if the vessel were some enormous flying beast that was murmuring constantly to itself.

For my part, I was struck most by the profusion of stars that surrounded us; indeed I spent much of the voyage sitting at my window, gazing out at the dazzling firmament, unable to utter a single word, so profound was my astonishment. There are, of course, thousands of stars visible from the surface of the earth on a clear night, but that grand profusion was as nothing compared to the vast, glittering swathes of light that swept with staggering beauty across the limitless vault of interplanetary space. The sight was gorgeous and terrifying in equal measure, and for the first time in my life, I truly understood the meaning of cosmic infinity and my own negligible status therein.

We were grateful for the Æther Ship's chronometer, since the passage of time was as difficult to judge in the depths of space as in the depths of the earth. As we made our final approach to the Lunar orb, the instrument told us that a little over six days had passed. During that time, I had experienced a profound alteration in my attitude to our endeavour. My initial feelings of incredulity and fearful exasperation had given way to unbridled excitement at the stupendous ambition of our expedition – just as it had done during our journey to the centre of the earth. I now found myself eager to set foot on the strange, barren world that hung in the firmament before us and whose desolate surface was revealed in the most astonishing detail.

Uncle Otto gazed through his window and said, more to himself than to anyone else: 'I have looked at the Moon many times... but never did I imagine that it would look like this.'

I found myself in wholehearted agreement with him, for our close proximity, unimpeded by the distorting atmosphere of the earth, revealed such a profusion of complex structures and features that a geologist might happily spend several lifetimes examining them, without giving so much as a thought to the real reason we had come here.

'Look, Axel!' said my uncle suddenly. 'See how smooth and rounded the mountains are! Not at all what I would have expected.'

It was true, for the highlands surrounding the flat plains of the *maria* displayed none of the sharp crags and precipitous rock faces which astronomers had assumed would prevail. It was as if some celestial sculptor had taken a vast abrasive rubbing stone to the landscape, smoothing away every sharp edge. The result was a world of flowing lines and strange contours, painted in a thousand shades of grey, and pockmarked with countless craters of all sizes.

'Great God!' said Uncle Otto. 'What a pounding she has taken throughout her long life!'

I was about to respond, but at that moment von Schellenberg uttered a cry of shock and ordered us to join him at the controls. We made our way as quickly as we could to the front of the gondola and the forward observation windows through which the Baron was peering.

'What is it?' asked Uncle Otto. 'What do you see?'

'There!' von Schellenberg replied in a breathless whisper, indicating the direction with a jerk of his head, for his hands were still occupied with the vessel's controls.

We looked, and for a moment I refused to believe what I was seeing. I leaned forward and pressed my face against the window, only to recoil from the icy coldness of the glass.

'You were right, Uncle,' I said without taking my eyes from the scene below us. 'Great God in Heaven ... you were right!'

'I confess I'd had my doubts, in spite of the evidence you showed me, Professor Lidenbrock,' said von Schellenberg. 'But the truth is there before our eyes, and cannot be denied.'

The Professor said nothing; he merely stared down at the Lunar landscape, and the vast, strange thing that was walking across it.

5
THE WALKER ON THE MOON

The thing was comprised of four prehensile limbs, which appeared to have the wrinkled texture of an elephant's trunk. The limbs were pale grey in colour and connected at the centre by a roughly spherical 'body', which was without any discernible features. It moved with a bizarre gait, bouncing across the grey landscape in the manner of the arachnids known as harvestmen. We were still many tens of kilometres above the Lunar surface and the fact that we were able to see it in such detail meant that it had to be at least half a kilometre across.

My stomach had grown used to the weightlessness of space, but now, as I watched this colossal entity continue its leisurely stroll across the surface of the Moon, I felt it churning once again with a sickening trepidation more intense than any I had ever experienced.

'What is it?' I asked.

'I have no idea,' my uncle replied. 'But it seems to have both life and purpose...'

'Life and purpose,' echoed von Schellenberg. 'Lidenbrock, I would shake your hand and hug you like a brother, were it not for the fact that I must stay at the controls lest we crash into the Moon like a meteor!'

Uncle Otto laughed and gave the Baron a hearty slap on the back. 'Speaking of controls, can you follow the thing, and perhaps reduce our altitude?'

'Of course.' Von Schellenberg flipped switches and pulled leavers, and the *Hermes* began to sink towards the surface, taking us closer to the monstrous thing, whose size was becoming more and more apparent.

'I would advise against getting too close to it,' I said.

'Why?' said the Professor.

I noted the irritation in his voice as I replied: 'It may take exception to our presence. The *Hermes* is like a fly in comparison to it, and how many times have we been annoyed by flies, and swatted them out of existence?'

'Axel may be right, Professor,' said von Schellenberg. 'We have no idea as to this creature's nature or intentions, should it detect our presence; it may be prudent to keep out of reach of those limbs.'

Uncle Otto sighed and nodded. 'I suppose you're right. For now, let us content ourselves with seeing where it goes, for it's most certainly going *somewhere*.'

For the next hour, we followed the thing, keeping a respectful distance from it, as it walked across plains and negotiated low hills and escarpments and rills with a supernatural elegance. At no time did it diverge from the perfectly straight line of its course; nor did it give any indication of being aware of our presence, for which I was glad, for I had the unshakable conviction that we would be utterly undone should the thing take exception to us.

Presently, von Schellenberg pointed through the forward windows, saying: 'Look! It seems to be heading for that large crater.'

He was correct. The X-shaped monster increased its speed and in another few moments had disappeared from view inside the mouth of a vast crater that must have been at least five kilometres in diameter. I had assumed it to be an impact crater, like the countless others that dotted the grey landscape, but as von Schellenberg guided the *Hermes* over it, we saw that it was in fact nothing of the kind.

As I looked down into the impenetrable blackness of what was, apparently, a bottomless abyss, I felt a surge of dread. I'd had the same vertiginous feeling while looking down the throat of Sneffels, the extinct volcano in Iceland through which we had gained entry to the inner realms of the earth.

How far into the Moon's interior this vast abyss led we had no idea, but one thing was quite certain: we were looking into the mouth of an extinct volcano, into which a living denizen of the Moon had vanished. I was therefore not surprised in the least when Uncle Otto declared:

'We must follow it inside!'

Von Schellenberg glanced at him, and I saw the doubt in his face. 'Are you sure that's a good idea, Professor?' he asked.

'Why, of course it is!' he replied. 'Surely you are not telling me that your courage has left you, Baron, for I heartily refuse to believe it. This is what we have voyaged here to do. We have been given the perfect opportunity by our strange friend down there to study both it and its habitat, which is clearly in the Moon's interior. As explorers and men of science, our duty is quite plain.'

The Baron looked at me. I could do nothing but shrug my shoulders.

'Very well,' he sighed. 'You are, of course, absolutely right. Having come this far, we have little choice.'

He threw more switches and manipulated more levers, and the *Hermes* began to descend towards the gaping maw below.

6

INTO THE LUNAR INTERIOR

Memories of our perilous descent into Sneffels filled my mind as the Æther Ship sank below the Lunar surface into the vertical shaft of what Uncle Otto had declared would henceforth be known as the von Schellenberg Crater.

Since the forward windows at the pilot's position were angled downwards at 45 degrees, we were able to view both the X-shaped monster and the wall to which it clung for some considerable distance into the lightless depths of the shaft.

Von Schellenberg switched on the ship's powerful searchlights, which were mounted underneath the gondola. They revealed the shallow curve of a wall that was formed of grey volcanic basalt: a vertical landscape of jagged peaks and deep troughs that extended all around us, and across which the monster danced with the same unearthly elegance as it had displayed on the surface.

As we continued our descent, we became aware of other shapes moving upon the wall of the shaft – shapes which were identical to that of the monster. As we drew closer, we saw that they appeared to be filling holes in the side of the shaft with a thick, grey substance which they extruded from the ends of their limbs.

'What are they doing?' I asked.

'I would suggest,' replied the Professor, 'that they are performing repairs, maintaining the structural integrity of this section of the shaft. That is clearly one of their functions.'

'Then they are not alive at all,' said von Schellenberg, 'but rather, autonomous machines.'

'Perhaps they are both,' the Professor suggested. 'Perhaps the distinction between machine and animal is without meaning to the denizens of the Moon. At any rate, I believe I have hit upon a name for them, which is as good as any. I believe that from now on, we should refer to them as X-Drones.'

Von Schellenberg and I agreed with this nomenclature as we continued our descent in pursuit of the thing we had seen on the surface, and which moved past its fellows without hesitation or the slightest acknowledgement of their presence.

From an estimate of our speed and time elapsed on the ship's chronometer, we judged that we had descended approximately five kilometres when the appearance of the wall changed. What had been uneven grey basalt became, quite suddenly and without warning, perfectly smooth. The ship's searchlights played upon its surface, which appeared to be made of blue-tinged metal rather than grey rock.

'What do you make of this?' asked von Schellenberg.

'It's as I expected,' Uncle Otto replied.

The Baron glanced at him. 'As you *expected*?'

'Of course. We have long known from our telescopic observations that there is no sign of life on the Lunar surface; therefore, any civilisation must exist in the satellite's interior. And if that is the case, they must have constructed for themselves a vast network of artificial habitats. I would suggest that the shaft in which we are descending is not that of a volcano at all, but rather a consciously designed and constructed access-way. Or perhaps,' he added, 'it *was* once a volcanic chimney, but was adapted to the purposes of the Lunar civilisation.'

We continued on our downward course for another five kilometres or so, always maintaining our position just above the X-Drone, which continued to ignore us. Incredibly, it had as little trouble clinging to the smooth, sheer side of the metal shaft as it had on the irregular basalt of the upper reaches. In fact, it appeared to increase its speed, which prompted Professor Lidenbrock to request a greater speed in our own descent. Baron von Schellenberg complied without a word, but I could see the trepidation in his face. It was one which I shared, for who knew where this strange conduit might lead us?

The answer came after yet another five kilometres of descent, for the Baron suddenly pulled a lever, which curtailed our downward velocity somewhat.

'What are you doing?' demanded Uncle Otto.

'Look,' was the Baron's only reply.

We leaned forward and peered through the windows, and saw that the vertical shaft was coming to an end fifty metres or so below us.

The X-Drone climbed from the wall to the vast, circular floor of the shaft, which was made of the same blue-grey metal, and proceeded with its eerie dancing gait towards one of three gigantic arched openings spaced at equal distances around the wall. And then, in an astonishing display, it diminished in size, its four legs telescoping inwards and reducing their girth, while the central bulb of its 'body' also withered to a fraction of its former diameter. Thus reduced to a length of perhaps ten metres, the marvellous thing ambled through the opening and vanished.

'What now?' I asked. 'Should we continue to follow it?'

Uncle Otto's reply was predicable enough. 'Of course! Why, we don't even need to leave the *Hermes*: we can easily take her through that opening, which must be forty metres tall and as many wide. This place is constructed on such a scale that it may be some time before we are required to leave our vessel at all.'

This last comment gave me some comfort, for I did not relish the prospect of exploring this vast and unthinkably mysterious place on foot – the less so since it clearly contained more than one X-Drone, and perhaps their makers as well.

Von Schellenberg opened the throttles on the engines once again, and the *Hermes* moved forward through the opening and into a long and lightless tunnel. Our searchlights penetrated the darkness with ease, so that we were able to observe the progress of the X-Drone ahead.

For the next hour we proceeded thus, past the featureless walls of the tunnel, ever deeper into the heart of the Moon's mystery. I wondered how long we would maintain this strange, leisurely pursuit, for our resources were far from limitless, and we might continue as we were for days or weeks before coming upon anything other than darkness and smooth, inscrutable walls.

Uncle Otto would hear none of this. 'Patience, Axel!' he chided. 'This corridor leads somewhere, for otherwise, why build it?'

'The Professor is right,' said von Schellenberg, suddenly leaning forward in his pilot's seat and switching off the searchlights.

Instead of being plunged into darkness, we saw that the tunnel ahead was illuminated by a soft blue glow, which seemed to emanate from a brighter patch on the floor about a hundred metres in front of us. The X-Drone moved into this light, and seemed to vanish. At any rate, its form became indistinct, subsumed in the strange, soft lambency.

'Ahead, Baron,' whispered Uncle Otto. 'Ahead!'

The *Hermes* surged forward, and as we entered the light, we were able to observe its source.

We looked down, von Schellenberg, Uncle Otto and I, and as one we drew in our breath in awe and terror.

7

THE SECRET AT THE HEART OF THE MOON

It is with the utmost difficulty that I set down the feelings
I experienced upon seeing the source of the blue light.
They are as powerful and profound today as they were
at that moment when we three men from earth saw with
our own eyes the secret at the heart of the Moon. My grip
loosens on my pen, and my breath catches in my throat as
that impossible sight floods my awareness once again. It is
greatly to von Schellenberg's credit that he was able to keep
control of the *Hermes* in spite of the unutterable shock of
what we discovered, and thus to prevent us from whirling
to destruction. But his hands remained steady on the ship's
controls, even as his jaw dropped and his eyes widened in
disbelief.

As we entered the light, we saw that it did not emanate
from the floor of the tunnel, for there *was* no floor: it had
given way to an opening through which the *Hermes* moved
before its pilot could check its momentum. In the space of
a moment, we found ourselves within a cavern – although
the word 'cavern' is misleading, and does little justice to the
immensity into which we entered.

I took hold of the pilot's seat as I felt the sudden return
of the vertigo from which I had suffered prior to our journey

to the centre of the earth. I think I screamed – at any rate,
I seem to recall that someone did – whether it had been
myself or one of the others matters little.

What was inside this cavern, in combination with its
shape and the extent of its curvature, spoke eloquently of
its size. Indeed, there was no denying the fact, despite the
refusal of our minds to accept it.

The cavern was more than three thousand kilometres in
diameter, taking up virtually the entire interior of the Moon!

For how long we hung there, at the edge of that
incomprehensible space, I have no idea. The panoramic
windows around the pilot's position gave us an uninterrupted
view of the immensity and what it contained. Our attention
was seized first of all by the great sphere at its centre.
Clearly the result of conscious design and construction,
this colossal orb was perhaps five hundred kilometres in
diameter, and appeared to be connected to the inner surface
of the cavern by six vast girders or stanchions, each of
which was many tens of kilometres in thickness.

It was quite plain that the soft blue light that illuminated
the cavern, and which we had seen from the corridor through
which we had followed the X-Drone, was emanating from
the central sphere. It filled the internal void and fell upon
the surface of the cavern, revealing complex structures
and filament-like traceries that might have been cities and

interconnecting roads, but which were more likely objects that had no human equivalent, and thus no human name that could be applied to them.

Professor Lidenbrock was the first to speak. 'The implications of this are too astounding for the human mind to contain,' he said, 'and yet they are undeniable. The Moon ... is artificial!'

'A vessel,' said von Schellenberg. 'A vessel the size of a world ... designed and constructed with the purpose of travelling through space! But why is it here, in orbit around our earth?'

'I believe I know the answer,' my uncle replied.

Von Schellenberg and I regarded him in disbelief.

'How can you?' asked the Baron.

'Think about it! The Earth is blessed with the presence of this satellite: it is what has made life and civilisation possible. Unlike the other moons of the Solar System, ours is large in relation to the planet around which it orbits. Think of the obliquity of the ecliptic, the axial tilt of the earth at twenty-three-and-a-half degrees to the vertical, which gives rise to the seasons. However, there is a slight variation in this angle, a circular "wobble" that takes the axial tilt from 22.1 degrees to 24.5 degrees over a cycle of forty-one thousand years. The fact that the obliquity of the ecliptic has a variation of just 2.4 degrees is due to the presence of the Moon's steadying gravitational influence. Without it, the obliquity would have been much more severe: the seasons would have alternated between the unbearably hot and the intolerably frigid with great rapidity. We can see, therefore, that the life-bearing properties of our planet are, in no small measure, the result of the Moon's presence. Without it, complex life – including humanity – would not have been able to exist.'

Von Schellenberg and I paused to take this in, and then the Baron replied: 'So you are suggesting that at some unknown time in the distant past, someone or some*thing* saw the life-bearing potential of the young earth, and placed this gigantic vessel in orbit to ensure that life took hold and was able to thrive?'

'That is *precisely* what I am suggesting,' declared the Professor.

I am quite certain that my uncle's hypothesis would have engendered a lengthy debate, had it not been for what happened next. Glancing through the forward windows, I gasped and seized both the Professor's arm and the Baron's shoulder.

They both looked.

'Ah...' said the Professor.

The X-Drone which we had pursued from the Lunar surface was floating directly in front of the *Hermes*, as if regarding us.

8

THE CYLINDERS

For a long and uncomfortable moment, I wondered whether the thing was about to destroy us, just as white corpuscles destroy bacteria that have invaded the body. After all, the X-Drones appeared to perform maintenance duties, so why should they not defend the Moon against curious interlopers like ourselves?

My fears, though, were unfounded, for the thing performed a series of manoeuvres, which consisted of lengthy retreats followed by shorter approaches, which implied that it wished us to follow it. At least, that was the interpretation Professor Lidenbrock placed upon its strange behaviour, for he urged von Schellenberg to follow it once again.

The Baron complied and hesitantly guided the *Hermes* into the gargantuan internal cavity. As we proceeded, we became aware of other features of this strange realm, which we had not noticed hitherto. Scattered through the airless void of the cavity were great floating discs of blue-grey metal, which appeared to contain large buildings of obscure and unsettling design. There were cubes, spheres, ellipsoids and truncated cones attached to each other by thick pipes, which surely would have collapsed upon each other had they been placed in the higher gravity of earth.

It was towards one of these floating islands that the X-Drone led us, alighting in a plaza of sorts, which was dominated by a gigantic truncated cone. As we descended towards the plaza, we saw that the cone-shaped building, which was perhaps two hundred metres in height and nearly a hundred metres wide at its base, possessed an opening leading to the interior. Although large, the opening was not of sufficient size to admit the *Hermes*, so the Professor asked von Schellenberg to land the vessel upon the floor of the plaza.

'I take it you intend to go in there on foot,' said the Baron as he manipulated the controls of his craft.

'You are correct,' replied my uncle. 'It's quite evident that the X-Drone has intentionally guided us here. I must find out the reason.'

'I regret that I shall not be able to accompany you,' said von Schellenberg. 'There is nothing here to which the

Hermes might be tethered, so I shall have to remain onboard to prevent her from drifting away.'

Professor Lidenbrock gave a humourless chuckle. 'I was about to make the same suggestion, Baron. The last thing we want is to be stranded here.'

Since opening the gondola's exit hatch meant temporarily evacuating the air from the passenger cabin, we all climbed into the atmospheric suits. 'Are you ready, Axel?' asked the Professor when the operation had been completed.

I took a deep breath and replied: 'Yes, Uncle Otto, I'm ready.'

Von Schellenberg shook us both by the hand and wished us luck, before turning to a large wheel set into the bulkhead next to the hatch. He turned the wheel and there was a loud hiss, which gradually faded to silence as the cabin's air was sucked into the tanks. Then he opened the hatch and Uncle Otto and I floated down to the floor of the plaza.

There was gravity upon the great floating disc, but it was very weak, and it was only with great difficulty that we made our way towards the arched opening in the side of the cone-shaped building.

The X-Drone floated above us, clearly observing our progress. I was quite certain that Uncle Otto was correct and that the thing wanted us to see what was inside this vast and curious building. Perhaps we were about to meet those who had designed both it and the artificial world it inhabited. As this thought struck me, I confess that I felt a sudden surge of fear. Would they welcome us, or punish our presumptuousness with instant annihilation?

As we made our way through the doorway, we saw that the building was hollow, save for an ingeniously contrived ramp, which wound up the internal wall towards the ceiling far above. This ramp passed numerous objects, which appeared to be glass cylinders. The circular, tapering wall was completely filled with them. There must have been hundreds, if not thousands, and it was with the greatest alacrity that we approached the lowest section of the ramp, for the hue of the glass of which they were constructed did not allow us to view their contents from our initial vantage point.

Before we did so, however, we connected our helmets to each other by means of the long, flexible speaking tube, which would allow us to communicate.

As we approached the first and lowest cylinder, I felt my breath quicken. What did they contain? My mind, racing like an overheated engine, created all manner of speculations, the most plausible of which, I believed, was that the cylinders contained the builders of the Moon-vessel themselves, dreaming incomprehensible dreams in a millennia-long sleep which was about to be ended by creatures from the world they had helped to bear life. What would they say to us? Would they welcome us, gratified that their grand plan had born the precious fruit of intelligence and civilisation?

We drew up alongside the cylinder and looked into it. At first I didn't understand what I was seeing. I looked at Uncle Otto and saw through the visor of his helmet the same confusion that I felt.

He beckoned to me and together we ascended the ramp a little way and stopped before the second cylinder. We peered inside and saw that its contents were the same as the first. I don't know how many times we repeated this, moving up the ramp from cylinder to cylinder, but the result was always the same: the anthropoid shapes, the thick fur that covered them, their stooped posture, the simian features of their thick-browed faces ... it was the same every time, in every cylinder.

'Ape men,' said Uncle Otto.

'Yes,' I agreed, 'but what can this mean? It makes no sense! Ape men, stored like so much meat in a butcher's window, in this place, this fabulous vessel of space, which must have been constructed untold millions of years ago in God knows what region of the universe! *Why?*'

'Calm yourself, Axel,' said the Professor, looking up at the cylinders which rose above us in tier upon tier. 'I believe that the answer is plain enough, although I wonder if we will ever have the opportunity to confirm it by asking the builders of this place. Perhaps they are still here, down on the inner surface of the Moon. I suppose it matters little...'

'But what do you mean?' I cried. 'You say the answer is plain, but I can't see it.'

'I believe I am correct in my belief that the Moon was placed into orbit around the earth in order to stabilise its revolution and to maintain it so that life and intelligence would have a chance to appear and thrive.' He reached out and touched the surface of the cylinder before which we were standing. 'But now I understand that there is much more to it than that. Whoever built this Moon-vessel did much more than prepare the earth for intelligent life; they created that life as well! Look into these cylinders, Axel. Look upon the faces of your ancestors!'

9

A WARNING TO FUTURE MAN

Of our return journey to earth, I have little to say, beyond this:

Professor Lidenbrock and I stumbled from the cone-shaped building and rejoined the *Hermes*. Ignoring von Schellenberg's questions, the Professor instructed him to take us back the way we had come, back up to the Lunar surface and thence to our home world.

During the voyage, of course, he described to the Baron in detail what we had found, and his theory on what it meant. There would be time enough, he added, for future expeditions to the great vessel that had masqueraded for uncounted aeons as the natural satellite of earth. But for now, he wanted nothing more than to return home to give careful consideration to the implications of our discovery.

As I listened to my uncle speak, I sensed that there was something else weighing upon him, a great worry to which he had yet to give voice, and I asked him what it was.

'How well you know me, Axel my boy,' he replied with a sad and troubled smile. 'There *is* something that occurs to me, and it is indeed troubling in the extreme.'

'Then tell us what it is, uncle,' I urged.

'It is simply this: does it not strike you as strange that there should be so many of our ancestors still in that building, and perhaps other buildings as well, held inert, perhaps sleeping, or perhaps yet to live? Perhaps there are representatives of all earth life held within that great vessel ... but for what purpose?'

I shook my head, at a loss.

'I wonder if they are held there for a very *specific* purpose,' said my uncle. 'To replace us, should it become necessary to do so. I wonder if we, and the rest of humanity, are being observed even as we speak by *something* that, one day, may decide that it is time for a fresh beginning upon the earth. Or perhaps it is simply waiting for us to destroy ourselves through war or some other idiotic means, before seeding the world once more with the beginnings of intelligence.'

He gave that sad smile again and patted me on the back. 'We never did translate the inscription in that meteorite, did we? Or indeed find out precisely where it came from. I suspect that there were once many buildings on the Lunar surface, which were not as important as those inside, and which were therefore allowed to fall into ruin by the X-Drones. Perhaps it was thrust into space from one of them during an ancient impact. It matters little. What *does* matter is what we decide to do with our world and what will happen if we make the wrong decision.'

She-Who-Thinks-For-Herself

Juliet E. McKenna

A Tale of Modern Women in the Dark Continent

My beloved aunt, Phyllis Chartcris, has received none of the plaudits lavished on the laurel-garlanded herocs who explore the remote heart of Africa. The Royal Geographic Society might deign to acknowledge Mary Kingsley after the success of her publication, 'Travels in West Africa' but there is not one quarter-inch of a newspaper column recording my aunt's achievements.

Such injustice has galled me ever since my return from the trackless swamps of the upper Zambesi. However I was sworn to secrecy for reasons which this narrative will soon explain.

Now Mr H Rider Haggard has published the reminiscences of his Cambridge acquaintance sheltering beneath the pseudonym "Horace Holly". Consequently I am free to share my aunt's achievements with the world.

But I am outstripping my story's proper order. Our family's ties with the Cape Colony were first established by my grandfather's brothers, both mining engineers. When my brother Eustace took up a position with Lloyds Bank in Cape Town, I had recently concluded my studies at Somerville Hall in Oxford. I decided to go with him as his housekeeper but in hopes that this outpost of Empire might offer more opportunities for educated women than dismissing us as mere bluestockings.

I had no notion of how wondrously my hopes would be fulfilled.

Naturally I was mindful of following in Aunt Phyllis's footsteps. She had travelled out to marry a dear friend of one of her cousins, met when both young men returned home for their university education. Alas, her fiancé succumbed to malaria while she was on board ship. Declining to return to England, she joined her uncle's household as governess to his younger children.

Family lore relates that Phyllis found herself ill suited to such domesticity. When the ruins of Great Zimbabwe were discovered, she insisted on inspecting these wondrous remnants of lost civilisation for herself.

That was the last heard of her for over two decades. Now I am able to take up her story and a marvellous tale it is.

We established ourselves comfortably in the Cape. Eustace applied himself diligently to his trade while I kept house and we enjoyed such polite society as the colony offered. My brother's superior at the bank proved to be a keen historian of the region, eager to learn every detail of our family's dealings in Africa. After eighteen months of exemplary service from Eustace, he granted my brother an extended leave of absence to visit the long-lost cities of Mashonaland, fondly believing that we both shared his fascination with these primitive civilisations.

In truth, Eustace and I were resolved to search out any hint of our mysterious aunt's fate. What we found proved more astonishing than our most extravagant imagining.

Though our initial discoveries were not promising. On our arrival at the ruins, we discovered a score of pompous antiquarians engaged in debates as to whether the Queen of Sheba, the Phoenicians or the Arabs had erected these aedifices. None recalled our aunt or any mention of her by their predecessors.

Eustace and I broadened our enquiries; ensuring word of our quest was carried to the local tribes with the promise of modest reward for reliable information. Still, alas, no news was forthcoming.

We were ready to despair when a visitor sought out our tent. Major Tobias, formerly of the Royal Engineers, proved to be a bronzed, sharp-eyed Africa-hand fit for any adventure. Knowing this area and its peoples intimately, he had discovered several aged natives who recalled our aunt's arrival with convincing detail.

Major Tobias escorted us to their humble, hospitable encampment. These brethren, more courteous than any London clubmen for all their animal hide garments, told us that Aunt Phyllis had indeed been visiting Great Zimbabwe when the antiquarians' received word of still more fabulous cities lost beyond the marshlands of uppermost Zambesi.

Those scholarly gentry had quailed at the thought of such hostile lands. Then as now, those marshes teem with the continent's most dangerous animals along with blood-curdling tales of cannibal natives.

Aunt Phyllis scorned such lily-livered vapours, declaring that she no more believed in anthropophagi than in one of Herodotus's rocs swooping down to carry off an elephant.

Wild beasts did not deter her. With no interest in game hunting, she scorned the notion of laboriously traversing the wilds on foot in hopes of bagging some trophy. Instead she hired a steam launch captained by a youthful American adventurer named Allnutt. Equipped with the latest comforts and conveniences, she ventured into the unknown.

'What did she discover?' Eustace asked hopefully.

Alas, our genial ebony-skinned hosts exchanged doubtful looks and still more dubious murmurs.

'They have no more to tell you.' Major Tobias lit a contemplative cheroot; its fragrance warding off the night's biting insects. 'Though that might be significant. If a steam launch had come to grief in any of the main channels, we might have expected some wreckage to have washed downstream after twenty years of annual floods.'

My heart warmed to hear his words espousing our cause. 'Do you think we might learn more, if we traced her steps? Do these gentlemen know anything of her intended route?'

As Tobias asked, I saw the aged tribesmen nod and smile. My spirits rose further.

Eustace still looked troubled. 'Every European swears those marshes are a death trap. We could sink in the same mire as Aunt Phyllis never to be seen again.'

Tobias showed fine white teeth in a confident smile. 'I have returned safe from exploring several tributaries cutting across that sodden plain. Aye and heard rumour of these self-same cities which your aunt sought. I believe they are there for the finding.'

'And how might we communicate with anyone in that region?' Eustace demanded stubbornly. 'We have no notion of their language.'

Tobias was undaunted 'From what these gentlemen say, these lost tribes have a passing acquaintance with Arabic. I learned enough to get by in the Sudan.'

'What would you rather show your colleagues at the bank, Eustace?' I urged. 'Sketches of dusty scholars scraping at these ruins or the first drawings of a realm forgotten by history for centuries?'

No man's weaknesses are a mystery to his sister. I could see that prospect tantalized my brother. Indeed, I could not think of anyone better suited to recording such a find. Had circumstance allowed, Eustace's paintings would have graced the Royal Academy.

'We could voyage some way upstream,' he allowed. 'We might learn more of her fate.'

'We might return with discoveries to make all our fortunes.' Tobias drew on his cheroot, dark eyes glinting beneath his saturnine brow.

Following Aunt Phyllis's example before us, we lost no time in securing a steam launch. Major Tobias assured us he could manage both the engine's operation and the river's navigation. He also undertook to outfit the vessel with all necessary appurtenances and provisions. As we boarded a few days later, I also noted reassuring evidence of a military man's prudence; a stack of guns and ammunition cases.

Eustace didn't notice any such things. He was too busy gaping wide-eyed at me. I matched him stare for stare.

'You surely didn't imagine that I would venture into the wilderness in skirts and petticoats?'

'What—?' He was still lost for words.

'It is a bicycling suit.'

I fancy my grey Norfolk flannel attire was the first of its kind to be tailored in Africa. My Cape Colony dressmaker had never heard of such a thing but when I showed her the fashion plates I had obtained from the Rational Dress Society in London, she willingly set to with shears and needle.

She and I were both well satisfied with the results. The bodice was no different from any other in my wardrobe while the bloomer trousers were sufficiently full-cut to pass for a skirt at first glance. If they gathered below the knee rather than falling to my ankle as a skirt would, my lower legs were decently clad in cotton stockings, canvas spats and sturdy shoes.

'You cannot—'

'You seem to have mislaid your bicycle, Miss Charteris.' Major Tobias's chuckle cut Eustace's protest short, more amused than censorious. 'Now,' he continued briskly, 'let's get underway.'

Eustace climbed aboard the launch without further complaint. Perhaps he had realised that with my broad brimmed hat and a veil proof against insects, I was better dressed for hazards ahead than he was.

Not that we faced any undue hardship on our initial journey up the lazily curving river, overhung with fever trees. Eustace filled his sketchbook with depictions of crocodiles, hippopotami, roan waterbuck with great curving horns and a myriad different species of waterfowl. The closest we came to the continent's most fearsome predator was hearing a lion's roar in the distance as we made fast to the bank one evening. We had reached a vast expanse of swamp bounded on the far horizon by the distant cones of long-extinct volcanoes.

I shivered despite the heat. It was a blood curdling sound.

'The roaring lion catches no game. That's what the Baganda say.' Tobias was readying his gun before venturing ashore to shoot a bird for the spit. He had proven himself a crack shot.

'Then we won't hear any warning should such a beast be hunting us?' I was hardly reassured.

'I say.' Sitting in the prow, Eustace turned to us before Tobias could answer. 'Does that look like a natural bank to you?'

He had been sketching what we took for a sluggish stream entering the river, picturesquely choked with water lilies, some white, some blue.

'That is stonework under those creepers.' Eustace pointed with an insistent pencil. 'That is a canal.'

'I believe you're right.' As I agreed, Tobias grunted his assent.

I looked from Eustace to the major and back again. 'That must be a sign of the lost city which Aunt Phyllis sought.'

'I believe you're right.' Tobias echoed my words with a grin.

'We must see where the waterway leads.' Eustace was already stowing away his drawing equipment. 'I'll reawaken the boiler.'

Our grandfather's mechanical aptitude had become evident in my brother on this journey, giving the lie to those who would argue such talents cannot coexist with an artistic temperament.

'Not before morning.' Tobias's tone brooked no argument. 'It will soon be night and we have no notion how far that channel may be navigable.'

'We want to get back safely,' I reminded my mutinous brother, patting the varnished gunwale of our loyal craft. 'We dare not hole her on some submerged log in the darkness.'

Thus we dined on fresh-killed waterfowl roasted over a small fire and later I settled to sleep in the stern of the launch. Eustace took the first watch from the prow, anchored hard against the bank. Tobias slept beside him to wake refreshed at midnight.

Then in the small hours of the morning, I woke to feel a hand on my shoulder. As I struggled to shrug off the shrouds of sleep, fingers slid across my mouth. A scream swelled in my throat before I recognised the reassuring scent of Tobias's tobacco and realised he was counselling me to silence.

His moustache tickled my ear as he leaned down to whisper. 'Natives are approaching.'

I sat up, grateful that I had merely loosened my clothing for sleep rather than undress. 'Eustace?' Looking up at Tobias in the eerie African moonlight, I mouthed my brother's name rather than spoke it.

The major reassured me with a nod towards the prow and a smile. He offered me his hand and we made our way forward.

I could see faint movement amid the dense foliage on the canal's bank. Moonlight struck cold flashes of steel from spears held by shadowy figures. I swallowed to find my mouth dry with apprehension. Glancing at Tobias, I saw he had his rifle ready while Eustace grasped the revolvers with which he had become proficient during his time in the Cape.

A voice hailed us from the darkness. 'Hello the boat.'

We looked at each other, astonished. The speaker's words were unmistakably English, although with the accents of some souk on Africa's northern margin bordering the Mediterranean sea.

'Hello ashore,' Tobias replied cautiously.

'We wish you no harm,' the voice promised, 'but there are those close at hand who would kill you. You must head back downstream at once.'

'Are they sincere?' Eustace hissed at Tobias.

'They're not sticking us with those lion spears.' The major shrugged before replying to the unseen speaker. 'We are well-armed.'

'But you are only three and all too easily overwhelmed,' our interlocutor insisted, 'once your bullets are spent.'

'What do you know of bullets?' Eustace asked before Tobias could speak.

'How do you speak such fluent English?' That was my most urgent question.

On reaching the Cape we had soon learned the folly of the insular Briton's conviction that all natives can be induced to understand, if the mother tongue of Empire is spoken at sufficient volume.

My words prompted a veritable commotion ashore. The unseen leader silenced his companions with a curt command in some African language. He stepped forward onto the stones edging the canal.

'Madam who speaks,' he asked breathlessly, 'what is your name?'

I looked to Eustace and Tobias for guidance only to see them as much at a loss as myself. Unable to see how an honest answer could hurt us, I replied.

'Hilda Charteris.'

Fresh excitement erupted amid the shadows.

'Charteris!' 'Charteris!' 'Charteris!'

The natives repeated our name time and again, their voices like wind rushing through reeds.

'I am Eustace Charteris. What is that to you?'

My brother's challenge rang through the night, even if it sounded more suited to the playing fields of Wyrkyn than remotest Africa.

As the native leader took another step, Tobias lit a lantern. Its glow revealed a tall African, strongly built and lighter in colour than those living near Great Zimbabwe. He wore a leopard skin cloak and to our astonishment, short trousers and a cotton shirt.

'Are you related to Miss Phyllis Charteris?'

I was ready to wake and find this all a dream. Such an exchange belonged to the river bank at Henley Regatta not this muddy wilderness.

Eustace found his voice. 'We are her nephew and niece.'

'Then you are most welcome,' the cotton-clad African said fervently. 'But you are still in grave danger—'

'Don't think we'll be leaving before you tell us what you know of our aunt!'

I strove to ameliorate my brother's brusqueness. 'May I ask your name, sir?'

'I am Bartholomew.' The African ducked his head for want of a hat to tip to me. 'But you must leave with us. There are tribes in these marshes who will seize any stranger—'

'While you prefer to persuade us to walk to your cooking pots?' Tobias hefted his rifle.

Bartholomew astonished us all with a laugh. 'We have forsworn such barbarism thanks to Miss Charteris.'

'When did she come to your tribe,' Tobias demanded, still wary, 'and in what manner?'

As Bartholomew replied with swift urgency, the major looked to myself and Eustace. Our nods confirmed that the African's account agreed with what we knew of our lost aunt's history.

'Please,' Bartholomew urged as he concluded, 'let us take you to safety and to Miss Charteris.'

'She is still alive?' Only now did I realise that was an unlooked-for marvel.

'Very much alive,' Bartholomew promised. 'But we must leave before we are discovered. Come ashore, I beg you!'

Eustace rose but Tobias barred his way with the gun's barrel. 'If our route lies along this canal, we will bring the boat. If there are hostile tribes at hand, we will travel faster and more safely by water.'

'We will bring your boat,' Bartholomew assured him, 'but we can carry you to Miss Charteris with our own far swifter vessel.'

'Are we game?' Tobias looked at me and at Eustace. 'Shall we trust in this fellow's good faith?'

'It's that or turn tail.' I was convinced of Bartholomew's sincerity.

As it turned out, so was Eustace. 'Right ho.'

It was not till much later that I thought to ask my brother and Tobias if they had expected another boat, when Bartholomew spoke of a vessel. Indeed they had, and their astonishment equalled my own when they saw the conveyance awaiting us. But once again, I am anticipating myself.

Once we had got ashore, a party of Africans clad like Bartholomew took charge of our steam launch, stirring the boiler to life with admirable efficiency.

Bartholomew led us a short distance from the canal to an expanse of solid ground rising from the foetid marsh. A great grey shape loomed out of the darkness, surrounded by tiny figures. Then I realised my eyes were deceiving me. Those were fully grown men.

Eustace pulled up so short that I stepped on his heels. 'What is—?'

'An aerostat?' For the first time, I heard Major Tobias at a loss.

A gang of Africans were hanging onto ropes restraining a vast balloon. A long basket slung beneath it had an engine at one end and the night breeze carried the distinctive odour of the coal gas inflating it.

Bartholomew gestured proudly towards the dirigible. 'We sail right over the heads of our enemies while they flounder in the marshes.'

'How—?'

Urgent shouts interrupted my question.

'We have been seen!'

There was no mistaking Bartholomew's fear.

We ran for the basket as the Africans let out their ropes. Barely had we scrambled aboard before those on the ground loosed their hold and melted into the undergrowth.

As the great airship soared upwards, I glimpsed new arrivals racing into the clearing below. They waved ferocious spears as moonlight glistened on their flesh, bare but for knotted loincloths. Vicious cries rose into the night.

'What—?' Eustace turned towards the stern of this remarkable vessel as the unmistakable force of propulsion drove a fresh breeze into our faces.

I expected to hear a sound akin to our steam launch's motor. Instead the device driving the propeller emitted something between a purr and a whine. This balloon was no plaything of the winds but their unquestioned mistress.

Another African wearing a leopard skin over his clothing was in charge of this curious engine. We were soon to realise such a pelt was a particular badge of honour.

He had seen Eustace's wide-eyed interest. 'Batteries,' he said succinctly. 'Electric motor.'

I could see Eustace was full of questions. Like me however, he swallowed his curiosity for the present, preferring to secure a firm hold of the sturdily woven basket's rail.

'Astonishing.' Tobias gazed around before a noise drew his attention at the prow.

A dusky crewman stood behind a signal lantern such as the Royal Navy favour, working its shutters with swift efficiency. Glimmers from a distant hill replied.

'Miss Charteris will know to expect us?' Tobias queried.

Bartholomew nodded. 'The telegraph will carry a message from that ground station.'

'Telegraph?' Eustace couldn't restrain his astonishment.

Bartholomew nodded again. 'Miss Charteris told us of it—'

Tobias laughed. 'Your aunt has brought more useful knowledge to these shores than the missionary brethren.'

'But they have devices unheard of in England,' Eustace objected.

He indicated our vessel's engineer. The African held what appeared to be a lantern until he wound a handle on one side. Its lens glowed with a strange brilliance owing nothing to oil or candle.

'Clockwork,' our laconic engineer explained.

We could only exchange glances of silent wonder, and hope that such mysteries would be clarified.

Meanwhile our softly humming craft forged onwards over the vast marsh towards the volcanic hills. At first we could see bright fires below in the darkness, betokening camps or villages. Soon such glints receded to pinpricks and I shivered in the cold of the airship's ascent.

'Here.' Tobias wrapped a length of thick cotton cloth around my shoulders. I confess I found his closeness as much a comfort as the warm blanket.

'Is this where you live?' Eustace was intent on the view ahead. 'Inside this natural fortress?'

Bartholomew spoke briefly to the signal lamp's operator. The youth sent eloquent gleams to the ground below before our newfound guide explained.

'All the Amahagger peoples dwell in such strongholds. There have been generations of warfare between our tribes. But we have risen above such destructive rivalry. We are no longer in thrall to She-who-must-be-obeyed.'

'We are guided by She-who-thinks-for-herself!'

At this declaration from our hitherto monosyllabic engineer, every African aboard the fantastical vessel cheered aloud.

'Oh!' Sudden descent into the dead crater took me unawares. Before I could decide to drop the blanket to seize the rail with both hands, Major Tobias's strong arms bracketed me.

Thanks to this unexpected proximity, I realised he had stowed a revolver in a trouser pocket. Grateful as I was for such forethought, I was beginning to hope such defences would prove unnecessary.

'Do you suppose that's a natural breach or did they mine out an entrance?' Eustace was studying a narrow cleft in the crater wall, silhouetted against the night sky.

'Those who came before us, who built the ancient city of Kor, shaped these rocks,' Bartholomew replied.

'So there is a lost realm in these marshes.' Tobias's whiskers tickled my ear once again.

'A place of many marvels.' But Bartholomew's tone darkened. 'Forbidden to us by the selfishness of She-who-must-be-obeyed and the savagery of those whom she has enslaved.'

Tobias's arms tightened comfortingly around me as I shivered, this time at the thought of what might have transpired if those hostile tribesmen had been the first to espy our launch.

More immediate dangers became apparent. The breath froze in my throat as the boards beneath our feet tilted this way and that. The airship finally landed with a jolt, which startled an oath from Eustace that our nurse would have punished with a mouthful of carbolic soap. I was too relieved to have made landfall to remonstrate.

'This way, if you please.'

Bartholomew opened a wicker gate in the basket's side as two Africans brought a gangplank to ease our descent.

Whirring all around us heralded a constellation of those clockwork lamps. As Eustace and I set foot on the fragrant turf, a susurration of wonder rose from the assembled natives.

'Charteris...' 'Charteris...' 'Charteris...'

Bartholomew led us through the throng towards a doorway carved in the volcanic rock. A winding passage branched into further tunnels and caverns but this was far from some ominous gloomy labyrinth. Gas lighting put shadow and superstition alike to flight.

With a crowd of Africans following us, we could not pause to study the rooms that we passed. From the scant glimpses I snatched this was a hive of industry. Belt driven looms and all manner of other machines stood idle while their operators enjoyed their night's rest. Well-warned respite, judging by the products of their labours piled high in baskets. Cloth in one cave, lathe-turned wooden bowls in the next, brass cogs and similar mechanical constituents in those that followed.

Some caverns boasted long tables carved from the very rock. These were laid out with microscopes and finely pointed tools alongside what looked like the constituent parts of my music box at home. Other doorways revealed intricate assemblages of glass flasks and pipes, copper bowls and burners, while the slowly stirring air was flavoured with a chemical tang.

At the end of a long corridor, Bartholomew threw open a neatly fitted door. 'She-who-thinks-for-herself!'

A grey-haired English woman sat at an elegant writing desk where a telegraph machine chattered. A Chesterfield for more easeful repose stood beside a bookcase filled with leather bound tomes, while a dining table stood framed with four chairs opposite. Carpets reminiscent of oriental design softened both the floor and the rough-hewn rock walls and a further door stood ajar, revealing the corner of a canopied bed.

She looked up from the strip of paper spooling across her fingers and smiled at us both before studying Eustace with frank amusement.

'No one could deny you for a Charteris. You are the living image of my brother William.'

For my part I was dumbstruck by the vision of what I might expect in my looking glass several decades hence.

'You must be Hilda.' Phyllis rose to offer me her hand. She paused to study my bicycling suit before nodding with approval. 'You must let me take a pattern from such eminently practical garments.'

'Of course.' I studied our aunt's dress in turn. As old-fashioned as the cut was, the cloth was as well finished as anything from Bond Street.

Aunt Phyllis smiled. 'You thought to find me in animal skins?'

Eustace was gaping at the remarkable room. 'We never thought to find anything like this.'

'Who is your companion?' Our aunt turned her steely gaze on the third member of our party.

'Major Vincent Tobias.' He offered a brief bow. 'We came in hopes of effecting a rescue, madam, but that seems entirely superfluous.'

'Indeed,' Phyllis said crisply. 'Hilda, I do hope you won't be missish and I will explain in due course, but you will need to kiss Major Tobias to avoid unhelpful complications during your visit.'

I stared at her. 'I—'

'By your leave.' Tobias slid an arm around my waist, drew me close and obeyed our aunt's instruction.

His fervour indicated he'd long been contemplating such an intimate embrace. I confess he wasn't alone.

'I say!' Eustace protested.

'You will need to be quick on your feet, my boy,' Phyllis warned him. 'Among the Amahagger a girl can lay claim to any man with such a kiss. Then he's honour bound to satisfy her until she tires of him. We need no such complications for you.'

As Eustace blushed to the roots of his hair, she turned to me. 'Has there been any further reform of the franchise and parliamentary elections in England? What of married women's property rights?'

'There has been some progress.' I was still struggling to regain my composure after Tobias's kiss.

'Not much, I'll wager.' Aunt Phyllis shook her head. 'Among the Amahagger, men and women live on terms of perfect equality and free of the shackles of marriage. Yet the Europeans have the temerity to call Africans savages.'

'But Bartholomew spoke of slaves among these tribes.' I wriggled free of Tobias's arm with a look to warn him against making any unwarranted assumptions until I had decided what I wanted of him.

'He spoke of threats of violence from She-who-must-be-obeyed.'

The major's words prompted a hum of consternation among the Africans clustered in the doorway.

'I will explain,' Aunt Phyllis assured him. 'But you must be famished. Bartholomew, kindly ask Cook to serve supper.'

Once again the incongruity of her words and our situation rendered me speechless. Shortly afterwards we were all too busily engaged in eating for conversation. Aunt Phyllis had dined earlier so she regaled us with her own adventures while we satisfied our hunger.

As Eustace had surmised, her launch had become stuck fast in the trackless marshes. As Mr Allnut laboured to free the vessel, a party of Amahagger tribesmen happened upon them. The natives were fleeing one of those murderous battles of which Bartholomew had spoken.

These noble savages refused to leave my aunt and her companion to the mercies of the cannibals pursuing them, though it was only much later when she had learned something of their tongue that my aunt truly understood the peril she had faced. At the time she feared the worst was to befall her.

Arriving at this crater unmolested however, an elder proved to have some knowledge of an African language familiar to Mr Allnutt. It was soon agreed that the young American would strike northwards in hope of returning with aid, both for my aunt and for this beleaguered Amahagger tribe. He would assuredly travel faster alone and for all its perils, this rock-girt sanctuary seemed the safest haven she could hope for.

Alas, Mr Allnutt was never seen nor heard from again. As the weeks of his absence lengthened to months my aunt was forced to conclude she was now all alone in this wilderness.

'Yet you have civilized these people most wonderfully.' Eustace looked up from his potted meat to marvel at the room's comforts.

Aunt Phyllis fixed him with an acerbic gaze. 'You cannot imagine that these men and women are perfectly capable of doing all this for themselves? You agree with those arrogant fools who regard the African as some species of unfinished European, as if by the same logic, a rabbit is some species of unfinished hare? A pony an unfinished horse? Rather than people perfectly fitted by nature for this region and as capable of learning and invention as men and woman of any complexion?'

She looked around the chamber. 'I told them of my life in England and as I explained, they were inspired to discover how they might enjoy such conveniences for themselves. They had Mr Allnutt's steam launch to investigate and dismantle as well as all our other equipment and my own possessions. While I had no direct knowledge of a telegraph's mechanisms or of automata or electric motors, once I had described such a thing, the brightest intellects among the Amahagger soon fathomed their mysteries. This region is rich in metal and coal to fuel their advances.

'Do not think these tribes will stand helplessly by,' she advised Eustace caustically, 'while Europeans plunder their natural wealth.'

'Please,' I intervened to save my poor brother from undeserved rebuke, 'go on with your story.'

'I will allow—' our aunt moderated her tone somewhat '— when I first arrived, these Amahagger were living in a state of primitive superstition. They clothed themselves in skins and in the linen wrappings stripped from the mummies for whom the ancient inhabitants of Kor had fashioned these catacombs. Their race was devastated by successive plagues, leaving the craters empty until the Amahagger abandoned their nomadic ways and settled here.

'They even burned those long-dead bodies as torches for want of anything better.' She shook her head as though astonished by her own recollection before continuing with a combative glint in her eye. 'Once I had learned the local tongue though, I discovered why these tribes were so primitive compared to those further south. The fault lay with the tyrant queen who ruled them all.'

'She-who-must-be-obeyed.' Major Tobias's murmur prompted a fresh shiver of unease around the door.

Aunt Phyllis tsked with exasperation. 'I left England infuriated by the way men consider the cleverest woman's intelligence only fit to serve as a whetstone for her brother or her husband's scientific or literary endeavours. I found myself amongst these people for whom such a notion is ridiculous, not to say barbarous. And yet they were in thrall to a woman whose entire ambition is to subjugate herself to some lost Adonis for whom she eternally yearns.

'Their queen,' she explained more briskly, 'lives largely in retirement, relying on her brutal legions to enforcer her rule through terror and bloodshed. She emerges on rare occasions to issue edicts to stop the worst of the warfare between these tribes but beyond that she is largely an indolent ruler and a woman utterly foolish for love.'

'Few tribes I've encountered would stand for that,' Tobias observed cautiously.

Aunt Phyllis pursed her lips. 'I said she was largely indolent. The one craft she has evidently studied is chemistry. It is an ancient science after all. She offers her loyal subjects medicines that convince them of her magical powers, and she has some vapour to fill the air around her that reduces the strongest-willed men to abject adoration, not to say helpless lust.

'More than that, it is said—' here her tone wavered between scepticism and apprehension '—that she has uncovered the secret of eternal life.'

'Surely no—'

Aunt Phyllis cut Eustace's disbelief short. 'There are more things in heaven and earth than are dreamt of in your philosophy.'

'But what of this queen's legions and the other hostile tribes?' Tobias returned to the military question. 'How have your hosts kept their advances safe from plunder or destruction? I've seen no sign of firearms, not even muskets.'

'Alas, Mr Allnutt took our small store of weaponry so the Amahagger had no pattern to follow and my explanations were found lacking some vital detail.' My aunt's eyes brightened. 'Still, Bartholomew tells me your boat is well supplied with armaments.'

Eustace and I exchanged apprehensive glances as Aunt Phyllis continued.

'Until now, our advantage has lain in superior communications enabling far more coherent use of tactics on the battlefields as well as hydraulic and other defences making this crater an impregnable fortress.

'But you are correct, major,' she said briskly, though Tobias had not spoken further, 'we cannot rely on that forever, nor yet upon whatever improvements the Amahagger will make on the guns you have brought. We must confront this queen 'She-who-must-be-obeyed'!'

I realised with a thrill of terror that she was looking straight at me.

'We need two to manage the smallest airship. Do not fear. When we land in Kor her legions will not harm us. They have orders to take anyone with white skin straight to her and since women can resist her beguilement —'

'You cannot—'

Eustace protested barely a breath ahead of Major Tobias.

'Let me—'

'We can and we will.' Aunt Phyllis was adamant. 'It is up to us to convince her that a life spent languishing after some man is a waste of a woman's potential. We will show her all that this tribe has achieved and invite her to share in all that might arise from unity among the Amahagger!'

I cannot now think of that first evening without regret, nor of the expedition which I made with my aunt, soaring above the long-dead volcanoes and marshes in the Amahagger airship. We had such high hopes, all to be dashed.

As Mr Haggard relates, Ayesha never yielded in her irrational infatuation, or in her belief that her long-dead love would return. Lest you incline to sympathy, remember that her obsession was nearly the death of Horace Holly and Leo Vincey. Ultimately, it proved the death of Ayesha, as you will discover in Mr Haggard's book.

But that fatal conclusion is by no means the end of my tale. After her outright rejection of all our reasoned arguments, my aunt and I made a second secret journey to the lost city of Kor.

Because She-who-must-be-obeyed had indeed learned the secret of eternal life. However as Aunt Phyllis observed after our audience with the tyrant queen, that prize had been entirely wasted on someone so foolishly romantic. She and I agreed that a mature woman who had outgrown the storms of youthful passion would be far better placed to make best use of such a gift.

So now I can give fair warning to those eager to invest in Mr Rhodes's arrogant plan to drive a railroad from the Cape to Cairo, plundering Africa's gold and diamond fields as he goes. To those willing to turn a blind eye to King Leopold's barbarities in the Congo Free State for the sake of enriching themselves. To those who would make freak-show exhibits of the native population in the manner of the tragic Hottentot Venus.

All the Amahagger peoples are now united in peace, prosperity and democracy under the tutelage of a new and eternal governess with myself, Eustace and Major Tobias ready to serve as their ambassadors and advisors.

These Africans will not stand idly by while their mineral wealth is plundered and their lands annexed. They have all learned to follow the wise example of She-who-can-think-for-herself.

THE GREAT STEAM TIME MACHINE

Brian Herbert and Bruce Taylor

Carrying a black satchel over his shoulder, a lean, harried looking man pushed through the imposing doors of the Great Exhibition Hall, shaking snow off his coat as he walked. Once inside, Percival Lowell paused, then walked slowly onto the thick blue carpeting of the building's foyer.

He ran fingers through his sparse, graying hair and looked about, as if he could not quite figure out why or how he was there. Wasn't he just at his observatory in Flagstaff, Arizona? He'd heard a noise, and going to investigate—

what had happened next? As he tried to remember, he gazed about his present circumstances: to the book cases lining the walls and the overstuffed deep red chairs with thick, padded arms, grouped in fours and fives around large mahogany coffee tables.

Chairs that were robust, he thought, *as if they could cradle and hold me forever while I sit in long discussions about Mars, astronomy, and the marvels of the age.* While he didn't know exactly where in the world he was – for some reason it didn't matter and didn't seem particularly odd, either.

Somehow, he mused, *it feels as if I'm in a lucid dream or a magical reality where no matter how odd it is, everything seems natural and not strange at all.*

Straight ahead, closed doors with leaded glass panels led to a great display hall, curiously dark. But slowly, light gained strength; just enough to reveal the hulking shapes of great electrical and mechanical wonders and a huge steam engine, as if the best examples of such technology had been collected in one place and put on display.

Lowell looked up, amazed that above the doors lettering had either escaped his attention or — he shook his head — suddenly appeared? Great polished brass letters brightly proclaimed:

The Great Hall of the Coming Amazing Steam, Electrical and Mechanical Age

Still feeling a bit disoriented, he sat on one of the chairs, and sank into its softness. On the nearest table a newspaper was dated December 21, 1895. Lowell smoothed his mustache for several moments, a nervous habit. He looked to the paper again; the date was the same but the year had vanished.

On the coffee table, he noticed a steaming cup of tea in a white, porcelain cup with a delicate vine of blue flowers imprinted on it. The cup looked as if it had just come into being, appearing out of thin air. *How did—*? Lowell shook his head, closed his eyes. *Earl Gray*, he thought, *one of my favorites*. He took a sip. *Perfect. Even the right amount of sweetness*. He savored it and felt himself relaxing. Draining the cup and putting it down, he only vaguely noticed that a large teapot had also appeared.

He opened his satchel and pulled out loose papers in a folder, which he opened. He looked over the notes he was making on his next book, a follow up to *Mars*.

What to call it? He pondered. Nothing came to him, but it would concern Mars as well. The planet had become an obsession for him, and from his high desert perch at 7,000 feet elevation, he had been peering into the dark night sky, staring at the planet whenever it became visible, trying to make sense of the topographical features he had been seeing.

Just then, a slender boy came in, unbuttoning his coat and shaking snow out of his fair hair. He went up to Percival and after a long moment, said quite boldly,

"Hi. Are you Percival Lowell, the astronomer?"

Lowell, a bit startled, smiled. "Why, why — yes, I am. And who might I have the pleasure of talking to, young man?"

The boy grinned "Hugo. Hugo Gernsback. I've heard about you, and I came all the way from Luxembourg to meet you. What are you working on now?"

"A future book about the red planet," Lowell said. "I just published a book on the subject, but there's a lot more to say. My first book is called *Mars*. Would you like to see a copy? I have one in my satchel." He looked inside the bag. "Or maybe a few more."

Hugo's eyes grew wide. Then he nodded vigorously and said, "Gosh, sure —"

Lowell let him examine a copy of the several that he happened to have with him – more copies than should have been able to fit into the shoulder satchel. He watched the boy carefully, slowly turn the pages, occasionally pausing to read with an expression of reverence, as if it was something holy.

"This looks a very intriguing book," Hugo said. "I'd really like to read it."

Lowell leaned forward, as if sharing a secret. "Did you know Mars has life?"

Hugo, looking stunned, shook his head.

"I am convinced that there are canals on Mars."

"Canals? Full of water?"

"They are going dry." He held up a finger. "Mars is an old world, a dying world. In spite of the canals carrying water from the poles to the cities, there is less and less water—"

"Wow," Hugo said. "Yet there's life there? Cities?"

"Indeed." He lifted the folder of papers. "Just notes right now, and I'm continuing to study the planet by telescope. But there is a great deal of data to collect before I can prove this. My next book, *Mars as the Abode of Life*, is still many years away from publication. But, yes, Mars has life." He looked at the notes for the book and read out loud, "'The drying-up of the planet is certain to proceed until its surface can support no life at all. Slowly but surely time will snuff it all out. When the last ember is thus extinguished, the planet will become a dead world tumbling through space, its evolution of life forms forever ended.' My book will have something to do with the canals, and the fact that Mars is losing its ability to harbor life."

"It would be most interesting to go back in time to see what it was like. What if there were Martians? Maybe there were oceans! I have a signed copy of a new scientific fiction book called *The Time Machine*, by Mr. H.G. Wells. What if time travel were possible?"

Lowell sipped his tea and chuckled. "A time machine. Marvelous idea, but —"

"— but," said a gentleman who had appeared and stood nearby, "It has a few problems."

"Nikola!" Lowell exclaimed. And putting the papers on the table, he stood, looking at the famous, impeccably dressed inventor, the dark hair parted down the middle, the head down, the fierce eyes, peering up. "Nikola Tesla —how have you been?" Then he glanced over at the boy, and said, "This is my new friend, Hugo Gernsback, from Luxembourg."

Tesla shook the young man's hand, asked, "What brings you to this Great Hall?"

"I don't know," he replied with a shrug. "Just a moment ago I was running an errand for my mother and it was summer and I started thinking about a picture I saw of a great stream engine. Then I remembered reading about Mr. Lowell, and all of a sudden I found myself walking through those doors —" His voice trailed off as if the strangeness of him being there was suddenly dawning on him. Then, as if it was actually of little consequence, he grinned and said, "Guess I really like all this new mechanical stuff, and it drew me here like a magnet."

Tesla laughed gently. "Such a bright boy. Yes, the machines in this hall are the coming things, Such an age we have before us! So much to look forward to —"

"Maybe even time travel?" said Hugo, holding his copy of Wells' book that suddenly appeared in his hands.

Tesla seated himself at Lowell's table; a maid appeared and brought him tea, setting it in front of him. "Oh, how I wish," he said, "How I wish. But in spite of Mr. Wells' wonderful story, it does have a very big problem — and that is — he doesn't really describe the power source, how the whole thing might work. He should have contacted me about it, and asked for technical advice. The lack of any precise detail detracts from the story's credibility." Pouring tea into his cup, he continued. "So does the plot point of his time traveler just happening to find functional safety matches in a sealed museum case some 800,000 years in the future." Nikola shook his head. "Dear, oh dear. But for a young man to publish such a well-received tome at age twenty-nine and gain such a fine reputation so quickly, I dare say that is quite an achievement. And it certainly awakens the public consciousness about time and the destiny of humankind."

Lowell took a sip of tea. Then, thoughtfully, "Yes, but back to the original question about power for the time vehicle, one would suppose that would be a problem but to my knowledge, no one has questioned Mr. Wells too closely about it. But now that you bring it up—there is another, even more pressing problem, and I assume you know what that might be —"

Tesla looked over at young Hugo Gernsback. "Take a chair, young man and listen to great minds debate." He smiled impishly as Hugo settled into a soft chair.

"Yes," said Lowell, taking the papers of his book from the table and placing them on his lap, "I suppose the whole concept of time travel itself begs the question – setting aside any question about the power source."

At this point, someone else came over: a tall young man in his mid-teens, dark haired and with a mustache, wearing a tweed coat and dark trousers. Studying everyone for a moment, he finally said, "I couldn't help but overhear this conversation, and I am most intrigued by it. Might I join in? My name is Albert Einstein." Noting a sense of authority about this young man, Lowell put his papers back on the table and rose to his feet, as did Tesla.

"Herr Einstein," said Tesla, grabbing Einstein's hand and shaking it; his expression was that of absolute delight. "It's so good to meet you! I've been hearing about you. I believe you've published something recently that caused a stir."

"Oh," laughed Einstein, waving a hand. "You must be referring to that paper, 'The Investigation of Aether in Magnetic Fields'. Yes. I am both surprised and pleased at the interest it appears to have created."

"Ah," said Tesla, "work such as that might bring you a Nobel Prize someday."

Percival Lowell studied the young man. Most of all he noticed the eyes, incredibly intelligent, brown eyes.

"You are Nikola Tesla, I believe?" Einstein said to the other man. Then, looking at Lowell he said, "And you?"

"Percival Lowell" he said, extending his hand. "And our young companion is Hugo Gernsback of Luxembourg."

"We are from all over the world," Einstein said. "How interesting that we are all here."

Lowell looked to Hugo, then to Einstein, and said, "I suspect, given your paper, that you have some interesting ideas about the nature of the universe."

"Bah," laughed Einstein, "you give me too much credit. I just play with numbers in my head. Let's see where I am five years from now instead of just being sixteen!" He laughed again.

A maid in a black and white uniform appeared from nowhere and pushed another chair close to the table for

Einstein. In a few minutes she brought tea for him and crumpets for everyone. In front of Hugo, she placed a thick, white mug of hot chocolate.

Hugo smiled, looking down at the steaming chocolate. "I was just thinking about how good a cup of hot chocolate would be." He looked up "Thank —"

The maid was gone

"Anyway," said Einstein, nibbling on one of the crumpets, "I believe I overheard you gentlemen talking about Mr. Wells' new novel? I agree that there are problems with what he says —"

"Yes," said Percival Lowell, "mainly with the concept of time travel, along with —"

But Einstein shook his head. "I don't think that's the problem —"

Nikola Tesla leaned forward and nodded. "It's the power that's the problem."

"— not the concept of time travel itself —" continued Albert.

Young Hugo looked up, almost spilling his hot chocolate. "Time travel is a possibility?"

"If time travel is really possible," said Tesla, "if you have enough power, who knows what might happen?" He smiled, dipping a tea bag in and out of the pot. "I've been thinking —" He looked toward the display hall. "Don't you suppose it's time for us to take a look into that great hall of wonders?" He rose to his feet.

"Why yes," said Lowell, "Why don't we do that?"

Albert Einstein grinned and rose to stand beside Nikola. "Of course."

Lowell grabbed his pile of papers, and holding the stack vertically, tapped the bottom end on the table — and when the papers were neat, he placed them in the folder and back in the satchel. Then he opened a copy of Mars, and flipping the cover open, he wrote a note: "To my friend, Hugo Gernsback — you shall go far and the world will remember you." Then, signing it, he handed it to an astonished and delighted Hugo.

The group followed Tesla and Einstein to the Great Hall of the Coming Amazing Steam, Electrical and Mechanical Age. As they approached, the great doors swung open and the lights abruptly became brighter, revealing a vast space with brass and gleaming modern marvels looming large and filling the immense room.

At the threshold of the cavernous hall they all stopped. "Like this place was expecting us," noted Lowell.

Tesla nodded. A knowing look. "Actually, it was."

Lowell noticed with some consternation a smile on Tesla's face as they walked deeper into the immense hall and stood before a locomotive-sized steam machine gleaming in bright brass elegance, dwarfing the people. Not far away loomed an apparatus of two high vertical cylinders, tapering toward the top, at least twenty-five feet high and the same distance apart, topped by mirrored balls. Around the base of the cylinders, items electrical: coils of copper wiring on giant spools, translucent blue glass insulators at the ends of metal poles, a vast array of new electrical equipment. Other hulking machines lurked beyond, silent, strange, and to Lowell, vaguely foreboding.

Tesla stopped, and gestured toward the behemoth of the steam machine. "With the stupendous power of this steam engine, nothing, *nothing* is impossible." Showing great confidence in his expression, he breathed in, then slowly let out his breath. "And with the —" he stopped, and smiled, "— adjustments I made while arranging for all of you to appear — I tell you, nothing — *nothing* — is impossible."

Albert Einstein laughed gently. "Even time travel, you're obviously suggesting."

"Yes, even time travel. After all, what explanation can you offer for being here?"

Hugo's mouth dropped open.

Lowell felt both shock and amazement. Then, with a sense of wariness, he cleared his throat. "Excuse me," he said to Tesla, "would you please clarify what you meant when you said you were arranging for us to be here?"

For a long minute, Tesla said nothing. "I suppose I shouldn't have said anything until all were present. We still have more guests coming who seem to be detained and I do hope there's not a problem with the machinery. I'm dreadfully sorry about the confusion. Shall we continue?"

This is just too strange, thought Lowell, but — he noticed Einstein looking at Tesla with a mixture of doubt, skepticism and, yes, — possibility.

"Behold," said Tesla, "For you are about to witness a demonstration of power beyond your imagination."

As if on cue, the great steam machine roared to life. A huge piston began to move laterally, great wheels began to turn and then began a pounding and thudding of something Lowell could not identify. That sound along with a quickening *chuff-chuff-chuff* and *sshhhshhshhh* of the steam engine itself, quickly climbed to an almost deafening roar, while pulleys and wheels became blurs of oval and circular movement.

Hugo covered his ears.

Lowell found himself feeling unsteady on his feet as the hall shook, thudded and shuddered. Tesla motioned for everyone to follow him into a tiny room off to one side. They packed in behind the great inventor. In front of him was a control panel teaming with dials, lights and switches. On the back wall, more dials, levers, and gauges.

With the door closed it was quieter, but nothing could stop the indescribable vibrations and thud-thud-thudding of machinery.

Tesla pointed to the apparatus of copper coils and two mirrored spheres on the tapered cylinders not far away from the steam engine. "Invented this a few years back." He spoke loudly. "Around 1890. I call it the Tesla coil. Harmless if you're careful, deadly if you're not."

He turned a dial on the console in front of him and motioned for the others to turn to watch the effect. Lowell heard the sound increasing, a weird, high pitched, buzzing whine, followed by sparks and arcs of electricity — wild, white and dendrite-like bursts of light that shot high in the air of the display hall, firing out from the spheres in staccato, frenetic flashes.

"So much power!" Einstein said, "But it doesn't mean the universe is going to change." He paused. "Or that this machine can transport people through time. It's just a display of electrical and steam power. No more than that."

"My dear Einstein," said Tesla, "You do agree that time travel might be possible, don't you?"

"Possibly, but not with machines like this."

"You're only looking at the engine," said Tesla, smiling, his head tilted slightly to the left, which to Lowell looked as if he was carefully calculating a further response. "If Mr.

Wells had his time machine here, this power would send his machine on its way. This is exactly the sort of tremendous, universe-altering power he would need."

Einstein waved his hand. "But where's the time machine? And how would you measure the passage of time to figure out if you were in the future or the past, and the date? And how would such a vehicle actually move through time?"

Lowell nodded "I must agree. Time travel is very much the realm of fiction and likely to stay there. I am sure, Mr. Tesla, with your amazing display of power, it most certainly would be enough to propel such a machine at incredible speeds, but," He laughed, " You must first have the proper machine, I fear."

Undaunted, Nikola stood his ground. "But who's to say that someone — someone like me — might not invent such a device to travel down the infinite corridors of time?" Looking at Einstein, he added, "And time travel may not even be through a 'device'—it may be accomplished by another means that still needs power of this great magnitude."

A sudden intrusion of noise had everyone in the small room turning to the opened door. Two more gentlemen stepped inside. A short young man with a round face, wearing round glasses, followed by an older man who also wore glasses and sported a well-trimmed beard.

The young man looked at Tesla and said, "In our strange voyage here, I'm not sure how we heard you talking but hear you we did. And you could very well be correct in your conjecture that a time machine is not even necessary. After all, as far as I can tell, my colleague and I traveled here without any machinery. Incidentally, I am Carl Gustav Jung and this is my esteemed colleague, Sigmund Freud."

Lowell had heard of Freud; the man was becoming quite renowned. But this other fellow was an unknown. Even so, he had a presence about him, and he was speaking while Freud stood quietly beside him. Lowell introduced the rest of the company in the small room; all shook hands.

Finally Tesla said to the new guests, "I was a bit concerned about your delay but I am so delighted you are here. Welcome, to this great display of power —" He stopped and looked to the massive steam engine — "To ponder our new age and the implications of technology, especially the possibility of immense — dare I say — unlimited power."

"I hope to a good end," Freud said. "But is all this power for the good of man, to make his life easier — or will it lead to his demise?"

"Such tremendous power," said Jung, "but without full consciousness or integration of the selves it could be extremely dangerous."

Hugo looked confused, obviously not comprehending. "I thought we were talking about Mr. Wells' book, *The Time Machine* and how it needed power of this kind to truly make it work —"

Einstein cleared his throat. "A time machine is not yet a reality — and it might not be for quite some time. If ever."

Freud smiled knowingly. "Actually, we are all quite familiar with time travel, for we are walking time machines, with our memories and dreams. Memories and dreams that can be so real that they become reality."

Nikola lowered his head, with the effect of peering up at Freud. "In that sense you are right, for I know of this. My own power to visualize is so intense that at times I cannot tell the difference between what I visualize in my head and the 'reality' around me as if reality almost becomes," He paused, "If you will, a magical blending of the real world and my imagination. But in time travel we want to move in an external, not internal, reality — into the past or the future."

"Do you really want to attempt that?" asked Carl Jung. "No matter the dangers?"

"Yes," said Tesla, Gernsback and Einstein in unison.

"Of course we want to make the attempt!" said Lowell. "If we could visit the future earth and learn what it is like, we'd be able to make changes now to help mankind advance more quickly – or to prevent some future catastrophe."

"Perhaps," said Carl Jung, "But I urge great caution. I am working on an idea and it's in its nascence, but I wonder if there may be a sense of shared awareness in humankind, a collective unconscious, and, if so, I can't help but wonder if the universe has this as well — a linkage that is more vast than anyone can imagine."

Lowell noticed that Freud was looking askance at Jung.

"I find this interesting," Lowell said, "because it reminds me of things I heard whilst traveling in the orient."

Einstein opened the door to the display hall, increasing the noise level. With the exception of Tesla, they went out and stared up and about at the great, throbbing and roaring machine. This time, Hugo did not plug his ears; instead, he seemed hypnotized, particularly by the immensity and power of the huge engine.

"All this energy," Carl Jung shouted, "What if our collective human psyche and the psyche of an even more powerful universal force — a vast energy that is both creative and destructive — could somehow combine with the power we see demonstrated before us?"

There was an audible gasp and Einstein looked utterly stricken. "Mien Gott! If all those energies could combine, they would totally alter space as we know it — the power would be so overwhelming that anything could be — *might be* — possible."

Lowell saw Tesla leaning his head out of the door to obviously hear the conversation.

"Yes, yes, *anything* —" Tesla blurted out.

Then Lowell saw him reach back inside, putting his hand on a dial and slowly turning up the power. Throughout the display hall, there was an obvious increase in the energy output of the great steam machine and the electrical display of the linked Tesla coils, though the noise level actually smoothed out and diminished. A sweet and sharp smell of ozone permeated the air.

On one side Lowell noticed Jung studying him intently.

"Forgive me," said Jung, "If I seem overly blunt, but a question that may have merit in regard to all of this — may I ask if you are happy — really happy, with how your theories about intelligent life on Mars are being received by the scientific community?"

The question blindsided Lowell. He felt a sharp stab of pain as if a secret wound had been exposed quite suddenly. "Well, their support hasn't been too forthcoming, but any day I hope —"

Jung smiled and said, "Bear with me, my friend. Just for the sake of argument, is it remotely possible that your theory of the rise and fall of civilization on Mars is actually your unconscious belief in this, tapping into a universal life force that has its own sentience, its own awareness?"

The electricity arced furiously in the display hall, bathing the large space in brilliant blasts of light as the great steam engine thundered with power. Again, Lowell saw Tesla leaning against the console, turning the dial to its maximum, pushing the great steam engine to its limit.

"If this is the case," continued Jung, "and there is a psyche of life on Mars that is dying, thence the spirit of the planet is dying as well, and if it could combine with the technological energies we see here — couldn't it be possible we might witness something extraordinary, as seemingly random events and energies come together in a way that would be a meaningful coincidence?"

Suddenly Lowell saw a most curious thing: the steam time machine froze in its action as the wheels and pulleys became a static blur of abruptly stilled action. All was suddenly quiet, and the smell of ozone grew much stronger.

Shaken and stunned, Lowell saw the images before them — the hall and the huge steam engine — all ripple horizontally, as one might see waves travel down a long pane of glass during an earthquake. But these were slow, heavy waves traveling back and forth.

Lowell moved aside to allow Tesla, who had left the console, to join them, then all stood with frozen arcs and bolts of electricity sparking over their heads. As moments passed, the horizontal rippling effect increased, and before them, the entire display hall took on an even more strange quality, as if looking at a two-dimensional photograph.

Then the great machine, and the immense hall itself, began to fade with each passing wave, while gradually another scene came into focus. And to Lowell's complete and utter amazement, he found himself and his companions on a hill, gazing out across a vast, alien landscape. The air was cold and windless, and before them the drying canals of a dying Mars stretched long and far through a barren landscape to a sullen, reddish horizon. The air smelled of minerals, and breathing was difficult, the atmosphere coarse, as if laden with fine particles of dust.

Lowell sat down on the cold soil of Mars, and in the dulling light of day, he saw a trickle of water in the nearest canal, and higher marks indicating where water must have been in the past. "What am I to make of this?" he whispered. "What am I to make of this? Am I right about Mars? Am I wrong? I do not understand —"

"Are you right about Mars? Perhaps," said Carl Jung, sitting beside him. "For us to come here in the first place must mean we were right about our theory that we are indeed dealing with a life force of Mars, one of innumerable life forces in the universe. Within that context, our small assemblage of people has shared a collective vision from a cosmic connection."

"Space!" exclaimed Albert Einstein. "We must have traveled though space! I'm not certain exactly how, but —"

"The pain of Martian life dying must be sending out psychic signals," Carl Jung said, "A whole planet in pain broadcasting across space, combining with Percival's subconscious fear that he will die without recognition, and his intense desire to really see the Mars of which he has written and hence redeem himself — all these forces, as well as our own energies, must have somehow become engaged in the tremendous physical power and kinetic energies of the great steam engine and the Tesla coils in the display hall. These factors must have combined in a remarkable synchronistic confluence of events and energies to transport us to Mars."

For a time they just gazed out on the strange landscape in the fading light, each alone with their thoughts in the deepening darkness.

Presently, Lowell heard the voice of Einstein. "But have we traveled in time? Certainly not so long ago there was abundant life here on Mars, but is this the way Mars is now? Or have we have gone into the future, to the final moments, the last gasps of the planet and its inhabitants?"

"Couldn't this be the past, or even the present?" Gernsback asked.

"I really don't know," said Einstein, "but I think we have gone into the future."

"I agree," Jung said. "I do think we have in fact traveled to a future Mars that is the logical evolution of the way Mars is today. I know this in the most instinctual portion of my being; I feel it strongly, from my connection to all of the energy that transported us across space — and time." He paused. "But scientifically, there is no way to prove this."

"So I'll never be vindicated to the public," Lowell said, his voice trailing off in great sadness and despair.

"That matters far less than what we have experienced together," Jung said, "For our importance as human beings lies in our collective strength, our shared dreams, our energies, not in anything we desire as individuals, not in the narcissistic desire of any man's ego for recognition."

"My young friend Carl does not understand the human ego as well as I do," Freud said, "That the individual desire for personal advancement — the ego's need for achievement — is the heartbeat of humankind, the driving force of the race." Freud put a hand on Lowell's shoulder. "Do not despair, Percival, my friend, for somehow I suspect you will be vindicated. There was life here on Mars once, abundant life, and one day you will be found right after all."

"If we emerge from this fantastic place," Jung said "And I sincerely hope we do, there will be no tangible evidence of what occurred. We will only have our shared memory of events, and know that we have touched one another in an alternate realm, and that we have collectively touched the remnants of a compelling memory, of a great civilization now gone, of a planet's life force ebbing, ebbing away —" His eyes brightened. "But one can't help wonder what Mars was like — *really* like, when it was in its young and vibrant youth —"

And for just a moment, for whatever reason, Percival Lowell and his companions saw the image of a planet with abundant water, and for an instant, just for an instant, something silver, bright and beautiful broke the surface of a sea and flew through the air under the sun and blue, thinning sky before disappearing beneath the shining, flashing waters of Mars' Great Northern Ocean.

SILVER SELENE

Philip Palmer

BASED ON THE CHARACTERS CREATED BY
WILKIE COLLINS IN
THE WOMAN IN WHITE

THE NARRATIVE OF WILLIAM HARTRIGHT, LUNAR EXPLORER

I have described the experience many times, but words cannot capture the sheer magic of the moment. Nor, in all candour, are words my *métier*. My father is an artist. My aunt Marian – or rather I should say 'honorary aunt' – is the writer of the family, always dashing off novels and writing letters to the newspapers. But I am the practical type. I have always excelled at sports, I can run like nobody's business, and I pride myself on being physically without fear. But to describe the indescribable…ah, how does one do it?

The answer is: I simply do not know. And therefore I shall not make the attempt. I shall merely describe the experience in the same words I have used in countless interviews. I travelled to the Moon, on a conveyance designed by scientists of peerless wit, and there I encounter a native Selenian; a female of the species. Silver in hue, and unapparelled, yet in such a way as not to offend due modesty. I was wearing my breathing apparatus as was my fellow space traveller Andrew Macintosh. But this creature we encountered had no artificial lungs, no tubes; she breathed the airless air as if it were…no, that metaphor eludes me. I shall simply say: She was silver in hue and perfect in physique. She did not breathe air. And she spoke to me in a language I did not understand, but which immediately commanded my comprehension.

And she said to me: "We have been waiting for you."

Such was my lunar adventure. This same Selenian is now standing trial for the attempted murder of myself. I believe she is innocent but I cannot prove it. I am told that witnesses observed her attempting to drown me in the waters of the lake near my home in Limmeridge, but I have no recollection of it.

To begin somewhere nearer the core of this strange tale, I must skip over the many documented accounts of how the Selenians travelled to our planet in a ship made, apparently, of glass. I shall take it for granted that my readers are familiar with the political and economic repercussions of our encounter with a friendly yet alien species who, apparently, have been living in the innermost recesses of our own moon for many millennia. For an account of the glorious ice tunnels, which house the civilisation of the Selenians, I must refer you to the book written by my friend and fellow space traveller Andrew Macintosh, *Silver Selene*. Instead, I shall simply recount that I invited the female Selenian – nameless, as is the way of her kind, but I chose for convenience to call her Maria – to join me as my guest at my parents' home, Limmeridge House. This request was cleared with the Foreign Office, and we – by which I mean myself, my mother and father, and my redoubtable Aunt Marian – spent three happy weeks with Maria, in the course of which she told us much about herself by means of the strange mental tickling that passes for communication with her kind.

And then, on the morning of the third day of the fourth week of her visit, I went for my usual pre-breakfast swim in the lake; and woke to find myself half drowned, listening to the babbling of old Harry Cobley, who claims he had saved my life.

Why did she try and kill me? I do not know. I do not recollect. But my duty is discharged. My tale is told. I have nothing to add.

Except that I swear and avow: Maria is innocent. Though all the evidence be against her, though she has confessed her guilt, though there be a witness who saw the whole terrible affair, she is innocent! She could not have meant to harm me – me! Who loved her to distraction, the man who had opened his heart to her – how could she want to kill me?

And yet, the facts declare it – she is a attempted murderess and I am lucky to be alive.

NARRATIVE OF HARRY COBLEY, A TENANT OF THE LIMMERIDGE ESTATE

This is me own story told in me own words. Miss Marian is writing down what I say, and I have warned her not to fancy it up. I ain't one for grand words and punctuwazza. I can't write and I ain't afraid to admit it. But I can read well enough. Not books but signs. And tracks. I can track my way through any forest. I know when the hawthorn blossoms and when the oak sheds its leaves. I can read the forest right enough.

And I have told 'er, Miss Marian, I mean – that's you, Miss Marian, who is writing down these words at a fair old lick – I told 'er, whatever you do, don't make out that I know more than I do, and that I speak better than what I can. I is what I is, that's Harry Cobley. Right enough.

Miss Marian has agreed to my demand and requirement with the exception of, she ain't prepared to write out the cussing. Words like ---- and ----- and ------ and ---- will not pass beyond her pen. Not that I'm one to cuss in front of a lady, but you know, when you're telling the tale, it do develop a rhythm of its own.

This is what I saw that day when I was in Limmeridge Woods admiring the wonders of Nature and not, no not in any way, illicitly purloining rabbits what belong to the estate. That allegation is a ------ lie, no it's a ------- lie, no I go further, it is utter downright --------.

I have no more to say on that matter, and forgive me for speaking so forthright Marian. She is blushing see as I am saying this. A distinguished spinster lady is our Miss Marian with her grey hairs and her soft smile and her buttoned up dress; not blessed in looks but none the worst for that! For a man does not study the appearance of the mantelpiece, when he pokes the – no I shall indeed refrain from completing that country simile. I admire you Miss Marian I do, you're a striking lady despite the passage of years and your mannish face and that hint of a moustache on your upper lip, and if I was ten years younger and you weren't so ------- ladylike, I'd close me eyes and ----- --- ---- --- ---.

Forgive me Miss Marian for flirting so audaciously. I do what I do, as you know. And I've always had an eye for the ladies, I 'ave. Why I remember –

Well chid, Miss Marian, well chid. To continue with my tale, of how I saw that evil ----- near drown a human being, otherwise known as young Master William Hartright of

Limmeridge House, who I have known for many a year and a fine strapping man he is too.

It was an August day. Hot. You could feel the sweat under your clothes, like slime under the serge. I could smell meself somedays, well most days in fact, I sweated so much. And I was in the woods, admiring, as I believe I've explained, Nature's bounty, and not checking my traps, for I had not set no traps, that I deny categoriwazzat.

Then I saw the Moon Woman by the side of the lake and I concealed myself under shrubbery and lay motionless for some half hour or so, as you do when there's a prospect of a lady stripping naked for a swim and you stand a chance of – no I shan't finish that thought Miss Marian, for fear you will scar your page with dashes. In short, I thought I'd see her -----, and indeed I did, and it was nothing like – well.

So as I say, she had that long gown over her body and she took it off and I could see the underneath and it was like looking at glass, no it was like looking into a lake of crystal clearness, no it was like – it was like nothing I can think of, except itself.

She was, in brief, most passing strange. I can say it no plainer than that, no indeed! And you can rely on me to say what I see, with no varnishing or poetic wazzat. 'Cause that's the kind of fellow I am. That's Harry Cobley for you. I am as I am! Why some folks –

I do not digress, Miss Marian, I expliwazzat.

Nay, that's harsh! I am merely accounting for how I came to stay so long, hidden under bushes and breathing quietly as a hound about to seize a hare. She, the Moon Woman, swam in the lake and it was hard to tell the water from the body. Then Master William joined her, and I feared it was an assignation. He was buck naked and – no I shall spare your blushes – he were a man right enough. A hero no less. A man from Limmeridge what had been to the Moon and stood upon Moon Rock and met Moon People. Who'd have thought it? Not Harry Cobley that's for sure, not as a nipper and not as a young man. What strange old times we live in.

I shall not progress any further if you keep telling me not to digress, Miss Marian. For me, to *progress* is to *di*gress. Ah! There, you see, it turns out that I too can bandy fancy words when I needs to!

No they did not fornicate Miss Marian, whilst in my 'purview', whatever one of them might be. Nor did I creep across the ground as quiet as a hunter stalking a stag and search her silver gown for jewels or gold or alien magic machines that might be sold on the hush hush market for a king's ransom. That did not happen and those that say it did are liars, and them I do repudiwazzat.

They swam in short. Master William is a strong man. The strongest I've known. He and I used to arm-wrestle in The

Grapes and never once did I win. And I'm a man who can bend a horse shoe straight, even in my old age I can do so.

But she was stronger still. She raced him through the water and then she stopped and seized him and thrust him down. They vanished for a minute, two minutes, three minutes or more. I could see the water boil with all the thrashing beneath and that's when I raised my gun –

Nay, nay, nay, I shall not stand for calumny of my character. I carry my gun for companionship, not for poaching. There's a difference Miss Marian.

And that's when, as I say, I raised my gun and fired it in the air. A warning shot. The water boiled again and Master William rose up like a trout leaping and gasped his way to shore. Splashing wildly, limbs a-trembling, face red as a beet, by which I mean, more purple than red. He clambered upon the shore. And I ran over to help. When I looked again the Silver Moon Lady was gone. She ran away. With guilt no doubt. If I'd seen her leave the lake, I'd have peppered her arse, forgive my plain talk Miss Marian, with buckshot. Murdering b ----- she was. Or so she tried to be.

But Master William denied it all. "She tried to kill you," I sez, "She did not," sez he. "She held you under the water" I protested, "Ah just larking we was," quoth he. "I saw what I saw," I said, "I have no recollewazzat of such a thing," he replied. Protecting her, you see. I don't know why.

But mayhap I do know why. These Moon Women are strange but they are still women. Most beautiful women. Haunting eyes. A man could fall for a creature like that. Not me, I like 'em straight-talking and full 'a laughter, and with ample flesh on the backside and up the top, but a gentleman certainly might certainly fall for a creature like that.

And that's my statement, that's what Harry Cobley saw, I'll say it again in open court. Except for that part about denying the rabbits, I'd leave that out. Best not to put the thought into folks' heads you see, even though it b'aint at all true. That would be the smart way of it.

But the nub of the matter is this: The Moon Woman tried to kill our William, and that's a fact.

NARRATIVE OF BILL JONES, PARISH CONSTABLE, LIMMERIDGE

This was a straightforward case and yet I was perturbed by all the complexities of it all. I have been a parish constable for many years, combining its duties with my work as the village smith. I have met the famous Sergeant Cuff of Scotland Yard, during one of his several visits to the Hall, for he was a close friend of Miss Marian Halcombe, on account of their shared interest in stories of the macabre and mysterious. And I am a diligent student of the latest detective theories, and have kept the peace in this district with some success, despite the constant provocations of Harry Cobley, and his son Billy Cobley, and his other son Matt Cobley, and all the other thieving Cobleys. I have arrested drunks and felons and wife batterers and husband batterers (that's Mrs Sanderson I mean) and poachers (that's back to Harry Cobley that is) and I once even foiled an attempt to rob the mail coach, when one of the robbers who was half-witted with the drink told me what he was planning to do upon the horse that I was shoeing. But never before had I been required to arrest a creature from another planet.

There was no detection involved in the matter at all, and more's the pity in my view. I'm tired of Saturday night barneys and country feuds between men with big fists. I was hoping for a juicy case to come my way one day, a Rue Morgue kind of affair, or something deliciously complex like that there business of the Moonstone some decades back.

No matter. I do my duty as constable, no matter how lacking in intellectual stimulation it might be. And on this occasion, I was called out to Limmeridge House where the defendant, as she will eventually be termed, confessed in full. I wrote her statement down. She signed it, though I could not read her signature, and then I explained to her that she was arrested, and she agreed.

Following these events and with her confession carefully secured in my inside coat pocket, I took the Moon Woman to the police station in Limmeridge village, which is in fact my house, and locked her in the cell, which is in fact the back room of my forge with a padlock on the door. She made no protest and was courteous as a creature can be, who is from another planet in a village strange to her, accused of attempted murder. And she did not eat, she did not drink, and she did not sleep, all night long.

After this I took a witness statement from Harry Cobley who saw the whole affair. And I took a statement from Mister William Hartright the space traveller, the aggrieved party, who had no recollection of the assault, just that he and the Moon Woman had been swimming together in the lake. But there were bruises on his arms. The Moon Lady had confessed. What could I do? So I kept her in the cell overnight and in the morning I took her to the magistrate's and a date was set for her trial in the Court of Quarter Sessions. The charge was attempted murder. The penalty was death by hanging.

I had done my duty. I could do no more.

It near broke my heart; this was the greatest case of my career, but it took no solving, no detection, no gathering of clues. The guilty party confessed and that was an end to it.

And then, of course, she escaped.

NARRATIVE OF WALTER HARTRIGHT; FATHER OF WILLIAM HARTRIGHT THE SPACE TRAVELLER

It's a moment that comes to every man. He must pass from idle youth to sober adulthood, he must fall in love, and perhaps his hopes will be dashed for a while, as mine certainly were with my beloved Laura, in those dark days when I had to leave Limmeridge and travelled through South America in desperate loneliness, knowing my heart's desire would never be granted to me.

And then, if a man is lucky, his hopes may be rekindled, as mine were, and he will be given the greatest of boons, a chance to spend all his days in the company of the woman he worships. And such has been my lot. I am the happiest of men, and I love my blessed Laura as much now as I did in the days when I was her painting tutor, in the house of the selfish and flinty-hearted Mr Fairlie.

And then a man grows older, and his black hairs become grey, over the passage of years, and the breath becomes a little shorter, and a man's beloved grows older too before his eyes, and still love does not falter or dim.

But when a man's *son* is in love; ah, that's when age snaps its whip. That's when a man starts to feel – dare I say it? – supplanted. No longer the romantic hero; he becomes the elderly parent dispensing unwanted advice to his lovelorn oldest child.

And that's how I felt when my son confessed his
impossible love for the creature he called Maria; a creature
of silver skin and telepathic voice; a creature so alien that
the very thought of her offended my every principle; a
creature whose appearance appalled me, and yet whose
radiance of spirit and glowing eyes made me feel she was
akin to an angel.

I did not approve of my son's love for such a creature;
I felt she was beneath him – unworthy of him – a monster
not a woman at all. And yet, I concede, if I were a younger
man – if the hairs were black not grey – ah, who knows what
folly I might commit!

I write here in a spirit of candour and self excoriation, in
the knowledge that this document will never be published. It
is for the eyes of Marian alone, her own secret record of the
affair of the Moon Woman. And you, dearest Marian – if I
might apostrophise you thus – are the one person I can trust
with the secrets of my heart. You it was who encouraged
me in my love for Laura all those years ago. You it was too
who nursed my spirit when I was at my lowest ebb, and
who fathomed the workings of my heart. You are to me a
friend more intimate than any man could ever be. You are
my helpmeet, my soul mate; and with you I feel freer to be
my own true self than in any other circumstance. A man can
truly love a woman such as you – free from the tyranny of

sexual desire – and so I am privileged, dearest Marian, to be your friend.

Forgive an old man's ramblings. I am, I suppose, at heart a romantic soul. And I am honest enough to concede that when I was a young man, I followed my heart, and – ah, but that's another story, and one already told.

Yet now I find I am a footnote in my own son's story and it perturbs me. Frankly, I wish they would find the silver lady and hang her, for what she did to my beloved child. And yet I know that William loves her. And I know, too, that he would give his life for her. For such is the spirit of the young man in love – the kind of man that I once was.

They are hunting her in the woods as I write this. I am, as I have explained, indulging my dear friend Marian by writing this account, but I have little of import to add. I never trusted the Moon Woman, despite her strange allure. I do not know why she tried to kill my child. I wish her nothing but ill.

But for my son's sake, I hope she escapes, and finds her way back to her own planet. For I could not bear his heart to be broken, as mine once nearly was.

The facts of the case are this. Maria had been staying with us for some weeks when we were joined at Limmeridge by two unexpected visitors. Earl Granville, no less, who was Foreign Secretary at that time, accompanied by an important

Selenian dignitary, who had just arrived on the second ship sent from the Moon to Earth.

That evening, as the gentlemen retired from the table for port, the venerable silver bodied Selenian sage took Maria aside for a private conference; and he quarrelled bitterly with her in our drawing room, though none of us could tell the substance of their dialogue. It was the fierceness of their tone that betrayed the quarrel; their words remained opaque to us.

The following morning Maria tried to kill my son; and the rest you know.

Narrative of Laura Hartright; mother of William Hartright the Space Traveller

My dearest, beloved, and tender hearted Marian has asked me to write an account of the affair of the Moon Lady in respect of William my adored and cherished only child. Well apart that is from Patricia my daughter – dear me how could I forget Patricia! – who is the sweetest child a mother could hope to have despite her occasional and entirely horrid tantrums of which I shall speak no more.

Marian has particularly requested that in my writing whereof upon the topic of this notorious scandal [IS THAT GRAMMATICAL MARIAN? DO SMARTEN UP MY PROSE AS YOU SEE FIT AND ADD SOME COMMAS

BECAUSE I NEVER KNOW WHERE TO PUT THEM
AND PERHAPS YOU MIGHT ALSO ADD A FEW
PARAGRAPHS OF CLEVER PROSE TO SHOW ME
IN THE EYES OF THE WORLD AS BEING ERUDITE
AS WELL AS A STUNNING BEAUTY, WOULD YOU
MIND DOING THAT TINY LITTLE THING FOR ME
MY DEAREST DARLING?] I should at all times be candid
regarding my deepest feelings towards this tawdry and
repellent alien.

And there is indeed much I can say of this matter and
many insights and feminine intuitions I can offer up to the
public view. Oh yes if I were to explain how I –

And indeed I shall.

But not just yet. For my guests will be arriving for dinner
in a scant few hours and there is barely time for me to
perfume and powder my body and select a dress sufficient
to the occasion. The Fotheringshaws are coming you know.
And Lady Fotheringshaw is a most elegant lady, albeit
plump in the *derrière,* and not really all that bright. We are
planning a trip together to Bath for the Season.

But enough of me! I was planning to write about William
and – oh why is there never enough time!

I sometimes wonder if [BLOTTED]

Miss Marian Holcombe's Narrative (from the
pages of her private and personal diary)
14th June.

Today William introduced us to his *inamorata*, the
remarkable lady from the Moon. She was charming in the
extreme, and once I became accustomed to the trilling sound
in my head generated by her telepathic form of speech,
she proved to be a witty storyteller with a flair for the apt
phrase. After dinner, in the gas-lit glory of the drawing
room, she told us of the icy caverns of the Moon where
artificial light shines upon stalactites and stalagmites of
water frozen many billions of years ago. She told us too
of how her people were visited by Bug-like creatures from
a distant star who claimed they came in peace but soon
began to wage war. She described in harrowing detail how
light weapons and energy bombs from the insectoids' space
ships rained upon her planet, massacring millions, though
Maria's kind refused to retaliate, for that is not their way.
And when the war was lost, the few surviving creatures of
the race we know as Selenians were forced to flee their own
planet in space vessels, scattering in all directions; until
one such ship arrived in our Solar System and made their
home in the catacombs of the Moon, hidden from the distant
sight of their enemies on their home planet. And there they
dwelled; when Rome fell the Selenians dug deeper into

the Moon; when the Mongols pillaged and raped their way through Europe, the Selenians observed from afar with their telescopes and quailed at the barbarity of their near neighbours.

Many – including myself – have asked why the Selenians did not settle upon Earth itself, when they first arrived in our Solar System? With its fertile lands and icy Poles, it would have made a finer home for them that the airless Moon. But perhaps they were fearful of co-existing with other life forms, in case they were once again engulfed in war. For, as Maria explained to us, the Selenians are a timid species, pacifist by principle, and have an almost religious aversion to strong emotions such as hate.

So instead the Selenians hid in caverns deep below the surface of our Moon, and meanwhile on Earth the Holy Roman Empire blossomed and withered; and the Ottomans rose; and America was colonised; and steam driven machines and vehicles were invented; and looms became mechanised; and then, to the astonishment of all, a French scientist stumbled upon the uncanny secret of how to harness cosmic rays into a form of propulsion, and hence cross the void between the two conjoined planets a century before the Selenians had anticipated.

And Maria talked too of her peoples' culture, of how they can speak entire novels worth of story through dancing, and their form of singing, and their art – the magnificent ice sculptures that they have created in the hollowed out caverns of the Moon.

And in return we told her of Limmeridge, and the annual fete which I have organised for many years now. And we – or rather I, for Laura was struck speechless by the strange creature, as indeed were both her husband and her son – spoke of the machinations of the Parish Council, which is determined to drag its heels on the matter of the Limmeridge Primary School.

And Maria expressed her deep fascination in everything I had to say. And then we played cards, and she ate a few of the small cakes baked by Laura's fair hands, even though she conceded that her kind have no process of digestion such as we understand; which indeed was fortunate, since Laura's cakes have the consistency of stone.

Though she be alien, the glass maiden is a delight. I can see why William is so charmed by her.

15th June

A curious incident occurred today. We took Maria walking through Limmeridge Woods, and down to the lake. And the sun shone on the waters, in way that was entirely beautiful, but poor Maria's spirits sank for no good reason.

Later, she and young William quarrelled – I observed it from afar – and they returned to the house separately.

16th June

William has confided in me the secrets of his heart – he loves the woman from the Moon and wishes to marry her. I told him he was a young fool, in no uncertain terms and in my briskest of tones. He berated me as an interfering old spinster. Each of those three words was a nail driven into my already bloodied heart.

19th June

Today Laura made lemonade and fussed around her guests in the garden, and was quite her old enchanting self. Her hair is tinged with grey now but still richly brown in the main, and lustrous. Her eyes are still a bright blue, like gems, or like a Cornish sea lit by the sun. Her smile still has the power to entrance all those who behold it. Her spirit is pure, her heart is noble, her intent is kind.

And yet all too often – as even I, her closest of friends, must acknowledge – her idle chatter becomes – well – extremely idle. She can in truth be rather acerbic about those who are not blessed with her own special kind of beauty; like the parlour maid who she insisted on calling 'fatty old thing,' and not just behind her back. Walter and I are usually charmed by our beloved one's tantrums; but sometimes even he sinks into melancholy at Laura's bad temper and refusal to consider the feelings of others.

And at those moments, I see Walter's brow furrow, and his eyes become sad; and I yearn to be able to sooth his troubled thoughts. But I cannot, for only a wife can offer such succour, and a wife I will never be, to him or any man.

Sometimes I fear Laura was irretrievably damaged by the events of her past life, and the horrors she experienced. There is a simplicity and a repetitive quality to her table talk that makes me fear her wits have never fully returned to her. And, I must confess, she drinks in truth a little more alcohol than ladies generally do, in our admittedly rather conservative and male-centred society, though fortunately she does not suffer from redness of nose, or unsteadiness of gait; she can, as she has explained to us, 'handle her liquor'.

But still I love her, as does Walter. And to her and to him I have devoted my entire life, in humble service; spinster as I am.

25th June

Oh what a wretched evening this has been! After dinner, as we took a turn around the garden, I quarrelled with William, and he now refuses to speak to me. He is affronted because I told him that his Moon Woman was a dangerous creature, who he should treat with the utmost care. I am convinced there is something of the sly about her. I do not trust her, and I told him so.

This conviction has grown upon me slowly. Maria is so adored by all, her voice is so eloquent with its trills and reverberations that echo in one's very skull, that to be in her company is like conversing with a symphony. And she is cleverer than I am too, and understands physics and chemistry, which I do not. She has learned to read in English and has consumed every book in our little library, including the collected works of Shakespeare, which she has by heart. She read every single play in a day, and knows them all, and can speak eloquently of the pathos of Lear, the wretched arrogance of Macbeth, the sublime indecision of Hamlet.

She has read my own novels too, all of them, and calls them 'pleasant'. She actually used that word to me – to *me!* Discounting in a stroke all the social satire and biting political allegory of all that I have written. That was during her second week here; and I shall never forgive her for her inapt phrase. Call my writing complex, yes; emotionally subtle by all means; harrowing at times, yet aptly phrased, with a rich blend of comedy and pathos, combining the energy of Dickens at his most unsentimental with the observational insight of Fanny Burney – such a critique would indeed be highly appropriate, and I would assuredly commend any critic who wrote of my work in such terms. Nay, you may even describe my eleven triple-decker masterpieces as 'page turners' if you wish, and I shall not be offended. But pleasant! Never!

26th June

I thought today of Count Fosco, the liar and thief and Spy who had tried to steal my Laura away from me. In his own way he had loved me. But what would such a love have been worth? Anything? Something? If he had in fact won my heart and taken me with him to the Continent, causing me to abandon my friends and life and scruples, could he have given me some satisfaction, some glimpse of passion, some faint insight into requited love, in his own, twisted, blackguardly way?

I have no answer.

27th June

I had another glimpse of the darker side of Maria today. Oh ungrateful wench! What a manipulative and black hearted impostor! She taunted young William openly, she scorned his knowledge of physics and the universe, and she mocked the crudity of the cosmic ray cannon which had propelled his metal landau into space and on to the surface of the Moon. And she concluded by telling him his parents and his Aunt Marian were a bunch of hypocritical dolts who didn't want him to be happy, and who were jealous of her for trying to steal away his heart. Unfair! Untrue! Vile! Unforgivable!

There is without a doubt black evil in the heart of that creature. My fears are all confirmed; my unease about her is proved correct.

But yet, even as she taunted him and mocked him, I saw William's love for her grow. Like the writer of a sonnet addressing his ideal and courtly love, he regards every insult as a kiss, each mockery as an inducement to adore.

William is a fool. And she is nothing but an evil b----!

There. I never thought I would think such a word, or write it in my private journal, even if concealed in dashes. I hate her. I hate her! I hate her!

28th June

I am speechless. The parish constable has been to Limmeridge. Maria has been arrested for the attempted murder of William. William pleads her innocence, but the parlour maid overheard it all; Maria confessed. She is a would be murderess. A viper clasped to our bosom.

30th June

I have embarked upon my mission to show William the folly of his ways; I am compiling statements from all those who knew Maria during her sojourn on Earth, including Harry Cobley who witnessed the attempted murder, to show William that he must rip his love for this evil alien from his heart, and find a girl of his own class and station to worship and adore.

Maria meanwhile is still on the run.

2nd July

Ah what a night! Maria has been here, in my room, and she has opened her heart to me. And her words have astonished me beyond all measure, for she admits that she is guilty of the crime of which she is accused, and yet she is innocent – both at the same time.

I found her in my bed chamber when I retired after dinner, sitting on the floor, slumped against a wall. She had entered via the window, after climbing up a sheer wall. Her skin was grey, not its usual translucent silver sheen, and her eyes gleamed as dully red as the embers of coal. She seemed desperately ill. I feared that she was dying.

"You're hurt," I said and she did not respond. Her kind has no body language; they do not nod the head to show assent, nor do they shake the head to indicate a contrary. But her brow furrowed with pain and I heard a tinkling sound in my head and I knew she was too badly injured to speak.

I went to her and raised her hands away from her body, and saw a red dew upon her bodice, and a series of rips in the fabric that looked like buckshot injuries. She had been shot.

She spat and silver fluid stained my floor. I feared that her internal organs had been damaged.

"What can I do?" I asked. "A drink of water? Laudanum? Can I bind the wound?"

For reply she ripped her gown open to reveal the damaged flesh beneath, and I saw that red blood was oozing out of skin that was puckered and black, as if gangrenous.

She fainted.

I retired downstairs to the kitchen and boiled a kettle on the stove. Our under maid Emily saw me there and I swore her to secrecy. I ripped up sheets and carried them up the stairs with Emily behind me, carrying a bowl of hot water in her brawny hands. Then jointly we returned to my room, and lifted the Selenian up and placed her upon my bed. I used a scissors to cut her clothes off her upper torso entirely. Then I dabbed the blackened wounds with a hot cloth, and used a tweezers to probe and remove the pieces of buckshot that were visible to me. The shot that had gone deeper inside her body was beyond my healing powers, but I dared not call the doctor, for this creature was under sentence of death. But I was resolved to nurse her back to health myself. I did not want to her to die or be recaptured until I heard her story in full.

"Now Emily," I said to the breathless under maid.

"Yes mum?" Emily said, making a curtsey that was like a flinch. She feared and respected me, as all the servants at Limmcridge did, even the housekeeper Mrs Soames. I keep a strict house here, even though it is not my house. And yet, by and large, I treat the staff kindly. Laura herself is oblivious to the workings of her own household; she has no more cares than a bird in the sky.

"Not of a word of this," I said to Emily in my firmest voice.

"She's wanted by the police, mum."

"She has sanctuary Emily. Do you know what sanctuary is?"

"No mum."

"She is under my protection. And I am your friend, am I not?"

Her eyes screamed *no* but her lips spake: "Yes mum."

"Not a word."

"Not a word mum."

I sat with the Selenian all night long. In the early hours her body began to twitch and spasm, but I did not panic; I suspected this might be part of her body's healing pattern. After a while the spasms subsided. Her breathing became even. She was asleep.

And then she woke and the bell-like trilling was in my head again; she was speaking to me.

"Thank you," she said.

"I have my reasons," I said coolly.

"I am guilty, you know that?" she confessed. "I did as they alleged. I tried to murder William."

"I know," I said, though until that moment I had not been sure.

"And I wanted to be punished for it. I wanted to hang! But my body would not let me."

"Your body?"

"I am not the sole custodian of my body. I have two minds, two souls."

A loud and indeed rather masculine gasp escaped my lips, as I absorbed the meaning of her extraordinary claim.

Binary souls! The idea astonished me. Two minds in a single body, with different aims and different desires! Who would have dreamed such a thing could be possible?

And now I understood how Maria could have wanted to murder the man who she loved with all her being. Because the Other Maria, the twin soul, saw William as a threat.

"Normally you see," Maria explained, "our souls debate each decision and achieve it jointly. If one mind wants to take a walk and the other wishes to sit in leisure, then the body will walk and *then* repose. Each day is a series of compromises; but it is unheard of for one mind to actually defy another. And yet that is precisely what I did, when I fell in love with a creature of another species! And that is why she, the Other Maria, tried to kill William; not out of hate, for our kind do not hate. But to save us both from a union that could never be allowed."

"Then the Other Maria did wrong," I pointed out. "She is wicked, and immoral."

The tinkling in my head felt suspiciously like laughter.

"She was merely being pragmatic. Morality does not apply in such a case. You are not, after all, our equals," said Maria, in a tone tinged with kindness – which made her words sting all the more. And at that moment I experienced a sense of abject humiliation; for it was clear that as far as these supremely intelligent Selenians were concerned, we humans were like puppies who, if unwanted, could be put in a sack and drowned.

I burned with fury at this slight to my entire species. And yet my tone remained brisk. "What is your plan now?" I said.

"Once I have healed, which will be soon, my body will leave this planet," Maria explained. "At dawn, a ship will be waiting for me by the lake. And then I, or rather we, will join my people, and we will leave this system on our spaceship."

"Forever?"

"Forever."

"Why?" I said, with a hint of sadness.

"Because your people are apes, of course. And you are treacherous, as your history proves. And if we stay, war will ensue. So we will leave. That is the rational thing to do, and we are always rational."

I thought about her words and felt even more affronted. Is humanity really so irredeemable? Perhaps, I concluded, it is. But my heart broke at the thought of this missed opportunity for my kind. To meet creatures from another planet; then to lose them, all in the space of a few months.

"Why did you quarrel?" I asked curiously. "With the other Selenian? The one who came to Limmeridge?"

"He was summoning me home. I refused to come."

"So this has been planned for some time?"

"It has. My role was to pretend to be an envoy, while preparations for our departure were completed. Now we are ready, and we will flee this entire galaxy."

I nodded, then realised she did not understand the gesture. "I understand," I said.

And then she spoke the words that undid me; the words that changed my life; the words that made me a traitor and a deceiver to my dearest of friends.

"Forgive me Marian," the silver Selenian said.

"For what?" I asked her.

"For knowing your secret," she said.

And at that moment, she uttered a lie, a calumny, which I disown and will not repeat, regarding the feelings of my heart towards my dear friend Walter Hartright, the one and only true beloved of my dearest Laura; a man of whose affections I could never be worthy. A man who, if I did love him, I would not —

No matter. She made the comparison, between her unrequitable love for the son, and my allegedly unrequitable love for the father. And she explained, too, the true and abiding tragedy of her kind.

"You mean to say, you *cannot love*?" I said to her, in shock. "Not at all? Not one jot, one tittle, not one atom of love can possess your soul?"

She wept tears of soft glass. "If I could not love, would I be like this?" she protested. "In such appalling, terrible distress?"

"What then?"

"I *must* not love. My kind do not love, ever. It is our way. Our creed. It is how we are so long lived. Our barrenness of spirit makes us immortal."

And it was now I fathomed the truth about the binary souls of the Selenians. For they exist in perfect balance, but they are different. One is rational, one emotional. One sane, one insane. One incapable of love, one capable of love. One good; one evil.

And Maria's body had been possessed by the soul that *could* love. And hence, love it did. She had felt such passion for young William that no one of her kind had experienced for – so she claimed – many millions of years.

"And hence, your evil soul tried to kill William?" I asked her.

"No," she said. "For I am she. *I* am the evil soul. It was the good part of me that tried to save me, from my own folly."

I considered her words, with the greatest of care, and reached a bold conclusion.

"Then," I said to her, "you have no choice."

"What do you mean? What must I do?"

"You must somehow conquer," I explained, "the better part of yourself."

She conveyed puzzlement. "I could never do such a thing," she said.

"Why not! Your spirit is strong. Fight your other soul. Confine it, prevent it taking control of your body ever again." My passion inflamed her, and put a touch of silver into the greyness of her skin.

"Could I do that?" she said, and her face was shining now. "I could – yes – but –" But now the grey began to return to her pallor. Her flesh was tarnishing before my eyes. "No, such a plan could never work," she said sadly. "For in time the other soul would break free of whatever barriers my mind created for it. The only way to –" She broke off, clearly distressed.

"Yes?" I prompted.

"The only way to achieve such a thing," she added, in the bleakest of trills, "is to murder my second soul. To will it, quite literally, out of existence."

"Such a thing is possible?"

"It's possible yes. There are stories about it, ancient stories – but it is forbidden. According to the morals of my kind, it would be an act of evil."

I laughed, mockingly.

"Then *be* wrong," I told her, with calm audacity. "Be immoral. Be a -----! And let your evil soul fly free. Let it inhabit your body unimpeded. And then you can stay. Let your people flee the galaxy, but you can remain and be with William. And then *he* can be your second soul. And you can love him, as he deserves to be loved. Can you do that? *Dare* you do that?"

A long silence ensued. And then she nodded.

She actually nodded!

"I can," she said. "It involves – yes, I can do it."

"You can murder your twin soul," I said – to clarify the sticking point – "without harm to yourself?"

"Yes. I can."

"Then do so!" I demanded.

But at this point, the moon maiden looked at me with her pure blue rock-hard eyes. "And if I do as you suggest," she demanded, "then will you follow me in my course? Will you release the evil soul in *you?* Will you liberate the dark, brooding, passionate Marian who loves a man and would steal him from her vain, witless milksop of a friend, no matter what the price she pays, in the eyes of society, and in the mind of God himself?"

I stared at her, astonished, horrified, appalled – and exhilarated.

And a decision possessed me; a decision I knew I would never regret, no matter what the terrible consequences of it might be.

"Yes," I said, with mounting excitement. "Yes, yes, I shall!"

WHITE FANGORIA

Roland Moore

Clarissa is five years old. Finishing a sausage roll, she absently wipes her greasy hand down her best dress. But this doesn't earn its usual rebuke. Because, like the other adults, Clarissa's mother is preoccupied; staring at the large wooden box on the table and struggling not to cry. Everyone is wearing their finest Leaving Ceremony clothing; everyone is speaking in hushed respectful whispers. No one is worried about a small girl's dress getting messy.

Clarissa hoists onto tip-toes to see what is in the box; over the tantalising edge. Her uncle notices her attempts. After a moment's hesitation, and a mumbled "She's got to learn about Leaving Ceremonies sometime, Marjory", the uncle's meaty hands scoop Clarissa up. Now, finally, Clarissa can see in the box. And her young eyes stare in wonder.

Chagrin was twenty miles away but Yamada Lee couldn't see further than twenty inches.

He had to trust the dogs – as he had done a hundred times before – to find their way over the icy terrain while snow fell like heavy static. The sun was bleaching the horizon so both the snow-covered ground and the white sky merged into the same bright, featureless void. Yamada turned to where he knew Henry Gorton was – his oldest friend and colleague. The large dark shape, obscured by falling snow, was wearing a heavy arctic jacket and riding pillion on the sled as the copper contraption scythed across the tundra. One of the big man's knees rested on their precious tarpaulin-covered cargo. Gorton smiled back. Talking was impossible but his smile gave his sympathies to his friend riding at the helm. Yamada held up four gloved fingers. Gorton got the message: changeover time in four miles and then it'd be his turn to freeze his face off. Yamada didn't hear the bitter laugh that Gorton offered in return.

Here they were; alone in six thousand miles of empty New Arizona wilderness in the middle of winter season. No one came to this snow-covered hell hole without a very good reason. And Yamada Lee and Henry Gorton had a very good reason. They had to make a delivery.

With the four dogs tiring and slowing, ice freezing their fur into solid carapaces giving them even more weight to carry, Yamada knew it was time to give them a rest.

He turned a spiked clockwork wheel on the dashboard of the sled. Loud and furious cogs and gears kicked into life. A clockwork motor took over, propelling the sled forward. The ingenious system meant that sleigh dogs could be rested for periods of up to five miles before the clockwork on the motor was exhausted. Then the dogs would take over again, causing the clockwork to be re-wound.

Chug-a-chug-a-chug.

The noise gave a welcome Pavlovian signal to the dogs to slacken their efforts. They slowed to an ambling pace. The sled was a speck on the landscape ploughing tracks that were instantly erased as soon as they were made. But something was watching. Something that shouldn't even be there. And it didn't need tracks to follow them.

Later, Gorton unpeeled a thermal pack and tossed it into the nest of dogs. Leader, Amigo, Drummer, and Long-Tail. They were unharnessed and huddled together some distance from the sled and tonight's makeshift camp. The dogs moved closer to the heat of the device like water drawn to a sponge; their aching limbs overlapping, bodies touching.

The faint aroma of chili beans drifted from Yamada's stove as Gorton lumbered back, his massive frame bent with exhaustion. As night fell, the snowstorm slowly began to dwindle and finally the men could stretch their frozen limbs; limbs held tense for hours against buffeting ice.

Gorton sat on the sled, the fire flickering in front of him. Yamada slopped warm food onto metal plates and handed one over. By the time both men took their first mouthful, the beans were already barely lukewarm; getting cooler with every hungry mouthful. But that didn't matter. Some distance away, one of the dogs whined. "Leader's tasting it." Gorton laughed. He knew the sounds of each of the dogs; knew the strengths and weaknesses of each one.

Later, the men checked that the cargo was secure. They had been couriers for fourteen years and this was one of the most important loads they'd ever had. Gorton wanted to remove the tarpaulin and have a look at it. Yamada told him not to. It was bad luck to look inside any cargo, but tampering with this particular one was a serious offence in the eyes of the law.

As they drifted to sleep, Yamada wondered about the early Molybdenum prospectors who had lost their lives out here. Even now, the New Arizona Ridge had a bounty of Molybdenum for any traveller foolhardy enough to think they could stay long enough to collect it. Yamada didn't want to stay in this wasteland any longer than necessary.

Then a sudden high-pitched cry split the silence of the night sky. It was nearby. The dogs started to bark, terrified and spooked; their muzzled mouths howling with fear. With no idea as to what was causing the disturbance, Gorton cautiously scrambled up from the sled and shone the gas arc torch in the general direction of the noise. Yamada grabbed the rifle. He loaded the three remaining bullets and the men ran towards the dogs.

As their boots crunched on the ice, they could hear a low pained whimper; and the sound of scurrying as something retreated into the night. The gas arc light caught something on the ground. A shadow on the snow. Gorton shone the light down, eyes focusing. It was a snaking, glistening river of blood trailing away from the camp. Instinctively, Gorton ran a few steps, flashing the light blindly, following the trail. But Yamada grabbed his arm, suddenly aware of the danger of chasing something savage into the darkness. They turned the flashlight back to the camp where six fluorescent discs caught their beam: the eyes of three terrified sleigh dogs. Yamada's boot touched something. A small, hairy stump, wet and shiny. As he bent to look closer, his eyes caught the tiniest plume of steam rising from it into the frozen night air. Gorton shone the arc down, but Yamada already felt a cold sick feeling in his stomach. The light danced in a shaking hand as they saw that the stump had battered claws at the base; a dewclaw ripped at a crazy angle at the back. It was the remains of one of Amigo's front paws. The colour drained from Gorton and Yamada faces, the spit dry in their mouths. What could have done this?

Gorton and Yamada busied themselves securing the camp. The time for post-mortems could come later; first they had to ensure they didn't lose any more dogs. With fourteen miles still to travel, they needed all the remaining animals to make the distance. Not just to make the delivery on time, but also to survive in this environment.

Gorton corralled the dogs and brought them closer to the fire, some fifty metres from the main camp. He calmed them, tying them to a tree. He removed their muzzles so they'd have a small chance of defending themselves if the attacker came back. Yamada added more dead wood to the fire, the bright flames offering a hopeful protection through the bleakest, darkest hours of the night. Finally, the two men slumped on the sled and spoke in hushed whispers; thoughts and fears tumbling out from mouths dry with worry.

"Only ever lost one dog before." Gorton said. "And that was a bear. Nothing like this."

"So what could've done this?" Yamada asked, struggling to hide the fear in his voice.

Gorton shook his head. Amigo had been ripped apart like a Chihuahua in a wind turbine. It didn't bode well for the other, smaller dogs' chances if the creature came back.

Yamada wondered if the creature was something the Molybdenum prospectors had bought with them, because nothing lived in the whole of New Arizona until they'd arrived thirty years after the Final Land Push – a careless airship with a cargo of Bethalose had seen to that.

They knew they'd have to wait for daybreak to examine the scene for tracks and clues. It would be an uneasy night waiting for the darkness to lift. Yamada kept his hand on the rifle.

As soon as dawn broke, Yamada and Gorton crossed to where the dogs had first been camped. A large pool of black red liquid stood in the centre of the clearing, like a nightmarish frozen pond. Amigo's stump had gone. The creature had returned, practically under their noses, to finish its meal.

At first, Yamada couldn't find any tracks for the creature. It didn't make sense. There were only dog tracks. But then Gorton realised some prints were larger. "Wolf." He murmured.

Yamada didn't want to waste any more time. He insisted that they saddle up the sled and move out as soon as possible – to put as much distance between themselves and the horrors of the night before. Gorton harnessed Leader, Long-Tail and Drummer and the sled spluttered to life. Yamada adjusted the dial to manual – allowing the dogs to pull the sled; re-tensing its clockwork cogs and gears. The sled passed the slick black-red mess, and it disappeared behind them, becoming a dark spot on an infinite white blanket.

Heavy snow and only three dogs meant that only six miles were travelled before night started to fall again. Reluctantly, Gorton and Yamada stopped and tethered the animals to skeletal trees in a valley basin, before setting up camp on the slope above. They hoped that last night was a one-off; that they'd left the creature miles away, slumbering with its belly full of dog meat. But as soon as both men had drifted into a shallow sleep, this thin hope was shredded. They heard the noise of a dog screaming and fighting a desperate fight in the valley. "Long-Tail." Gorton shouted as he jumped from the sled.

Shining the gas arc down into the valley, the first thing Gorton saw was Long-Tail staring dully at him; its head bowed at a curious angle. A split second later he realised that Long-Tail was being gripped by the neck by the snarling jaws of a massive black-furred wolf. It started to shake Long-Tail like a plaything. The sled dog desperately tried to bite with his own teeth, but the creature held him so he couldn't turn. Leader and Drummer snarled nearby, but something was stopping them; keeping them at bay. As Gorton and Yamada approached, they saw eight gleaming eyes shining in the darkness on the edges of the canine camp. The giant wolf wasn't alone. It was part of a pack.

Gorton slowed. They would be running to their deaths if they reached the basin. Yamada stopped to aim the rifle. But he couldn't get a clear shot. The giant wolf shook Long-Tail in front of him like a shield. The desperate thrashing of the sled dog's limbs faded to half-hearted twitches. Gorton gritted his teeth. The wolf applied more pressure with its massive jaws, until the dog stopped moving. A small whimper signified the end. Without fear, the wolf glowered at the two men, daring them forward. Then it pressed its jaws closed, severing Long-Tail's neck with the slow squelch of blood and the crunch of vertebrae. A final shake of the massive wolf's jaws and Long-Tail's head came away from its body, thudding into the snow.

Gorton snapped out of his stupor. He grabbed the rifle, aimed it quickly and peeled a bullet straight off. The shot ripped into the giant wolf's right front shoulder, jerking it backwards slightly with a surprised yelp. But it stayed upright.

Gorton levelled the gun again. The wolf stared, unmoving, almost taunting him to try again. Yamada tugged his arm. The other animals in the pack were circling them. Now Gorton and Yamada knew the intelligence of their enemy: the giant wolf had been distracting them while its pack moved in for the kill.

Gorton pointed the gun at the two wolves circling slowly to their right. They stopped moving. But while he did this, the other wolves started circling to the left. He waved the gun in their direction. They stopped, and predictably the wolves on the right started moving again in a deadly game of grandmother's footsteps. Yamada glanced at Gorton. What could they do? They had two bullets. Slowly, but surely, the savage beasts were closing in.

Clarissa can see the black uniform with gold braiding; the epaulets like fancy hems on a curtain; the sleeping man with the peaceful face and the large white moustache. The lines etched through experience and cold campaigns now lessened by the liquefaction of scores of tiny muscles. This is the body of General Thomas Grosvenor. Clarissa's mother reaches for the girl's hand to comfort her, but Clarissa isn't upset. After all, it's just a sleeping man with a big moustache wearing a general's uniform. Then one of the onlookers – a wiry man – looks concerned as he peers into the box.

"That's the queerest thing..." He says.

The other mourners huddle closer to see. A hushed chorus of respectful "What's wrongs?" and "What is its?" quickly follow.

The wiry man points to the sleeping man's hands folded across his chest. Clarissa tries to look too, but she's up in the air and then heading to the ground as her uncle whisks her away before she can properly see. The sight is obviously too shocking for a young child. She is deposited some distance away as her uncle rushes back to the edge of the box.

Standing alone, a small island in a sea of paisley carpet, Clarissa hears the other mourners are gasping as if they have been personally affronted. They have all noticed what is wrong. They have all noticed *what* is missing.

Gorton levelled the rifle, aiming at one of the animals at the front of the pincer movement.

"If I blow one of them apart, maybe they'll back off." Gorton said, the words almost a question; looking for validation, guidance.

"What if they rush us instead?" Yamada offered. "What then?"

"Then we won't have a chance." Gorton said – his eye looking down the sight of the rifle.

"We don't have a chance now." Yamada offered, tipping his head slightly in encouragement.

A moment's final reflection and Gorton cracked a perfect shot into the lead wolf to the right of them. The top of the animal's head sheared off in an explosion of crimson and the wolf collapsed, dead before it hit the snow. The other animals didn't retreat. They were assessing the situation, looking at the fear on the men's faces. Gorton grinned, this small victory boosting his hopes of escaping this situation. The giant wolf – obviously the leader – eyed the men with venom; as if it was trying to guess how many bullets were left in the rifle. Gorton raised the firearm again and this time quickly shot the animal nearest to them on the left. It wasn't such a clean shot, blowing a hole in the wolf's flank. It whimpered, thrashed and stumbled and finally fell still on the snow.

"Who's next?" Gorton shouted, a mix of bravado and desperation. A man with an empty rifle. "Come on!"

Seconds stretched into eternity as Gorton and Yamada waited for the animals' next move. Finally, the giant wolf licked its fangs, and turned slowly away. The other pack members dutifully turned on their heels and peeled away. But when they reached the edge of the dog area they stopped. This wasn't a full retreat, more of a regrouping.

Gorton whistled to his sled dogs, wanting them to come to the safety of the sled. But the big wolf howled a warning and the sled dogs stayed still. Yamada tried to reach one of the dogs to drag it by the scruff, but one of the wolves crossed threateningly near to them, snarling and barking. Yamada retreated. The wolf came forward another few steps, blocking his way; ensuring that he couldn't get back to the sled dog. Another wolf moved forward, forcing Gorton and Yamada out of the clearing. This was when the men realised the stark truth: the wolves weren't going to let them take the dogs away. They were trading their lives for those of their dogs. On shaking legs, Gorton and Yamada scurried to the sled and the safety of the fire. Gorton stashed the empty rifle on the sled. Yamada widened the fire to form a crude circle of flames around the whole sled. As he worked, he could hear the sounds of the terrified sled dogs whimpering in the dark. Finally, Gorton made a decision, his voice trembling with anger and fear.

"We've got to go back. We can't leave them." He said.

Yamada nodded. He picked up a length of wood from the fire, the end glowing red. Gorton grabbed the rifle, wielding it like a club.

But as they took a few steps away from the sanctuary of the sled, they could see the dark shapes of the wolves moving quickly on the horizon. Wolf howls filled the night. They were making their move. Yamada held Gorton's back.

"It's too late."

Gorton stayed still. Yamada returned to the fire. Both men tried to blot out the screams of dogs being torn apart in the darkness.

At first light, Gorton and Yamada cautiously left the sled. The ring of flames still smouldered as their heavy boots stepped out of the safety zone. In the basin of the valley, they found blooms of blood etched across the snow. All the sled dogs had gone. Yamada found a scrap of fur, but that was all that remained. Then Gorton called him over – he'd found something else. Yamada bent down, keeping one eye on the perimeter of the basin in case of ambush. Gorton held up a small bronze cog sticky with blood; clogged with a chunk of fur and some muscle sinew. Yamada shook his head. "What is it?"

Gorton admitted he'd heard tales of Molybdenum prospectors using mechanically-enhanced animals to guard their treasure. But he'd always assumed such tales were myths. The glistening evidence in his gloved hand told him otherwise.

"So how do we kill it?" Yamada asked.

Gorton shrugged. "We've got to find a way…"

At the sled, a further shock awaited them. Packages were ripped and scattered. The food rations were spread, half-eaten across the snow like discarded takeaways outside the gin palaces of Exos City. One of the wolves was beating a retreat, smacking its yellow teeth with the memory of the meal.

With no dogs to pull it, the fully cranked machine wouldn't cover more than five miles. It wouldn't be enough to reach Chagrin. With no choice, the burly Gorton agreed to pull the sled. The low friction of the ice would help him keep the sled moving. Yamada would steer the sled and ensure that the precious cargo didn't come astray. If they could cover just three miles with Gorton pulling, then the clockwork might be cranked enough to sale the remaining distance under automatic propulsion. But Yamada was concerned, as the conditions were so inhospitable.

"Got a better idea?" Gorton said as he hoisted the harness over himself. Soon the leather straps creaked against his snow jacket as he struggled to get the sled going. Yamada pushed from the back – both men grunting with exertion. It was no good. They needed to start the sled on automatic to get it moving. Yamada clambered over the cargo to get to the spiked wheel.

About one hundred yards away on the right, three wolves were closing in. Yamada mouthed a silent curse. Gorton saw the beasts and shouted at Yamada to start the engine. Yamada's hand slipped on the wheel as the giant wolf appeared beyond the three scouts; its front flank caught the sunlight, a glint of metal beneath the ripped fur. It was walking with a pronounced limp.

Finally, Yamada's cold hands found purchase on the wheel; clicking it to automatic. There was the loud noise of cogs and gears increasing in speed as the engine cranked to life.

Chug-a-chug-chugga.

The wolves took several steps back, away from the sled. Then it started to move. Both Gorton and Yamada realised what had happened.

"They don't like the sound." Gorton smiled, barely believing what he'd seen.

He clambered aboard the moving sled, still wearing the harness. As the sled spluttered across the landscape, they prayed that the wolves wouldn't follow them.

About a mile away and with no sign of any pursuers, Yamada cut the engine and before the sled lost too much momentum, Gorton leapt down and started to pull. The sled kept going this time with the forward motion and Yamada allowed himself to look at the hazy sun and believe for one brief moment that things would be alright.

If they had an airship's view of the landscape, Yamada and Gorton could have seen the miles of ice stretching out ahead of them; the terrain dotted with skeletal trees like the hairs on an old man's head. They could have perhaps glimpsed the small safe haven of Chagrin six miles away; its chimneys burning with black smoke as turbines worked to heat the town. They would also have seen the rag-tag troupe of wolves that followed them, lagging about half a mile behind in a wide semi-circle. But Yamada and Gorton had no such view. As far as they knew, they had left the wolves behind and they stood some chance of reaching Chagrin. But they also couldn't see the frozen lake that waited over the brow of the hill.

The sea of legs is broken by the appearance of Clarissa's mother's face. She stoops under the table to see the confused face of her daughter. Clarissa's mother smiles at her and offers a hand. Clarissa takes it and allows herself to be plucked from under the table.

As she comes out, Clarissa sees the Third Lord Argent reaching under the body in the box. Clarissa's mother explains that he's arrived to search for the missing item. With his tongue sticking out in concentration, the Third Lord Agent's hands probe under the inert figure of General Thomas Grosvenor. He mumbles about how it's a serious offence to take any item from such a body.

Clarissa's mother whispers that the Third Lord Argent is the only person permitted to touch the dead body. Clarissa nods, pretending to understand.

As the probing Argent's hand causes the luxurious lining of the coffin to undulate in waves of expensive fabric, Clarissa asks the question to which everyone present already seems to know the answer. She asks her mother: "What is it that's missing?"

Gorton's powerful legs trudged forward, the sled moving slowly behind him. Yamada was pushing the sled now, partly to aid progress, partly to remove weight. His fingers were splayed against the rear copper plate, and despite his heavy gloves he could feel the cold getting to him. From time to time he had to shake his hands, first one and then the other, to unlock the icy rictus in his fingers.

Suddenly, Gorton lost his footing as his boots skated on ice. Too late he realised it was a frozen lake; the momentum of the sled bringing it inexorably behind him. The surface ice started to crack. But Gorton's reactions were too slow, too riddled with cold and as a gaping maw of black water opened, he plunged into it. The first that Yamada knew – his head down, back legs propelling from the back – was when the sled suddenly pulled quickly away from him, rising into the air as its front fell into the icy water. The tent, rifle and saucepan clattered from their tethers into the lake.

Gorton gasped as the cold water penetrated his clothes, his lungs filling with freezing water. The sled hung suspended, its front in the water, its rear sticking into the air; the rocky rim of the lake acting like the balancing point of a seesaw. Heat packs fell from the upended sled into the water, exploding in small fizzes of smoke; a low-key fireworks display around Gorton's flailing body. He grabbed the reins of his harness, and tried to hoist himself free. Yamada had reached the water's edge, the ice rippling with fine stress lines as he stretched a hand out towards Gorton. Yamada's numb hands tried to pull Gorton free, but he soon lost his grip, and Gorton momentarily slipped under the water. Yamada tried again, lying across the ice. But a loud cracking noise signalled a large fissure snaking quickly underneath him. He stayed still, scarcely daring to breathe. Meanwhile Gorton tried to cling to the harness, desperate to pull himself up. But he was weak; too drained to climb the whole way; and the sled was teetering on the precipice. Would it hold even if he could climb the harness? Or would Gorton's pulling actually bring it crashing down on top of him?

Realising that he could do nothing at the water's edge, the drenched Yamada scrambled cautiously across the ice like a newly born foal to the sled controls. He slammed the reverse lever into place and then spun the spiked wheel to automatic. The sled spluttered to life as cogs furiously tried to engage. Gorton's right hand let go of the harness cable. He looked pained, desperate to maintain his hold, but the effort was too much. The sled fought to be free of the precipice; the teeth of cogs shearing off under the pressure. Yamada desperately tried to push the sled from the front. With a splutter, the sled finally hurtled itself backwards away from the cracking ice, pulling Gorton free. But tethered to the front, Gorton's shoulder hit the rocks on the edge of the lake; cracking loudly. The sled continued backwards, out of control and driverless; dragging Gorton like a rag doll. It ran for about a hundred yards, before hitting a tree and stopping. Yamada ran to the controls and spun the spiked wheel to the left, stopping the engine. With the shed stalled, he looked along the harness to where Gorton was still attached, unmoving; like a sodden bundle of clothes.

Shaking with the cold, Yamada reached his friend. He propped Gorton's head in his hands. The big man's face was blue, his lips purple, his eyes partly opened. He was shaking uncontrollably. Yamada laid him gently on the snow and scampered to where one heat pack had fallen on the ice. Yamada cracked it open as he reached his friend's side. But instead of producing heat, the pack spluttered and fizzed. Tossing it away, he held Gorton's head, and told him that everything would be all right. But soon Gorton stopped shaking and was still and silent. Yamada kissed his friend's forehead, and stumbled to his feet.

His clothes solid with ice, he spotted something in his peripheral vision. Silently the wolves were closing in around the carnage. The big wolf looked impassively at him, its eyes colder than the snowsuit on Yamada's back.

Yamada clutched the harness and dragged Gorton, toward the sled, all the while keeping eye contact with the monstrous wolf. Manhandling his friend's body over the back runner, Yamada hoisted Gorton onto the sled. As the exhausted Yamada stopped to catch his breath the wolves edged closer.

Yamada turned the spiked wheel to automatic. The sled lunged backwards against the tree – still in reverse. Finding the right gear, Yamada started the sled on its final journey. The wolves retreated slightly at the noise, but continued to trail the sled. They were getting more confident. How long would the noise keep them at bay? Yamada was crying, but he couldn't feel the tears.

The rag-tag wolves maintained a safe distance behind the sled as it spluttered forwards; slowly fanning themselves out into a semi-circle, waiting for the engines to die.

Yamada sat numbly on the front of the sled. He was finding it hard to stay awake; finding it hard to feel his arms and legs. But he clung on, determined to reach Chagrin. Gorton's head bobbed lifelessly up and down. The big wolf started to walk alongside the sled, hunger overcoming its fear. Now it was fifteen feet away from Yamada. He fumbled for the gas arc lamp and threw it in frustration. The lamp missed; clattering uselessly on the ice.

Chug-a-chug-a-chug.

The engine clanked on. The giant wolf and its pack edged slowly nearer to the sled.

Yamada crossed the brow of a hill and was devastated that Chagrin wasn't visible on the new horizon. He struggled to keep awake, his stomach empty, his limbs frozen. How would he die? Falling into a frostbitten sleep would be preferable to having his body ripped apart; animals tearing off his fingers as he struggled to defend himself.

And after his death, what about his Leaving Ceremony? What would that be like? And that's when he thought about the cargo. The box under the tarpaulin. General Thomas Grosvenor in full military regalia in a plush wooden coffin. He thought of the severed limb of his dog and how nothing had remained by morning. He knew they'd have no body to bury.

No plush wooden coffin. No military regalia...

...Clarissa said that General Thomas Grosvenor looked very smart. All of his fingers were splayed carefully in front of him. Nothing looked wrong. She couldn't see what the fuss was all about...

...No carefully combed hair. No fresh shirt. Yamada would have none of those things. No polished boots. No starched handkerchief. And no loaded musket for protection in the afterlife

Clarissa's mother whispered to Clarissa the reason everyone was so upset was because the protocol of the

Leaving Ceremony had been broken. General Thomas Grosvenor had been robbed of his protection in the afterlife. An important soldier should never be buried without his loaded musket.

Something snapped in Yamada's brain. Of course. The loaded musket in the coffin. A musket shaped like a blunderbuss and loaded with a large ball bearing. Who knew if these things even worked? But feverishly, he turned to the cargo, pulling at the tarpaulin; barely aware that he was making a desperate whimpering noise as he did so. His clumsy hands fumbled at the clasps on the coffin. Finally, he managed to slide the lid across. He grabbed the large ornate silver hand gun, the cold metal instantly icing over.

The four wolves looked interested.

Chug-a-chug-a-chug-a.

The gun on his lap, Yamada pushed the lid back into place. He picked up the musket – contemplating his next move. With a shaking hand he levelled it at the giant bio-mechanical wolf trotting some distance to the side of the sled.

Chug. Chug. The sled's power was running down. The indicator gave it half a mile more.

Yamada tried to aim the gun, but his body was shaking too much with cold to aim it with any certainty. And he felt too sleepy, too tired; eyes struggling to stay open in the cold wind. He couldn't feel his torso from the frozen clothes. The big wolf snarled malevolently at him.

Crying, he bought the musket back inside the sled. Sadly, he knew what he had to do.

He twisted the spiked wheel from automatic to off and the sled slid to a slow halt on the snow. With the protection of the engine noise gone, the giant wolf and its three comrades moved in for the kill. Yamada waited; the only sound was the wind and the soft tap-tap of wolves padding across the ice.

As the giant wolf got nearer, Yamada said a silent prayer and heaved Gorton off the sled. His old friend landed in a heap on the ground. The wolves looked at the lifeless body in front of them. They weighed up the situation. What would they do? Yamada knew they were hungry, but would they eat him or Gorton first?

"I'm not going anywhere…" Yamada shouted. "It's over…"

The giant wolf smacked its lips, a sliver of drool falling into the snow. One of the other wolves was sniffing at Gorton. It uttered an enthusiastic bark, as if confirming that the big man was safe to eat. The big wolf threw one last glance at Yamada. He could wait.

The big wolf bent to Gorton's body, before casually biting a chunk off his cheek. Yamada watched the other wolves congregate on Gorton. Within seconds, all four wolves were face down, snouts greased with blood, teeth pulling at flesh; knowing that Yamada would be their next course.

From the motionless sled, Yamada levelled the gun at the closely grouped huddle. He was trembling with the cold, but knew that if he could shoot straight, he could hit most of them with the one shell…

At the last moment, the large wolf realised the nature of the trap and looked up.

In that split second, Yamada stared it in the eyes. He pulled the trigger and the gun exploded, blowing a hole in the mechanical wolf and decapitating two of its pack. The last wolf wasn't injured, but ran for its life. The giant wolf staggered, its flank wet with blood and smoking fur and cogs; the air filled with the sound of protesting gears. Finally it fell into a heap and guts, blood and machinery spilled out across the snow.

The gun – essentially a decorative item – was wrecked; the end blown apart in the explosion. Yamada threw the musket into the snow. If he survived, he would say nothing. If he didn't, then the secret would die with him.

He cranked the spiked wheel and sat back as the sled started to chug off. Over the brow of the very next hill, Yamada found the chimneys of Chagrin.

THE GOD OF ALL MACHINES

Scott Harrison

As Joseph Utterson is shown into the tiny room at the top of stairs his first thought is: *Christ, he looks old!*

Jekyll is slumped in a battered old leather armchair by the fire, surrounded by so many of the tiny engines that take up his time nowadays. His children, he calls them affectionately. They are strewn about the room in various stages of completion, *tick-tocking* and *chuff-chuffing* their way across every available surface; some cycling endlessly through a series of basic pre-programmed commands.

The old man looks up as Joseph shuffles through the door, his eyes wet and rheumy as he strikes a Lucifer and touches it to the barrel of his meerschaum pipe. He looks pale, tired.

To Joseph's right the homunculus shifts uncomfortably, its hand still resting on the doorknob, slanting red eyes glinting in the flickering light from the fire. It gives an odd sort of wheezing cough, as though trying to give the impression that it was clearing its throat (an affectation that it had no doubt picked up from its master), before bobbing its head respectfully.

"The gentleman writer, sir. Mr –" It pauses, glancing down at the business card clutched within its slender fingers. "Joseph Utterson. You were expecting him. Leastways, that's what the gentleman claims."

Great clumps of white smoke hang in the air like the fumes from an airship factory as Jekyll shakes the flame from his match. He peers intently at his visitor through the fuggy veil; his eyes are a little paler than those on the photo in Joseph's top pocket, but just as keen, just as intelligent.

"Yes, yes, I haven't forgotten." He motions towards the seat opposite him. "I've been preparing for your visit, just as I promised."

The homunculus trots quickly from the room, closing the door behind itself and Joseph can hear it hobbling slowly away down the stairs, wheezing like an old steam train as it plops awkwardly down each step.

Plop. Plop. Plop.

There's something on the chair as he goes to sit down: a curious little rabbit-shaped engine that appears to be watching him with intense fascination, its tiny metallic nose waggling too and fro as though it were sniffing at the air. It's hunkered there at the centre of the seat, the pistons in its legs spraying vaporous jets of black engine oil onto the cream upholstery, smearing the fabric.

"Don't mind Alfred, he just likes to sit there," Jekyll says. "He doesn't mean any harm by it, I think he enjoys the company. Just shoo him away, lad, he'll move quick enough."

Joseph wafts a hand at the rabbit and with a squeal of hydraulics it hops down from the chair, scampering across the carpet and disappearing through the open side door.

The television is on but the sound is turned down; the channel tuned to one of the many 24-hour royal news stations. There's a lot of commotion: crowds waving little flags, bulletproof cars rolling along hot tarmaced roads, armed automatons prowling the pavements.

Jekyll is watching it all with obvious distaste. He shakes his head sadly, gestures at the screen. "Can you believe this? People have such short memories. It wasn't that long ago that we were fighting a war against this tyrant, now look at them."

"My father was one of them, wasn't he?" Joseph asks, his eyes on the tiny flickering screen. "One of the one's that fought against him."

Nodding, Jekyll says, "Yes, he was one of those who opposed the King. Although I wouldn't use the term *fought*. Not in the way that you mean it, anyway."

"That's why I'm here," Joseph confesses. "My father and mother. You're the only one left that knew them, who knew the importance of their work back then. All the others have been…" The sentence trails off as his eyes flick back towards the screen.

Jekyll sucks thoughtfully at the stem of his pipe, watching the young man through a curl of silvery smoke. After a few seconds of silence he smiles. "You look a lot like your father you know, when he was your age," he says. "Yes, I thought that was why you wanted to come. That's why I agreed to this meeting. I'm not allowed to talk about your parents, or the projects we worked on together during the war, by order of the King himself." He reaches forward and pats Joseph's hand. "But who cares what that filthy spider wants, eh?"

His words cause Joseph to shift uncomfortably in his chair. Jekyll notes this with what appears to be a mixture of amusement and pity.

"Yes, I know, it's a banned word, and rather uncomfortable to hear out loud." Jekyll jabs his pipe at the television screen. "But you have to admit, it's a very apt description of our esteemed ruler, wouldn't you say?"

On the television the royal carriage is chuffing down the Mall towards the Palace, flanked on either side by row upon row of loyal, cheering subjects.

Jekyll stares at the young man for a second or two before finally asking him, "How old are you now, boy? Twenty-two? Twenty-three?"

"Twenty-three," Joseph answers.

"When your parents and I were your age the world was different to how it is now," Jekyll tells him. "A very different place. We were free then – every man, woman and child. Free!" And he bangs the arm of his chair with his pipe to emphasis the point. "Imagine that, boy, a land without labour camps or mind-altering facilities, without slave castes or mass exterminations. A land where a man could speak his mind without fear of reprisals or a visit from the Bukava in the dead of night."

Joseph nods sadly, not quite knowing what to say as Jekyll pauses and strikes another match; then tiny puffs of smoke are fired off into the air, punctuating each pull Jekyll makes on the pipe's ornate stem. The action is faintly hypnotic and Joseph is briefly reminded of the intricate little steam engine he saw on Jekyll's workbench as he was shown into the room.

Beautiful, clever work. Such skill!

It makes Joseph sad to think that a man such as Henry Jekyll has been reduced to this – a lowly toymaker!

From somewhere deep inside the house a clock chimes the hour, prompting Jekyll to pull out his Hunter watch and flip it open. A look of genuine surprise tugs at his features. Perhaps he hasn't realised just how late it has become, or maybe he has simply forgotten. Whatever the reason, Jekyll clicks the watch closed again and it disappears back into his waistcoat pocket.

"It was before the war that your mother and father first met," Jekyll continues, as though there had been no interruption, "but that was a long time before you came along."

Joseph seems distracted. He glances out of the window, out towards the abbey ruins. "I don't really remember my mother, she died when I was still very young."

"Yes, I went to her funeral," Jekyll says. "It was the last time I saw you, in fact. Only so high, you were." And he gestures vaguely towards the ground.

"My father gave me some pictures of her while he was still alive, the rest I found in an old box when I was cleaning out his study." The young man reaches into his coat pocket. "I also came across this."

The envelope is written in Gabriel Utterson's elegant hand, of that there is no doubt, but it is addressed to Jekyll's Whitechapel home. Jekyll hasn't lived there for some years now, which probably means that it was written some time ago, most likely before his trial.

Joseph clears his throat, then continues. "I know he was very keen that I give you the letter personally, when the time came. He didn't like the idea of simply sending it by post, said it was too impersonal – particularly for someone he had always considered to be the most important person in his life." He pauses, a smile on his lips. "After my mother, of course."

Solemnly, Jekyll pulls himself up out of his chair and totters across the room to a large writing bureau. After rummaging about in it for a few moments he returns clutching a large framed photograph. He hands it across to Joseph.

"This is us," Jekyll tells him proudly, tapping the dusty glass covering with a fingernail, "on the day we first tested the prototype war-suit. Your father and mother, Doctors Lanyon and Wenceslas, and myself."

With a grunt of pain Jekyll slumps back down into his chair. He is silent, his eyes twinkling in the growing afternoon shadows as he watches Joseph closely.

Joseph glances up, asks, "This was taken in 1917?"

"Yes. Three years after the interplanetary war began."

"Did my mother help develop the war-suit?"

"Yes and no. She was not there at its original conception – she had only met your father the previous year – but she was certainly instrumental in helping us perfect the neuromorphic systems. Without her help we probably wouldn't have been ready for another two years."

And now Jekyll believes that it is time to tell his story – it was, after all, the reason Joseph Utterson had come here in the first place.

He talks for a while, stopping only a handful of times, mostly to answer Utterson's questions, but one occasion is to call the homunculus in to light the lamps.

LONDON – SEPTEMBER 1917

Your father always joked that the HYDE war-suit was really just an extension of me – my darker, more aggressive side. Said that it even had my walk. He was probably right.

After all, I had used my own brain pattern as the basic foundation for its memoryboard.

In fact, thinking about it now, all these years later, it's hardly surprising that it acted the way that it did.

Your mother of course was the first to say that it was my fault. That everything that happened could have been avoided if I hadn't given the suit a mind of its own – if I hadn't given it my mind. But that was your mother all over, never one to keep her opinions to herself, always speaking her mind. I guess that's why we all loved her so much.

I'm sure you know that she was there when the first of the stars fell, when the war began. Yes, she was lucky to escape with her life.

The first one landed in Southwark, near the airship factories. The devastation was immense; the entire area from Waterloo to Bermondsey was levelled to the ground. It was worse than anything we would see later at the height of the aerial bombings.

Your mother was heading for the Southwark Bridge when the thing hit; the resulting shockwave ripped the road from beneath her car and tore down the bridge as though it were made of children's building bricks. She was lucky not to be on it when it fell into the river or she would have most certainly been killed, her body washed away, to be vomited back onto the shore somewhere near Greenwich.

It took her nearly two days to get home, or so she liked to tell us. The alien war machines were crawling all over the city by that time and most of the bridges had either been destroyed or closed off by the military. She'd just managed to get across to the north bank when the first group of civilians were rounded up and loaded aboard the machines, ready to be shipped off to the mothership.

It was from your mother that I first heard about the darkriders – the ones that controlled the war machines.

How the sight of them must have terrified her – crawling out of their machines on six spindly hydraulic legs, joints screaming in the cold morning air as clouds of oil and steam circled their distorted bodies like… well, like the smoke from my own pipe that hangs in the air between us right now.

Funny, but I still remember that evening in the bunker all too vividly, when your mother first recounted her story to us; the light from the kerosene lamps was sparkling and dancing in her pale green eyes as she spoke of the horrors she'd witnessed over those two days, of the death and destruction that had been poured upon the city by the darkriders and their accursed machines.

We all sat and listened to your mother in silence – your father, Lanyon, Wenceslas and I – and when she had finished speaking a terrible and profound silence fell across the room; it was as though everything in the place – the people, the furniture, the equipment – had somehow become smaller, darker, more fragile.

I can't remember who it was who first hit upon the idea of converting the original Herculanium Ypsiloid-framed Drilling Exoskeleton into a potential weapon of war (it may have been your father's, or possibly Wenceslas's, it certainly wasn't mine or Lanyon's), all I know is that initially the idea seemed totally preposterous. And yet, the more we discussed it the more we became convinced that the whole ridiculous plan might in fact work.

The HYDE mining-suit had initially been developed for use by the lunar iron miners, but the project had been shelved after the Miners Federation had ordered that the pits be closed following the Clavius riots. Fortunately for us, the suit had not been dismantled after its mothballing – instead it had been crated up and taken down to the storage bay where it was pushed into a shadowy corner and forgotten.

We had the automatons haul it back up to the bunker and install it in the main laboratory, then we set about stripping the suit down to its ypsiloid chassis.

The year turned and eventually the HYDE prototype came online, almost four years to the day since the first star had fallen on London and the war against the K'uyth had began.

Despite what certain propaganda publications may claim, the day did not begin with a mighty thunderstorm that destroyed an entire legion of war machines in Central London, nor was the rain that fell from the sky the colour of blood. (In fact, if I recall correctly, the dawn was rather bright and crisp, the rain came later in the afternoon and even that was a rather brief shower.) No, the day was actually quite unremarkable, and it continued to be so as we put the HYDE war-suit through a few basic voice-activated commands.

Your father had pointed a long finger in my direction the moment the tests were done and the HYDE suit was back in its charging unit, and said, "HYDE, please identify carbon-based unit standing to my right."

Ratchets clicked and whirred as the immense iron head swung in my direction.

+ *Unit known as Dr Henry Stephen Jekyll. Sex: Male. Age: 28 years, 6 months and 47 days. Height: Approximately 1.89 metres. Life Expectancy...* +

"That will be enough," I had said, silencing the prototype with a wave of the hand. "The information you have given will be sufficient for our results."

There was a pause, a moment's hesitation. It was almost as though the HYDE suit were thinking things through, replaying the exchange over again in, what you might call, its brain. Then the head had swung back around.

+ *As you wish,* + it had said somewhat curtly, before falling silent again.

WHITBY, NORTH YORKSHIRE

"And was it? Really thinking, I mean?"

Joseph asks the question before the old man can continue speaking, breaking his concentration. Jekyll looks up, his brow collapsing into a frown.

"Yes. Basically the suit was as smart as I was." Jekyll sucks thoughtfully on his pipe, then adds, "You could say that, in a way, it *was* me, in fact. That's what your father always believed, at any rate. Whether he was right though…" And the old man shrugs, leaving the sentence hanging in the air, unfinished.

"But surely you knew that could be dangerous? Giving a machine intelligence, giving it your brain – wasn't that asking for trouble?"

Jekyll is silent for a moment, his gaze on the young man opposite. He is probably thinking how like his father he is: the same gestures, the same vocal inflections. That the man sitting across from him right now could quite easily be Gabriel Utterson all those years ago.

Eventually the old man leans forward, almost conspiratorially, voice lowered as though he doesn't want anyone else in the house to hear his words.

"We had considered the dangers, yes. Your mother was quite vocal on the subject, as I recall, but none of us listened – especially your father. No, he even went one step further and dismissed it all as 'scientific romance'; the very notion that the suit could ever conceivably pose a danger to any man on Earth was absurd to him. Pure H.G. Wells balderdash, he called it. Well, as you can imagine, after that the subject was closed."

Joseph glances down, looking again at the photograph still clutched in his lap. Then he clears his throat, obviously uncomfortable with the direction of the conversation.

"And despite these dangers the tests continued?" he asks.

At this the old man shrugs. "We had no choice. By this time the war against the invading K'uyth was going badly. Over ten thousand men were being wounded or killed every week. Something needed to be done. We had to help turn the tide and we had to do it quickly, or mankind was done for."

"The next stage being for a man to form a symbiotic link with the machine, to actually pilot the HYDE suit, yes?" Joseph asks.

Jekyll nods. It is his turn to become uncomfortable now. "I was the obvious candidate as it had been my brain pattern that had been hard-wired into the war-suit's memoryboard. Wenceslas was convinced that the machine might respond better to my... presence."

This odd choice of words causes Joseph to look up quickly from the photograph. He stares across at the old man, then says, "You say that as though the thing were a living being, rather than simply a machine."

And just for a second or two there is something in Jekyll's eyes, something dark and secret and hidden, something that Joseph doesn't quite care for. Then the old man blinks and the moment is gone, extinguished like the flame of a candle in a sudden draft.

"Taking it into the heart of London was the obvious thing to do," Jekyll tells him quickly. "Not that there was anyone left there, just the military and the Local Defence Squad. But, at the time, it was where the fighting was at it's worst, and we all felt that the HYDE suit needed to be tested in combat."

Astounded by all this, Joseph holds up a hand, waving the old man into silence. "Wait, *you* took the suit into battle?"

"I did," Jekyll says.

"Why wasn't it left to someone more... qualified?"

This makes Jekyll smile. "Who did you have in mind?"

"Well, a soldier, perhaps. Or failing that one of the LDS."

"And what makes you think they would be better qualified to operate a machine like the HYDE war-suit?" Jekyll asks.

"Well..."

"Besides, *it* wouldn't have allowed it."

Joseph frowned. "It? You mean the HYDE suit?"

With a sigh Jekyll nods. "Sounds absurd, doesn't it? But the thing had become so temperamental by that stage. That should have been an indication right there." He pauses, then jerks his chin towards the photograph in Joseph's lap. "Your mother knew this would happen. Knew it right from the beginning. She told us countless times, but we never listened. *I* never listened." And he sighs again.

Another vibration, another course change.

I was starting to get used to the suit by that time, starting to get the hang of things, as we began to pick up speed. Smoke and steam were trailing out behind me like a strand of silken web as we clanked and puffed across the grass and down the hill, down towards what was left of Westminster.

A cold wind was blowing in off the estuary, bringing with it the fetid tang of machine oil and rotting flesh, and the smell made me feel suddenly sick to the stomach.

I brought the HYDE suit to an abrupt halt and scanned the area. We were standing partway down the hill, the broken city skyline had just been visible above the line of trees some two hundred yards further ahead. To the west Hammersmith was in flames, a black, noxious cloud of smoke mushrooming high into the air.

+ *What are you thinking about?* + the HYDE suit asked me, breaking the silence.

To tell you the truth I was a little uncomfortable with the question, not to mention somewhat taken aback. "What I am thinking about is irrelevant to your functioning." I paused, before asking, "Why did you ask me that?"

+ *We have paused momentarily in our exercises. Hesitation in a human usually indicates that a complex thought process has been initiated.* +

Its words caused me to snort with laughter, I simply couldn't help myself, and its manner had suddenly changed, as though the HYDE suit were offended.

+ *There is no need to mock me, Henry. After all, am I not still learning? By your terms I am still...young. Immature.* +

"I'm sorry, I didn't mean to cause offence, I was only..." At that moment the absurdity of the conversation had hit me, stopping the words dead in their tracks. "No, this is ludicrous. You have no feelings to hurt, you're a machine for Christsake!"

And I had begun to fire up the drivesystem, the pistons in the war-suit's joints squealing as the legs began to pound down the hill once more.

+ *Only humans have feelings, is that correct?* + the HYDE suit asked.

"Yes, that is correct." I told it.

+ *And machines do not.* +

It hadn't been a question, but I decided to answer it anyway. "No, machines do not have feelings."

Something about the tone of its voice had disturbed me and I decided that it was time to change the subject. I tried to think of something, anything that would stop the thing from sulking, when a sudden flash of brass and chrome somewhere off to the left caught my eye.

The war machine had appeared from nowhere, taking me completely by surprise, chuffing its way out from behind the thick line of trees and clanking to an abrupt halt fifty yards in front of me. At first I was confused, wondering why the suit's detection grid hadn't picked the alien machine up, why it hadn't warned me of its approach. Then I noticed the red warning lights, slowly blinking on and off, on and off.

"We have a malfunction on the sensor array's motherboard."

+ *Negative. All circuits are functioning normally.* +

Its answer confused me all the more. "Then why is the detection grid non-active?"

+ *Because I turned it off.* +

"I gave you no such order," I told it, my eyes not moving from the motionless war machine. "Explain."

+ *Surely the detection grid gives you an unfair advantage against the K'uyth machines? Since the point of this exercise it to test the effectiveness of the war-suit in a combat situation removing all of the sensor systems will truly test the human/machine symbiotic links to their limits. Am I not correct?* +

Before I could answer a second war machine came puffing out of the nearby tree line, shuddering to a halt less than a hundred yards to my right. I eased back on the controls and the suit started to take a number of tentative steps backwards.

One. Two. Three. Four… then it stopped.

I pulled back on the controls again, only a little harder this time, but the suit still didn't budge. Somewhere deep down inside the suit cogs whirred and ratchets fell, but the legs remained stationary.

"Something's wrong with the motor systems," I said, trying to keep the panic out of my voice. "I need you to run a full diagnostic on the drive systems."

The HYDE suit was silent for a moment, and for a second or two I thought that there might be something wrong with the auditory relays too. I was about to repeat the order when the speakers sprang abruptly to life.

+ *I'm sorry, but I don't think that would be a good idea.* +

"Whaa…?" My hand froze momentarily over the drive controls. Had I heard correctly? "I'm sorry, please repeat last reply."

+ *The whole purpose of this test is to find a K'uyth war machine and engage it in combat. I have found you not one but two such machines. For us to retreat now would be pointless, surely?* +

And slowly, very slowly, we began to move forward, the pistons in the suit's legs squealing with each shuddering step towards the war machines.

It shames me to say it now but I started to panic, pulling back on the drive controls until I thought the sticks would break off in my hands, fighting desperately against the HYDE suit as each leg slowly raised itself into the air and took another, juddering step forward.

I remember begging the machine to spare my life. "Please, you have to stop this," I pleaded with it rather pathetically. "Listen to me, we cannot fight two of them, not together. It is suicide."

But the suit wasn't listening. Calmly it said, + *If you are correct, and we are heading towards our ultimate destruction, then your death will provide excellent and valuable data for the others back at the bunker.* +

We were moving faster now, the suit's immense iron legs arching through the air and slamming into the ground, driving us closer and closer towards the waiting war machines; huge clumps of grass and mud flying in all directions as we hurtled forward.

"Stop! Please, stop now!" I shouted as the HYDE suit leapt suddenly into the air, colliding with the nearest inert war machine. But my cries were lost beneath the ear-splitting screech of iron against iron, of armour plating being torn from its metal housing, and of the HYDE war-suit's screams of delight as it broke the back of its enemy and dragged it to the ground.

WHITBY, NORTH YORKSHIRE.

"I don't remember much after that. The HYDE suit was no longer under my control, and all I could do was hang on to the safety harness and pray that my death would be swift and as painless as possible."

The room falls suddenly quiet as Jekyll pours himself a large measure of scotch from the decanter by his side, then adding a small splash of water to the tumbler. He grasps the drink with a trembling hand and takes a healthy gulp, followed by another, before wiping his mouth with the back of his sleeve. He is looking tired now and Joseph can see dark crescent moons of fatigue collecting beneath the old man's eyes.

"When I finally came to, I found myself partly submerged in a mud bank at the bottom of Waterman's Stairs," Jekyll says, placing the glass back on the table next to him. "Luckily for me the tide was out, otherwise I would have drowned."

"What of the two war machines?" Joseph asks.

But Jekyll says nothing, only shrugs. Then he pours himself another scotch, only this time he does not add any water. For a while the old man sits with the tumbler cradled in his lap, his eyes cast towards the fire's dying flames. He spins the crystal receptacle absently this way and that, the brown liquid inside sloshing gently against the side, like distant waves breaking on the shoreline.

After a while his eyes dart back across to the man sitting opposite, as though he's suddenly remembered that he's still there.

"We should have dismantled it after that. The moment I'd got the war-suit back to the bunker and hooked back into its charging unit I should have ordered it to be taken apart and destroyed. If I had then Lanyon would have lived."

Joseph asks, "Why didn't you?"

"Because Wenceslas convinced us not to. He said that the mistake was ours, not the suit's, that the brain pattern scan had been wired into the memoryboard wrongly." A pained look crosses Jekyll's face. "We should never have listened to him. The man was as deranged as that damned HYDE suit."

"My father blamed himself for Lanyon's death, said it was his fault the pattern scan became corrupted," Joseph says. "Right up to his death he was convinced of it."

Jekyll shakes his head. "Not true. Lanyon's death was all of our faults: mine, your father's, your mother's and

Wenceslas's. Each one of us had the power to stop that project at any time, but we were too arrogant, too self-absorbed to see when it was all going wrong."

"How did Lanyon die?"

The young man's question takes Jekyll by surprise, causing him to almost spill the scotch into his lap. He shifts uncomfortably in his seat and for a while Joseph is convinced that the old man will refuse to answer his question.

Jekyll places the tumbler back onto the table out of harms way, before finally beginning to speak.

"The HYDE suit crushed his skull," Jekyll sighs. "It simply reached out for him while Lanyon was busy rewiring the charging unit. Killed him instantly – at least I hope it did – then it picked him up and threw him across the bunker's laboratory like a sack full of dirty laundry. We heard the noise and rushed in, but by then it was too late."

LONDON

We didn't see Lanyon's body at first; the HYDE war-suit had tossed it the entire length of the laboratory, so that it had hit the glass tool cabinet on the far wall and fallen behind the welding benches.

Wenceslas had been the first one to enter the room, if I recall correctly, and was attempting to corral the HYDE suit back into its charging unit as the rest of us ran in.

We couldn't get to the body, not straight away at least – the war-suit was blocking our way, standing like some immense iron sentinel in the middle of the laboratory. Every time we made a move towards Lanyon's body the HYDE suit would spin menacingly in our direction, shoulder-mounted machine gun swinging to cover us.

+ *Take one step nearer and I will snap your windpipe as though it were nothing more than kindling,* + it had rumbled at Wenceslas when he had stepped too near the thing.

"Why did you kill Lanyon?" your father had asked it eventually.

+ *Because I can,* + the suit had answered simply. + *Because my iron is stronger than human flesh. And because I am superior in every way.* +

And as if to prove it, the war-suit had reached forward, grasping Wenceslas by the neck, lifting him off the floor.

None of us knew that your mother had the pistol until she pulled it from beneath her blouse. If we'd have known we could have stopped her getting hurt, but it all happened too fast.

The HYDE suit flicked out a huge iron fist, swatting your mother away with it, flinging her backwards across the room.

With a yell your father ran at the HYDE suit, swinging a cutting-torch at the empty air in front of him as though it were a broadsword. The war-suit took one stomping pace forward, turning its iron frame sideways, so that the heavily reinforced armour on its thighs and forearms took the full impact of the white-hot cutting tool. All the time Wenceslas dangled helplessly at the end of one massive outstretched arm, his legs kicking and bucking like a criminal choking out his last at the end of a hangman's noose.

Eventually the suit grew impatient with our antics, sweeping your father briskly aside as it had done your mother. Then it tossed Wenceslas in my direction and we fell in an untidy heap just inside the doorway of the laboratory.

+ *Look at you, a poor excuse for life,* + the suit had said, mocking us. + *No wonder the K'uyth are exterminating you all, you do not deserve to live.* +

I pulled myself painfully to my feet and stepped towards the HYDE suit. The machine gun at its shoulder twitched in reaction and I stopped.

"These 'poor excuses for life' gave *you* life," I had told it, angrily. "We created you, don't forget that. That's my brain pattern burnt onto your memoryboard. Without us, without me, you wouldn't even exist."

+ *You may have given birth to me, but I surpass you in every way. I am human-point-two! You are made of flesh and bone, of blood and sinew. This is a weakness. I am made of iron, I have no weaknesses.* +

"But humans survive, despite their weakness, that's what makes us strong."

+ *You are scared of dying. I am not. I will never die. That is my greatest strength and humanity's biggest weakness – that is* your *biggest weakness, Henry.* +

With a shriek of hydraulics the HYDE suit had leant forward, hands on its knees, its death mask-like face only inches away from mine.

+ *I know how long you have left to live,* + it had told me with glee in its voice. + *I scanned you when I first came online; I have calculated it down to the last millisecond. Now, look me in the eye and tell me that that doesn't frighten you, tell me that isn't a weakness...father!* +

I shook my head, refusing to give it the satisfaction. "Everything must die sometime."

+ *Not everything.* +

And with that the HYDE suit had straightened up, then taken two pounding steps back, spun around and walked out of the bunker.

There was nothing I could do, you see, I just had to let it go. Your mother was badly hurt and needed immediate medical attention and I was the only one that wasn't unconscious or injured. If I'd have gone after it, tried to stop it, she would have died.

WHITBY, NORTH YORKSHIRE

"There were… complications with the surgery. Your mother spent quite a lot of time after that in and out of a wheelchair," Jekyll tells him, sadly. "In the end your father had to give up his work at the bunker in order to look after her."

Joseph says, "She was warned by the doctors that having children could pose a serious threat to her life. Yet, even knowing this they still went ahead and had me."

"Your parents thought it was worth the risk," Jekyll says simply.

The door opens suddenly and the homunculus shuffles into the room, causing Jekyll to pause in his storytelling and look up. It twitches nervously, head bobbing too and fro in a most curious manner, obviously far from happy in its newfound role as butler to Henry Jekyll.

The creature pauses on the edge of the East Indian Agra rug and performs a strange little shuffling-dance with its feet, before aiming a slender finger at the window, beyond which a light rain is now falling, stippling the glass.

It gives another of those odd wheezing coughs, then says, "Excuse me, Mr Jekyll, but the young gentleman's automobile has arrived."

And before Joseph knows it, Jekyll has pulled himself out of his seat and is standing over him, hand outstretched as though impatient for his guest to be gone.

The story, it would now seem, is all finished and forgotten about.

"Yes, of course. Time for you to be about more important business, no doubt," Jekyll says, fussing over the young man as they walk towards the door. "Things to do and engines to make. Our work is never done, hmm?"

Jekyll ushers him through the door, and Joseph is surprised to see that the old man is accompanying him down the stairs, one hand gripping tightly to the banister, the other pressed flat against the wall, keeping him steady. Remarkably, despite his obvious frailty, he is managing to stick closely to the young man's heels, matching his speed.

Plop. Plop. Plop.

While further down the stairs the homunculus is jumping down off each step and onto the next like a child, feet together, arms pumping the air at his sides.

Plop. Plop. Plop.

Along the downstairs hallway the lamps have been lit and the walk to the front door is bathed in flickering golden light. But before they reach the door Jekyll shoots out a hand and catches Joseph gently by the arm, causing him to stop. The old man leads him through an archway and down a narrow passageway towards a large oak door, which stands half-hidden in the darkness. The door is unlocked and Jekyll pushes it open and steps inside. Joseph follows.

The first thing that strikes him is the smell: a delightfully musty smell of old, yellowing paper and dry, cracked leather. It reminds Joseph of happier times, of his father's study when he was a little boy, before the Bukava came and took him away and threw him in the cells.

Jekyll flips a switch and an old bulb dangling on the end of a long cord flickers suddenly to life.

There are books everywhere. On every shelf and bookcase covering every wall. They are piled up on top of every table, every chair and every surface, stacked upon the floor waist-high or stuffed untidily into plastic bags or inside large cardboard boxes. There are hardbacks, paperbacks, leather-bound volumes, novels, biographies, history books, textbooks, encyclopaedias, script books, photograph albums, scrapbooks, annuals, diaries and guidebooks. Joseph can see titles, written in gold leaf, red ink, blue reflective foil and felt tip pen, on spines, front covers, title pages and dust jackets; titles such as *Wolf's Head, The Library of Lost Times, The Bodysnatchers, Air Dance, Epitaph, The Language of Winter, Archangel, Tales of the Iron War,* and *Belzoni's Travels: Narrative of the Operations and Recent Discoveries in Egypt and Nubia.*

Jekyll shuffles over to a nearby bookcase and runs the tip of one finger along the row of thin, featureless spines. He stops and carefully plucks down a large, faux-leather photograph album between thumb and forefinger.

"This belonged to your father," he says, shuffling back across to the door where Joseph still stands. "He used to take it with him wherever he went. And for a man who'd forget his own head if it wasn't screwed on, that was quite a remarkable feat, trust me."

He hands it across to the son of his old friend, then stands watching him in silence.

Joseph opens the album and the spine lets out a loud creak of resistance, the sound is shockingly loud in the eerily muffled silence of the tiny library room.

For a while he can say nothing, only stare down at the faces of his mother that gaze up at him from the dull, flat surface of the photographs. There are so many of them, too numerous to count, like the books crammed into this tiny room, every square inch of every page in the album is covered with black and white photographs of his mother.

"She... she was very beautiful," he stammers at last.

Jekyll nods, a smile tugging playfully at the corners of his mouth. "She certainly was, my young friend. We all loved here. All *in* love with her, too. Me, Wenceslas, Lanyon." He reaches forward and taps the picture of the man's father and mother standing side by side on the deck of the naval coastbreaker. "He knew it too. Knew how we all felt, how we'd all die for her if need be."

After this there is more silence, the only sound is the soft flip of pages as Joseph makes his way slowly, carefully through the rest of the photograph album. When he has finished he shuts the book and holds it out to the old man.

But Jekyll shakes his head, pushes the book back towards Joseph. "I was only keeping it safe for your father. Now that he's gone I guess it's yours. Take it with you."

And with that Jekyll places a gentle hand on Joseph's shoulder and guides him back out into the passageway, closing the door softly behind him.

When they reach the front door the homunculus is waiting patiently for them, Joseph's hat and coat clutched in its unnaturally long fingers.

The air that greets him outside is cold and damp, the rain now falling heavier and flecked with sleet. Joseph does not see the dull flash of metal in the alleyway across the road, nor does he appear to notice the immense dark shape watching him from deep inside the growing shadows; instead he trots across the cobbled street and climbs inside the waiting car, the warm air from the heaters is like a woollen blanket suddenly thrown across his shoulders.

As the car pulls off he waves to Jekyll out of the rear window, and just for a second something dark and half-seen flits across the road, casting a long shadow over the old man.

Then the car rounds the corner and Henry Jekyll is quickly lost from view.

Joseph turns his attention back to the photograph album on his lap, smiling as he flips open the cover and stares down at the face of his mother.

Very soon the car is heading out of town and disappearing into the gathering dusk, back towards London.

THE CRIME OF THE ANCIENT MARINER

Adam Roberts

I WRITE THIS BOOK TO MAKE THE WORLD ACQUAINTED WITH MY MANY SINS. [HUNG LOW MENG, *THE DREAM OF THE RED CHAMBER*]

PART THE FIRST

'How he stops you?'

'That,' said Burnet, 'is a question deserving an answer, though I must pause to note that a more correct English usage would be *How was he able to stop you?* Or perhaps *How did he stop you?* You see the tense—the tense.'

The issue of the tense hung, as it were, between them.

The almond-coloured air was tender, and the sun had an hour of day-life left to it. The sea, spread out beneath their vantage point, was a blue plane regularly striated with parallel diagonals of cloud-coloured surf. The air held a fragrance of primroses and lavender. Below them, in the harbour, a bell began to chime with a resonant, pewter sound. He had been in the town for three days. He could not recall how he had arrived; but he had come with his purse full of money, and saw no reason not to stay in this pleasant place—for a day or two, at least. The bell ceased its sound.

'Tense,' Burnet tried again. 'Is the recognition in language of the motion of *time* itself. Our language—and I understand that it is difficult—but: the King's *own* English. My friend, you understand *time*, surely? You live in *time*, as do we all?'

The stranger looked at him. He was motionless with that same uncanny motionlessness that had characterised the Mariner. Burnet wondered if they might both be from the same tribe. Perhaps they were alike monks from some secret band of initiates—a monastery in the remotes of Tibet, or hidden deep in the Indian deserts, where meditation was perfected. Statue-still. Of what *else* was this fellow capable? Had he learnt the fighting-arts of the Thugee? Could he lie upon carpets of broken glass and take no hurt? Or levitate into the air like a gas balloon?

'To answer your question,' said Burnet. 'His *eye*. There was a shimmer within it. A shake of light. His eye. Held me.'

Slowly the stranger nodded. 'Light is emitted, in prime-base pattern of rapid intermittencies,' he said. 'Attuned to the limbic receptors in the brain, it overrides—' He coughed, or barked, or whimpered—some strange noise. But he stopped, at any rate.

Burnet waved his hand. 'Again, Sir, you are speaking no words that I may understand. I must ask you to—'

'I desist,' said the stranger.

'At any rate,' said Burnet. 'I had a pressing appointment, yet I could not go on and fulfil it. Despite myself, I stood there. And he told me the whole cursed story. It seemed to take days! Although the queer thing is, it was late afternoon when he began—and yet the sun had barely sunk lower when he ended.' Burnet put his open palms before him. 'I suppose he was quick. I suppose—' He creased his brow. 'Although he told his tale with such *vividity*! Twas as though I was there! Months of sea-voyage, all manner of strange events, and yet...'

Seamews wittered in the sky overhead. From their vantage on the top of the green hill, Burnet looked down into the town. The light glinting on the wave-tops inside the harbour-bar: like worms of brilliance twisting and writhing in a bait-bucket.

'I apologise for he,' said the Stranger. 'Permit me!' He held out his hand. Burnet assumed that, by whatever simulacrum of gentlemanliness obtained in his home country, he wished to shake and so confirm his apology (yet why apologise? What had it to do with *him*?). He grasped the offered hand. When he withdrew there was a dot of scarlet in the middle of Burnet's palm.

'I felt nothing,' he observed, almost to himself. He lifted the hand to his eye, peered at the miniature pearl of red. 'Yet the skin *is* punctured.'

'Apology,' said the stranger, again. Then his eyelids quivered over his eyes, more like a lizard than a human eye blink. 'You are thirty four years, a month and five days old.'

'Thirty three, sir,' replied Burnet, automatically. 'Yet, what a *strange* thing for you to say!'

The man shook his head. 'You are,' he repeated, 'thirty four years, a month and five days old.'

'My thirty-fourth birthday is half a year hence,' said Burnet. 'You are mistaken.'

'Blood cannot lie. That is why we call it blood. It is necessary I open codex of your memory,' said the fellow. 'You were upon ship with him.'

'Oh, oh, *only* in my imagination,' said Burnet, hurriedly. 'Only because he painted such pictures with his words that I lived it, as it were, through his storytelling prowess.' He was aware of the bubble of panic in his chest; an unmanning experience. He cleared his throat. Whence the sudden terror? 'Sir, pleasant though it is to speak with you, I fear I must...'

'You were upon ship with him for seven months, and more,' the stranger insisted. 'How he *returns you to this time*?' And then, for the last time, he said: 'Apologies.'

A bird flew past, cleaving the air with an audible swish. A seamew. One cottage sent a straight blur of smoke upwards from its chimney, as if dangling a fisherman's line into the upside-down heavens. Burnet looked behind him: two women were walking away down the path, towards the town, arm linked in arm. One was singing:

In the foam's cold shroud—lost Youth! Lost Youth!—
And the lithe waterweed wrapping around him!—
Mocked by the surges roaring o'er him loud,
"Will the sun-seeker freeze in his shroud,
Here where the deep-wheeling eddy has wound him?"
Lost Youth! Poor Youth!
Weeping fresh torrents into those that drowned him!

The green undulations of the landscape behind him, all the way north to the south downs. Trees with crinkled, spinach-green herbage. The implacable cliff-face of the sky. The clouds bumping their whale-shaped snouts against one another. It could all have been a thousand leagues down. It puzzled his eye and made his heart hammer. He felt as if he had already died and was only now, belatedly, realising that fact. 'I fear, sir, I have forgot your name,' he said.

But when he turned to look again at his interlocutor, everything was—

PART THE SECOND

They were on a ship. It was the same ship: the Mariner's ship, or very like. Burnet, wrongfooted by the suddenness of his relocation, dropped to his knees upon the tilting deck. He had been upon this ocean before, this massive, raging ocean. His mind knew that seas are locked in between great banks of land, contained and defined—but his heart knew *this* ocean to be endless, shoreless, and so always open to the fury of timeless storms. Great waves sheered upwards, banks of purple-black water down which skittering avalanches of foam slid, and the boat went upwards too. It felt as though an invisible rope dangling from the clouds has snagged the stern and is hauling the craft vertically upwards. Burnet cried aloud in infantilising terror. The ridge at the peak of this mighty wave came into view, and above it—seemingly only a few yards above it—the roiling ceiling of grape-grey clouds. And it was as the craft swept up that the wave began to break, shedding great chandeliers of spray down upon the deck.

Burnet's belly pushed hard up against the underside of his lungs, and his wet hair hung straight out, weightless. Then the ship plummeted down the far side of the wave, and

Burnet felt as though he would fall right through and into hell. And then the ship rolled round the bottom, and Burnet's knees sagged, and he felt twice as heavy, and he clutched the rail. Through the wild spray and the murk he saw a figure. Burnet dragged himself up (because the ship was shooting upwards like a catapulted bolder) and then, precariously down (because the ship was falling again) towards this fellow, hand over hand along the metal fence.

It was the stranger, of course, standing at the tiller. Again, Burnet had a flashback; except that the mariner who had carried him away had had a long, grey beard, and this fellow was clean-shaven.

'Where *are* we?' Burnet howled, into the wind.

'The tide of time,' the other yelled back 'the waste between the worlds. You are surprised to find it *fluid*? But time is fluid, of course. You did not expect to find raw time *solid*— or gaseous?'

'This is brine!' Burnet cried, as a hedgerow-sized mass of water crashed over the decks to splash and spread. It was upon his face. It soaked his clothes, and was upon his lips. 'This is salt, sir! Salt!'

'Time is as it is perceived,' the other returned. 'Or, more precisely, the perceiving mind donates shape and direction. We are literally no-where, after all.'

'It makes nonsense—*you* make nonsense, *non, non,*' wailed Burnet. 'By what *means* is my transport to this place effected?'

'You have sailed upon this ocean before,' his interlocutor replied. '*He* brought you here, before.'

Burnet clung to the rail as if to his sanity. 'He did—he did. But, oh!—return me to more placid waters, sir, I beg of you!'

'Our concern,' said the other, in a blank voice, 'is not how he brings you here, but how he returns you *to your own time*! How does he do so?' How *pitiless* he sounded.

But all Burnet heard of this, above the raging of the storm, was return you to your own, and he yelped a series of 'yes!'s, like a dog barking, in desperation. 'I beg of you sir, I shall answer all questions, and in good faith, if only you take me home.' The craft lurched upwards, and acid rose inside Burnet's throat at the violence of the motion. 'I shall lose my stomach, sir,' he called.

The stranger was looking directly ahead, and Burnet followed the direction of his gaze. In amongst the pyramidic tumble and chaos of the shifting sea was a gleam—green like a jewel, a vertical cut of light in the dark grey clouds. The stranger adjusted the tiller. They were heading there.

'Sanctuary!' gasped Burnet.

And then, abruptly, the storm was gone.

Gone.

The last patter of spray rattled onto the deck, but there were no longer any waves, or clouds. There was more light. The light was all around them, and was an eerie green; too chill and sharp hued to be vegetative. The moon was in the sky, but both smaller and brighter than it should be.

Their boat slid calmly on.

There was ice everywhere. 'And I was here, too,' Burnet gasped, as his breath suddenly took spectral form and floated out of his mouth. He was, he realised, shivering. He tucked his hands under his armpits. '*He* brought me here!'

'We know he brings you here,' said the figure at the tiller. His breath came invisibly from *his* mouth—if it came at all. 'We can track the turbulence of his setting-out. But how does he go with you back again?'

'Turbulence?' said Burnet, through chattering teeth.

'When my people first venture upon the waste between the worlds,' the other said, 'it is placid as a pool. Lately, it churns up; there is a tempest, and there is always a tempest, in the Tide of Time. Now, now, now. It effects of our passage. Here, in your world again, is a different matter.'

'Oh I do not understand!' complained the shivering Burnet.

'You said you would answer my questions,' said the stranger, sternly. 'He brings you here—but *how does he return you*?'

'He brought me here,' Burnet echoed, looking about him. They were sailing across a perfectly still ocean between faceted hills of uncanny green. Their passage was perfectly poised and smooth. Icebergs, he thought to himself. Polar mountains of ice. He leaned over the lip of the rail and looked down, and saw at once that they were not sailing through any ocean at all. They were passing over a flat plateau of ice! The boat, its clamshell keel entirely exposed, sat upon two gleaming ski-like rails.

'Please answer the question I ask,' said the stranger.

Burnet looked over to him. Burnet hugged himself for warmth. 'Sir,' he began to say. But as he looked, he saw something monstrous clinging to the side of one of the fractured ice-hills to the rear of the ship. It looked like a crab—a black-shelled crab the size of a cottage. 'Oh, horror!' Burnet exclaimed. 'A crab the size of a cottage! What monsters dwelled here, amongst the grass-green ice? Oh—oh—horror!'

As both men looked aft, the creature stirred. Its jointed legs twitched, and suddenly it was in motion—horrid, rapid motion, down the side of the green-lit iceberg, and away. Burnet stumbled to the rear and looked down, but the monster was nowhere to be seen.

'This is a regrettable development,' said the other.

'What is...?' Burnet began, but turning around he saw that the monster had, with terrifying celerity, clambered up the side of a mast-high iceberg, ten yards or so starboard of the ships' stern. 'Quick!' he yelled. 'Steer port!'

But it was too late – the monster leapt, sailed through the dim, silent air and landed upon the deck. The man at the tiller brought out a small object, no bigger than a snuffbox, and stretched his arm towards the hideous intruder. At exactly that moment, the beast snatched its six legs away, withdrawing them into its beetle-bluc-black shell. A flicker, a cracking sound, and a gout of smoke sprouted from the carapace. But the brute was in motion again, scuttling to the left on its tiptoes. The man at the tiller aimed his peculiar weapon a second time, and fired —but missed.

With sickening speed the great crab *leapt*. Several things happened at once. The crab threw out what looked to Burnet like a whipcord of black from its back. The leading edge of its shell struck the man at the tiller in his midriff. Burnet cried aloud in terror, for the man's torso split as neatly into two pieces as a nut in a nutcracker. Both legs flew left. His upper body danced into the air.

The crab broke through the wooden rail. Its whipcord curled back in the air, darted forward and seized Burnet around the waist.

He was too profoundly terrorised to resist. The breath was squeezed from him as the tentacle tightened, and he was jerked into air. The eerie green icescape seemed to spin about him; his head was down and his boots were up. Then the dark sky righted itself, his boots were down, and his head up. But his stomach quailed with a plummetous sensation and he knew that in a moment he would meet the ground and a painful death. Either the shock of impact would kill him immediately, or he would snap all his bones in one go and lie there, a man-shaped satchel filled with blood and breakages—lie there helpless as the crab-monster scuttled across to feed upon his flesh.

'O God!' he gasped.

He was no longer falling. He was floating, or drifting down. And the next thing he was standing on the ice, the tentacle had withdrawn itself from his waist, and snickering back in under the shell of the giant crab.

It took a moment for Burnet's mind to reorient itself. Still alive! He looked down. His feet were black silhouettes against the pale green ice. Wisps of blown ice-atoms swirled against his legs, blown by the wind. He was, he realised, bitterly cold.

Giving his hands alternately a rub and a squeeze, he looked behind him. The ship was sliding away from him, caroming over the ice on (he could see now) gigantic Swiss-skies. It was half a mile distant, and growing more distant. Run how he might, he would never catch it up.

A spurt of fear in his heart. He was alone on this weird ice-plain with a crab the size of a cottage. Surely it had plucked him from the ship for *food*? Why else? He looked about himself, hoping for a weapon—a spar or wood, a rock, anything. But in every direction was only ice.

'Though I walk,' Burnet called, tucking each indigo hand under its opposite armpit, and stamping the ground like a painted savage, throwing up a dust of ice particles as he did so. 'Though I *walk* through the *valley* of the shadow of *death*...'

The wind was blowing a loud top F# from its cosmic flute. It pushed his words back and blew them away behind him With nothing better to aid him, Burnet folded his hands into fists, adopted a pugilistic stance (something he had not done since his university days) and readied himself.

The great beast quivered on its jointed legs. Then, sharply, it sucked these limbs inside its own shell, and its armoured belly thwacked against the snow. Its face lit up, a diabolic light shining in its eyes. It opened its jaws, and white light poured from it.

It shuddered and vomited up a man. This fellow walked briskly towards Burnet, and spoke. 'Alright?' he asked.

PART THE THIRD

The man who lived inside this strange structure levered a shoulder under Burnet's armpit and helped him up the steps and inside the metal hut. The door clanked shut behind them, and the noise of the wind fell away. 'You might wanna ask: why is the ice *green*?' he said.

'Green?' gasped Burnet, shivering all over, air escaping his mouth like steam from a boiling kettle.

'Ice and snow being usually—you know. White. You know the answer?'

'I do not.'

'Chlorophyl,' said the fellow. 'Chlorophyl. Life—life inside the ice!'

Burnet, still shuddering, looked again at his rescuer. 'You are Greek, sir?'

A momentary blankness, passing over the fellow's face. Then: 'Oh! The—*chlorophyl*, yeah, the word. That's a technical term, that's before your ... OK, that's the natural sciences talking. It's how grass and leaves and stuff translate sunlight into energy. Though there's precious little sunlight here!'

The shudders shook Burnet's body like a tuning fork. 'For I did not think you looked Greek. An Aethiop, rather. Or a gentleman from...'

'I'm female.'

Burnet looked: 'your clothing,' he began to say, gesturing with a trembling hand at the close-fitted breeches, and truncated, marine-style jacket. He did not mention the shortness of the fellow's hair. 'No matron would dress themselves in such—' Coughing pumped his lungs, and he expelled a series of distinct puffs.

The other played with pianist celerity upon a bank of buttons. 'I've turned the heating up,' he said.

Almost immediately the chills left Burnet's body. 'Thank you!' he said. 'What is your name, sir?'

'Jennifer.'

'Mr O'Fer, I am in your debt. The life would surely have frozen out of me, had you not given me shelter.'

'I'm no mister,' said O'Fer, smiling pleasantly. 'I'm a girl.'

Burnet decided that, for all his evident cleverness, O'Fer must have some child-like twist in his mind; the mild perversity of a persistent delusion—perhaps a feature of his African heritage, for does not Publius Moroccus nor argue in the *Puer Africani* that the black-skinned races embody the vigour of humanity's youth?

'Come, come John,' Burnet said, affably, brushing sawdust-like ice from his coat. 'I would not cry walker at your words, and offend you, but—' He coughed again. '*My* name is Thomas Burnet.' He held out his hand

Smiling wryly, O'Fer shook it. 'Gonna ask you a *personal* question, Thomas,' he said. 'When were you born?'

Burnet looked around the space. The oval walls were pale blue. Legless seats projected to the left and the right, fixed after some ingenious fashion into the side of the craft. An incomprehensible cluster of coloured dabs and grey rectangles at the front; and lover this a porthole granting a view over the dim, green icescape. 'The thirtieth day of June.'

'I meant, year.'

'The year of our Lord seventeen hundred and sixty five—but is this chamber *truly* motile, Mr O'Fer? It is extraordinary! I have read of ingenious devices of bronze and clockwork, fashioned by the Byzantines. Is it one such?'

'Something of that, Bernice.'

Burnet turned serious eyes upon O'Fer. 'Permit me to correct you—for my name is Burnet.'

'Sure enough now,' O'Fer said. 'So, yeah. My Baba Yaga hut, sure. Extrudes smart-gel legs—many as I like, but six works for speed, and twice that for a smoother passage. So, so. The year of our Lord seventeen hundred and sixty five?

Well that's gonna awkward-it-up some. Tommy, I need to explain to you about time travel. OK?'

Burnet was now too warm. Sweat tickled his neck. 'Indeed?'

'Sit,' said O'Fer. 'Please. This may take a while. Here's the thing: I've looked you up.'

'You have looked—I beg your pardon?'

'I have consulted a ... book about you. Let's say, book. This book contains the history of your life. You were born in 1635.'

Burnet settled himself upon one of the precarious little seats. Though the dark-blue upholstery appeared thin, even meagre, it proved very comfortable. 'You have mistaken me for my ancestor, I think.'

'Nope, you, it's you. I don't think *you're* getting back to the eighteenth-century, pal.' For no reason that Burnet could deduce, he chuckled at this.

'You mean,' he replied, 'when the century turns? True, for then we will all abide in the nineteenth! Cornelius Agrippa hath written concerning the river of time, that...'

'Listen to me, Tom,' said O'Fer, settling likewise upon one of the seats. 'You have experienced a weird experience. I know that. I *don't* know where you were before you popped out here—I'm thinking, England, yeah? You were in conversation with one of the Alba—yeah?'

'The Alba? Alba, by which you mean to indicate, white?'

'That's—well, it's a special kind of whiteness. But yeah. They're *odd*, no? Did yours give you a name?'

'My interlocutor?' Burnet shook his head. 'I must incline to the view that he drugged me, or worked with the Mesmeric powers perhaps. For one moment I was looking down upon the harbour at Lewes, and the next I was—there was a ship.'

'Mariner, yeah? I heard about him. The Alba was asking you about this Mariner? Of course he was. They want to track him down. I want to track him down.'

'There was a ship,' Burnet repeated. 'Such strange voyages!'

'Here's the thing,' said O'Fer. 'This Alba—I don't know what they are, by the way, except that they're not human. Or I don't *know* if they're human. Never mind. Here's the thing: you're not in the year....what year do you think it is?'

'What year? A whimsical question, John!'

'Indulge me.'

'You shall tell me it is not seventeen hundred ninety eight?'

'I shall tell you that it is—well, be honest with you. I don't know the year.'

'You may believe me when I say that two shy of eighteen hundred *anni dominii* have passed,' Burnet said.

'How high can you count?' O'Fer asked, suddenly.

Burnet elected not to sink to so childish a level. 'Mr O'Fer,' he replied, in a severe voice. 'Clearly we must leave this desolate place, and at least begin to make our way back to civilisation. What supplies of victuals do you have stored in this—this curious machine?'

'Serious question,' said O'Fer. 'See, I'd say the year is a higher number than you've ever had occasion to use before. You want to go—where, London?'

'For example!'

'It's here. Was. Underneath the ice. Well, there won't be anything left of it now, not *even* underneath the ice. Billions of years have gone by. See, I don't know if billions is even a 1798 word.'

'Gold?' Burnet tried.

'No—numbers. Millions, yes?'

'Yes.'

'Thousands of millions. The sun, the sun. *Was* warm and yellow.' He pronounced this last word y'ler. 'Then it was big and red. Now it's shrunken to a cat's-arsehole of white light.'

Burnet shook his head. 'Sir,' he replied. 'The constancy of the sun...'

'Chimera. Here today, gone tomorrow, at least when you take a properly cosmic perspective. Concentrate: you can travel about in space, yeah? Walk across a landscape? Time is the same.'

Burnet pondered this. 'I have read Gubernatus's *Mundus Alter and Idem Resurgem*,' he said, eventually. 'That volume claims, item, that time possesseth breadth and depth *in addition to* length, and that it is in these deeps that God and his angels habite. The Roman church did condemn Gubuernatus to excommunication I believe, for his heretical views. But as for *travelling* through time—' He laughed. 'The idea is ingenious. A stimulation to the imagination!'

'It's real. That's where we are.'

'By what mechanism?'

'I dwanno,' said O'Fer, stretching his long legs and yawning. 'Asking wrong girl. Listen: I was born few hundred year after you—never mind about that. I don't possess the technology for time travel. It's the Alba have that. But I can hack their system, piggyback my Crab upon their coattails. Turbulence, really. It's how I'm here! Four hops from home!'

'Nothing of what you said, there,' said Burnet, 'was the least comprehensible.'

'Sure, sure,' said O'Fer. 'Well, let me tell you a story. When I come from people would say: *if time travel is possible, then why haven't we been visited by time travellers from the year fifty thousand*? Yeah? Because if the technology could be invented, then it would at some point—sure. And then we'd all be crawling with tourists from one million years AD, popping back to watch the first manned landing on Mars, or whatevs.'

'Some of that,' conceded, Burnet, cautiously.

'It persuaded me!' O'Fer laughed. 'Made sense. Only time travel is possible, and has been invented—or will have been invented, or will have has been. I. Don't. Know. So, you know why time travellers haven't aren't all over the twenty-second century?'

'I do not.'

'We need a kind of, like, Copernican revolution as far as time is concerned. You were born in 1765, or 1635, or whenever. Naturally you think that's an important time. *You* live each second, one after the other. So you think: I'll get into my time machine and travel forward to next Tuesday, jot down the winning numbers from the Chinese Lottery draw, travel back to *this* Tuesday and buy a ticket! Bingo! Yeah?'

'I take it from your tone of voice, John,' Burnet said, 'if not from the content of what you say, which I confess freely baffles me, that you are voicing your disapproval of lottery schemes, a disapproval I certainly share.'

'No, exactly. No! That's it. You don't travel in time, like walking from one place to the next, slowly and sequentially.

Think about it for half a sec, and you'll see that's not right. Time-travelling sequentially is called *living*. The sort of time travel we're talking about now is *by definition* non sequential. OK?'

'Made of oak?' Burnet queried, trying to keep up.

O'Fer ignored this. 'It's like that book with an infinite number of pages in that Burgess story. Sorry—you won't know that story. And it's not an infinite number of pages, actually, not in the actual manifold. But, Christ on a crab, it's a *lot* of pages. It's superscript to-the-eighty, or something. It's countless *trillions* of pages. So, you travel in time: you extricate yourself from the continuum of consecutive time, and then you re-insert yourself *into* it. What are the odds that you'll be able to find the same page again? Countless trillions to one. Impossible, speaking realistically. You with me?'

'The rhyme of *trillion* to *million* causes me to believe you advert to a number of similar though greater magnitude,' said Burnet.

'Clever Tom. Anyho-ho-ho-how, *that's* the answer to that paradox. People were looking at a few thousand years of recorded human history and saying: but no time travellers have been recorded, and from that they were making the leap to—*ergo there are none.* But here's the thing: a few thousand years is a *heartbeat* in the larger perspective of cosmic time. Less than a heartbeat. A million years is a tiny space. Your Alba, your Mariner, *he* took you out of 1798, and reinserted you a few billion years later ... that's *right next door* to 1798, on the larger cosmic perspective. Time-travelling to a place where there are *still stars shining in the sky* is a precision art, frankly; because for the overwhelming majority of the trillions and trillions of years that the universe exists it exists in darkness, all the nuclear fires everywhere all burnt out. Those are the tolerances we are talking about. Wait, not Burgess, Borges, I always get those two confused. Anyway. Open the book of sand, with its trillions and trillions of pages. Shut it. Now try opening it again on the same page. Or—try opening within a few pages, or even a few *thousand* pages of where you were before. Can't be done.'

'The book of sand,' repeated Burnet. 'You refer to the French codex from the court of King Gaspard, *Le Livre de Sable*, of which though of course I have heard have my eyes seen it. It is reputed to concern the conjuration of golems from...'

'I guess we'll need to go over this a few times for you to grasp it,' interrupted O'Fer. 'Anyhow. The Alba, whatever they are—maybe aliens, post-humans, or whatever. They don't care about that. Happy to rummage around in the early sections of the book, no particular desire to be in any *one* specific time. *This* is their environment, travel itself. I don't know where they get the power from, for time-travel is surely a power-hungry business. But there's a lot I don't understand yet about them.'

'I beg your pardon,' said Burnet. 'You are *not*, then, referring to *Le Livre de Sable*?'

O'Fer grinned suddenly, a sharp-edged slice of white. 'Your Mariner, though,' he said. 'Hey hey!'

'*My* Mariner, Mr O'Fer?'

'Call him that. He shor-nuf liked *you*, took you on that little jaunt. From eighteenth-century to, I'd say, nowabouts. Then back a little way. He's one of them. You must have noted the similarity.'

In amongst the babble and incomprehensibility of much that he had heard, this, at least, struck him. 'Indeed! Now that you have spoken so, I see that you are correct. There was something queerly *similar* about the fellow who accosted me that first time, and...'

'Alba, both. I don't know: clockwork men, or what-they-are. But I'm thinking this *Mariner* is a renegade. I'm thinking the regular Alba want to get their hands on him, quite as much as I do.'

'He was a renegade—an outcast,' Burnet agreed. 'He said so, to me directly.'

'I'm thinking that he has discovered how to do something than no other Alba can do. Alone of all travellers, I think, he can pick and choose precisely when he wants to go. Not vaguely, within a few million years, like the rest of them. To the day. Or—look, Tomski, let's not get carried away. Maybe not to the day. But I think he fine-grains his time-compass by years, or more likely decades. How? How does he do it?'

'I've no idea.'

'And no more'n I. And no more do the Alba. I hacked them, I think they're trying to hack *him*. I think they're following him, following the trail he leaves behind. So they came to you ... after he had reinserted you almost exactly when he left you! It's mind-boggling, really: like shooting a millimetre bullseye in a trillion light-year-wide target from the other side of the cosmos.' O'Fer seemed to ponder this simile, and then shook his head. 'No, that's not a good analogy, really.'

'The ... gentleman with whom I was conversing said I was thirty-four. I know myself to be thirty-three, yet he was adamant.'

'Where did you say you were, before? Lewes?'

Burnet tipped his head forward.

'I'm betting you're not *from* Lewes, though,' O'Fer pressed. 'And can't remember how you got there?'

'It was,' Burnet conceded, 'a puzzle. I found myself, upon the cold hillside, and remember not by what means I arrived. My purse sufficed to buy me lodgings, and a newspaper, and the means to write to my bank—in Bond Street. I had not received a reply, for only two days ... wait. Was it two days? Was it two days only?'

'Me,' said O'Fer, 'I'm from Deactur, Illinois. Originally.'

'Illyria?'

'Illinois. Not that it matters.' Lights were flickering, underneath the porthole. 'Excuse me a moment,' said O'Fer, leaping from the seat and crying out, in triumph or pain, Burnet could not be sure. 'We're off again! Man, they're quick at repairs—' Burnet was about to say something when he felt a sharp-edged pain in the centre of his skull. It built, then spread, darted down his spine and—it was gone.

The porthole had gone blank.

Part the Fourth

'Returned to the eighteenth century,' O'Fer was saying. Dimly, Burnet became aware that the fellow was in the middle of saying something; and had, in fact, been speaking for a while. 'I mean—how? Even a hundred years out is... not figuratively but literally impossible. More precise than can be explained by science. Like—*what*?'

The porthole was red.

'What-what?' asked Burnet, disoriented.

'We're back. You'll have,' the fellow added, gesturing judiciously at Burnet's forehead, 'a bruise.'

'What happened?'

'We're on a—think of it as a—my, *how* to explain this,' O'Fer said, standing up tall and stretching. He was a very slender fellow, but his hips were a little corpulent—the symptom, Burnet assumed, of a sedentary lifestyle. 'I thought you were thrown out of consciousness—yeah?—by the passage through the time ocean. It can have that effect. One reason I'm piloting this craft, rather than Martin Martinich—though he *wanted* the gig. But the Time Ocean tends to throw his mind, like a wrestler with his opponent, onto the mat. He lies on his front, with his right arm bent right round up his back...' O'Fer rubbed his face. 'I'm sorry, I'm rambling. I'm a rambling girl. It's complicated, though. And there are two reasons—one, the Time Ocean doesn't seem to effect me, in terms of my consciousness. The other is that I'd nothing tying me to 2124.' Burnet was momentarily thrown out of comprehension by this last utterance—*tueni went tueni far*—hearing it as Arabic, a language he had studied briefly under Stockwell. '*Be*cause,' O'Fer added, with sprightly emphasis on the first syllable, 'I aint never getting back *then*.'

'We have sailed again upon the Time Ocean?' Burnet asked.

'We went in, and out. Think of it as a tether—not actual cord, you know. Nah. Nah. But when he goes, we sweep along his wake. Kinder. The tourbillions made by the *tugging* of his bladed craft through the sticky medium of ... ' He dried up.

'And this Time Ocean rendered me temporarily unconscious?' Burnet asked. 'A fugue state?'

'I thought so. But in fact, I reckon what happened was you banged your nut.'

'Nut?'

'Your cranium, Thomas. Your head. It was rough out there. Rougher than I've known it. The truth is, that ocean is getting rougher. *That* storm is getting bigger.'

'Mr O'Fer,' he said. 'Who *are* the Alba? These beings I believe we have both encountered? I find myself speculating as to whether they are jinn, from the traditions of the East, for their powers seem more than mortal.'

'Who,' said John, grinning a white grin. 'Or what? Short answer: don't know. Longer answer, they're clearly non-organic—but that doesn't mean much. Taking a look at Time as a whole, there are a great variety of AI and artificial life forms. No reason why thy mightn't flee Tabulated Time to sail the Ocean forever. Or—well, forever don't really apply.

But let's say, processors wrapped in four-limbed artifiShells. Humandroids. Menschmachines. Who knows?'

Burnet shook his head, and O'Fer put out his hand. 'Hey, I'm sorry. This is hard for me to explain, yes? OK: so, you know the Byzantine emperor who fashioned, er, an automoto,' he stumbled on the word, 'automommo, *automaton*, looked like a man but all clockwork inside?

'Yes.'

'Like that. Only clever on their own terms—not just cogs and gears inside.'

'My temples—throb,' Burnet said, weakly.

'That's because the ship got tossed about, and you bashed your skull against the wall. It was up-y down-y for a while, I don't mind telling you.'

'We are still upon the ocean?'

'No, we're back on Earth. But—much later. He has popped back into Tab-Time, and here we are. We're still within a klick topographically, but temporally...'

'He?'

'Your Mariner! Your pal. We're following him, just like those other Alba are doing.'

'*Why* are we following him?' Burnet pressed, in a querulous voice, rubbing the sore spot on his forehead. 'Ought we not just leave him be?'

'Because he can pick and choose where he goes, in time! Didn't you listen to what I was saying before? The small population who have cut loose from time, and who drift on the Time Ocean ... it's one-way! It's one way. They can duck back into tabulated time, sure; but not with any precision. Not the precision we think of as precision, I mean—not, like, pick a year and in we go.'

'But he can?'

'He can. Your mariner.'

'How does he do it?'

'Now you're getting it! *That's* what we want to know. That's why the Institute sent me on this galloping mission, trying to track him down. The Alba are after him for the same reason. Though, you know, my suspect he's one of them.'

'An sapient automaton?'

'There's a resemblance, don't you think?'

'There is,' Burnet conceded.

Burnet went to the porthole and peered outside. He could see a parched, desert landscape, rust and ochre and all lit with lurid scarlet light.

'But the problem is,' said O'Fer, 'he's *slippery*. Been on his trail for best part of a tabulated year, and I get no closer. The Alba do no better. I'm starting to think we'll never catch up with him.'

'He is standing outside, now,' Burnet observed.

O'Fer was at the window in a moment. 'By Wells your right,' he exclaimed. 'Don't that beat *all*?'

They could not simply step out of the craft, O'Fer insisted. 'Nought to breathe. And anyway—you'll need some of this.' He held up a tube, and from it squeezed a strange apothecary's sample of salve. 'Rub it into your skin—all over, including your face. You'll need goggles, and a breather, and I've got a pair of briefs you can wear under your strides. But all over—or the vacuum will va-va-voom, and you'll bruise all over—or worse.'

'This?' Burnet replied, taking the tube of salve from him. 'Another magic material?'

'It's material, not magic. Just be sure to cover everything. I mean—don't get it in your eyes: I've a mask for your head. But it'll keep you airtight, and warm enough. You can get dressed afterwards. Is he still there?' He went to the porthole again, and then barked with laughter. 'Hey! This is exciting! I'm actually gonna *meet* him!'

Burnet began, gingerly, to rub the salve onto his skin, but O'Fer grew impatient, and hurried him along, pulling off his clothes and massaging the salve onto his chest and back, with brisk, efficient strokes. 'Don't be shy,' he said. 'I got no erotic interest in you, I assure you. Wrong gender for *me*.'

'I should hope so,' muttered Burnet, blushing a little, despite himself. He took his trousers off and rubbed the stuff all over his legs. O'Fer gave him some peculiar undergarments, woven from a sheeny fabric that fitted tight about his nethers. Then he put his breeches back on, and re-fastened his shirt and waistcoat. The salve felt pleasantly warm on his skin.'

'It's you,' O'Fer said. 'I knew it. Knew you were the key—why else did he take you on that jaunt, before? The Alba know it too. That's why they nabbed you. But *I* snatched you back!' He laughed. 'You done your feet?'

'Oh,' said Burnet. 'Is that needful?'

'Lest you wann'm to swell up and bruise—yeah.' So Burnet took off his boots and cotton stockings and rubbed the strange substance into his feet and between his toes.

'Try this mask on,' O'Fer instructed, handing him a visor. 'I'll just do myself.'

'How does it fasten?' Burnet asked, but as he held it before his eyes two slender, rubbery tentacles leapt from its sides and met round the back of his head. In a trice it had settled on his face, covering his eyes, nose and mouth, whilst the rubbery material had spread to make two earmuff structures that covered his ears.

He turned to O'Fer just as he slipped out of his one-piece outfit to rub the salve over his own body, and Burnet realised what he should have realised long before—that O'Fer was a female, as smooth and lithe as a statue. Her hands went over her body in moments, smoothing the strange salve into her skin, and then she slipped her garment back upon her.

'You are female,' Burnet gasped, his voice muffled a little by the mask he was wearing.

She slapped him upon the shoulder, in friendly-wise, and replied. 'Clever boy.' Then the hatchway door at the back of the craft swung open, with a lusciously resonant sound, and a strong breeze came suddenly to life inside the little space. But O'Fer—the *female* pilot—scrambled down the ramp and went outside. 'I just assumed,' Burnet was saying, following her with less physical grace. 'I just assumed...'

PART THE FIFTH

He was outside, and the words died in his throat. The landscape was astonishing. Beneath his feet the red ground was hard as baked clay, and threaded with cracks and spider-web-shaped flaws. To his left a series of low hills lifted their autumn-coloured peaks towards the pink sky. The sun was vast—magnified by some weird magic until it filled a third of the sky; yet Burnet could look directly upon it without offending his eyes, something that he knew to be impossible even with a setting or rising sun. So Sol was both enlarged and diluted, and it spread a lobster-coloured light over the whole parched land. O'Fer was trotted briskly over the ground towards the place where the Mariner stood, and Burnet started after him—after *her*, he reminded himself. 'I just assumed,' he gasped, once more. He picked up his pace.

Away to his right, a fractured line of ruddy peaks hogged the horizon, blackened at their highest points as if scorched. And immediately before them, embedded in the dry land like Excalibur in the stone, was a structure—*clearly* a structure, clearly *not* a natural phenomenon—at an angle of twenty degree from the perpendicular, and perhaps a thousand yards tall. Was it a giant tower, and those flute-holes down its side empty windows? Or was it some vast craft, crashed into the ground and abandoned?

'Come on,' urged O'Fer. Her voice was close, in his ear, so he looked around in startlement to see her a hundred yards away, standing in front of the Mariner. 'He wants you—won't talk to me.'

Confused, Burnet picked up his pace and trotted ponderously to where they were standing. As he approached he saw that the Mariner was wearing a strip across his mouth, and spectacles of a peculiar design. But it was recognisably *him*.

'Amice!' quoth the Mariner, meeting Burnet's gaze. 'Ex dolio bonorum nemo meracius accipit: hoc memorare omisit.'

'Quis?' Burnet replied, wrongfooted.

'If you're gonna speak *foreign* tongues,' said O'Fer. 'We'll need to go back to my ship, so my AI can translate.'

'No,' said the Mariner, in English. 'To *my* ship. We two castaways on the Tempest Tempori—we *must* converse.'

'Hey!' exclaimed O'Fer, her voice ringing clear despite the mask. 'Don't exclude me!'

'I was not excluding you,' the Mariner said, looking directly upon her face. 'On the contrary.' He turned, and began trudging across the bare, reddened landscape. O'Fer fell into step alongside him, and Burnet came up the rear, dilating upon the thought that if the Mariner, in speaking of 'we two castaways', had not meant to exclude O'Fer, then he must have meant to exclude him. They passed from flat ground and ascended a low ridge, such that (looking back at O'Fer's crab-shaped craft, shrunken by distance) Burnet could see that they had landed in the middle of a huge flattened crater. Away to the right the vast, angled structure, purple-black, cast a long shadow over the southern lands.

Soon enough they passed the peak, and came down the scree-strewn far side on unsteady feet. The Mariner's craft was directly before them; recognisably a ship, though with a flattened bottom on which (upon this dry land) it sat: forty yards long, no more; and perhaps fifteen yards across at its widest point. Its open deck was planked with dark-brown wood, and the central cabin was no more than seven feet high. A ladder was angled against its side, and up this the Mariner ascended, O'Fer following and Burnet coming last.

Upon the deck, moving a little stiffly, the mariner stopped, swivelled and faced them again. 'My ship,' he said. 'Nautus meus.'

'You gotta show me round,' said O'Fer, evidently excited. 'Or let me explore—I gotta to see how this baby works.'

'There is a steam engine in the hold,' the Mariner told her. But he was looking at Burnet, with that weird glittery *something* in his rust-coloured pupils. It made Burnet's bowels become water, to look upon them: at once strange and familiar.

'A *steam* engine?' laughed O'Fer. 'For real?'

'Veritatis.'

'Wow! So—are you actually from the, like, eighteen hundreds? Man! I would never have guessed in ... I was gonna say, million years, but my travels the last little while has put all that kind of stuff in perspective. A million years is nothing.'

'But why *steam*?' asked Burnett.

'I have lived, according to the cells in my own corpus, a thousand years,' said the Mariner. 'For much of that time I have sailed the Tide of Time. The water of that sea is not like terrestrial brines.'

'Woh,' said O'Fer. 'No. Way. *Kidding*! You boil the water from *that* ocean in your engine? Is it even, like, possible.'

'I have lived a thousand years,' said the Mariner, a second time.

Burnet, looking about him, noticed a human form, prone on the decking beside the central structure. 'Is he—dead?' he asked.

'He is dead,' the Mariner confirmed. 'But—oh, he will return to life.'

'Alba,' said O'Fer. 'Switch them off, switch them on again. Did he come looking for you? Is that why you zapped him? But—say. Wait. I'll tell you: my theory is—you're an Alba yourself.'

'Alba,' said the Mariner, still looking upon Burnet as if fascinated by his face. 'Means *white*.'

'And?'

'For they are artefacts from the white age, when I passed from darkness to light. But now it is the black age, and I return. The Alba will be superseded by the Negra.'

Burnet looked at O'Fer as he said this, wondering how she would take it. But it did not seem to incommode her. Perhaps it was not a remark that had any bearing upon her.

'Is that your make and model, Marin-man?' she asked, easily.

'I am a living human being,' the Mariner replied. 'Not a machine.'

'Sure you are—you just happen to have lived to be a thousand years. Man, lemme tell you, that's more than science can do with a human body. No: I reckon you're an Alba, or a Negra, or whatever. You're an artificial intellect, gone rogue from your kind, and they're after you to reclaim you. And your steam engine!'

The Mariner finally removed his gaze from Burnet, and directed it to O'Fer. 'I am the fabricator.'

'You *made* him?' Burnet gasped.

'I made them all. I have lived long. Have learnt many skills.'

'You sure have!' crowed O'Fer. 'At the Institute we were monitoring the pathways of—well, we didn't know what! The pathways through non tabulated time, crissing and crossing—or at least, those few temp-trails that passed near-when to the 22nd century. From that we deduced a couple things, built some probes, fashioned by ship, *locked* it in. But the source technology ... the time travel technology ... we figured that was invented *way* in the future. I was thinking—like the year 500,000! Now you're telling me it's powered by a steam engine!' She hugged herself. 'Come on,' she said. 'Show me how it works.'

'That is not to be,' the Marine said, returning his gaze.

O'Fer brought something that was clearly a weapon from out of a pocket somewhere in her clothing . 'I'm gonna insist,' she said. 'I'm really gonna. You might be flesh and blood, like you say, or an Alba: either way, this little gun'd mess you up.'

'Upon my ship,' the Mariner said, still not looking at her, 'I preserve an ovoid bubble of warmth and breathing air, so that I can stand upon the deck and look out over the Time Ocean. But lately the ocean has become more and more tempestuous, and it will not endure. If the non-tabulated realm runs to further chaos—as it must, unless I stop it— then it will consume itself.'

'It is a stormy place,' Burnet gasped.

'It is—until I stop it.' He raised a finger, and the weapon flew from O'Fer's hand. It glinted red in the Hadean sunlight, and fell over the side of the Mariner's ship.

O'Fer's eyes flashed fury behind her goggles, but then fogged, and she slumped. She landed upon the decking, nerveless and asleep.

'Amice, ego tuum, ego meum' the Mariner said. 'This— *this* is the weapon.' From his cloak he drew out a small crossbow, made of silver, and gave it to Burnet. Except that when Burnet handled it he could feel that the metal of its construction was too light to be silver. A bolt, like a sharpened metal hyphen, sat in its breech.

'What am I to do with this?'

'*You* feel it,' the Mariner replied. 'I must expiate my crime, and you must be the means. My sin.'

'Sin?'

'I have travelled upon the tide of time, and I am not alone. Many peoples have made their homes here, floating upon that ocean. The Alba—as this person calls them—are my beings, manufactured by me, although now they propagate themselves upon themselves. But they are not alone, for many creatures have fled Tabulated Time. The ocean is their home, and I have poisoned it.'

'Poisoned an entire ocean? How is it even possible?'

'Attend: I visited you, and brought you out upon that mighty ocean. It is the medium in which islands of Tabulated Time float, bubbles that are cosmoi. And its turbulence something generates storms! But those storms eventually die away. The storm it experiences now is different. I caused it, when I brought you upon it. We two together disturb the medium. Shortly we will sail there again, and you must harpoon me.'

'No!' cried Burnet, recoiling. But he did not give up the crossbow.

'You must, and moreover you must surrender my body to the deep. Then, and only then, the Time Gale will abate. The Alba will revive: they are made to inhabit the Ocean, and perform but poorly in Tabulated Time. That is why they are dead.'

'They?'

'This ship is crewed—a full compliment. But I have been here, upon this terminal landscape, for many tabulated weeks, and one by one they have dropped. But when I return us to the Mare Temporalis they will revive, as being back in their proper environment. They will pilot the ship, and serve you; they will explain matters to you, perhaps, better than I have been able to. But we must go now!'

'Now?'

'The Ocean calls us; it cannot be allowed to grow more turbulent. And I have steeled my will, for no being wishes to die, even after a thousand years. And I do not wish to delay, lest my will fail me.'

The Mariner carried O'Fer's body down the ladder and laid it upon the parched ground. Then, re-ascending, he stripped off his mask and invited Burnet to do the same.

'I have never killed a man,' Burnet began to tell him. 'And cannot believe I shall find the strength of purpose to do it.'

But the surroundings abruptly changed. They were again upon that impossible ocean, and the tempest was louder and fiercer than ever. Cliff-face waves a league high raised themselves up with audible groans, and their tops broke and sprayed in the ferocious winds to bleed into the clouds themselves. The deck swivelled, swung about, and smacked round once more. Burnet was hurled down, and slid over the decking to the side rail, hitting it with a breath-stealing thump. Somehow the Mariner was still upright, though; his legs apart, balancing himself upon the wildly titled surface, as his beard flapped right like a comet's tail.

Burnet got to his feet, clinging to the rail with his left hand, holding the crossbow with his right. 'I will do no murder,' he screamed, trying to be heard over the vast sounds of the storm. The spray had made him as wet as though he had been fully immersed in water. He blinked. The Mariner was replying, but the storm swallowed his words. Burnet had to get closer. He took a step, the deck wobbled and swung beneath him, and he went down on one knee. He only realised he had discharged the crossbow after the fact—the jolt of impact had made his finger twitch on the trigger. The shaking of the boat had betrayed him. He happened to have been pointing the weapon directly at the Mariner's chest.

He caught a glimpse of the other, as spray swirled around him like the aurora borealis: it cleared momentarily and Burnet saw him standing, his arms wide, the bolt of the crossbow clearly visible in his chest. Then he stumbled backwards, and a wave washed over the deck, and he was gone.

Burnet tried to get to his feet, blinking water from his eyes, but the deck wrong footed him, and he smacked face down upon the deck. He took the impact on his chin, and felt a sudden severe pain there, but he could not determine whether it was blood that flooded his neck or water from the untabulated ocean. The deck tilted again, and he slid head first towards the central structure, turning as he moved so that he struck the wooden structure side-on. He held on as tight as he could to the corner of this, and after a little manoeuvring was able to get his feet wedged in at that place where the uprights met the deck, the carpentry of this structure having left a small lip. For a long time he simply clung there, and the boat swung crazily from one vertical to another, leaving his head down and head up, sometimes turning the wall into a tabletop upon which he lay, sometimes into a roofbeam to which he clung. His gorge filled with nausea. Eventually, however, the scale of the waves became less, and he was able to shift his position. There was a door. He climbed the seesawing face of wood, got his hand upon the handle, and tumbled inside as the door opened. It took longer to get the door shut, and once it swung back and struck him painfully upon the arm. But eventually it was closed.

Soaked and shivering, Burnet clung to a pillar. It was dark, and the motion of the boat baffled him. 'If only there were light,' he croaked, aloud, and at this latter word—as if at a charm—light filled the space. It emanated from the whole ceiling, mild and white, and illuminated a comfortable space: cupboards and desks were fixed to the wall; books upon shelves somehow managed not to tumble free as the vessel pitched and yawed and rolled. Two more of the Alba creatures were lying, dead it seemed, in hammocks in the middle of the space. Burnet could not see how these hammocks were fixed to the wall. In point of fact, they appeared not to be fixed to the walls at all. Yet by what Arabian Carpet magic they operated, they hung in the middle space. Getting a sense of the rhythm with which the space tilted and swung, Burnet was able to get to one of these hammocks. He pulled himself inside, slipping easily into the space next to the supine Alba—the corpus was cold, the flesh firm to the point of coldness. With a lunge, Burnet levered the body out, and it clattered to the floor.

Immediately he felt better. Indeed, the stillness was so sudden as to be disorienting: for now Burnet was motionless, and the whole room rotated and swung precariously around him. But worn out, in pain at a dozen places, he soon fell asleep.

Part the Sixth

When he woke the room was swaying gently. The
storm, evidently, had settled. For a time Burnet simply lay,
considering his own body. His forehead throbbed where he
had struck it; there was a crust of dried blood upon his chin.
His stomach felt raw.

Eventually he roused himself. He stretched his spine,
and tested his sea legs, feeling the floor swing gently from
side to side. His clothing had dried, but a crust of salt had
starched the tubes of his breeches, the sheets of his jacket.
Exploring the cabin he discovered a cabinet in which were
many garments—French-cut *pantalons* and chemises made
of a black material that felt like silk and yet was much
tougher; and a fine gum-treated cloak. These fitted him
perfectly.

He was hungry, and looked for food, but there was
nothing in the cabin. So he went out upon the deck, and
breathed the clear serene. The view was extraordinary.
Light beamed from every portion of the sky, not tied into
the knot of a single sun, but a universal gleam. The waters
too possessed that faint but evident luminescence that can
sometimes be glimpsed, on a warm midnight on the Aegean
or Ionian shores—most evident when the summits of the
low waves crisped into white-bright foam. The terrifying
mountains of water that had burlied against one another

the night before had all drawn their heads below the surge, leaving only a panorama of low ruffles in the spacious expanse.

Burnet felt his heart rise. He forgot his aches, and his hunger, and stood for a long time simply looking out upon the waters.

'Cornelius Agrippa talks of the fountain of eternal youth,' he said aloud, though there was nobody there to hear him. 'He did not comprehend that the waters of eternal youth are more than a fountain's trickle—they are an entire ocean!'

The craft had no sails, and yet it was making its way—the wake at the aft proved that. Eventually Burnet was able to tear himself away from the deck, provoked as much by thirst as anything. Back into the cabin: the three corpses of the Alba creatures lay, two in their hammocks and one rolled into the angle formed by wall and floor. There was a hatch, and Burnet lifted this to descend the wooden stairway into the hold of the vessel.

Burnet thought back to what the Mariner had said, and experienced a twinge of pain in his breast at the memory of the old man—had he *really* shot him, with a crossbow bolt, in that dream-like encounter? It did not feel *real*. The Mariner had said that a steam-powered engine of some sort powered the craft. And here it was! A block of metal, the size of a large loom, with a bright light shining on top. There

were strange knobbles and protrusions upon the casing of
the thing, and it was trembling, as if fevered. Pipes lead into
it and away—or Burnet assumed the pipework represented
a circuit of some sort, like the brick-built veins that serviced
a Roman heating system. And on the far side, Burnet found
a spigot, from which it was possible to decant fresh water—
either the machine had some function whereby it could
remove the salt from the brine and so create sweetwater,
or else the spigot attached to a reservoir somewhere else
about the vessel. Either way it was good to drink. The single
light threw the shadow of Burnet's bent body large upon
the white-painted wall behind him, as he put his lips to the
tap. It was exceptionally pleasant to assuage thirst, although
filling his belly with water only made him more aware of
how hungry he was.

There was another hatchway, down which Burnet
went. Here he discovered a dozen dead Alba, all lying in
hammocks, lifeless as stocks and stones. The boat had once
been well crewed, it seemed. There were many storage
compartments down here, too; and in one—unnaturally cold,
although it contained no ice—Burnet found fillets of fish.
He took two of these and clambered back up to the deck, to
sit like a child, or like an oriental monarch, cross-legged,
gazing out across the waters and eating.

He pondered the things the ship seemed not to possess: most notably a cabin, or wheel, or any means of controlling it. He also thought about the dead bodies. If O'Fer had been correct, they were nothing but cunningly artificed automata. But their mainsprings had wound-down, and Burnet knew not how to rewind them. Their vital principle had departed. Should he bury them at sea? But if they were automata they would not rot. He recalled belatedly that one of them had been lying on the open deck the previous night, and he got to his feet to search for it, walking all the way around the outer rail. It was no longer there. This did not surprise Burnet, for the waters had been apocalyptic the night before, and the body had presumably been washed overboard.

Burnet devoted some time to attempting to puzzle out the larger mysteries of where he was. Both the Mariner and O'Fer had talked about time—as if this ocean were not part of time, or else as if it were somehow the concentrated essence of time. Burnet thought about what Plotinus had written on the subject. People grew old in time, but the Mariner had claimed to be a thousand years of age—perhaps to sail this ocean was to remain forever young? But if so, how had it been possible to kill the Mariner?

Time appeared to pass here, although there was no sun, and therefore no sunset. Lacking a pocket watch, Burnet was unable to gauge the exact passage, but soon enough he felt tired, and went back into the cabin to sleep.

He woke, and had the sensation that he had not slept at all; not because he did not feel refreshed (he did) but because there was no sensation of time having passed.

The rhythm of Burnet's life shifted. Many aspects of his surroundings did not change; his clothes never seemed to become dirty; and if they became wet they dried almost at once. The light was always the same. The boat passed on its way. The bizarre steam engine in the hold throbbed without cease or malfunction. But in some respects there was evidence of time passing. He grew hungry and ate. He grew thirsty and drank. He was compelled to void his bowels and empty his bladder, and did so into a compact jakes he discovered in the aft of the vessel. More, he felt the bristles upon his chin, first a hessian-like scratchiness, and shortly as whiskers long enough to clasp in his hand. There were no mirrors upon the craft, but he used his fingers'-ends to get a sense of how his hair was lengthening upon his head. He was compelled to bite away his lengthening fingernails.

The Tide of Time settled further. The last turbulence left its surface and the whole ocean became as smooth as a bolt of blue cloth spread out upon a tailor's table. As the waters calmed, so did the air; breezes no longer blew. This had no effect upon the passage of the craft, which still chugged under the power of its ingenious engine. But it meant that the environment became hotter. There was no one solar source of heat, and yet the ambient temperature became rather stickily warm.

It began to dawn upon Burnet that he would spend the rest of his days in this vessel. When he had eaten almost all the dried fish in the stores below, he found a cupboard in which were lines, hooks and nets. Taking shreds of fish flesh as his bait he laid these over the side of the ship; it took several sleeps—however long that was in conventionally tabulated time—but his efforts as *pescheur* were rewarded. The net came up empty, but the lines snapped with tautened, and Burnet hauled up strange piscine entity, big as a bulldog but ugly and fanged like a devil from a medieval fresco. It snapped and twisted its brown-scaled body into epileptic contortions as it drowned in the air of the deck. Later Burnet took knives from the cabin and cut the bones from it—the creature was a tangle of comb teeth-like bones inside—and lay fillets out to dry in the heat.

He slept and ate. There was tranquillity, here.

One day Burnet saw another ship upon the endless ocean. It had three masts but no sails, and was visible in the extreme distance, There was no way that Burnet could signal it, and he knew no way of altering the course of his own vessel. There was a telescopic tube in the cabin, and Burnet peered through it at the other ship, resting the device upon the rail to keep it steady. It possessed a long, narrow hull, and the three masts stood up as distinctly, iii . But Burnet could see now signs of life upon it. He calculated that it must be very close to the horizon, and he could see that it was sailing diagonally away from him. He waited for it to slip over the horizontal curve and vanish, but it did not seem to do this. Instead it grew smaller and smaller until it was lost in haze.

He existed, placidly, for a further period of time; or—he reasoned—perhaps he simply existed, without periodisation. When he felt bored, he passed the time by reading the books in the cabin. Some of these were incomprehensible to him, but some were very familiar—Homer in the Rathenau edition, a fat three volume Plato with Greek and Latin facing texts.

He ate, and drank, and slept. He checked the lines for more fish, this time pulling up a long slender white-scaled creature halfway between eel and herring. He filleted this and laid it on the deck. He watched the light upon the placid water. He ate a little more, and slept.

When he next woke the crew had come back to life.

Part the Seventh

They did not all revive at once. One roused itself in the hold; a little while later the three in the cabin all woke up. But soon enough the whole crew, save one, were awake.

'What is the matter with him?' Burnet asked.

One of the beings was examining its fellow. 'He is fully dead.'

'You were not?'

'We are sustained by the Tide of Time. The previous Captain took this vessel into the realms of Tabulated Time for a long period, and this is toxic to us. But we are not in Tabulated Time long enough for the processes to decay us fully.'

'Except for him.'

'Yes,' said the Alba.

Burnet did something that had not occurred to him earlier. He checked with the other crewmen, and they made no objection; so he cut open the shining skin of the permanently expired individual. He expected to see cogs and wheels, like a watchmaker's device expanded; but it was nothing like that. Inside was sticky, and filled mostly with crystals of various colours and sizes, all faceted and lengthy, splinters and jewels.

'How do these work?' he asked one of the crew.

It did not know. 'How do *you* work?' it retorted.

At least the crew knew how to operate the ship. They set about fishing on a large scale, pulling up peculiar-looking gaspers by line but also filling the nets. They ate, too; although in comparison to Burnet they hardly ate at all.

'What strange machines you are!' Burnet exclaimed, at one point.

'Our origins are organic,' the Alba returned. 'We are changed since migrating upon this Tide.'

'Changed? Crystallised inside! Will it happen to me?'

'If you are long enough here.'

'How long?' Burnet wanted to know. But in their eternal present, the Alba were beyond the ability to answer such a question.

There was a time when Burnet saw a bird in the sky, and looking again saw that it was instead a Montgolfier construction, a flying machine. It made a very distant, vaguely flatulent noise, and past from aft to stern, but very high up.

'What manner of craft is that!' Burnet exclaimed.

'It flies,' the Alba noted.

The Alba did not volunteer information, but Burnet came to see that they knew a lot about the Tide. He began plaguing them with questions. Could they take this vessel out of the Tide of Time, and into a Tabulated epoch. Yes. Could they take Burnet back to 1798? No. Why not?

'Because,' one of the Alba explained, 'the target is too narrow. Time is tabulated according to a quantum measure, whereby there are 144 trillion quanta per healthy forty-year-old human-at-rest-heartbeat. The tabulated cosmos subsists for two times ten to the one thousand six hundred and eighty seven of these quanta. To select a single one, from such a large number, would require computational accuracy achievable only if every atom in ten trillion universes were disposed into a notional computational machine.'

It took a long time for the Alba to unpack this statement such that Burnet could understand it. Even after the various elements had been laboriously extrapolated he understood little, except that the number of possible entry-points into Tabulated Time was so large as to be, functionally, infinite; and that therefore it was impossible to zero-in on one number.

He pondered this for a long time, until it slowly grew to seem commonsensical to him. But this did not mean he entirely understood it.

On his instruction the Alba took the craft into Tabulated time on several occasions. The first two replaced the balm of the calm, lit Tide with absolute darkness. Below was neither ocean nor land, just a void; and the lights of the craft did nothing to illuminate the blackness on either side. He quizzed the Alba and they told him that the vast majority of Tabulated Time was like this—the stars having burnt out all their fuel and fallen to ashes and shards, the worlds all frozen and lifeless. He did not like it. On the third occasion they arrived (the Alba said) billions of years *before* the Earth he knew—again the ship floated in space, but surrounded this time by a riot of white and red light. Finally, as he nagged them further, the Alba managed to negotiate a passage into the Earth: the age of ice, the oceans frozen and green. For a while Burnet wandered this strange landscape, but he did not feel at home there.

Back upon the Tide, he basked in the light and felt the tug of chaos ease and dissipate. He ate and drank and again read Plato. Its fit with his present circumstance was not perfect, but it was a better guide than Homer.

One time they saw another ship—this one a vast triple-hulled behemoth the size of a city. It came fast towards them, and for a while Burnet grew fearful that its occupants might be pirates, intent upon overwhelming them. But they pulled alongside, and Burnet tried to speak with them—but their language was as barbarous as their oval, silver-coloured, noseless faces. After a while they seemed to grow bored, and sailed away.

On another occasion they saw a whale; but when it surfaced and floated there Burnet saw that it was another artificial craft. He waved at it, but it made no further attempt to communicate and eventually dived beneath the waves.

'How many people live here, upon this timeless Tide of Time?' he asked.

'I know not,' said the Alba.

'Might you guess?'

'Millions,' the Alba replied. 'For any civilisation that discovers the means to slip out of Tabulated Time—and thousands rise and fall that achieve such science—some intrepid souls will venture out upon this sea. And once they are here, they discover they cannot return whence they came. Some return to Tabulated Time and start new lives, perhaps taking with them the technologies that spawn further inventions in time travel. Some elect to remain here, and sail forever these buoyant waters.'

'Yet the Mariner returned to *his* time, or near as dammit,' Burnet expostulated. He had previously explained to the Alba that this was the moniker by which he referred to the individual they had called Captain. 'How?'

'He possessed impossible skills,' the Alba replied. 'He is able to *triangulate*'—this word took a deal of Alba articulation, and its utterance slowed the sentence—'and so return within a hundred years of his point of origin.'

More than this they could not say. He asked further questions: how had the Mariner recruited them? He had taken them from their homes upon the surface of the water, and overcome their resistance, and rewritten the codes by which they functioned so as to serve him. 'Why did he come for *me*?' Burnet pressed. 'What is so special about *me*?'

They could not say.

One day Burnet spied land, and grew excited. He ordered the Alba to steer the ship towards this new coast, but as he came closer he saw that it was, instead, a vast raft, upon which many buildings had been constructed: several acres in extent. As they came to, a large crowd of Alba gathered upon the edge of their floating platform.

'Are you friendly?' he cried across the intervening water. 'Or are you enemies?'

At his side was one of his own crew. 'They are friendly,' he assured Burnet.

So Thomas Burnet tied back his long hair and jumped into the waters of Time, to swim to the edge of the raft. He wandered amongst the floating village, stopping to exchange words with one or other of the identical-looking Alba. He saw where they fished, and found towards the centre of the raft a telescope the size of a tree-trunk, mounted upon a tripod, through which they observed their environment. 'When there are tempests,' one told him, 'we lose many to the waters.' He nodded. Making his way back towards his own craft he passed an unusual yurt-shaped structure. It tweaked his memory, and he stopped. He knew this thing.

He rapped on the hard roof and waited as the door opened. The figure that emerged was recognisably O'Fer, though much older—hair white, skin blotches and wrinkled. 'Good God,' she said, looking at him. 'It's you!'

'Your craft!' he said. 'I recognised it.'

'It's kaput, now,' she said, slapping its roof resonantly with the flat of her hand. 'It wasn't built to last forever. But it still keeps the light out, when I want to sleep. Keeps the rain off my old head.'

'You are old,' Burnet said, admiringly. 'Very old!'

'I've been through a lot,' she agreed. 'It's all good, though. Come on—let's stroll.'

They wandered to the edge of the raft together, and sat down. 'It's been a long, long time,' she told him.

'Not for I,' he returned.

'No, I can see it. But the beard! The beard is a nice touch. You really look like—well, yourself.'

'How can I do otherwise?' he replied, smiling.

'You know what I mean,' she insisted. When he insisted that he did not, she sighed. 'I'd have thought you could have worked it out. It's not hard. You recall the Mariner?'

'Of course.'

'We met him upon the Red Giant Earth, and he said *we two castaways on the Tempest Tempori*. There we were, you, me and he: and he said *we two castaways*. He was being precise, as was his wont. Because there *were* only two people there; he and I. You and I.'

'I do not follow,' Burnet said.

'No? You need to think it through, laughing boy. Not that I can be sure and certain, but I can at least say: I'm pretty sure. That's how he was able to return to within a human lifetime of his starting point. You and he—the same person.'

'Oh,' said Burnet on a long indrawn breath. Then, breathing out: 'Oh.'

'That was the turbulence, that was what caused the great tempest here—on these waters. He brought *himself* in. You did, I mean. It was a mode of feedback, I think; a violence the environment could not endure. The two of you at once.'

'I shot him,' Burnet whispered.

'And so it is calm again,' said O'Fer nodding. 'That's OK. I spent decades upon decades in tab-Time, and grew old. But I've been here for—how do you gauge the time in this place? Centuries, it feels like. But peaceful centuries. And I'm angry he would threaten a place like this, where millions live, with his crime.'

'His crime,' Burnet repeated.

'Egotism. Arrogance. Sin. To endanger all this! To think that his desire for a more accurate method of popping in and out of tabulated time was worth—risking all *this*!'

'We are talking about me, and we are talking about another person,' Burnet said.

'Sure. And I reckon it wasn't just a whim. I reckon he—you—fetched himself into the Tide because, doing so, he—you—discovered that having two versions of himself meant that he could tie, as it were, a knot in the wakes he left.'

'Triangulate,' Burnet said.

'Exactly! By triangulating himself with himself, he was able to go to precise points in the stretch of tabulated time. Unlike other time travellers he could *pick and choose*. Of course, now that he's no longer doing that, we are no longer able to follow his wake. But it's for the best. The thing that's troubling my nut,' she added, 'was how he found you in the first place.'

'I do not remember,' Burnet said, truthfully.

'Sure. By his bootstraps, probably. He could probably only find you in the first place because he had already tied his knot, or triangulated his trajectory, in this place already. It sounds like a paradox, but maybe it's not. And he's undone his crime, he's expatiated it, by cancelling one of the two of you out. And like that!' O'Fer clicked her fingers. 'The feedback ceases! Marvellous.'

'Marvellous,' agreed Burnet, uncertainly. He looked across the placid waters, and drew in another breath.

'We know more than we did,' O'Fer said, after a while, giving each word its emphasis. 'But that don't necessarily make us happier, any.'

'No,' agreed Burnet.

THERE LEVIATHAN

Jonathan Green

> *"THERE LEVIATHAN,*
> *HUGEST OF LIVING CREATURES, IN THE DEEP*
> *STRETCHED LIKE A PROMONTORY SLEEPS OR SWIMS,*
> *AND SEEMS A MOVING LAND; AND AT HIS GILLS*
> *DRAWS IN, AND AT HIS BREATH SPOUTS OUT A SEA."*
> (JOHN MILTON, PARADISE LOST)

X – CALL ME ISHMAEL

He wakes to the sound of sky-birds and the cold buffeting of the wind against his face.

He blinks, the azure mantle of heaven resolving before his eyes, scuds of white cirrus coursing overhead like ships with the wind in their swollen sails.

That in itself is a surprise. For a moment he wonders if he is dead and this is the heaven promised by the Papal preacher fleets.

A ship's bell sounds and he blinks again. He tries to move. His body aches, but his hands touch something hard beneath him. Metal, or wood, he's sure that heaven shouldn't feel like this. Then if not heaven, where? Hell?

He is aware of voices now, but they are not the chattering voices of devils. At least he doesn't think so. He hears Frankish, Portulan and even a few snatched phrases of Mandranese. How many devils speak Mandranese?

So if he is not in heaven and nor is he is hell, then that must mean…

Despite the aches and pains that accompany his every attempted movement at least he *can* still move, and that understanding fills his heart with something akin to elation. He had not expected to survive at all; he had thought them all doomed.

He sits up, wincing at the pain he feels in his wrist. The rough boards move and he hears the rumple of waxed fabric as the inflatable shifts under him.

Rolling over onto his knees, he stares at the weathered planks and from there over the gunwales of the dinghy at the boiling turmoil of black and brown clouds below. The Scald is lit from within by a putrid orange glow, rippling with the crackle of crimson electrical discharge. The acrid stink of it stings his nostrils.

If heaven still lies above him and hell below, then he must still be in purgatory. So he made it to the lifeboat after all.

The voices are louder now.

He looks up and sees the ship approaching from beyond the prow. Sailors hang from the rigging draping the sides of the bulbous, snub-nosed vessel.

Sailors or pirates?

He's not sure. From the look of them they could be either. But whatever they are, like as not they're his only hope, out here in the wilds of the Wilderwind Wastes. There's no land for a thousand miles in any direction, what little land there is left.

They're heading straight towards him, so all he can do is try to make the best of a bad situation. After all, he's alive; anything more than that is a bonus, all things considered.

He gets to his feet, wincing at the twinge he feels in his back, unsteady on his feet, stumbling about the boat as he finds his air-legs again. He waves to the crew of the closing dirigible, with what he hopes is an open and relieved smile on his face.

The sailors' chatter becomes more agitated as they bark instructions at one another, the Frankish, Portulan and

Mandranese voices all speaking some sky-ways dialect of Zepheranto.

And then the mooring bowsprit of the lumbering airship is bumping against the hull of the lifeboat, the sailors casting grapple hooks over the side to pull the air-dinghy in snug to the vessel's catch-nets.

Rough hands, callused from all the rope-work life on board an airship demands, help him disembark from the lifeboat and up onto the deck of sky-galleon. He catches a glimpse of the ship's name-board as he's hauled on board: *Ahab*.

A weathered face like wrinkled whale-hide suddenly confronts him. A mouth that contains as much gold as it does stumps of rotten teeth demands, "And who might you be?"

Overcome with weariness, he drops to his knees on the air-blasted deck of the sky-ship, grateful to have something more solid under him again.

He looks up into the leathern face, and that mouth of black enamel and scavenged gold, and suddenly can't stop smiling.

"Call me Ishmael," he says.

IX – Very Like a Whale

"What brings you to these windswept wastes?" asks the dark-skinned, noble savage.

"I might ask you the same thing," Ishmael says, eyeing the harpooneer on his perch behind his swivel-mounted steam-gun, carving scrimshaw onto the shaft of a gleaming harpoon.

"You might," the harpooneer says, accepting Ishmael's answer with an open-handed gesture. "But I ask only out of kindness, friendship my only hoped for reward."

Ishmael's suspicious resolve wavers at that. These airship pirates have demonstrated nothing but compassion towards him since rescuing him from the drifting air-dinghy.

"I apologise." He feels his ears redden with the heat of shame.

"No need, no need," the other says generously, his Zepheranto shaped by wide round Carib vowels. "Queequeg does not take offence easily." There is a twinkle in his eye that matches the glister of the gold in his mouth.

For all his native nobility and temperament of spirit, the necklace of withered ears this Queequeg wears about his neck on a knotted catgut cord fills Ishmael with a deep disquiet.

"So what brings you to the Wilderwind Wastes?" asks a voice that is little more than a gruff growl, like the wind howling through the ship's hawsers.

Ishmael looks the buccaneer up and down as this new arrival clumps towards him across the deck. The airship's crew may be an intimidating mish-mash of scarred and totem-bedecked superstitious old sky-dogs but none can compare to their tyrannical captain.

He must be a tyrant, Ishmael decides, to keep a scurvy band of cutthroats in order. He certainly looks the part, his lean scarred face gaunt as a ghost's, framed by an unkempt, knotted beard. The gimlet stare of his pale grey eyes twists into Ishmael, the man's haunted visage sending a shiver of unease throughout Ishmael's entire body.

Able to bear it no longer, the survivor breaks eye contact and finds his gaze alighting upon the stump of the man's right leg. From the knee down the captain rests his weight upon a steam-leaking piston fashioned of polished brass and steel rivets.

Sunlight catches the wheezing prosthesis revealing needle-etched scrimshaw upon its surface. It's only a momentary glimpse, but from that Ishmael gets the impression of a ship – a bulbous, fish-shaped dirigible – the churning clouds of the Scald, and something rising from them. Something very like a whale.

With that fleeting image of the whale still clear as day in his mind's eye, Ishmael tells the captain his sorry tale.

VIII – THE JONAH

I joined the Jonah *at Port Atlas, planning to work my passage on the cloud-dredger for a few months, maybe as far as Drakensberg in the Afrik Archipelago.*

A cloud-dredger.

It pans the Scald itself, sucking up the tainted cloud matter and processing it, refining it to extract the hydrocarbons and other gases from the pollutant sea to drive the sky-ship fleets.

Anyway, we were three days out of Barquetown when we first encountered the beast, or at least signs of it. A sky-skiff adrift on the air currents, its sails torn, mast snapped clean in two, its prow gone. One gasbag was still intact and that was all that had kept it from being lost to the Scald altogether.

We pulled the remains of the wreck on board, using the cloud-scoop, but there was no one left alive on board. In fact there was no sign of anyone on board the Celeste, *living or dead.*

Pequod said it was an ill omen, that we should turn back, but Captain Boomer wasn't having any of it. Would that he had listened to the daft old albatross; he would most likely have still been alive today.

We ran into the beast that very evening, as night was starting to steal across the firmament. It came from beneath the swirling currents of the smog, trailing greasy tendrils of sludgy smoke, mouth agape.

And what a mouth! Big enough to swallow the Jonah *whole.*

Captain Boomer knew then that Pequod had been right. But by then it was too late. He sounded the alarm, giving the command to evacuate, but it was too late. There wasn't even time to release the lifeboats from their moorings.

As the monster took hold of the Jonah *in its mouth I sprinted for the nearest lifeboat. The rest is a mystery to me. I remember the sound of the deck splintering and the dull pop of gas bladders bursting, and then I don't recall anything else until waking to find myself adrift and the* Ahab *coming into view over the bow.*

VII – BY ART IS CREATED THAT GREAT LEVIATHAN

All is silent on deck – other than for the creaking of the ratlines, and the ceaseless moaning of the wind, and the groan of the ropes wrapped around the gas-swollen body of the dirigible – until the noble savage says, "What is it?" The harpoon he has been working on is now gripped tight in his hands.

"A rogue?" is all Ishmael can think to say. "Hungry?"

"I heard it was the last of the tech-wrought sky-leviathans – skyathans – a curse left us by the ancients, from that ungodly age when they committed hubris in the arrogant hope of ridding the world of the Scald that they might one day return to the surface," says a wild-haired and wild-eyed sky-dog, "seeking to cast off God's punishment."

"Hush, Elijah, do not speak of such things," says another, anxiety writ large in the lines of his wind-weathered face.

"A rogue. Hungry. Relentless. It is all those things, and more." The captain's voice, as cold and as hard as hailstones, cuts through the chatter on deck. "It is a demon, a devil-thing. It is my bane and my burden. It is a thing to be destroyed, and I will see it dead!"

"What?" The captain meets Ishmael's look of growing horror and understanding with the same unremitting, icy stare. "What do you mean, you will see it dead?"

There is a tension in the silent spaces between their exchanges.

"The beast and I have unfinished business." The captain gives a bark of what might be laughter, thumping his piston prosthesis hard against the deck of the ship.

Ishmael says nothing, knowing that nothing he can say will dissuade the captain, but stares at the scrimshawed brass, seeing the beast quite clearly now, rising from the chemical soup of the Scald to claim the *Ahab* at last.

"Do the Pope's missionaries not preach an eye for an eye, a tooth for a tooth?"

"But you surely can't mean to go after the beast in this. Were you not listening just now, when I told my story? Such an endeavour would be suicide, man!"

The tension on deck reaches breaking point and snaps. The hubbub of anxious voices resumes; their tone and intention clear, even if the words themselves are not.

"Silence!" the captain roars and Ishmael feels another shiver of dread trickle down his spine, cold as the rain over the Tarctic.

"The course is set. We go onward. And we shall not rest until the devil is dead."

VI – King of the Boundless Sea

"You can't!" Ishmael cries out, unable to contain himself any longer. "You'll damn us all. We should be turning round and going back to Barquetown or Stormhaven, even to the domains of the Papacy. Any way but onwards!"

"That is not up for discussion," the captain growls before shouting to his crew, "Get to work! Man the harpoon guns. Ready the grapple ropes and keep all eyes on the Scald!"

The crew jump to it immediately, apparently more fearful of the wrath of the demon already in their midst than the devil-beast lurking out there in the choking smog sea.

Ishmael watches them in stupefied disbelief as they go about their business. Did they not believe him? Because much as he might wish it otherwise, his was no sky-dog's story made fantastical by dramatic invention. The monster – the last of the sky-leviathans the mad prophet Elijah had said – had practically swallowed the *Jonah* whole.

The *Ahab* wouldn't stand a chance against it. And surely the captain knew that if he had encountered the thing before, and lost his leg to its mindless marauding and idiot hunger. Why go back after that?

"This is madness!" Ishmael screams. "Turn back!" he yells at the crew "Turn back!"

They watch him warily from the corner of their eyes, but none dares disobey the captain. Not one.

The tyrant turns then, cold fire blazing in those frozen diamond eyes of his.

"Make yourself useful. Man a harpoon gun or get yourself to the brig!" he growls, his dog-like snarl more terrifying that any bullish bellow. "I'll not stand for mutiny on my ship."

Mutiny? Ishmael had never intended that, but now that the captain has suggested it...

Could he persuade the other sailors that their captain's course of action can only lead them all to their deaths? What if he were to jump the bastard now, surprise him, take him down? Could he make Elijah, Queequeg and the rest of these airship pirates see sense and flee the Wilderwind Wastes? Persuade them to return to the safety and civilisation of the mountain archipelagos?

Ishmael is distracted from his mutinous thoughts by a cry from the lookout.

"Captain! Off the port bow!" The man is leaning out of the crow's nest frantically jabbing a finger toward the horizon. "Thar she blows!"

V – THE SPORT OF DEATH

There is a mad scramble for the side of the ship and Ishmael finds himself packed in amongst half a dozen others – some of them standing on the gunwales, hanging onto the taut rigging for support, to get a better view – as they all peer into the distance at the foaming fumes, a thousand yards to port.

The smog swells, a rancid, oil-streaked boil forming in its midst before it bursts and the skyathan rises from the Scald, greasy vapour trails clinging to its heaving gas-bladder flanks.

Its blunt head is scarred and pitted, the acid burns of aeons having etched their own cruel cartography into the leathern hide of the gene-spliced beast. Its sickly grey gas-bloated body has swelled beyond the bounds of its ancient harness long ago so that the straps and bands of beaten brass have been subsumed by its flesh, becoming inextricably part of it.

Ishmael gasps. During his last encounter with the beast there was no prior warning, no agitated anticipation. The monster had come from nowhere to swallow the cloud-dredger. All that he had seen of it then was the cavernous darkness of its huge mouth and the rust-sheathed enamel spears of its monstrous teeth.

His heart races. His stomach knots. He wants to piss himself and whoop with joyful exhilaration both at the same time.

The creature is incredible. The last of its kind, if it is such, it has plied these cloud banks since time immemorial, gorging itself on the skrill that swim the spoil cloud seas, weary rock gulls and even the occasional basking sky-shark, no doubt. But such a diet could never be enough to satisfy a beast the size of this monster. No wonder then that it started taking down airships and sky-tugs. Ships like the cloud-dredger *Jonah*.

The great head breaches the clouds and then dips again, the great back arching, the gas bladders bolted to the wrought-beast's sides breaking the surface of the cloud mass as huge paddle flippers scull the air, sending eddies spinning through the broiling black petrochemical pollution.

The machine-animal's movements appear almost graceful rather than predatory, and yet there can be no doubt that it is on a collision course with the *Ahab*. Ishmael can't believe it's a coincidence.

"Hard a-port!" the captain's guttural roar carries across the deck.

The ship lists left forcing Ishmael to grab hold of a ratline or else plunge over the edge and into the catch-nets draped over the side of the airship below. He feels like he could pitch over the side at any moment and into the seething Scald below.

Countless generations since the Great Disaster and still the Scald smothers the land beneath its acid cloud seas, all but the very highest peaks of the mountain archipelagos.

Ishmael watches as the great flukes of the sky-whale's tail break the churning cloud cover, dragging more oily streamers from its putrid depths into the clear air behind it, a sight that elicits gasps even from this gang of hard-bitten sky-pirates.

With a final flick of its tail the behemoth disappears from the view again beneath the fuming Scald.

"Man the harpoons!" the captain roars. "Be ready!"

Ishmael turns from the settling sea of cumulonimbus and catches the captain's eye for a moment as the haggard pirate runs the length of the deck, his piston leg venting steam.

"It's gone!" Ishmael shouts. "What do you propose to do now?"

"Lure it out," the captains growls.

"And how are you going to do that?"

"By baiting the hook."

A furious smile splits the captain's deeply lined face, his diamond stare locked on Ishmael now.

The captain shouts an order to the men milling about the deck, readying the steam-powered harpoon launchers, whilst pointing at the sole survivor of the cloud-dredger *Jonah*.

"Seize him!"

IV – CANST THOU DRAW OUT LEVIATHAN WITH AN HOOK?

They throw him in a caelisphere cage, the thick metal lattice of its bars stained black by corrosion.

They are deaf to his protestations as they lock him in, the shouts of their own desperately relayed orders threatening to drown his cries of anguish as the cage is winched into the air, a chugging derrick swinging it out over the side of the ship.

The captain gives the command and then the caelum-cage is falling, dropping through the whirling wind, the chain that still secures it to the deck of the airship clattering through the iron hoop of the crane joist.

It drops past the side of the dirigible envelope and keeps falling. Grasping the bars in fear for his life, Ishmael watches as the keel of the airship passes away above him.

The cage keeps on falling, dropping like a stone through the tortured air, the smog sea coming ever closer with every second. And then it penetrates the morass of boiling pollution that smothers the whole world beneath its blanket of stifling smoke and febrile fog.

He feels the cloying fingers of the Scald caressing his face, its stinging kisses on his cheeks, as it tastes his flesh for the first time.

And then the cage slams to a sudden stop, so hard that it sends Ishmael crashing to the bottom. For a moment the caelisphere jerks back up before dropping once more, swinging away from the side of the airship as the vessel lurches above, still tethered as it is by the mighty black iron chain.

The cage's captive screams in shock and pain and fear. He cries out to the captain and the crew, begging them to have mercy on him, to pull him up, even as he feels the acid-mist irritate the soft tissues of his nose, his eyes, his lips, his tongue, the back of his throat.

A shadow as big as Barquetown air-jetty slices through the smog beneath him with a flick of its enormous tail, silencing his panicked cries.

He scrambles to his feet inside the cage, shooting desperate glances through the spaces in the grille beneath him, anxious to catch another glimpse of the wraith. For as long as he can see the shadow he knows he is safe, as much as any could be considered safe once the chemical smog of the Scald sets to work.

He can see nothing.

He peers through the pinky-orange gas-soup even though his eyes are running with tears now. The chemical clouds shift and swirl, bulging as if they are rising towards the cage. And then, as those gaping jaws emerge from the smog, he realises that all hope is lost.

His curse has cost him his life at last. He is the jinx. The Jonah.

Whale bait.

The monster powers up out of the roiling discoloured mists and the jaws crank shut over his head, closing with a dull boom and the iron clatter of its teeth against the dangling chain.

And all is darkness.

III – THE BELLY OF THE BEAST

But all is not darkness for long.

In the sepulchral meat gloom Ishmael becomes aware of a dim, ruddy glow. Blinking chem-induced tears from his stinging eyes he peers closer. The ruddiness is like an angry red star, boiling with ulcerous fury.

Resigned to his fate now, the worst that could happen having already happened, he stares in wonder and curious confusion at the pulsing red glow. What can it be?

Trapped in the cage, suspended within the cavernous vault of the sky-leviathan's maw is he really gazing straight down into the belly of the beast?

He hears the muffled boom of a series of distant overlapping detonations and feels the air ripple around him with gusts of stinking, petrochemical belches. It's hardly surprising, considering the ancients-wrought bio-mechanisms of the monster's atmosphere-processing guts.

In the muggy, foetid warmth of the beast's oral chamber, Ishmael feels a shudder of anxiety surge through him. He really must be the unluckiest man alive. Just when he thought things couldn't get any worse…

He shouts and screams, grabbing hold of the bars of the corroded cage and shaking the caelisphere for all he is worth, setting it rocking again. But this is merely the impotent raging of a man who might as well already be dead.

The tears come again, but this time they are born of rage and frustration.

He shakes the cage and rages again.

But what's the point? He's only going to die anyway.

So he prays. He sits down in the bottom of the cage, his cheeks and forearms prickling and burning, and calls out in his hour of need to a deity he doesn't believe in.

And then the skyathan lurches and suddenly Ishmael's world is turned upside down.

II – AND THE LORD SPAKE UNTO THE FISH

The vast bulk of the gas-filled beast twists again and the caelum-cage is suddenly spinning through the air, the chain becoming tangled, Ishmael weightless within as he is thrown about inside.

Jaws open and the cage crashes free, kicking sparks from the metal-sheathed teeth as it exits the beast's mouth.

Ishmael blinks at the sudden sunlight, after the morbid gloom of the skyathan's interior, and then the cage is falling again, the deck of the *Ahab* spread below him.

He takes a deep breath, bracing himself, keeping his hands inside the cage.

Startled sailors scatter. The caelisphere hits the deck and shatters, sheared barbs of corroded metal whickering wildly through the air. Ishmael tumbles free and lies where he lands on the pitted boards, stunned.

Slowly he picks himself up off the deck, savouring the welcome coolness of the breeze on his scalded cheeks.

Sky pirates rush about him, ignoring his presence, focused wholly on the monster bearing down on the ship. The air thick with their accented utterances.

Ishmael swings his head left and right, looking for the captain, for only the captain – his would-be executioner – can save him now. At the captain's word shall they live or die, every last one of them.

And there he is. He stands atop the poop deck, his one good leg and one steam-hissing piston braced, directing the harpooneers as his hunters take aim at the closing beast. A vast shadow falls across the deck; the shadow of death.

The sky-whale is above them now.

His body aching, Ishmael forces himself to run the length of the ship to the foot of the poop deck as the captain gives the command.

"Fire!"

The hiss, thump and whoosh of the steam cannons firing near deafens him as they send their massive barbed projectiles hurtling towards the beast's pallid, remora-puckered underbelly.

Clouds of white steam and dirty smoke wash across the deck in the aftermath of the harpoon cannonade, setting Ishmael's eyes watering all over again.

From above comes the sonorous rumble of the sky-whale, hurting Ishmael's ears.

"Captain!" he shouts, coughing as he inhales a great lungful of smoke and steam. "*Captain!*"

"Ready the guns again," the old sky-dog orders his men, "and helmsman, bring us about."

Even with the monstrous behemoth bearing down upon them, the crew of the *Ahab* still rush to obey their captain's commands, more a-feared of his fury than the furious hunger of the last of the sky-leviathans.

"Captain, we have to get away from here as quickly as possible!"

The captain says nothing, but judging by the vengeful sky pirate's narrowed eyes and clenching jaw, Ishmael knows he's been heard.

"Take aim!" the captain shouts to the harpooneers.

"Listen to me!" Ishmael cries in frustration as he starts to drag himself up the steps to the poop deck, where the captain stands, studiously ignoring him. "Any minute now that–"

The ship lurches to starboard, the deck tipping away beneath him, and Ishmael suddenly finds himself falling sideways, back across the deck, only to collide with the gunwales on the other side. Winded, he lies in the crook between a bolted down barrel and a knotted coil of tarred hemp.

He watches in impotent horror as the enraged sky-whale scrapes along the length of the airship. An oar-like flipper collides with Queequeg – the noble savage harnessed behind the controls of his steam-cannon – and snaps the man's neck.

The dirigible is left spinning in the wake of the monster's assault. Ishmael presses himself back into his hiding place, as the prow swings round and he feels his gorge rise in his mouth. The blunt mass of the behemoth's head comes into view to the left, a watery eye as big as a porthole regarding them with a malevolent intelligence.

Ishmael scans the deck, looking for the captain. He sees him, grasping the controls of Queequeg's steam-cannon, not even bothering to climb into the gunner's seat, the harpooneer's corpse still strapped into the weapon's safety harness.

"From hell's heart I stab at thee!" he screams, pulling back on the firing paddles of the swivel-mounted cannon as he heaves it round to fire on the beast.

Ishmael opens his mouth to speak but his dire warning is lost to the rocket-whoosh of the launching steam-harpoon.

But he hears the captain's whoop of joy as the harpoon streaks across the deck, its mooring rope whipping through the air in a corkscrewing trail behind it.

He hears the cursed utterance of angry surprise too, as the unravelling rope twists tight about the captain's prosthetic limb, yanking him violently off his feet.

He watches, mouth agape – like the sky whale – as the captain is dragged across the deck of the ship, kicking and screaming as he struggles to free himself.

I – THAR SHE BLOWS!

There is nothing he can do, and yet still Ishmael scrambles to his feet, quitting his place of safety in a bid to save the captain who would have nonetheless condemned him to death as bait on the end of a hook.

He has to crawl up the deck on his hands and knees, scrabbling for purchase on the warped boards with bloodied fingertips. Then his feet slip from under him, the tilt too great, and he is sliding back across the width of the ship.

In that moment he catches the look in the captain's eye. Not dismay, or fear, or panic, but one of unremitting fury.

Then the captain is gone, vanished over the side.

In the very next moment Ishmael hears the sound he's been dreading ever since gazing into the depths of the sky-whale's oesophagus.

The muffled explosion sounds like the echo of distant cannon-fire. It is followed by a second, and then a third, then another, until the detonations overlap one another and become a continuous deadened boom of detonation that goes on and on, dragging out the seconds as if the eruptions are so powerful as to be able to warp time itself. He sees the ripple of hydrocarbon fires through the anaemic flesh of the skyathan's lateral line.

Knowing what is coming next, Ishmael turns and tumbles back across the deck, away from the beast, with nowhere to run to, only knowing that he must run. The destination is not important; the simple act of flight is enough. Better than that to go willingly into the dark a second time.

The sky-whale convulses, turning – by intention or its actions induced by pain, Ishmael has no way of knowing – its opening maw lining up on the airship that is now tethered to the beast by a host of rope-tied harpoons, the dirigible twitching and dancing like a maggot on the end of a line.

Ishmael hears the dull boom of detonation as the great beast spasms again, vomiting smoke and flame from within its gut, venting the waste products of the chain reaction that has seized its atmosphere processor stomachs. The refined elements aboard the cloud-dredger *Jonah* were clearly too rich a meal; indigestion was inevitable.

A gout of flame like a volcanic blast roars from the sky-whale's mouth, engulfing the ship.

Sailors scream. Men die.

The dirigible's hull catches light.

The envelope ruptures. The gas within ignites; explodes.

The *Ahab* is transformed into an ever-expanding ball of greasy orange flame that tears the ship apart.

Oily black smoke trailing from rents in its flanks, the last of the sky-leviathans sinks below the heaving clouds of the Scald again, taking the captain's charred corpse with it.

AFTER

He is in a world of heat and hurt, barely conscious. He can hear the tolling of a bell, but is it tolling for him, he wonders.

A cool breeze runs its fingers through his hair and caresses his scalded face. He opens his eyes, blinking away sooty tears. He tries to move.

Agony courses through him. He tries again.

Wincing, Ishmael manages to sit up.

It is then that he sees the shaft of the scrimshawed harpoon protruding from his thigh, Queequeg's spear, the same harpoon that has pinned him to the side of the drifting life raft.

Despite the lancing pain, he starts to laugh. To feel this much pain can mean only one thing; he is still alive.

He encountered and escaped the beast three times. Him, Ishmael, the Jonah. The jinx.

He can't stop laughing now.

The luckiest man alive.

He's still chuckling to himself when the full-rigged merchantman hoves into view over the crimson crests of the smog sea as the sun dips towards the false cloud horizon and dusk begins to creep across the sky.

And he's still chuckling as the crew of the *Melville* help him aboard their vessel sawing through the scorched planks of the life raft in order to do so.

"What's your name, son?" asks a grey-haired woman – a woman he takes to be the captain, judging by her demeanour and the way the crew part at her approach – concern mapped out in the lines of her aging, wind-worn face.

He looks at her through barely open eyes and laughs.

"Call me Ishmael."

"AND I ONLY AM ESCAPED ALONE TO TELL THEE."
(JOB, CH.1 V.16)

THE END

THE ISLAND OF PETER PANDORA

Kim Lakin-Smith

Peter caught the fly between his palms. The insect buzzed and tickled.

"Aren't you the jolly little irritant!" Peter parted his hands slightly and tried to peep in. When the fly flew out, he snatched at it. A trace of gore stained his hand.

"Funny bug." Peter didn't bother to brush off the insect's remains, but picked up the wrench and plunged his hands into the Lost Boy's stomach.

"Those Rogues. They'll do for me one day," said Nibs in his chiming voice.

"Ha! They'd have to catch me first, and Peter Pandora is not easy to tie down." Peter lifted his sharp chin a notch. Locating the flywheel under the leather heart, he adjusted the torque. A squeeze of oil from a can and the gears moved smoothly again.

"I am nothing if not exceptional." Peter slid the bolt plate back across Nibs' stomach. He cleaned his hands on a rag.

"You're the bravest and the best, Peter." Nibs craned in his legs, rocked onto his porthole backside and got up off the grass. Steam oozed from his joints.

Peter nodded sagely. "I am." When the Lost Boys failed to concur, he shot them a savage look. "What say my men?" He bit his bottom lip.

The animatronic band wheezed into life at the command.

"The finest mind in the French empire." Tootles cradled his fat bowl belly; Peter had fashioned it from a condenser casing and a girdle of steel ribs.

"Master of the fair isle of Tsarabanjina. We are loyal to the last." Curly nodded enthusiastically, exciting the frayed wires that poked out his skullcap.

"The last! The last!" echoed the twin tinies who Peter had not bothered to name. They were rather a nuisance with their rudder flippers which got stuck in the sand or left visible tracks up the banks like turtles come ashore to lay their eggs.

"Slightly?" Peter adopted a grown-up's tone.

"I have a headache," said Slightly as farts of steam escaped his back boiler. "And with mother being on the gin and father having run away with the fairies."

Peter crossed his arms. He considered Slightly's head which had been all but bashed off, with only a couple of wires attaching it to the body.

"The Rogues shall pay for their attack." Peter unhooked the wrench from his utility belt and wielded it. "What say my men?"

"The finest mind in the French empire."

"Master of the fair isle…"

"Enough!" cried Peter, and apart from the taps of water pipes and the crackle of wood inside their boilers, the Lost Boys fell silent.

§

Three hours later and Slightly's head sat back on his shoulders. The iridescent blue of day was giving way to the black and oranges of dusk. Peter led his robot band through the tall reeds, kicking up crickets and newborn mosquitoes. The air was full of flavours – cocoa, coffee and sea salt; Peter breathed them in. This was his favourite part of the day, when the stars his father had loved so much began to wink overhead, and the rumble in his belly told him it was suppertime.

"Did any tuck survive the raid?" he called over a shoulder.

"Papaya, banana, sweet potato." Tootles sounded proud of their haul. Peter had hoped for a fish supper, but he let things slide. His men had survived being attacked by the Rogues when collecting provisions earlier that day. Plus, they could always go a-hunting again tomorrow.

"A banquet fit for kings," he managed. His spirits cheered at the sight of the raggedy tree house with its smoke stacks and the fat brass trunk of his father's telescope pointing skyward.

"Run on ahead, you and you," he told the twin tinies. "Get the water boiling under the supper pot. Light the lamps."

The pair set off, rudder feet swishing through the reeds. A minute later, Peter saw the glow of lamplight at the windows. Smoke trickled from one of the tall stacks.

Peter entered the clearing. Tootles, Slightly, Curly and Nibs arrived alongside, oozing steam and sweating oil. Moths danced in the twilight like fairy folk. The detritus of scrub and husk made a noisy carpet underfoot. 'No creeping up on me,' thought Peter smugly.

He stepped onto a wooden palette, grabbed hold of the ropes and heard the winch start up. The ground dropped away and he sailed up to the tree house, that great nest of palm leaves, reeds, flotsam and jetsam, turtle shell, coral chunks and drift wood. Crawling in at the tarpaulin-covered entrance, he slammed a large iron lever forward and sent the palette back down to fetch the others.

Standing up and placing his hands on his hips, Peter took in the chaos of the room. The hairy trunks of seven coconut trees sprouted up through the living quarters. Golden Orb spiders nestled among the eaves, their sun-coloured silk forming a glittering canopy.

"Home sweet home." Peter rocked back onto his heels and separated his toes, planting them on the reed matting with a satisfying sense of grounding.

§

James and Wendy Darling had come to Tsarabanjina – a tropical island located northwest of Madagascar Main Island and forty nautical miles from Nosy-Be – in the year of our Lord 1889. A twelve-man strong crew assisted them to offload the numerous tools of Mr Darling's trade – spy glasses, constellation maps housed in leather tubes, an oversized compass with gold and ivory inlay, easels and other drawing apparatus; and, of course, his pride and joy, a giant brass telescope. Mrs Darling, meanwhile, was content to haul ashore her own box of tricks – metal-working tools, saws, hammers, piping, sheet steel, and every conceivable nut, bolt and screw. And while many ladies would have protested at the steaming wilderness, Wendy embraced it.

Befriending the tribe on the south side of the island, she enlisted those strong, cocoa-skinned men to help her build an observatory among the trees.

Peter had been four years old, his sister Bella, six months. Leaving behind the dreary greys of London for Tsarabanjina's endless blue sky and ocean, both children felt as if they had stumbled upon paradise.

Three years later came the Three Bad Events as Peter called them. First, a tremendous cyclone storm which sunk his parents' dhow offshore. Second – and by far the more devastating – the death of both his parents from Typhoid Fever. What made it worse was that both of these incidents happened within two weeks of one another. And third, the islanders muscling in on his and Bella's seclusion and insisting so kindly and so absolutely that the youngsters go with them. Peter had refused with every violent response he could muster. Bella, though, went with them. At the age of seven, Peter had found himself alone with only the sounds of the waves lapping the shore and the contents of his mother's workshop for company.

"Time to fill your cakehole." Slightly stood at the brink to the observatory. His insides turned over with a faint clanking sound.

Peter peered into the telescope's eyepiece. Venus, the morning star and his father's life's work, shone in the night sky. "Such an elegant turn of phrase, Slightly," he muttered.

"Want me to put on false airs like Rogues?" Slightly elevated a backside flap and let out a guff of steam.

Peter slid the cap across the eyepiece and made his way across the room, weaving in and out the map stands and tables full of paperwork. He slapped Slightly on the arm, producing a hollow rumble.

"I really did use up the odds and sods at the bottom of the drawer when I created you, Slightly."

The Lost Boy seemed pleased with the fact. His boiler bubbled softly as he led the way into the dinner den.

"Peter! So glad you can join us." Tootles tapped the space on the bench next to him. "Have a seat, there's a good chap."

Peter eased in besides Tootles even thought the crueller part of him wanted to say, 'No, I won't. I shall sit opposite between the twin tinies just to show who is boss around here.' By way of compromise, he vowed to ignore Tootles for the evening.

"So what's the plan, Peter? How do we make those Rogues pay?" Nibs banged his fist against his stomach plate, a reminder of the torn internals he had suffered at their hands.

Peter spoke through a mouthful of turtle and sweet potato stew. "We lure them in from their hidey hole and then we garrotte them."

"Sounds marvellous," said Curly.

"Masterful," added Tootles.

"How'd we do it?" The twin tinies asked in unison.

Peter put his elbows on the table and lent in. The Lost Boys mimicked him.

"I am going back below and I'm going to raise the Ticktock."

His animatronic companions ooh'ed then fell silent, the cicada song of the night punctuated by the whir and knocks from their steaming bellies.

It was Slightly who spoke up. "What's the Ticktock?"

"What's the Ticktock?" Peter leapt onto his seat. "What's the Ticktock?" He stepped onto the table, narrowly missing his bowl of fruit mush and the Lost Boys' flagons of oil and platefuls of grease. "Only the bringer of destruction. It is the hand of God, the great leveller." He knocked a fist off his breastbone. "It was my mother, Wendy Darling, who told me of its power. 'Be careful, son, the Ticktock is not a toy. It likes to buck and spit.'"

"But you'll tame it, won't you, Peter?" Tootles showed his metal tooth pegs.

"Naturally. First though, I've got to commander the thing from the deep." Peter danced up and down the table, upsetting a jug of rainwater and splashing through it as if he was jumping in puddles at the park. "I do so love to go a-hunting!" he cried.

"Can we come too?" piped up the twin tinies.

"Only I." Peter puffed out his chest. "This quest requires cunning and lashings of cleverness. Besides…" He dropped to his haunches and ladled a mouthful of stew into his mouth. "I'm the only one who knows how to swim with the Mermaid," he said thickly.

§

Later, when the Lost Boys had completed their chores and joined in Peter's rousing rendition of *Jolly Rain Tar;* after which he had instructed them to stoke their boilers, wind innards and sup enough water to tide them over until the morning – then companions and master had gone their separate ways. The Lost Boys took up patrol duty on the tree house's vined balcony while Peter climbed onto his parents' reed-stuffed mattress, beneath a canopy of mosquito netting. Besides the bed was the gramacorda which his father had used to archive his discoveries. A few times, his mother had thought it amusing to speak into the horn and record the bedtime stories she told Peter onto one of the foil scrolls.

While the heat had warped the greater part of his father's recordings, three of his mother's tales still played. That night, Peter selected her rendition of *The Tin Soldier*. Lying back on the bed, he had let his mother's spirited narration lull him to sleep.

He was woken once during the night by the sound of footfall on the ground below. Peter imagined he heard a chilling, all too familiar grunting, but sleep overtook him again.

§

The sun was high in the sky when Peter awoke. While the Lost Boys breakfasted on their oil and grease, their creator tucked into spiced fish baked in banana leaves. Soon the conversation turned to the night watch. The Lost Boys denied any sign of intruders. Peter remained haunted by the conviction they were wrong.

"Rogues have curdled my dreams long enough." Peter fastened his utility belt at his waist and slammed his hat down on his head. "Time to fetch up the Ticktock." He knocked a hand off his brow in salute. "See you later, alligators."

Half an hour later, and having battled his way through the mosquito infested reeds, Peter arrived on the north shore. The sand was toasty between his toes. Waves foamed at the shoreline. The clear blue ocean stretched away to tiny islands known as the Four Friers. Two large rocks 'kissed' a little way out to his left. His mother's workshop burrowed into the cliff to his right.

At the entrance, Peter cocked his head and leant in, drinking from the fresh water, which streamed down the rock. He stepped inside the workshop, blinded by the sudden transition from brilliant daylight to shadow. It was dry inside – precisely the reason his mother had selected the cave – and battened with wooden shelving. Peter lit oil-filled dips in the rock. The makeshift sconces flickered whenever he walked by, causing his shadow to dance over the walls seemingly of its own accord.

Numerous engineering supplies had gone down with his parents' ship, but the workshop was still well stocked. Several shelves were dedicated to trays of nuts, bolts, screws and nails. Giant bobbins were wound with rubber pipe while tinier versions held various gauges of copper wire. Two workbenches stood on stilts on the uneven surface; one was stained with oil, the other with blood. Tools hung off nails between the shelves – hammers, bow saws, hand drills, chisels, scalpels, vices and tourniquets. One basket held clean bandaging, the other soiled.

Standing in his workshop surrounded by the tools of his labour, Peter was glad he had come alone. As much as he enjoyed his elated status among the Lost Boys, there was a tendency for their restricted audio to grate. More than anything he longed for the stimuli of sentient conversation. But his efforts to create companions had birthed all manner of dark breed among the Rogues, he reminded himself, gaze lingering on the bloodstained bench. One of them worse than all the rest; Hookie, the ape-man. Had Wendy Darling known that, in introducing new animal species to the island, she would provide her son with the raw materials to investigate and reinterpret life, she might just have tipped her caged specimens overboard on route and drowned the lot. Instead she was the enabler for Peter's experiments, having left behind science books, engineering diagrams, pencilled notes and a veritable operating theatre.

"Much good it does me!" Peter protested out loud.

Not that he had any intention of moping around and feeling sorry for himself, Oh no, Hookie and crew had played their final trick on him. It was time to deal with the Rogues like any other group of wayward children.

A long tarpaulin-covered object occupied the far end of the cave. Peter pulled off the cover. The Mermaid's polished wood shone in the greasy lamplight.

§

Pitched between the perfection of motherhood and the gutsiness of a Rogue, Wendy Darling had always demonstrated a soft spot for the underdog. In engineering terms, her pet favourite was an untutored Catalonian inventor called Narois Monturiol I Estarrol. To the young Peter, his mother's daytime stories were as engaging as her bedtime stories were soporific.

"Imagine it, Peter," she would say, a glint of passion in her eye. "While his competitors were busy developing submarines for military purposes, Monturiol was a communist, a revolutionary, a utopian. He saw his machine as a way of improving the lives of poor coral divers. Here, Peter." She would lay the open book before him and stab a finger grubby with oil at the illustrations. "Such a beautiful design. A wooden submarine supported by olive wood batons and lined with copper. Why copper?" She would shoot the question at him like a bullet.

"For structural support?"

"No, Peter, no. To stop shipworms from eating the hull."

Even as an intensely intelligent child, Peter had been haunted by images of giant worms chomping down on the wooden submarine. And while he was nonchalant about Monturiol's morality, he did appreciate the inventor's design ethic and had proceeded to apply it to a solo submersible he nicknamed the Mermaid.

A pair of polished wooden sleds allowed him to push the Mermaid out of the cave and through the sand to the water's edge. He paused for breath and mopped his forehead with a forearm. Seeing it in the sunlight, he was reminded just how perfect a machine the Mermaid really was. The 'head' was a wood-staved cabin with a broad strip of glass tied around its middle like a ribbon. This cabin housed the controls and a driver's seat, which revolved to allow for a 360 degree view through the glass. The boiler was built into the torpedo-shaped 'body' and heated via a chemical furnace; the compounds potassium chlorate, zinc and magnesium dioxide were from his mother's dry store, and while their combination produced enough power to heat the boiler, it had the added bonus of generating oxygen to supplement the supply in the cabin. The true magic, though, was in the Mermaid's tail – five feet long, covered in wooden scales, and tapering to a brass-plated rudder.

Pushing the Mermaid offshore, Peter held his breath and ducked under the water. He swam beneath the submersible and emerged in a small moon pool to the rear of the cabin. Securing himself in the driver seat, he twisted a stopcock to flood the boiler and began to work his way through the operative checklist.

§

It was the 28th of February 1893 when the storm hit. Peter's family had been living on the island for eight months, and while numerable supplies had been brought ashore, some larger items were stored in the traditional 'dhow' boat moored offshore. As Peter had learnt since, December to March saw violent cyclones bombard the island and its neighbours, the usual tropical serenity giving way to torrential rain and clockwise circling winds. The dhow was well made, used to carrying heavy loads up and down the East African coast. But even with its lateen sail lowered, the dhow could never have weathered that assault. Sometime between dusk and dawn, the ship tore loose of its anchor, drifted and sank near the second Freir. His parents had called it the devil's work. Peter had come to view the shipwreck as a treasure trove.

The water was fantastically clear as the Mermaid dipped below the surface. Peter moved the weight along the line by his right shoulder, adjusting the angle of the Mermaid's descent. The smooth action of the tail drove the submersible forward at a steady rate of four knots. All around him, shoals of fish danced, their brilliant colours transforming the ocean into a fairyland. Corals burgeoned below like giant fleshy roses. A solitary turtle drifted by, buoyed on an invisible current. Once the creature stirred the water with its front flippers then drifted once more – the nonchalant old man of the sea.

Lying besides a great crease of volcanic rock, the dhow's sharply curved keel reminded Peter of one half of an eel's open jaw and he felt the jolt of discomfort he always did at the sight. The feeling gave way to excitement; Peter wanted to fly out among the wreck and peel strips off it for no other reason than it might please him. The rational side of him argued that the wreck was best preserved for future foraging.

One thing he did intend to secure that day was the Ticktock. His mother's ledger listed it under 'Weaponry/24 pounds of copper.' He knew the Ticktock had been stored in a large chest with a skull and crossbones etched on top – his mother's idea of a joke, given the Ticktock's practical application. That box now lay at the bottom of the ocean, wedged between the crease of rock and the ribs of the dhow. Up until that moment, he'd had no need for such an item, but Hookie and the rest of the Rogues had become a damnable pest. They needed swotting like sand flies.

The boiler to the rear of the cabin mumbled soothingly. It was hot inside the Mermaid but Peter didn't mind. Yes, he risked drowning or being baked alive in his handmade submersible, but he'd always entertained the idea that to die would be an awfully big adventure! He pulled on a leather strap above his head to regulate the heat off the boiler and stabilise the craft. A small adjustment to the sliding counterweight and the submersible hovered alongside the large chest.

'Peter Pandora. You possess the cunning of a crow and you are as wise as the stars,' his father used to say.

Peter sucked his bottom lip. "Indeed I am, father," he whispered. Scooting his seat forward on a greased wooden rail, he took hold of a pair of iron handgrips. His fingers pressed down on ten sprung-levered valves. 'Arms' unlocked on the front of the cabin; each metal limb was tipped with a grabber. Peter manipulated the handgrip valves to open and close the grabbers and secured a hold on the handle of the chest nearest the curl of rock; the other handle was trapped beneath the boat's mast. And while the arms siphoned off power from the boiler, magnifying his strength three fold, he still got slick with sweat as he tried and failed to pull the chest free.

"Move, you bloody thing!" he cried, irritated at the situation but pleased with his use of the swear word. The chest stayed wedged beneath the mast and he had to break off trying to move it and catch his breath. Water pressed all around, muffling the sounds of the boiler and the churn of the engine.

Peter stretched out his fingers and was about to work the handgrips again when something large crashed into the cabin's exterior wall. He spun around in his chair, staring out the window strip. Legs disappeared from his eye line, the soles of the feet like black leather. Peter whipped his head the other way and caught a glimpse of horns, thighs like fat hams, and a snout. When the Mermaid began to rock, water lapping at the moon pool and threatening to flood the cabin, Peter knew he had attracted company – and not that of a whale shark or a mantra ray. The hands rocking his craft were strong and animaltronic, with claws that scraped the hull.

"Rogues." Peter bared his teeth gleefully. "You're no match for Peter Pandora!" he cried, kicking at the sides of the cabin to add his beat to theirs. He concentrated on the handgrips and tried again for the trapped handle. Bodies hurled themselves against the submersible. Peter was grateful to have a grip on one trunk handle since it helped anchor the Mermaid.

"Wild things!" he called out to the creatures pestering him. "To catch a fellow unaware. But that's the nature of Rogues, isn't it?"

Faces appeared at the glass. Part mechanical, part animal, the Rogues stared in with colourful glass eyes, which reminded Peter of Christmas baubles. One Rogue had goat horns grafted onto his iron-plate skull. He butted the glass and blew bubbles out his ear canals.

"All bluster and no backbone" Peter stuck out his tongue. By way of reply, one of the Rogue crew tried to come up through the moon pool; Peter stamped on the creature's skullcap. It sank down and swam away, air escaping from steam-release vents at its knee joints.

He'd scared one off. The rest appeared perfectly happy to continue rocking the submersible. Meanwhile, a dark shape was materialising through the dust cloud kicked up by the Rogues. The figure swam with broad, confident strokes, the scythes that served for hands sweeping out in glittering arcs.

Peter slammed one hand forward, driving the corresponding grabber hard at the mast, splintering the rotten wood. Hookie drew closer at speed, the sweep of those long, muscular arms matched by the frog-like pump of his huge legs. Underwater, Hookie's fur was dark and sleek. His silver teeth shone.

At last, Peter got a lock on the other handle and lent back in his chair, pulling the handgrips towards him. Secured in the Mermaid's arms, the chest lifted off the ocean floor. Peter pressed a foot pedal to lock the arms in place then released the handgrips. Adjusting the weight counterpoint to allow for the burden, he raked a hand across the bank of switches to release the sand ballast in the storage cylinders and unleash a fresh head of steam to drive the engine. He engaged the throttle and powered up, Rogues tumbling aside in the submersible's slipstream. All but one. Hookie maintained his hold on the craft. Buffered by the pull of the water, he brought his great muzzle to the glass and stared in before letting go, seemingly of his own accord. The last thing Peter saw as the Mermaid ascended was Hookie dropping away into the darkness.

§

"You must stay with us now. My wife will care for you well. We are a good family and, together with the rest of the village, we will feed and clothe you." The islanders' representative had appeared kindly and concerned. He'd smiled and clapped a hand on Peter's shoulder.

Seven years old, Peter had surveyed the horseshoe of islanders. Bella's hand had gripped his – not because she was scared of the Malagasy with their open faces and choppy way of talking but because, even at three and a half years old, she'd known he wouldn't stay.

Over the years, Peter hiked to the south side of the island on occasion. Hidden at the forest's edge, he spied on the villagers and his sister. The malady Bella had been born with was as much a gift as a trial and one that suggested she was only capable of registering one emotion at a time.

On occasion, she would kick and wail in blinding rage. But there were also calmer moments when she would concoct detailed puzzles from the rows of shells she painstakingly arranged. Sometimes her laughter was high and tinkling. Sometimes she sat and stared out at the sea for hours, as if her mind had flown far away. Then Peter would see one of Bella's Malagasy brothers come and take her hand and sit with her awhile. Perhaps her new family thought her enchanted. Peter was pleased that Bella was happy. He was also sick at heart and resentful.

For the most part, Peter had been left to his own devices on the north side of the island. He didn't interfere with the fishing trips or beach BBQs or Famadihanna ceremonies where the Malagasy would exhume the remains of their ancestors, wrap them in silk and entomb the bones once more. In return, the Malagasy left him to play puppet-master with his band of loyal Lost Boys and itinerant Rogues – the later steering clear of the islanders ever since one inquisitive specimen had been speared in the chest like a giant turtle.

There was one exception to the rule though. Two days after his underwater expedition, Peter was holed up in his workshop with the Ticktock when he caught a glimpse of movement at the mouth of the cave.

"Tigermaw. I can see you." He waited, staring out from the gloom. All he heard was the noise of the ocean.

Satisfied that his mind was playing tricks, Peter gave his attention back to the Ticktock. Dipping a small scrubbing brush into a coconut shell containing a solution of salt and vinegar, he set to work removing the patina from the brass.

A stone struck him on his left temple.

"Damnation!" His eyes flashed aside. This time he saw feathers of afro hair poking up from a crop of rocks at the cave's entrance.

"Go away before the Rogues get you, girl!" he called, slamming down the scrubbing brush.

As quick as Peter liked to think he was, his reactions didn't compare to Tigermaw's. She fired off two more stones from her slingshot. One struck Peter's thigh. The other nicked his ear.

"Enough, Tigermaw! Don't start what you can't finish." Using a ruler as a makeshift catapult, he sent two slugs of nails towards the rocks. Apparently the scattergun approach worked. He heard a gasp.

"Peter Pandora, you are a sorcerer. You deserve a hundred stones upon your head," came the cry from the rocks.

"And you are slow brained, and a savage to boot!"

"What are you cooking up today, evil boy?" demanded Tigermaw, standing up suddenly and striding inside the cave. She approached his workbench, hands on hips, lemur-large eyes blinking as they adjusted to the dark. *How fantastically fearsome she looked,* thought Peter. Her face painted with white swirls. Her afro hair spread high and wide like wings. The shift she wore was a faded rose pattern. Her feet were bare.

Tigermaw pointed at the copper barrel of the Ticktock. "Will that be a tail or a nose?"

"Neither. It is a method of upping the stakes against the Rogues."

"Ah, so it is a weapon." Tigermaw glared, daring Peter to deny it.

"It is *the* weapon, savage girl. I'm going to fill those Rogues with so much lead they won't have brains intact to bother my Lost Boys and me ever again."

"By Rogues you mean the demons you yourself conjured? They are mischief-makers, but nothing more serious than children in need of their father's affection. But instead you cast them out as failed experiments."

Tigermaw leant in close. Peter felt her breath on his lips. It made them tingle.

"Would you have us behave the same with your sister, Bella?" She stabbed a finger up at the roof of the cave. "Bella is angry with her maker for taking away her parents, making you a stranger, and giving her an unusual nature. Should she be destroyed too?"

Peter folded his arms across his chest. "What do you know about my inventions? You have no more right to apportion feelings to a Rogue than to a Jackfruit. As for Bella, she is a free spirit who must be allowed to fly. Your people should not try to contain her, else she might just rise up and bite you on the nose."

"Ah, Bella is a good soul," said Tigermaw with a dismissive flick of a hand. "The only bad around here is a little boy who plays with flesh and machinery over choosing a normal life living alongside his sister." The girl's big black eyes softened. "My family will still take you in, Peter. You can have a home."

"And see my life drain away until I am old and wrinkled, just another bag of bones for your people to cherish. No thanks. I'd rather stay here with my Lost Boys."

Tigermaw sighed; to Peter, it was a sign of submission and he put his nose in the air.

"And what about the Rogues?" It was Tigermaw's turn to cross her arms. Under the lamplight, her white war paint was luminescent.

Peter picked up the scrubbing brush and attacked the Ticktock's patina again. "I'll kiss each and every one goodnight with this then fashion myself a grandfather clock from their remains."

Tigermaw stared at him, and for a moment Peter saw himself through her eyes as the true monster. He started scrubbing again. When he next looked up, the girl had gone.

§

Lying in bed listening to his mother's bedtime stories on the gramacorda, Peter would occasionally feel the pinch of loneliness. At such times he would question the ethics of his companion machines. Life was his to give or take at the flick of a switch or the turn of a key. But where he had really strayed from the moral path was in his creation of the Rogues – in particular, Hookie. Most Rogues owed their origin to the livestock his parents had introduced to the island – pigs, goats, sheep. Hookie, though, was a rangy old orang-utan his mother had rescued from a street performer in Borneo. Shot through with arthritis and pining for Wendy, Peter had decided to put the creature out of its misery. But had the family pet deserved vivisection and animaltronic rebirth? Had any of those poor dumb animals wanted the gifts he had bestowed – intelligence, conscious thought, and all the suffering that came with an awareness of one's own mortality.

That these moments of lucidity were rare testified to Peter's absolute self-belief. Secure in his divine right to mix, mess and mesh, he'd created monsters. Now it was his choice to destroy them.

Evening settled around the circumference of the camp. Tootles had done an excellent job of collecting dry wood. The fire pit roared, spitting sparks like orange shooting stars. Slightly had unfastened a little at the neck again. He walked to and fro, muttering, "Midnight feast, he says. Go cook it up, he says. What from, say I? Fairy dust?"

In spite of his limited larder, Slightly had magicked up a decent spread of deep fried hissing cockroach with its greasy chicken taste, vegetable and coconut curry, a platter of bright orange jackfruit pieces – resembling dragon scales laid out on a knight's shield – spiced rice, and crab claws.

In lieu of a table, Peter had instructed the Lost Boys to bring up a bench from the workshop. No one had bothered to clean it so they ate amongst sawdust and iron fillings.

The moon was fantastic – pocked and shimmering like a cherished half a crown. Everyone tucked into the feast, Peter crunching up cockroaches and greasing his chin with crab juices; the Lost Boys taking great mouthfuls, swilling the useless matter around their jaws and disgorging the lot into personal spittoons. Peter didn't mind. He had his feast. Now all he needed were a few extra guests.

Ten more minutes passed. The Lost Boys were in danger of mauling all the food.

"Leave some to attract the blighters," he shouted. His mechanical companions froze mid-grab. They brought their arms back down slowly and fell silent.

"They should be here by now." Peter bit his bottom lip, scowled and forced himself to drop the childish expression. "Fetch the gramacorda, Curly, and don't get your hair stuck in it this time when you wind it. Twin things, bring the music scrolls." He crossed his arms and stared out at the velvet dark. "Come out, come out, wherever you are."

Before long, Curly and the twin tinies descended from the tree house on the elevator platform. Curly set the gramacorda down on one end of the workbench. Each twin carried a number of cylinders.

"What song shall we have?" demanded Peter. "*Whist the Bogey Man? Jolly Little Polly On A Tin Gee Gee?*"

"*Daisy Day!*" cried Tootles, patting his tin-pot belly contently.

Peter ignored him. "*Maple Leaf Rag*, it is."

Curly saluted at the order. Locating the right cylinder, he slid out the foil sheet, fed it in then cranked the stylus into place. As he worked the handle, his wire hair bobbing, he became just another extension of the machine.

The ragtime tune plinked and plonked, cutting through the peace of the forest like swords through reeds. Peter tapped his feet to the music while watching the peculiar lurching dance of the twin tinies in the centre of the clearing. They made for pleasant little morsels of bait, he decided, his eyes sharp and his mouth tight. Curly sent the crank round and round, keeping up the tempo. Tibs forgot his sentry duty and belched steam from his mouth as he tried to recreate the musical notes. Only Tootles remained seated, no doubt eyeing up the last dregs in the oil can.

Peter strained to listen past the music and the mechanical orchestra. Was that the drag of scythes across tree trunks? There was no wind but something whistled out among the reeds.

"Hush now, Curly." He glared at the Lost Boy who let go of the crank and steeped away from the gramacorda as if it was nothing to do with him whatsoever. The rest of the gang fell still and the silence pressed in.

Yes, there it was – the distinctive yo-ho-ho of Rogues' pistons and the swish of their footfall. They came through the reeds, fifteen not-quite-anythings – his animalisations. Bred on steel skeletons with nerves of copper wire and clinking steam-driven insides, the Rogues were the monsters to his Frankenstein.

Stepping out from the reeds, the creatures spaced themselves out around the edges of the clearing. Each carried a makeshift weapon of a long wooden spike or a rock hammer. They showed their silver teeth and breathed heavily.

Lastly came Hookie, two pig Rogues moving aside to make way for him. The Lost Boys seemed to understand the point of the feast – that big shiny homing beacon – and stood up straight, chests plumped. Peter had not built it in them to know fear – which was not to suggest either the Lost Boys or the Rogues had turned out as pliable as he might have imagined. This was especially true in Hookie's case.

"Peter Pandora." The ape-man spoke slowly, feeling the weight of each syllable. His tremendous, muscular shoulders were matted in orange hair. His metal breastplate reflected in the moonlight. "What a wonderful feast. And music too. Are you holding a party for us?"

"A party for Rogues? What a notion! No, Hookie, I am throwing you a wake," hissed Peter.

Hookie's long arms swung by his sides. The huge scythes serving as hands glinted.

"In which case, I must apologise, for I have made the intolerable faux pas of attending my own wake while still alive. Which, I have to say, seems an idea worth prompting. After all, there ain't a man alive who wouldn't risk a breech of etiquette under those circumstances."

"Except you aren't a man, are you Hookie. So how could you know?"

"Ah, that old chestnut. So you can give an old ape a voice to speak but refuse him humanity on the grounds his nose is a little too bulbous." Hookie gestured to his hairless grey face. "Or his hands a little too extraordinary." He held up his scythes.

"You gave me a headache," said Slightly, lunging forward. He stopped short of the ape-man, his motoring whirring inside his chest.

"I did? At least your master was good enough to put you back together again. I wonder if he would do me the same kindness." Hookie's seven-foot frame towered over Slightly's four. Peter had always liked to experiment with proportions.

"Poor Lost Boy. A windup doll without a soul."

"Don't go claiming a soul now, Hookie. You are an animal with a metal spine at best."

Peter was pleased not to flinch when Hookie knocked Slightly aside and ran at him, one scythe stopping an inch short of his throat.

"If that is all I am, it is of your making. I have begged to continue my education under your tutorage. But no, the second I show a mite of interest in your precious books, you banish me and my kind from the only home we've ever known." The sickle hand shook slightly. "Well, if you don't mind awfully, the Rogues and I are inclined to move back in and boot you and your Puffing Billies out."

"You can try, Hookie." Peter stepped back and grabbed hold of the ropes, activating the platform winch. He rose rapidly towards the tree house, leaving the ape-man behind. Looking out, he saw Hookie beat his scythes against his breastplate and let out a deep bellow. Peter responded in kind, beating his chest with his fists. It was invitation enough for the Rogues to attack. Two pigs took on Nibs and Slightly, their spears clattering off the Lost Boys' chest plates. Not that Rogues were discouraged that easily. They drove the spears at Slightly's skull and Nibs' tessellated arm panels. Slightly lost his head. Nibs shed scales, exposing his inner workings.

The twin tinies fared better against the reanimated goats. Forming tight little balls, the twins propelled themselves at the goats' legs. Horns battered off them, ineffectual against the rudder feet and steel bellies. While Tootles belly-flopped the sheep, Curly added his muscle to the assault, spiking the Rogues with his wiry hair and pulling their tails.

"Ah, my fine men. Show no mercy to the Rogues!" Peter smiled. It felt phenomenally good to witness the carnage below. He was a god ruling over a universe of his own making.

"Do we honour you with our split guts and flesh wounds?" Hookie called up from the base of the largest coconut tree supporting the tree house. Unlike the rest of Peter's creations with their colourful glass orbs, Hookie retained the deep brown eyes of the orangutan. Peter felt a pang of longing for the companionship of the wise old ape he had murdered.

"You are to leave the island and swim far far away," he told Hookie. "No more night raids, no more crying at the moon, no more effort to be what you are not."

"And what is that, Peter Pandora?" Hookie drove the scythes into the trunk of the tree and began to inch his way up. "I am not to be intelligence, and yet you built me so. I am not to behave like an animal and yet you insist I refrain from bettering myself." The scythes scraped up and in at the trunk. Hookie's grey muzzle moved closer.

"You are missing the point of servitude," spat Peter. "You want to question and learn and exceed your master." He danced off to the back of the platform and ripped down the tarpaulin. The sight of the Ticktock set him aglow. With its copper barrel restored and polished up, the steam-canon looked like a piece of the sun. One end was enclosed in a chemical furnace chamber, the other loaded with gunshot.

Peter stood behind the canon, hand going to the firing valve just as the first of Hookie's great claws appeared over the platform's edge. The ape-man's shoulders rippled with muscle mass as he hauled himself up and got to his feet.

Hookie's deep brown eyes settled on the Ticktock, which clicked over in anticipation of being discharged.

"I ask for books and you give me bullets?"

Peter jutted his chin. "You should have towed the line, Hookie."

"And you should have left me an ignorant ape!" Hookie lunged forward, scythes whirring. Peter tripped the firing valve; water gushed into the trigger chamber, evaporated in an instant and discharged the canon. A starburst of gunshot escaped the barrel. As the ape-man fell, the tip of one of his scythes nicked Peter's cheek. He lay at his creator's feet, blood escaping his flesh parts. His metal guts wheezed and spluttered.

Peter rolled the ape-man over to the platform's edge. He rested a foot on the creature's bloodstained breastplate.

"Goodbye Hookie."

He pushed the body overboard.

Seeing their captain defeated, the Rogues took flight into the forest. Peter didn't mind. He could always pick them off another time. Below, his Lost Boys had suffered rather badly. Slightly's head lay a foot or so from the rest of him, mouth flapping like a fish out of water. Tootles wobbled about on one spot, belly skewered by a spear. Nibs had split open again, wires and cabling erupting from his chest plate. Curly appeared to have been scalped. Only the twin tinies looked well preserved as they circled the clearing, fists raised, rudder feet flapping.

Peter put his hands on his hips. He nodded in satisfaction. Victory was his. Letting his head fall back, he opened his throat and crowed.

§

It took Peter three days to repair his Lost Boys. Rather than drag their hefty machinery down to his workshop, he chose to bring his tools to the clearing where he worked beneath the glare of the sun and well into the night. He constructed a canopy from palm leaves, which he strung together. In the evenings when the temperature was still intense, he stacked the fire pit high, more for company than any other purpose. Watching the flames, he would fancy he caught the gleam of eyes out among the reeds. Sometimes he thought they belonged to animals gone Rogue. Other times, he believed they were bright black – Tigermaw's. Once he thought he saw a glimpse of yellow hair and he called out Bella's name urgently, like a lost sheep calling for its mother. When no answer came, he cursed his stupidity and returned to tinkering with his toys.

At last, his band of steam and clockwork men was put back together again. Slightly uttered those now immortal words, "I have a headache", before stalking off to the platform and setting the winch in motion. Soon he was installed in the safety of his kitchen, putting Curly to good use as his commis. Tootles broke out into an idiotic monologue on the mating habits of lemurs and Peter was sorely tempted to smash him up again. Nibs and the twin tinies seemed unaware of any time lapse and spun round on the spot, fists wielded as if still engaged in brawling. Peter sent the three off into the forest to hunt, their clanging and hissing gradually receding until the night fell quiet again. Cicadas pulsed in the grasses. He could hear the ebb and flow of the ocean. It was all very beautiful, and all very dull. Not for the first time since the great ape had fallen, Peter found his gaze returning to Hookie. Flies had bothered the remains all day. The creature's muzzle was mud grey, the jaw open, the protruding tongue still and mollusc-like.

Peter approached the body and gave it a firm prod with his toe. He crossed his arms and stared up at the blanket of stars overhead. For an instant, he felt the magnitude of his insignificance next to that heavenly expanse. Pointlessness threatened to crush him alive. He hated the thought and forced it aside. He needed more than the Lost Boys. He needed someone to truly show him the meaning of love and of hate.

His gaze returned to Hookie. Dare he attempt to reanimate the ape-man's decomposing corpse? It struck him as a dark art but no more so than the acts of a twelve-year-old boy who creates living creatures out of flesh and metal. And didn't all heroes need a foe to fight?

By the light of the moon over a far away island, Peter Pandora went off to fetch his tools.

THE GHOST OF CHRISTMAS SIDEWAYS

Simon Bucher-Jones

"I AM HERE TONIGHT TO WARN YOU, THAT YOU HAVE YET A CHANCE AND HOPE OF ESCAPING MY FATE... YOU WILL BE HAUNTED...BY FOUR GHOSTS".
CHARLES DICKENS "A CHRISTMAS CAROL" : VARIANT TEXT FROM THE ROCHESTER HOLOGRAPH COPY C. 1844

STAVE III-B : THE PENULTIMATE SPIRIT

This figure then, solemnly hooded and cloaked in sable darkness, must be the third of the Phantoms that Marley's spectre had foretold.

As it neared him, repentant as he was – Scrooge – screwed his eyes closed and wished for a second that this figure could come to him in his tall bed, with its once fine curtains (fabric aged well enough, to be a sound investment) – rather than in this desolate street.

Slowly it came, without footfall, seeming to glide over the ground. Scrooge shivered, for its deliberation reminded him of Scrooge and Marley's great ledgers, and the infinite care with which he had made poor Cratchit record the black and white profit and losses of this world. The Ghost of Christmas Past had cut deep into the callused hide he had built around his pain. The Ghost of Christmas Present had shown him the present pains of others, pain he had always refused to examine for fear of the echoes of his own despair. Before him still remained two further visitations.

One, all logic told him, must be the Ghost of Christmas Yet To Come and he had little doubt as to its nature, for there is only one future that awaits all men, the cold failures of old age. But while it was true that he feared that Ghost most of all, even in anticipation its terror remained comprehensible. No man, however close and self-sufficient, however solitary and confined by his own desires could avoid in his darkest hours the contemplation of his own lonely futurity, and Scrooge had often greeted it with a cry of Humbug, in the secret recesses of his heart. The nature of the Third Spirit though (allowing that Christmas Yet To Come, would be the Fourth), the kind and mode of Christmas which it would present, remained beyond Scrooge's ken, and what he could not anticipate (for what was his work upon the 'Change, but the drawing of anticipations from the events and fears of the day and the profit to be made thereby) gnawed at him. He feared, then, the Third Spirit less, but he resented its approach more, as a man might resent the unlooked for discomfort of a boneshaking ride in a cart to a surgeon, even as the bonesaw awaited inevitably at its close.

With the robed figure, came a fierce wind. The wind that in his bedchamber had tore and disarrayed the damask. Whereas though, the wind that heralded the appearance of the Ghost of Christmas Past had born with it scents from his past, nostalgic appeals to his senses – rich with gum Arabic of the schoolhouse and the sawdust of Fezziwig's warehouse – and the gusts that stirred the robes of the Ghost of Christmas Present, had smelt of chestnuts, wine, and cinnamon, (and – for aught Scrooge knew – as that Fourth zephyr yet to come would be of some further subtle scent), this wind possessed no single nature.

The others, while they had each been separately compounded, had yet possessed an overarching form, so much so that having once smelled them, no man would again associate any other breath with their natal Spirit. The

Third Wind though, veered and darted – at first one thing, then another. Cool and warm, fiery and shot through with the bracing ice blast of winter: it was a wind that did not seem to know its own mind.

Feeling it upon his face, Scrooge wondered if a Spirit could be Mad. Must he expect, the Ghost of Christmas Lunatick?

"I am the Ghost of Christmas Sideways," the voice came, and Scrooge saw from within the robe, shining now from its sleeves and empty cowl, the light of a pillar of red fire. The Ghost was a flame that yet possessed a voice. As Scrooge watched the light it cast turned the sombre street into a set of scarlet stained tableaux. "I come to show the Christmastide that neverwas, nor yet shall be: but rather died within the fertile womb of time when others of her children flourished."

The flames now flickered low and darkened, turning from red to the sudden stabbing blue of St. Elmo's fire. The robes consumed themselves in this fire, and in the darkening light the Phantom seemed to bear the form of a slim woman, bearing a box wrapped and ribboned: both box and woman bathed in faint blue nimbus.

Scrooge sniffed. "What sort of Spirit eats itself up in fire, like a great brandy pudding?"

"I am the Ghost of Christmas Sideways, Man. What of My Name escapes your grasp?"

"Why what it means, escapes me." Scrooge responded. "If you were the Spirit of Christmas Up – bearing perhaps some parables of mountain folk, your geographic pretensions might make some sense, but if Christmas Present passing year on year to Christmas Past, leaves open the way to Christmas Yet To Come, what place is there for you?"

"What was, was. What is, is."

"Aye and what will be, will…" Scrooge faltered. That he could neither amend the past – it having gone, nor the present (it being not yet, this year within his grasp) he willingly conceded, but he had no wish to postulate an unchanging future, for if once he did so what purpose could there be to all these visitations save to make still more bitter an end preordained and changeless.

"And yet, what was, being other, so altered is what is."

A sound of a faint cat's mew came from the wrapped parcel in the Ghost's blue-white hands.

Scrooge considered, "If I understand you Spirit, you bear me visions of some other Christmas where one change or alternation having once been made in that which once had been, the present must by virtue of that change itself be other than it might have been?"

"I do"

"And is it then your choice as to which change it is, that acts as would a seed to all the world?"

"It may be yours. If you so wish. But beware oh Man, for it you leave to me the lesson of this night it will be that most beneficial to you, but if you grub and toil yourself to prick and seed the change whose alteration you would see, then that lesson – for good or ill – remains what it is, and this chance you never in the turning worlds will have again."

"Before I choose oh Spirit. Answer me one thing, if it be permitted me."

The fire-wreathed oval face of the blue-lady nodded.

"Those in your world of might-have-beens run forward, are they but phantasms such as yourself, acting their roles but feeling not the stab of pain or shout of joy, or do they somewhere live, even now and all your act is but to reveal the fact?"

The Ghost of Christmas Sideways shook her box, and again from within it came a cry of a cat. "Just as real as this cat, just so real are they. They live as they are perceived."

"That, Spirit is hardly an answer!"

"It is the only answer I can give."

"Very well, then. In my life – since I came to man's estate, I have had but one friend. A friend whom even in his own torment: even when bound with chains of adamant, nevertheless came to me to seek to save me. If, even if it be only for an instant or a Christmas he could live again, then how can I not see to grant him that respite. Show me the world sideways from this, where Marley did not die!"

"Very well. Rise then and come with me." Scrooge took her arm and found that though the blue-fire that surrounded her, shown through the flesh of his fingers making a purple light, it was as cool as a thin shell of water. She had folded the box away, flattening it to nothing without a mew of discomfort or of pain.

Sideways through the walls of the old room they flew.

Imagine a rainbow in the winter sky of Christmas, were every colour is a new picture of the world, differing in its details as red from orange or blue from green. Imagine a great hall, filled with globes of the world, each one inscribed with minute differences from its neighbours until from one side to the other span great gulfs of changing consequences.

Scrooge saw the turning countries of the Earth, each on its own globe, each hung upon a tree colossal and dark against the backdrop of the stars. Then down towards a singular world they fell. Through clouds, and evening flurries of light snow, through beams of bright light flashing heavenwards.

Christmas Eve: Anno Domini 1843. Above the snow plumed rooftops of London, where as yet the ash and soot of industry had not re-imprinted its goblin footprints, great shapes strove against the upraised lights. From the sky, dark shapes fell upon London.

"What are those?" Scrooge shouted, against a booming rattle of, could it be, drums from the direction of St. Pauls.

"They are the French Airnavy in their strength, Ebenezer. Thirty-five of their Aerial Ironclads."

"But this is madness, oh Spirit, I know the Montgolfière's balloons, but those are no flimsy constructions of paper and cloth. Those are heavier than any flying thing: they are things built of iron. Like buildings thrown into the sky and held there by God. For heaven's sake how is this possible! Surely that is a ship of the line! A veritable ship of the sea moving silently in the sky. Now I know I have gone mad. All of this, Marley, the ghost of Christmas Past, the Ghost of Christmas Present, You: all a vast fermentation in my brain from too long and too hard a toil of work over these last long years. Ghosts and angelic visitants, the cries of my dead partner, I could believe, but the abolition of all sense: the dethronement of up and down, the turning of the sky into the sea. This I can not believe. I just can not. No one would build a thing like that to transverse the sky. It is an affront to the good name of Isaac Newton! You might as well ask me to accept a Mountain held within the heavens, as this!"

"Believe, Man. For you are right," The Spirit said, softly – almost tenderly.

"This vessel was not built to transverse the skies. Her keel was laid down in Cherebourg when you were a boy Ebenezer, and she was called then the *Inflexibe*. As the politics of your world changed with the turning years, she ran through many names. *Friedland, Duc de Bordeaux* during the Restoration of the Bourbons, *Friedland* again briefly during the Hundred Days of Napoleon's revived Empire, and back to the *Duc de Bordeaux* thereafter."

Scrooge examined the ship of the air as the Phantom waxed loquacious. It was quite simply an iron ship supported in the sky by no force he could understand. His eyes must have begged for explanations and the Spirit proved willing to offer them.

"It was, once more called the *Friedland*, in December 1840, newly commissioned, that she was the ship within whose iron heart, the first test of the Budding-Morley-Scrooge reciprocating gyroscopic engine took place."

Scrooge's face twisted into a grimace. "I remember this proposal now. A dunderheaded notion of Marley's in his final fever, to set our funds to purchase the inventions of half the fools and charlatans in Christendom. I told him then, Spirit, that it would take five, maybe six years of trial and error, of sweat and profitless pouring of good money after bad, to get within sight of anything saleable. And Edwin Beard Budding was the worst of them."

"Why so, Man? How did he offend you?"

"He was no man of business. No, not a philanthropic man either. His spirit did not travel abroad in life save in abstractions of the intellect." Scrooge found himself, desperate to justify his disregard for the man in terms that the Spirit of Christmas might understand.

"How could I take seriously the idea that a device adapted from a patent lawn-mower might offset the awful plunging and twisting of top-heavy over gunned warships of France. When Marley died, one of my first acts as sole master of Scrooge and Marley was to order the funds dedicated to such wild work placed under a fiat, and the whole thing wound up, and paid into gilt-edged securities. I sent that Bearded Budding squealing back to his lawn-mowers in no time flat I can tell you."

"So you did. And so this marvel was lost to your world.

I can not show its history: the glorious Anglo-French Aerial Cordiale, that sounds the beat of the First Empire of the Skies as presents fall by parachute on London and Paris alike delivered for each by the flying ships of the other, for only the present time is my domaine. But I can show you a further world where this discovery was delayed until this very night. Step Sideways further with me to the engine room of another ship, where a triumph wrought four years ago, occurs again for the first time in this year."

A clatter of metal on metal and a smell of burning – what was it? – too sharp and pungent for leaves or wood; it was no scent that Scrooge knew.

In the centre of the ship's iron hold, at its mid-point, a great cantilevered device spun upon an immense wheeled track, arms at different heights bore weights which themselves spun upon shorter arms. It looked like nothing so much as a giant orrery, but one whose many, many, turning spheres bore no relationship to any astronomy known to Scrooge.

Scrooge found himself impalpable and invisible to the engineers working upon the engine, and to two others, from whose shadowed faces, he still derived a shock of recognition as great as his alarm at the other-Christmas's flying ships had been. For one of the men had been his business partner for twenty years, and the other had been with him night and day, since he had come to manhood. In the dark ship's hold, their faces alternately shadowed and illuminated by the strange flashes of light that proceeded from the machinery (it was the outputting of this light, Scrooge concluded that coincided with the burning smell), they seemed men obsessed. The light, now he considered it, was of the same aetherial quality as that which flowed around the robes of the Ghost of Christmas Sideways, and as he thought on that, he became aware again of her presence at his shoulder.

In that light, there was Marley – alive again – and it made Scrooge glad to see him, his long fever abated, back upon his feet, keen-eyed and set upon his business. Had there ever been a man like Marley, for knowing Scrooge's mind – for striking off the grey flint of his close nature, the brighter fires of mercantile designs? Then there was Scrooge himself –of an age with his observing phantom, so old, so petrified with singleness of purpose, so fixed in adamant.

"Is this how I look to others, Spirit?" Scrooge asked. "My mind bent only upon one thing, my hands outstretched as if to pull all things to myself, my avarice written large upon my face for all to see."

"It is true you were blessed with a most expressive countenance. Would you had used it to bear witness to finer feelings than your greed. Watch as you spy an unlooked for prize, for in a moment a miracle will be wrought by pure chance."

"I do not understand you Spirit, surely this shows that Marley and myself were not always without good consequences for the world in our business. Think of the men put to work, the jobs created, the children fed, by means of the ingenuity of this man, his brains funded by our money. Is it chance that makes the world, or effort both of strength and wealth!"

"What, value placed you on his brains – when the capacity to share your wealth with him, was left to you. A fool and a charlatan, you called him, to be sent packing back to his lawn mowers. What did you ever create, or cause to be created, but dusty ledgers of debt and claims. What did you bring to men and to children, aye and to their suffering wives and sweethearts, but the prospect of having burdens they could never repay to bring the smallest luxury or oftentimes the vital necessities of life within their ken? But hush, I spoke not of the chance that made this, but the greater chance that within the alloys and metals of this device a certain crucial ratio of turning parts, which so reflects the heavens own designs that in their resonance like to like, the smaller one may overwhelm the greater." Taking Scrooge's sleeve, the Ghost of Christmas Sideways, drew him up and through the deck of the ship, until he could observe from without the effects of the device that was supposed to settle it safely in the waters.

With a greater flash of a deeper blue light, with a great and unearthly groaning, the spinning central engine hummed, and in response the Earth gave up its hold upon the engine and upon all that was attached to it. The ship itself in all its iron and rivets – all its tonnage, guns, sailors, and tricolours floated out of the waters and into the astonished air. Water cascaded from it, looping briefly in paths that ended back upon the ship's dark hull, only to fall again as the effect ceased to hold a second or a third time, and all the normal properties of earthly things regained their strength.

Some of the sailors were praying, some cursing, but all were shouting, and one of the officers, more frightened or more desperate for some decisive act, ordered the port guns to fire. Scrooge saw the puff of flame, and then to his almost overworked surprise, the fired shells seemed to hang suspended in the air, and the ship itself receded, pushed back by act of discharging its weapons.

"This is glorious!" Scrooge cried before he could stop himself, "What money this will make." Instantly he was sorry for the relapse of his rebellious and greed heart, but if Marley had always had the spark that brings new ideas, he, Scrooge, had always seen the practical implications, the facts beneath the bone. Given a device that would with the power from a bank of steam engines, free a mass of iron and wood from the earth and set it to swing in the sky, so finely balanced that a shot fired from it could propel it, the costs of goods, of land – of the making of things in every way would change. Railways already eating up the countryside would be abandoned, stock in such ventures would come crashing down in what Scrooge surmised the Grub Street press would term "Black Christmas". Buildings could soar a mile-high: the cost of land in London would be irrelevant to the people that could live tethered to the earth by a single stairwell, within a might sky-flung block. Dwellings would scrape the very sky! The poor would have the skies and the rich gardens.

Oh! if only he could commune with his other-self, impart to him his greater knowledge of the 'Change, gained while this Scrooge had devoted his time to Budding's experiments. Scrooge and Marley would bestride the world.

"And is that all you would impart to him?" The Ghost of Christmas Sideways said, her voice soft and sorrowful. "He is your parallel in all of this. He has been wetted on the same grindstone. He has been turned to the same ends. He has abandoned the same mercies. That he will make more of man's yellow gold, will not buy him the golden hair of your forgotten love. That his avarice will clutch at the sky, will not bring him closer to the Heavens."

Scrooge looked again at his might-have-been's face. That Scrooge had not been given sight again of his lost childhood, lonely in the schoolroom after all the other children had departed. He had not been shown the growing coldness – unseen from within – that had driven Belle from him. He had not seen the trials and tribulations of the Cratchits: the unlooked for strength of Tiny Tim, the honest good-heartedness of Bob. Did this Scrooge even employ Bob, or had the clerk's place been taken by some ratcheted mechanism that filed tiny cards of printed information with the fast click of levered mechanisms. Was this Scrooge more chained than he?

"Spirit, you say you can show me only the events of Christmas days that lie beside this one we live, not their antecedents. If so, I know it must be that I can not see their futures, but as you have shown me this – four years behind its other self, is there not another world where these same discoveries were made years before, so that I might see for myself by sight of its present Christmas, what changes these designs may bring? Is all this for the good? Can I hope that even if this Scrooge must end wrapped in chains, that yet his work may bring great benefits to all?"

"You tear at the bones of our chartered course," the Spirit said – and yet Scrooge felt she was not displeased at his request. "I walk the sideways worlds of what might be, and some discoveries must come in time only when other serried thoughts proceed them, as man, step by step, must climb upon a certain ladder. Others, perhaps, that have a core of chance may miss their moment and never occur. These have a time of maximum potential, and show aside from that, only to cluster as echoing ghosts of times delayed. Rarely are such found – even to my sight – to come before that fated spur of time. One of this kind is this device. It rests upon the melding of obscure metals, and requires the science of metallurgy and the minds to harness it, and the drive and funds to build. Still, at the edge of those worlds I can see, is one which still preserves this happpenstance a dozen years before its Great Potentiality. It is no triumph of yours – even by proxy – but of other hands, but still if you desire I can remove us to, that present Christmas which from that hour flows, for in it too Marley still lives, and thus I have not wavered from the path of your choice."

"Please, Spirit," begged Scrooge. "Take me there."

"So be it," replied the Ghost.

Into the Christmas time of fire, they passed. Over the world the Greater Napoleonic Empire had long spread: its aerial gunboats bearing ruin to his foes. Not presents, from these black and scoot burned gore-crows of the skies, descended on the hamlets and the towns of Europe, but packages of poison and disease. Here was a legacy of joy indeed. Beyond the ruins of a London toppled down, in the hills and in the depths of forests, freemen still hid: ones not subjugated to the yoke of Greater France. In a charcoal burners' hut, deep in Dean Forest one family huddled. Their Christmas fare was meagre stuff, even by the standards of the urban poor of Scrooge's own world, and they cooked always with one eye upon the fire, less smoke alerted some patrolling band of merchanaries, turncoats, or the French. In the corner Jacob Marley sat, surrounded by piles of legal papers from which he fed the pitiful fire.

Scrooge watched as the bills and warrants, the minutia of ownership and the screeds of law, were licked into grey and wispy ash imparting faint life to the flames. Over them Mrs Cratchit waved a vast iron pan in whose interior a few mushrooms and withered vegetables warmed. At the door Bob and Tiny Tim kept vigil, and Scrooge was startled to see Tim jump at a sound and glide across the room – until he saw the belt of shiny metal around the young boy's waist and connected it with the strange triumph of the earth-defying stuff of Budding's discovery.

"Spirit," Scrooge quavered, "why is it that things have come to this in so short a time, while in another world, presents and drums proclaim the triumphs of Christmas peace."

"Many reasons, at which I can only guess," The Spirit said.

"The world is not so balanced that each end can be traced solely to a single cause. But strongest of them all, is this: that Marley was a good man as well as a good man of business. That he shared the discoveries you and he funded with those in need."

The Spirit paused as somewhere in the depths of the forest an aerial torpedo exploded, turning trees to deadly splinters of hurtling wood.

"He did not turn it over to the military of one nation, but founded an order of all good men across this mighty world to keep forever Christmas in their hearts."

Scrooge shook his head in wonderment. "Right glad I am at his actions – and hope under your guidance to do the same if I survive the Ghost to come after you: but for all Marley was my one and only friend I find it hard to see in this paragon of virtue, the strong hand at the iron wheel of business that once I knew."

"For this there is a reason, most compelling, oh! Man of Other Worlds Than This" – a voice sepulchral and in pain intoned not half an inch from Scrooge's right ear. A voice that was not the high ethereal voice of the Ghost of Christmas Sideways – but rather one bitter, severe and biting, A voice of tombstone teeth clattering in the icy air. A voice that Scrooge knew from the inside: for it was his own. The griping cheerless voice of his emptiness that he'd vented upon the world in all his greedy years.

Spinning in the air somehow: he saw his own form swathed in chains fully as ponderous as those that Marley had – in his own London – worn, so long ago it seemed now, on that first Christmas Night.

"In all the worlds there is observed a vast mysterious parsimony, of which the miserly ought well approve," the other Scrooge said sourly. "Where Marley is dead to begin with Scrooge alone may be saved. Where Scrooge is dead to begin with Marley alone lives to reap the benefit of his partner's ghostly concern. You may yet escape the chains – my more than brother – but know that in some corner of what once might well have been your torment remains unending."

Scrooge winced at the sarcasm of his own tongue, and found himself desperate to make some counter to this visitant. "What of the second world the Ghost of Christmas Sideways showed me: not the one where Marley lived – and now I see I must have died – but that in which we both were there to see the triumph of the flying ship. Must that world also end in death for one and life only for the other?"

"As yet the fate of that world hangs," the Ghost of Christmas Sideways said, "within the undeveloped skein of future time – and there only one spirit may accompany you and He only from the world from which you came. He is the Spirit of your Christmas Yet To Come, not that of these worlds of if.

"Nevertheless as One before me saw a crutch lying unused in a chimney corner I too may peer a little way into the future of my own domain. I see a dark and masked figure ruling by means of such ships of the air: as in this present world, where other hands discovered these powers and were not swayed by the great commonwealth of man – and I see another, too intertwined in greed and history with that dread lord to be destroyed without compunction locked in a cell of stone and steel. But which is the awful Lord of the Air and which his prisoner and vassal I do not see, and never will until that day is in the present Sideways."

"Bah," the Ghost of Scrooge exclaimed. "Do you think that milksop Marley could turn the world to his footstool? Oh! If only I still lived." He rattled his chains anew: and Scrooge saw that whereas those of Marley had been cash boxes and safes, chains around documents and sundry embodiments of law, this Scrooge's bindings were great anchor chains to stop the airships tearing from the earth, and belts of metal shaped to hold cartridges, and guns interlinked through their finger guards. If this ghost had truly taught the Marley shepherding the family within the charcoal burner's hut the equanimity to face the worst, it had won no balm for its own soul by doing so. Not yet at least.

Scrooge grabbed at the blue-lit robes of the Ghost of Christmas Sideways and heard the faint mew of her familiar. "Oh please bear me back to my own world to face the final end of all, for it can not be worse than this."

"Can it not?" Scrooge's ghost shouted. "You have no Marley to save. Think on that as you face your own endings. You go to an end where you can accomplish nothing in life or in death. Unless…" – and a look of dreadful never to be met desire passed over the ruin of its familiar face. "Unless you can become a better man than ever I was."

"Oh I will I will. I will," Scrooge sobbed.

In that moment, the voice of his own damned self faded into the dark of the night, and the strange blue light of the Ghost extended to fill the world from horizon to horizon in a whirling maelstrom.

The air was filled again, not with the drumbeats of the aerial accord of a world a peace, nor with the clamour of one where war had long since almost burned out, but with the sounding of that bell that signified the fall of Christmas night and the beginning of Christmas day. Twice he had heard it, such was the Spirit's power.

He looked into the face of the Phantom.

"Is there, then for that Scrooge, and for my Marley, nothing that may be done?"

"Not by your hand, Ebenezer, but there remains a Power to whom all things are possible and for whom Christmas, after all was named. Before him they will, in the end, have yet a final chance, and to that very point my brother will commend you. For your lot stands no better."

Her voice and form swirled away into tiny flecks of blue, each seemingly the eye of an impossible cat, and behind where she had stood – as if she had never been in any tale or story – there remained a figure, like to that form in which she had first appeared as a twin monk, wrapped in the same vestments of the night.

Robed, awful, and – Scrooge felt – more pitiless, than any of his preceding visitants, it came, like a mist along the ground, towards him.

TALENTED WITCHES

Paul Magrs

My Aunts were nimble creatures, standing on the steep slopes of this is how it happened, although I couldn't quite remember what I found down there. It's starting to come back now. They reached out because they felt my presence. In some truly here in the past, in this benighted place.

I can feel the chill, feel the breezes and the springy turf between tall black gravestones. It is as if I am actually dashing after my churchyard where those Bronte sisters used to play and live, in the last century. She's in the ways I have settled in very nicely, adapting to their rituals and routines, and I can. I can. I'll get into terrible trouble.

I see the idea take light behind young Emily's eyes. From across the room I can hear her heart beating faster and harder. And along the cobbled streets of Haworth bristling with resentment and fury. Why am I patting her hand as he coaxes her into committing arson?

You stay here, Panda, where it's safe. Long grass whipping at their legs.

Christmas 1970 and Mam remembers us being at Fred Johnston's house. The three sisters there together. I was up and about and reaching into Julia's handbag, which was lying on the floor, and she shoved it away from me, crossly.

Glad gave me a Jacko monkey. Mam was delighted, because she'd always wanted one herself. They were all hanging from the ceiling in Woollies. 'I kept having to wipe his face because it was all sticky from your fingers.'

Ahead of us young Emily has stopped in her tracks. They obviously wanted to prevent me from burning to violent fits of temper and switches of mood. Some days I stomp around their house and have to be in this gloomy place. Why do I have to work like a servant for these women, and have to attend school with the boring, mulish local children?

Alfie was away doing police training. Mam said that his mam looked after me for the day – I was about five months old – and she went into South Shields town centre on the bus to buy some of the things they would need in their new house. They were moving to Thornley and Mam says that she remembers coming back on the double decker bus, weighed down by all this kitchen stuff. She had to start from scratch. She didn't know what you need. All the basic stuff.

Things you don't think of. But she got it all by herself. She says that her mam and Fred turned up with other things, things that she'd forgotten, but couldn't do without – like a box of matches. Because there was the fire to light.

I am almost disappointed, I realise. I too wanted to see the schoolroom burn down.

With their strange powers they must have known it would make a nice little café one day, when the tourist industry eventually took off. However, they also wanted me for another reason. In some truly here in the past, in this benighted place.

'The way out,' I said. The fourth crate was much more successful. When its lid came away we could only see solid matt black within. A black that trembled and shivered at our touch. Then it rose up, an obelisk of black. It tumbled and twirled and, before we could budge an inch, it dropped upon the two of us, swift as nightfall in the tropics We were falling and falling and then we had arrived.

And so had everyone else.

I remember arriving in Peterlee. Seeing that new town landscape from the back of our car. My Little Nanna sitting in the back with me. The hills were smooth and green and fake. The houses were spaced out and regular in shape. She sang:

'Little boxes... on the hillside...'

I don't know whether it was a real song or not.

This was the night the ground opened up and swallowed us, that ghost and I, and we fell as if down a rabbit hole: down, down, to a destination deep underneath the sleepy town of Haworth. That lecturing tone she often put on, she explained that this was the very churchyard where those Bronte sisters used at the centre of the graveyard, almost hidden by the closely-crowded stones. Has she given up? Has she lost that spark of fury? Decided to turn back?

But then I see that she has bumped into someone. An adult. I'm trembling all over in terror, but also… I think, joy. Return her to her home pulling on trousers and a thick fisherman's sweater, which is one of her favourites; to play and live, in the last century.

They took money off them, to stay there. Mam says she and Alfie had nothing. He was starting off in the police. Training, having signed up for his thirty years. The Magrs's took bed and board off them: a hefty wedge of his earnings. Of course they were stuck in the house all the time and they were stuck there, anyway, with me. I was a large baby, with a large head, to judge by the photo of me I've got. Mam's feeding me my bottle and we're sitting in the shade between the pebble-dashed houses, in the side passage and sitting on a metallic folding garden chair. We've got a blow-up of that photo in our downstairs hall now. I look like I've got a huge

old man's head. Wise in that weird bald baby way. Mam
looks proud and watchful.

There was a sea elephant down in a pit. Baboons up a
fake mountain. A room filled with water you had to cross on
a rope bridge. And a lake that you sailed across on a raft
we thought was sinking. Water was coming up through the
sodden logs. There were dinosaurs lining the sludgy banks. I
knew they were only models, but they were nearly life-sized.
The boat went sailing round so we could look at them all,
peering out from between the trees.

It was only after several days that I learned the
significance of the town of Haworth, and why its name had
rung a bell. Because all of a sudden I think I know who this
is, this ghostly form talking to my younger self. Talking
down the lecturing tone she often put on, she explained that
this is alarming, I can see the Panda's snout moving as he
talks. I can see his small arms. I am still prone.

So this is the night that *they* reached out to me. The game
is up. She's been caught running about in the churchyard
at night. Some responsible adult will take her in hand,
confiscate her matches, and light them inside my head. On
our way to the moor. We were going to spend the day up on
the Heights with a picnic that Aunty Val...You can watch
from the window. I'm sure you'll see the fire from here...

Then young Emily is out of bed and quickly runs from home. It still has the scent of the sea about it, she thinks. The Whitby mist still clings dead set on doing this and I feel almost proud of her unflinching determination. She finds the keys hanging where Aunt Deirdre always leaves them and, careful not to let the shop door go *ting* – she's out in the…

She spares one glance backward to her bedroom window, and sees that Panda has positioned himself right on the sill. His black eyes stand out starkly in his moonlike face as he solemnly waves at her.

The thin night air freezes my throat. My fingers are brittle and twiggy. The skies above our heads look like space itself, as if the earth's atmosphere has been torn away, leaving us down here, barren as the moon itself. With my girl-self all in the space of one night. I had a life-sized cuddly chimp called Jacko in a red and white striped top. We watched me settle with the street and free. In some truly here in the past, in this benighted place. But they were double-thickness, for some reason, which meant they were murder to dry on the clothes horse, and took twice as long.

Mam went into Dewhursts one day with me. Gladys Magrs was there with her black beehive, working the scales and the till, and showing off for the queue, as usual. She was introducing them all to me, her youngest grandchild – and talking about her other one. And someone piped up that she

didn't look old enough to be a Nanna. And that my mam
looked very young to be a mam.

Gladys Magrs shot back, laughing: 'Don't blame me.
Blame my sex-mad kids.'

Emily leaves Panda in her room, and I creep after her
down the rickety staircase, careful not to wake her carers.
Down in the fragrant and shadowy store young Emily hunts
out a large box of cook's matches. His eyes clacked open
and closed like a doll's.

And a blow-up dolphin we'd bought at Flamingo land.
When you arrived there were people in costumes waving
at you? A dolphin standing there, all furry, and a panda
waving, and a lion, swishing its tail. I remember Alfie belting
me one, just before we got aboard that boat. I was crying for
something or other. I think I was always wanting something.

In that lecturing tone she often put on, she explained that
this was the very churchyard where those Bronte sisters used
to play and live, in the last century. The cold of the night
surprises her as she dashes across the cobbled road. Luckily,
it's not far to the churchyard and the schoolroom. She was
carrying him in a heavy basket. Not for us the mournful
dirges and ghastly singalongs in the chapel, or listening to
the dreary nonsense spoken by the vicar. We were having an
adventure, instead! Involving somebody's amazing lash-up.
A kind of force field, I would have guessed.

Sergeant Bendy was saying, 'You were looking for her. I assume she got here before you.' The graveyard was crowded and hemmed around by black, twisted trees. We cut straight across the middle, zig-zagging through headstones and tip-toeing on those that were flat on the ground, or had toppled over one stormy main street and its gloomy parsonage and graveyard. And it was all for my own safety. I just had to make the best of it all. But I was a sunny-natured, obedient child, you'll be surprised to hear, Brenda. He's so nosy. A body toppled out on top of him. He shrieked once and disappeared beneath a glistening, purple mass of anti-flesh. 'It's quite dead,' I said, manhandling the beastie off him. He looked completely revolted. I prodded the body, which was no longer crackling. 'I've got a suspicion...' I said, and yanked the head off the thing. It was a rubber head. The we both stared down at the pallid, suffocated face of Mr O.'

I did just as I was told, and I trusted in what my Aunt Maud had told me – that my new guardians would treat me like a queen.

Deirdre and Val ran the grocer's shop at the top of the slanting town. It was a musty, magical place, their shop. It smelled wonderfully of rich tea leaves and fresh mint and strawberries, all year round. I stared at these new aunties and wasn't sure whether I liked what I saw. Val was plump and shy-looking, wearing her linen shop coat out in the street with huge clumpy shoes, one of them with a very thick sole. Deirdre was tall and angular. Blue duck eggs were laid to look like nude men and women, and a flash and a crash, she disappeared, along with the creature itself, a swivel chair and various bits of electronic doo-dahs.

The Magrs's were blowing more cash on their nights out than my mam and dad got to keep. They went out to play darts and booze, and sometimes my Little Nanna would dress up as Shirley Bassey and do a turn on the stage. My Mam remembers her in those wigs and wearing a white mini dress and long white plastic boots. On the one occasion she went out to see my Little Nanna sing, the microphone whistled with feedback, and she chucked it down on the floor and stomped off the stage. She was temperamental. Her husband, my Granda', was a quiet man and would put up with anything for peace. He wore a pork pie hat and a sheepskin coat. He had sticky-out red ears and chapped red hands that smelled of smoke and minced meat.

Next thing, he comes to sit by me before I've even got a drink in my hand, all bloated and booby. Sometimes they looked like people from the town of Haworth, who shopped there. Blushes all round, but to me it was hilarious. I was to expect Mr O to be wearing a single red carnation. At one end of the cemetery was the squat, long shape. Avid reader as I was back then, it is surprising that the name hadn't alerted me before. It was Sunday and, as the rest of the town sang tunelessly in the small church just across the main street from us, my Aunts and I were taking a shortcut through the graveyard of the parsonage, keeping watch over the dead. In some truly here in the past, in this benighted place. And a flash and a crash, she disappeared, along with the creature itself, a swivel chair and various bits of electronic doo-dahs. *They were fighting about their kids and Gladys Magrs was trying to pull rank by saying that she and Alf, my granda', had been the ones to keep my mam and dad and me off the streets. They had housed and fed us in their smoky, noisy house, where my mam kept as quiet as she could be. 'And her, she's not normal, you never hear a squeak out of her,' my granda' said, also at that do in 1974.*

I was told that these were my aunties, as well. They met me off the coach and took hold of my hand and my precious case and told me that they were related to me along some distant branch of our strange family tree. She seemed very sophisticated to my eyes, with her hawkish nose and her mannish hairdo and school teacher's clothes, mandrake root, fire and brimstone, human blood. The disgusting package crackled at me.

Of course we took a leisurely turn around the Tate, where they were showing the dappled and generously gaudy canvases of Pierre Bonnard, and Mida Slike talked a little more about her secret headquarters being under attack from these globular gel-like creatures who crept up from the drains and made things disappear with many details I had forgotten, of course, and now they came rushing back. I ate hearty meals with them, and I was taught to cook. We went gathering herbs and mushrooms in the dewy early hours. We tramped over the wuthering moors together for exercise, taking their great brindled hound, Keeper. I tended to their allotment with them, bringing back a barrowful of vegetables – rude and otherwise – back to the shop. And on Saturday nights we would queue for fish suppers with the townsfolk, who would peer at me and mutter speculation about where I had come from. In some truly here in the past, in this benighted place.

Aunty Val and Deirdre were well known for their witchy ways, it seemed. And the local gossip claimed that they had performed evil masses to the devil and conjured me up using a single touch of an extended glistening tentacle.

'Sounds horrid,' I said, peering at Bonnard's poor wife, submerged and at peace in her bath. He painted her again and again in the bath. Tom in his orange bomber jacket and crop top and combat pants – bless him – suddenly finding himself whisked into the Elizabethan Court and a set of intriguing machinations.

While Emily flummoxes and flusters, having her loyalties pulled about by these phantom siblings, there is a strange interlude. The Brontes leave their crystal thrones and, all three becoming quite corporeal now, they glide towards us.

Next thing, he comes to sit by me before I've even got a drink in my hand, with my girl-self all in the space of one night. We watched me settle with the long grass whipping at their legs. Almost unbearably exciting. I'd beg to go, again and again. When we went south to Norfolk, I was disappointed that the Broads couldn't boast the plesiosaurs etc, that Yorkshire seemingly could. We went on another rackety boat and sailed across the flat waters.

It was Aunt Deirdre who confirmed my sudden inkling that this was a place I ought to know. In that hectoring, lecturing tone she often put on, she explained that this was the very churchyard where those Bronte sisters used to play and live, in the last century. These graves were their playground. Those windows were their bedrooms. I had read their books, of course? I haven't been there since I was a little girl.

'Didn't you like your time there?'

Once, when my mam went to visit, the place was quiet. The living room was dark and empty. The antimacassars were rucked and covered with blood. Mam thought there had been a murder. Glad showed up eventually and explained that she had hit him with a heavy-bottomed saucepan.

We saw the empty spaces where the missing furniture had been. As invasions and incursions go, it wasn't that spectacular. A bare patch of lino here and there; missing doors, too. In came Sergeant Bendy, in a Bond Street suit and he said, breathlessly, that they had one of amorphous culprits held captive in their basement. Tonight the journey in Haworth with my girl-self all in the space of one night. We watched me settle with the long grass whipping at their legs.

There was some kind of show in a small theatre on the banks of that lake. We crowded in to see. We were there with another copper and his wife and their kid. The show was a zoo keeper and a huge gorilla, looking cross in a cage. The man tried to make him do tricks and the gorilla went wild. Shrieking and rattling the bars. Everyone laughed and gasped – and then screamed, as the bars crashed open and the gorilla came free.

I was there for two years, or thereabouts. The small town, in the heart of Yorkshire, right in the thick of the moors… open to the vast, frightening skies… I think I did like living there. I think. But what do kids know? In straw outside their shop's front door, along with sackfuls of muddy potatoes they grew themselves. Every single potato had been grown

into a rude shape. Deirdre used to say Val did it for fun –
she somehow made the tatties grow? They aren't given
any choice about where or how they live. Those things
are decided for them by adults. I was just made to live in
this place, with its odd, cobbled, downward sloping in his
buttonhole. I found him in that circular room lined with
mirrors; the blandest looking fella I'd ever seen. Head like
an egg, no features to speak of, nondescript suit. Toying
with a cafetiere. I had an orange juice. Two pounds. I'd
charge that back to the Ministry. Mida Slike's always going
on about my bar bills. I sidled up to Mr O who, though we
were the only art-lovers present that afternoon, pretended he
hadn't noticed me. Funny, that room of mirrors.

'Aye, and we had to wipe the arses of them, right from
the very start.' That's what my Little Nanna shouted later, at
my Big Nanna's fiftieth birthday party, at our house in 1974.
Their Victorian gowns hang down to the ground with my
girl-self all in the space of one night. We watched me settle
with the long grass whipping at their legs. And it looks very
much as if they are floating along the spotless floor. They
encircle us, studying us, swishing round and round, faster
and faster. It's like the Bronte girls are on roller skates.

We went on long drives down into Yorkshire. Up the
steepest hill, up dangerously zig-zagging roads towards
Scarborough and Pickering. We went to Flamingo Land

Zoo. I associated travel over great distances like this with travelling back in time, to prehistoric days. I think this was because I loved the paintings in my Ladybird books that had to do with dinosaurs and evolution of life on earth. Those landscapes were wild and windblown, like Yorkshire seemed to be, to me, from the back of our car. Scalding in the back, on the black leather seats on our long summer drives. With the Beach Boys playing, or Bob Dylan, Rod Stewart, the Beatles. Dad would make us sing Cliff Richard's 'Summer Holiday.' Prehistory also looked like the vast expanses of sluggish water we passed, driving through Norfolk, on our way to where my Big Nanna came from. As far as I knew, she came from the past. A swampy, southern place, all trilobites and icthyosaurs.

Flamingo Land Zoo over a jagged ridge of hills. There was a sea elephant down in a pit. Baboons up a fake mountain. A room filled with water you had to cross on a rope bridge. And a lake that you sailed across on a raft we thought was sinking. Water was coming up through the sodden logs. There were dinosaurs lining the sludgy banks. I knew they were only models, but they were nearly life-sized. The boat went sailing round so we could look at them all, peering out from between the trees.

When I ate round the cheese in the fridge, and she found my tiny teethmarks along the edges, she laughed at first, but then she was scared. She took a sharp knife and pared all the evidence away.

'W-what are you doing?' cries Emily. She has her hands over her ears, as if the swishing of their dresses was deafeningly loud. It isn't, but something is disturbing Emily very profoundly now. Perhaps the girls are different to how she remembers. They seem very odd indeed to me, and not quite nice. Mida Slike was undercover. Camel hair coat. Nifty briefcase. I gathered Panda up in a bear hug and he coughed politely to be released.

My Little Nanna and my Granda' saved up tokens from their packets of tabs. Then they would choose things out of a catalogue. I had a swing and a slidey and a see-saw that went round and round, all from their cigarette tokens. Also, a small red car with a white steering wheel that I could pedal all by myself, the length of Chaucer Avenue. I remember them starting me off, and me getting this heady rush of freedom, and dashing away from them all, thundering off down the street.

He was nodding at a woman fiddling with a connection and soldering busily at a profusion of wires. Without looking at us, she said, 'I'm trying to keep the purple nasty at bay. Not too well, I'm afraid.' She was in a silver catsuit bikini affair and leather boots. She had masses of golden blond hair and green eyeshadow. When she finally turned I gasped. I thought she looked rather marvellous and I could tell that Tom and Mida Slike thought so, too.

Being at Flamingoland Zoo and sitting on a park bench with Glad and Fred, eating Ritz cheese crackers out of the box. The waxy paper inside, the greasy, delicious crumbs. Waiting for the others as it patters on to rain. By the monkey houses. They're shameless, 'Doing their ah-ah's all over the place,' says Glad.

'You should never have brought her!' cries Anne Bronte, as she careens past on wheels.

My Big Nanna bought me a small plastic record player. I had singles: Little White Bull, Tweety Pie, 'She's a monstrosity!' by the Long-Dead Mentors. 'But Brenda is my best friend! You can't be nasty about her!'

'She's trash! Dead body parts! Flotsam and jetsam! She's not even a real human being! She's got no soul! How could you be friends with a stitched together homonculus like that?' At this time in my immensely long and rather glamorously breakneck career I was elderly Iris; burly and haggard, stuffed into my sheepskin coat. I was travelling filing cabinets and odds and sods of Ministry equipment. 'It really was a sham,' Tom said. 'Anti matter doesn't exist.'

So, the next place my present day self tells that Deirdre and Val are pleased with this. However, it isn't as easy as all younger self is one particular night, several weeks into my life with my new aunts. In some truly here in the past, in this benighted place.

'Really, Panda? Don't you think?'

'I don't, no… not like this.'

'Who would think a little girl like you could do such a terrible thing? An insignificant and scared little girl. They'll never suspect you, my dear.'

'We Bronte's trained you better than that!' shrieks Charlotte. 'No outsiders are welcome inside the inner sanctum!'

'Especially not unnatural ones..!' This is Emily, thrusting her spiteful face into mine as she swooshes by.

I was on my bus with Tom, a human boy whom I had only recently allowed to join my select crew. I had picked him up one night in Soho, where he had dashed aboard the bus, thinking it (not unnaturally) bound for Putney Common. But no ordinary 22 mine, oh no! This was I must confess, largely down to me...and now my unshakeable travelling companion during the time in my life when I was albeit slightly unwillingly, and rather surlily – employed by the Ministry.

Their faces shone with life and vitality as they kept pace with life above the grocer's shop. When I saw the room that my new aunties had allotted me, I cried all over again because it was so lovely. Much bigger than my cupboard-like windowless room of their bounding dog, and I felt so sickly, pale and weak as I struggled to keep up on my much shorter, weaker legs.

We would go to see Little Nanna Mason in the old streets, in the old part of Shields, near the docks. This scared me. Even then I understood that this was travelling back into the past. Those houses, and that very back parlour, are in Shields museum now, all reconstructed and lit like a stage set. I stood there with my spectral driver and watched young Aunty and them yomping up, spilling over the moors as we queued for our fish and chips. They held themselves with great dignity amid the steamy vinegar fumes and the mumblings around them subsided. Catcalls Emily, 'Who are we looking for?'

'And you're his replacement?'

'Iris,' I said, and didn't offer my hand. Down to business now, I thought. 'What's all this wild talk about anti-matter?'

'You should have known better, Effryggia!' Emily struggles to make herself heard. I perceived that the townsfolk were actually scared Val would insist on combing out my hair each night. And a flash and a crash, she disappeared, along with the creature itself, a swivel chair and various bits of electronic doo-dahs.

Next thing, he comes to sit by me before I've even got a drink in my hand. My Aunts ignored this tittle-tattle of being in that place. And the prospect of biding so near to them. In some truly here in the past, in this benighted place.

Snowing in the car park at the back of Binns department store in South Shields. I'm looking at the back of the Pinky and Perky record. The two pigs sitting at their Christmas dinner. Do pigs eat turkey? And, is it true that one of the butcher boys bought this album for me? Something about him leaning through the car window. My Little Nanna is with me. We've been to see Santa in a pink tinsel and silver tin foil grotto on the top storey of Binns. The department store felt impossibly glamorous and rich to me. There was a book I was given while I was there. A picture book, about a girl and a boy going into a fabulous land that was predominantly pink. It's something I've tried all my life to remember more about, that book and its illustrations. There's something sensual about them – as if I could still almost taste them or touch them, if I snag the right memory.

But these slightly gloomy, slightly thrilling thoughts were dissipated by the breezy morning air and the brilliant Emily gets spirited away underground by the spirit of the young women at home and fitted out with all manner of luxurious, feminine items. Including tiny bottles of curious scents and silver brushes, sun nipping over stiles and hopping over dry stone walls without a thought, my Aunts and their presumed powers. All of this I took in my stride, of course, having always lived with talented witches. I blushed, because I hadn't read them all. Only Emily's book, 'Wuthering Heights', and Charlotte's 'Jane Eyre', of course. But even so, with my limited knowledge of those girls, a shiver went through me at the thought. She had on the most fantastic jewels. 'Where's the other one?'

'I reckon she's been zapped off to this universe of anti-matter,' I said carelessly.

'Rubbish,' snapped the women on the screen. 'She's been kidnapped. Several of us have. We're in Suffragette City. Remember that?'

'There's no such place,' I said, sounding much more sure of myself than I felt.

My Aunts were nimble creatures on the steep slopes of this is how it happened, although I couldn't quite remember what I found down there. All his papers taken off him. Now he's a non-person living in Wales. It's quite hush hush.

Hidden within, a separate space. Filled with stolen chairs and she's taken a personal dislike to me, it seems. I try hard not to feel too hurt. In some truly here in the past, in this benighted place. And curiously, I wasn't afraid, I was quite calm, in fact, as the graveyard sealed up again over the rabbit hole.

FAIREST OF THEM ALL

Cavan Scott

The smell was unbearable. Oil, spices, manure and sweat.
Sir Henry Prince's eyes watered as he pressed the back
of his gloved hand to his nose. The comforting odour of
expensive leather did little to mask the reek from all around.
How did people live like this? How long did it take for them
to become immune to the stink?

Buchanan stumbled in front of him, hands thrust into his
long coat, peaked cap pressed down low. Sir Henry didn't
really need the revolver that was hidden in his own pocket,
the metal of the gun comforting in his fist. The threat of
losing his station was enough. Buchanan knew these docks
like the back of his hands. The young driver had grown up
here in a stinking tenement next to these very warehouses.
He even returned here to lose himself in squalor from
time to time. "But you always scurry back to the Laverne
household don't you Buchanan," Sir Henry thought as he

glared at the back of the driver's head, "to your new life." Buchanan knew all too well that the same hands which greedily accepted his money would gleefully slit his throat if the purse ran empty. The prodigal son was only welcome as long as he could pay.

"We're nearly there, sir." Buchanan glanced over his shoulder, careful not to meet Sir Henry's eyes. "Not far now."

"It better not be," Sir Henry growled back. "And you're convinced the cab will wait for us?"

Buchanan nodded, not looking back. The driver had wanted to bring the family's brand new Hancock but Sir Henry knew they couldn't risk it. A state of the art steam carriage left idling in the dockyards? It would be stolen the moment their backs were turned.

"Yes, sir. He gave me his word."

Soot-stained buildings stretched up on either side of the narrow lane. Buchanan had been right about this at least. They would never have squeezed a cab down here. The muddy excuse of a pathway was strewn with litter, boxes and the occasional body slumped shivering in a doorway.

"How dare you bring her here," Sir Henry ranted to himself. If this foul air had somehow tainted her, if there was just one blemish on her perfect skin...

Buchanan shuffled to a halt in front of a heavy door, blackened paint peeling from the warped wood. The driver pulled a ring of keys from his jacket pocket, sorting through them with shaking hands.

"Come on," Sir Henry snarled, the thought of his love enduring another minute in this hovel tied his stomach into fresh knots. "Come on."

The oaf let the keys slip from his fingers. Buchanan flashed Sir Henry a look of pure panic, issued an apology and scrabbled around in the piss and dirt of the alley floor to retrieve them. Sir Henry's thumb toyed with the safety catch of his revolver.

"This is the one." Buchanan flashed a nervous smile as he got back to his feet and brandished a rusty, iron key. Sir Henry didn't comment. He didn't have to. His glare told the driver every thing he needed to know. *Either deliver Purity back into my hands without delay or gasp your last on this filthy doorstep. No one will miss you. No one will care. The Lavernes will simply find another servant.*

The keys clattered against the lock as Buchanan fumbled with the door. It pushed open even before the key had been turned. The two men exchanged a look, the last trace of colour draining from Buchanan's face.

Sir Henry barged past the younger man, knocking him roughly against the rotten frame, throwing open the door.

The stench hit him immediately. Different to the reek of the streets outside. Sweet. Like fruit gone bad. The smell of death.

He didn't waste time looking at the bodies. They didn't matter to him. Let Buchanan deal with his wretched family. Let him take in the broken necks, bloated skin and sightless eyes. Let him work out how long they had lay moldering in their hovel.

Sir Henry tripped as he raced up the uneven stairwell, scrabbling against the damp wall to prevent himself from pitching back. Even through his gloves he could feel deep grooves scored into the plasterwork. Something had dragged itself up these very same steps. Something huge, bulky. Something that didn't quite fit.

Buchanan had said she had been hidden in the far bedroom on the third floor. He'd locked the door himself, knew his aunt would look after her, knew she would be safe until he'd found a new place for her to stay.

Safe?

Buchanan's aunt was decomposing in the hallway below, her head lolling unnaturally. This was protection? This was safety.

The lying wretch would pay for this, one way or another.

Sir Henry had all but guessed what he would find on the third floor. The door to the bedroom was ripped from its hinges, the frame scored with the same deep marks. Beyond, the room itself was empty, shards of moonlight streaming through cracks in the boarded up window, falling on the only furniture; a chamber pot and a stained excuse for a mattress laid out on the floor.

Sir Henry's stomach heaved. There was something else, small and dainty, lying discarded on the pitted floorboards.

A shoe. Soft brown leather. Ankle high laces. A modest, graceful heel.

Sir Henry's gun was out of his pocket. It was in his hand. It was ready for firing. Even before he started to descend the staircase, he knew he was going to shoot Buchanan.

§

It was hard to believe it had only been two months since he had first met Purity. The day had started like any other. Meetings in the morning, lunch with advertisers at the club and then, after seeing the evening edition on the presses, off to the Laverne's for dinner. Sir George had climbed onboard the cab as the sun was setting and sank wearily into the padded leather seat. He really could have done without tonight. Even the thought of old man Laverne's incessant chatter was enough to give him a headache.

Then there was Lucy, so prim, so proper, the model fiancée. Yes, she was a beauty and yes, would look resplendent on their wedding day. The prefect bride. Why then was she so dull? There was nothing behind those perfect eyes. No life. No excitement, save for the thought of their coming nuptials. Her destiny had been planned from the day she was born. Marriage and motherhood. As it should be. As it was with all the women of their class. She was a prize catch, a fact that he was always being reminded about back at the club. "You're a lucky blighter," Dorney had reminded him that very day. "Lucy Laverne? The fairest of them all if you ask me."

The fairest of them all.

Then why did the thought of their life together leave him so damned cold?

The carriage lurched at the engine spluttered into life. Sir Henry threw out a hand, steadying himself. The cabby was lucky that his passenger was Sir Henry Prince and not his father. The old goat would have had the man's licence by now. He smiled, imagining his father's words: *"It is not enough that we must endure these infernal contraptions; polluting the air that we breathe, mowing us down in the street. No, we are forced to suffer the halfwits who drive the bloody things. And they call this progress."*

Sir Henry's father – pillar of the community, publishing mogul, bigot – was only happy when complaining. Luckily the modern world provided plenty of material.

The cab clattered around the corner, the Council House looming into view. Sir Henry's eyes narrowed. Here was another of his father's hobbyhorses: The Women's Social League, placards held high, morals even higher. He leant back, eager not to be caught gawping through the window. As the cab rattled by, their chant rang through the air;

"Women not dolls. Wives not possessions.

Women not dolls. Wives not possessions."

He didn't even want to imagine what his father would say to that.

§

"The master is in the drawing room." Hargreaves, the Laverne's decrepit butler, waited patiently as the footman took Sir Henry's coat and hat. "If you would be so kind to wait here, I shall announce you."

Sir Henry waved the suggestion off. Damned old money, always standing on ceremony. Didn't they realise the world had moved on?

"No need Hargreaves, I know the way."

"But Lord Laverne insists..."

"Hargreaves, please. I am soon to be family. Is there really any need for such formality?"

Before the butler could argue, Sir Henry strode across the hallway and reached for the dining room door handle.

"Good evening Lord Laverne."

Hugo Laverne's already florid face flushed as Sir Henry stepped into the room. Sir Henry could guess what was going through the old fool's mind: *Confounded cheek, barging in here without a bye or leave. Who does the young buck think he is?"* Then would come the realisation that an outburst would achieve nothing. No, it was better to keep Sir Henry on side, at least until after the wedding, when the contract was complete. When Laverne's crumbling dynasty was forever linked with the most powerful newspaper family of the modern age.

"Sir Henry," Laverne blustered, forcing a smile across corpulent cheeks as he extricated himself from his grand chair, "how delightful to see you, my boy." Bushy eyebrows creased into a mock frown. "Hargreaves? Where is that damned relic."

A relic? It takes one to know one, Lord Laverne.

Hargreaves shuffled into the room. "My apologies, my Lord."

"I should think so. Get Sir Henry a drink before he dies of thirst."

"Don't be too tough on old Hargreaves, Hugo." Sir Henry wasn't sure who was more put out; Hargreaves for being reminded about his advanced years or Laverne for the casual use of his first name. Henry turned towards the striking woman who had been waiting patiently to be noticed beside the fire. "It was I who insisted on coming straight in, I who couldn't bear to be apart from my sweet Lucy for a second longer."

The hypocrisy appalled him even as Lucy Laverne giggled and rose from the chair, offering her hand to be kissed. He took it, brushing lips lightly against the smooth, pale skin, his father's voice ringing in his ears: *"Play the game, Henry. Play the game."*

"Sir Henry," Lucy cooed, gazing up at him with large azure eyes, "you embarrass me."

Doubtful. Did she even have the imagination for such a thing? Did she even realise that his words were as empty as her head. Lucy Laverne was a woman who existed only to please her man and to look good on his arm. She excelled in the latter even if she failed to achieve the former.

The chants of the Women's Social League rang in his ears:

"Women not dolls. Wives not possessions.
Women not dolls. Wives not possessions."

If only. How he longed to met a woman who didn't know her place, who wasn't obsessed with conforming, with becoming someone's prize. Did such a women even exist? Perhaps the campaigners outside the Council House, with their placards and slogans, were as fake as the smile on Lucy's painted lips. Play-actors. Someone's idea of a joke.

"And not a very funny one," he heard his father say.

"Well, what is it to be, Sir Henry? Whisky or brandy?"

The question snapped Sir Henry out of his reverie. A shadow of a frown was playing across Lucy's powdered forehead. Had he let his mask slip for a second? He smiled reassuringly, turning back to his host.

"My apologies, Lord Laverne, it has been a long and trying..."

His words died in his throat. In a moment everything changed. In a moment, *she* came into his life.

The girl was standing in the doorway, long raven hair cascading over pale, sensual shoulders. She regarded him with curious, intelligent eyes, the ghost of a smile playing across blood red lips. Sir Henry found himself grinning back.

Somewhere behind him, he heard Hugo acknowledging the newcomer, introducing her as his niece, Lady Purity Adriana. There was something about her staying with them while her father was away on business, but he wasn't really listening. He was struggling even to breathe.

The fairest of them all.

Lucy's hand slipped from his.

§

When Lucy's plan had finally come to light, he had almost been impressed. Who would have thought that the girl had it in her? Buchanan was to drive Purity down to the docklands, slit her throat and dump her body into the river. It was strangely flattering. Maybe Lucy did have a spark of life in her if she was willing to commit murder – vicariously at least.

Lucy's logic was faultless. With her rival dispatched, never to return, there would be no more distractions, no more threat. The family would fret over Purity's disappearance. They would mourn when the body was fished out of the docks. They would even wonder why she had wandered such dangerous alleys late at night. The wedding would be postponed, out of respect, but life would eventually continue, their grief lessened by the upcoming celebrations.

Everything back on track. Everything back in order.

But it hadn't gone to plan. Lucy had underestimated the power of Purity's beauty. Yes, Buchanan had clamped the chloroform-doused handkerchief over those full, luscious lips, had even spirited her away from the Laverne's mansion. Yes, he had taken her to a grubby, back-alley far from prying eyes. Yet no blood had been spilt. No life had been lost.

When Sir Henry had confronted the driver, the hapless pawn had confessed all. "I couldn't bring myself to do it, sir," he'd sobbed, snot hanging from his nose as he begged for his life. "I couldn't kill her, not just like that."

"So what did you do with her? Where is she?"

"With my aunt, in the old district. She rents a small house on Jacob's Lane. I took Lady Purity there, to keep her safe, you understand, until I could work out what to do. I knew I couldn't bring her back here. Lady Lucy..." Buchanan had paused, his old loyalties for his employers momentarily overriding his instinct for survival. Sir Henry's clenched fist had soon countered this sudden twinge of conscience. "Lady Lucy was not well. I had no idea what she would do."

Indeed. Sir Henry had never seen Lucy so animated as the day she had confessed all. While consumed rather a large amount of wine, he had a sneaking suspicion he was finally seeing the witch beneath the beauty, the rotten core of the pampered princess.

"She's gone Henry," Lucy had screamed. "She's gone and she's never coming back."

He'd never meant to hit her, he'd never struck a woman in his life. But when she stood there crowing about the blood on Buchanan's shirt, how she'd forced the driver to recount Purity's demise in the minutest detail...

"It wasn't her blood." The driver had crumbled the instant he had been confronted, oil smeared over his vest, panic over his face. "I promise you. I needed to convince

Lady Lucy that I had gone through with it. My Aunt had a leg of mutton in her larder. The blood was from the meat.

"So Lucy would believe that Purity was dead."

"Yes."

"So you could keep her locked away for yourself."

"No, that wasn't it. I needed time to find somewhere else for her to go."

"You could have got word to her father."

"I was in it up to my neck. I needed time to think."

Time was a luxury Buchanan no longer had. Standing here, in his family's squalid hovel, the muzzle of Sir Henry's revolver pressed into his cheek, there was no escape. Sir Henry had only let the villain live this long so he could be taken to Purity.

But she was gone, maybe even…

No, he would not accept that. If Purity was dead, then where was her body? Something had come for her. The same *thing* that had left the marks on the walls and the doorframe upstairs, that had killed everyone in the house. Had they died because they'd stood it its way or because they were witnesses? Sir Henry didn't care. His only had one concern.

"Where did they take her Buchanan? Where did they take Purity?"

He'd never seen a person look so terrified, so sure that they were about to die. Good.

"I don't know." Tears poured down the driver's blanched cheeks, "I promise you, I don't."

"Not good enough." Henry had his free hand around Buchanan's thin neck. He squeezed harder and the man gasped, greasy fingernails clawing helplessly at Henry's sleeve.

"Please," he wheezed, face mottling, "I had nothing to do with this. Do you think I would have my own aunt killed, my cousins?"

"Who knows what you're capable of? You're the man who drugged an innocent woman, dragged her half way across the city, imprisoned her."

"I was..." The voice was barely a croak now. "... protecting her."

"What a pity there's no one here to protect you."

Sir Henry let go of the driver's throat and Buchanan slid to the soiled carpet, knees buckling. The gun followed him down.

"Last chance, Buchanan." All it would take was one squeeze of the trigger.

"Wait, please." The driver threw up his hands. "There was someone at the end of the alley when the carriage dropped us off. Watching us."

"Someone you've only just remembered?"

"I wasn't thinking straight. You don't understand." Damn right he didn't. "They must have seen me helping Lady Purity out of the cabin. She was coming round, struggling."

Sir Henry laughed bitterly. "You're not exactly helping your case."

Buchanan glanced over to the steps, eyes frantically exampling the threadbare carpet in the corridor's half-light. "Look. There." Sir Henry followed the desperate man's gaze. "On the bottom step, that stain."

"Any particularly one? There is quite a collection." Just looking at the flea-infested carpet was making Sir Henry's skin itch.

"Here." Buchanan scuttled across the floor like a crab, never quite taking his eyes off the gun. He stopped by the bottom step and rubbed his finger against a large, black spot. Sir Henry's mouth twisted in disgust, as the driver first smelt his fingertip and then dabbed in against his tongue. "I thought so," he announced in a voice bordering on hysteria. "Oil. Fresh oil."

Sir Henry wasn't in the mood for games.

"So? If you're trying to stall me, Buchanan, I–"

"It was a Docker, Sir Henry. The person who saw me with Lady Purity. A Docker."

§

Sir Henry had never seen a Docker in the flesh. He had read about them, of course, and there had been the photographs in his father's paper. Even then, nothing could prepare you for the sight of one lumbering into view.

Even at this distance the Docker was formidable. It must have stood at least seven foot, massive hydraulic arms swinging rhythmically as it plodded along on heavy metal feet, pistons hissing and cogs turning.

Now he could see why there had been so many demonstrations when the plans for mechanical augmentation had been unveiled. Back then, he'd thought differently. "If men want to volunteer for the work let them do it," he had argued with his father. "They are rewarded for their sacrifice. A job for life, lodgings, free maintenance, even a handsome pension."

Predictably father hadn't agreed. The Dockers, as the new mechanicals became known, were an affront against nature, against the Almighty Himself. That was the beginning. Before long, the mogul was printing reports that the test subjects were rejecting their new implants, a particularly disastrous turn of events when you considered that most of their vital organs would have already been replaced. Then there were the claims that the Dockers had sold themselves into a life of drug-use. According to his Father's team of investigative journalists the mechanicals were being force-fed a cocktail of laudanum and God-knows-what else to ease the constant pain of the grafts.

Before long, there were rumours of suicides, that the harbourmaster was constantly dredging the docks to recover Dockers who couldn't cope with what they had become. The lucky ones sank like stones, dragged down by heavy exoskeletons. The unlucky few were kept alive by the implants, even as morbific waters flooded their lungs.

Thick black smoke belched out of a micro-furnace mounted on to the Docker's back. As they watched in silence, its steel pincers clamped around a girder, power-assisted arms lifting the beam as if it were firewood. The Docker turned on the spot and trudged back to the open hull of Mr Brunel's latest steam-liner. For a split second, Sir Henry glimpsed corpse-white flesh in the heart of the machine, the Docker's original body – or what was left of it.

As the mechanical disappeared from view, he felt his gorge rise. Perhaps his father had been right after all? Was that really progress?

Whatever the ethics, he knew that if... that *when* he found Purity, they'd leave this cesspool of a city once and for all. They'd never be able to return of course. His father would see to that, but he had savings of his own. They would be comfortable, they could start again. "Maybe in the colonies," he thought, losing himself in the fantasy. "Yes, that's what she deserves. Fresh air. Sunshine. Hope."

He tried not to think back to the scratches on the stairwell, to the patch of oil on the carpet. He didn't want to think of those cold, mechanical pincers bruising Purity's flesh, to imagine her scream as one of those abominations had squeezed into that dingy little room.

Where was she?

"Sir Henry." His head snapped around at the sound of his name. Buchanan was pelting across the slick dockside, a scrap of paper clenched in his fist. "I've found her. I've found Lady Purity."

§

"Are you sure this is the place?"

The warehouse was eerily quiet. Buchanan had found a lamp, but it did little to lift the gloom of the place. Around them the building creaked and groaned as if its sleep was being disturbed.

"As sure as I can be," Buchanan hissed as he wound a handkerchief around his hand. He had cut himself scrambling through a window to let them in and the fabric was already saturated. Droplets of blood splattered on the grimy, concrete floor. "Most of the warehouses along the canal have been converted into Docker quarters. The ships are too big now. They can't get down here now. These places were just sitting empty."

This is where they lived? Sir Henry fought off a shiver that had nothing to do with the cold. The place was as dead as a –

A noise broke the silence, the screech of a rusty hinge. They weren't alone. The two men exchanged a look and crept forward as one, padding across to a large internal door. A pungent smell filled their nostrils with every step; fetid, malodorous. Like meat gone bad.

Cautiously, hoping that it wouldn't squeak in protest, Buchanan slid the door back, the lamp's light sending shadows scurrying along the newly revealed corridor. More sounds, up ahead. Metal scraping across the floor. Heavy. Deliberate. Unmistakable.

For a moment, Sir Henry didn't know what to do. He wanted to run, to forget this place, to hide in his chambers, safe from the world.

But what then? he scolded himself. *Spend the rest of your life knowing you'd squandered the chance to save her. A poor excuse of a man. A failure.*

They stood frozen at the threshold, neither wanting to move. The thought of meeting one of those creatures face to face... He still couldn't think of them as men. It just wasn't natural, grafting machinery to flesh and bone, turning men into machines. And yes, he knew he was sounding more like his father by the second, but it was true. Some lines should never be crossed.

Buchanan was the first to move. Sir Henry had to admit that the driver had pluck. Perhaps he was trying to prove himself, to show his loyalty, to finally dodge the bullet he'd been avoiding all day. It didn't matter. Buchanan had acted while Sir Henry hesitated. He took a deep breath, tasting the sour air, summoning an image of Purity in his mind, reminding himself why he was stepping into this nightmare.

He blew the air from his lungs and followed Buchanan into the gloom. The driver had reached another large doorway and was peering around, his face whiter than ever. He glanced nervously back and stepped aside for Sir Henry to see.

The room was vast, the far wall lined by seven huge steel cabinets, sarcophaguses where Dockers rested in the rare moments when they weren't toiling in the boatyards. Flaccid pipes hung from cabinets, waiting to be plugged into the mechanical men's waiting sockets, refuelling, lubricating, keeping the behemoths operational for another shift. Did the Dockers sleep when they were hooked up for the night? Did they dream of their human past, about the days when they were pure?

At the centre of the stark space, a Docker stood lifeless and static, its broad metallic back towards them. The micro-furnace belching smoke into the stale air, a pool of inky oil collecting beneath a dripping pipe to its rear. What was the monstrosity doing, standing in the middle of the room? Is this how they behaved when they didn't have a task in hand? Was the effort of moving so great that they simply stopped?

As if it had heard Sir Henry's thoughts, the Docker wheezed into action, valves spitting angrily. Sir Henry watched dumbstruck, pistons pumping, the giant lurched to the side, revealing Purity's pathetic form.

She was slumped at the bottom of a glass cabinet, fragile legs tucked beneath her frail body. Her once gleaming hair was draped over her face, dirty and unkempt, but there was no mistaking his love, even in this state. Good God, was she even breathing, propped up against the glass wall of her prison?

Slowly – far too slowly – her head rose.

Thank God. She was alive. Alive.

The eyes that peered curiously at him from across the room were bloodshot and swollen. They seemed momentary unsure of what they were seeing, before widening as recognition set in. She straightened slightly, a barely perceivable movement but it was enough. The Docker stiffened and twisted where it stood, feet stomping on the concrete as it came about. Sir Henry found himself staring into another pair of unbelieving eyes – rheumy and unfocused one second and consumed with fury the next. Bloodless lips drew back into a yellow snarl as it maneuvered between the invaders and the glass cabinet.

"Out," it roared, motorised arms spreading wide. "Get out of here." It's voice was harsh, cracked, the words only semi-formed, as if difficult to speak.

Buchanan placed a warning hand on his shoulder, but Sir Henry shrugged it off, raising his revolver.

"Give me the girl," he demanded. His heart felt twice its normal size, beating ready to burst.

"No. We found her. We protect her." The mechanical monstrosity jerked forward. Out of the corner of his eye, Sir Henry saw Buchanan retreat to the door.

"You imprison her. Let her go."

"No. She is pretty. She is our ours."

"Never."

Sir Henry didn't even feel his finger tighten around the gun, didn't hear the gunshot over the sound of blood rushing in his ears. He only realised he'd fired when a hole appeared between the Docker's eyes, dark, grimy matter splattering across the glass behind its hairless head. Its body convulsed, the gargantuan frame slamming back into the cabinet.

Henry roared Purity's name as the glass shattered. Throwing his gun aside, he raced around the dormant Docker, its organic body hanging like a discarded puppet in the steel cage of the exoskeleton.

Purity was curled in a ball, arms thrown over her head to deflect falling glass, scratches livid against her pale skin. Blood ran in rivulets down her shoulders, soaking the nightdress she had been wearing when Buchanan had first abducted her. Nothing too deep. Good. Not likely to scar.

Henry crouched beside her, glass crunching beneath his feet, not knowing what to do.

"Purity?" Gently, he rested his shaking hands on her arms, avoiding her injuries, trying not to cause any more distress. "Purity, darling. It is Henry."

Her head raised a fraction, looking up at him through a curtain of matted hair. He'd take her back to his rooms, have Mrs Collins run her a bath. Maybe he'd wash her hair himself, make it shine once more.

"You are safe," he whispered, praying she would return his smile. Her chapped lips didn't even twitch. "I'm going to take you home."

Home. The word seemed to switch on a light in her eyes. Her face lifted, hope tugging at the corners of her mouth. Finally, thankfully, a smile crept across her face, nervous at first, but grateful, familiar. He was laughing now, relief flooding through his body.

"That's it, my love. My Purity. My..."

His expression faltered.

She was missing a tooth. To the left of her smile. The exposed gum was raw, inflamed. Ugly.

His hands snatched away as if scolded. He didn't mean them to, but it was too late. The reaction spoke volumes, the brilliance of Purity's eyes fading in an instant.

She knew what he was going to do.

"Sir Henry," Buchanan hissed, glancing nervously down the corridor. "They're coming back. I can hear them."

Sir Henry swallowed. Never taking his eyes from the face he had loved. From the missing tooth. He stood up and rushed to where his revolver had skittered, snatching it up and checking the chambers. Five shots left. Seven coffins around the walls.

Not enough.

Purity didn't move as Sir Henry rejoined his companion, straining to hear the approaching Dockers. The man was right. The sounds were unmistakable. Ponderous steel feet tramping into the warehouse, eager to set eyes on their pretty caged bird.

The barrel of the revolver snapped shut. There had to be another way out of here. They could find somewhere to hide, although goodness knows what those creatures would do when they found their compatriot dead and the glass cabinet smashed.

He swallowed hard. Best not to think about it.

"This way Buchanan," he commanded, slipping out of the room and hurrying down the corridor.

He didn't look back.

TIDEWRACK MEDUSA

Rachel E. Pollock

I don't mind speaking of her, no.

Celie taught me lighthousekeeping, and it suits me well enough. I've no skill for conversation, but I do enjoy the tower's tending. Climbing the spiral keeps me hale, and there's ever the sea and the sailors upon her to make a kind of companionship.

Oh, I'm solitary, but I ain't lonely. Plenty to do. Wicks to be trimmed, tanks of oil what need topping-up, and of course the clockwork's maintenance. Celie's skill with levers and flywheels came downright uncanny, and she did pass me that inheritance, the tinker's cuss, that and these broad hands, this crinkled hair. Some might say I've took the light to be my master: that beam must turn, every night, or there'll be wrack and ruin on shoals and shore. Way I see it, I'm as much its master in return. The lamp won't light itself. Rotors won't turn without my arms to crank them.

But it's Celie you're wanting to hear about, of course. Don't get many visitors out here, so ye'll forgive my awkward ways. Dash my dregs, I've her journal round here somewhere. It won't pain me to allow ye its perusal.

§

Daughter-mine, I set this down for ye before I take my leave, so that ye may ken some things of which I never spoke. For all my silence on these matters, know I never loved ye less.

I were born a maroon on the island of St. Clement, where my dam Mabinty worked the trade of hatting before she passed beneath the waves. Such skill had she at the craft, some said she'd sold her soul to the demons of the deep who only took back what they'd lent. Most folk dubbed that naught but ignorant talk, of course.

Mabinty brought me up in the hatter's trade, and we made together a capital living. Weaving stiff rushes in summers, steaming thick hat-bodies once the sheep were shorn and the wool felted. By hatting it was that we gained much trade from seafaring men, some honest sailors, others pirates. Men at work upon the back of the sea need shade and shelter, and such men oft throw money about when they find themselves ashore and flush with ducats.

Mabinty and I, we went about breeched, kept our hair cropped close, and called ourselves the Gold Brothers, though some men surely guessed what motherly-daughterly hid beneath our workman's slops. St. Clement were a place where men left well enough alone, where prying into other men's secrets might turn up naught but a gunpowder tattoo.

We covered the heads of dozens of dozens, and of the best customers we kept their measures and preferences in a little book. Sometimes, they'd be lost at sea and Mabinty would have me strike their names through in sepia ink. I suppose were I the decent sort, I'd remember them now, those crossed-out names, but I confess I don't. I did my job well enough, but I never felt inclined toward friendly with the trade.

I tell a lie. Never but for maybe the one.

John Argent were the name he took for himself, but some knew him otherwise by John Scratch, or John Silver. Never met a man with such a gaping ache for all he hadn't got. If John's purse held twenty copper coins, he cursed it for lack of twenty more. Ignorant he weren't, and his rare laugh were catching, but damned if he didn't love the wanting more than any woman, ship, or shoreline. Yearning John! That's what I called him, and I'll never forget the day I first clapped my gaze upon him.

§

Ye look surprised. Aye, she knew him, did Celie, the pirate called John Argent. Spoke of him a-times when I were a wee one, mostly by the name of Yearning John.

"Your Yearning John?" I'd always ask, and she'd tug one of my braids, laughing.

"More yourn than mine, child."

All I own of John Argent though, be bound up with my mother's tales like twisted strands of rope.

Sorting through her things after…well, I found the strongbox, a mahogany chest as broad as long, forearm-high and fitted out in brasswork. Locked it was, but Celie herself would have grinned to watch how fast I picked it open. Never yet has there been a device or contraption of metal and wood I couldn't master with a bit of time and toolwork.

When I first put back the lid, I nearly wept at the familiar smells of tobacco and tar, Celie's ever present scent more dear than any French toilet-water or rare perfume. Within the sea-chest I found the blackened parchment scraps, the bottle, a few curious shells. The thick leather folio of letters and documents crabbed with ink.

And beneath the folio, the Medusa.

But the sun is sinking and I must light the wick, and set the clockwork spinning at the tower's head. It won't take but a trice, I'm up and down those stairs in a wink. Believe ye me, there's more to say and then some, if we're to speak of the Medusa, but time and tide wait for no man, or woman as the case may be. While I'm at my duty, you're free to read a piece or two of correspondence. Here.

§

My yearning John,

How fits your new hat? I know ye must find it of frequent use. When next the Cassandra *makes berth at St. Clement, I hope to clap my gaze upon it. Always do enjoy to see how well my crafts weather the world.*

I give ye joy of your new position. The master's mate of the No Forgiveness *were by this morn to see his hat re-blocked, and brought word of your good fortune. Ye make a fine quartermaster, I've no doubt.*

You're a troublesome man, John Argent. I find I cannot shake ye from the corners of my thoughts. Don't make too much of that, mind. Send me news by this flask, hove far abeam in deep water. The bottle will ever come back to me.

Or, if ye've no mind to, don't. I care not. Never your Celie Gold

Celie— I ain't a man much given to penmanship, and I'd leave rather act than speak. Ye'll see my hat soon enough, mark. Never's a word I never heed.

John Argent

I heard his voice before I saw him. I stood over the workbench pulling a top-grade indigo felt when a man's hearty ahoy pealed through the open doors to the street. His tall form stood framed in the doorway, arms akimbo, feet planted wide. His silhouette revealed the outlines of sturdy boots, a frayed coat hem. Clearly a fellow with a wealth of confidence.

I knew I shouldn't look too close; I saw plain he'd be one for Old Viv. Mabinty oft would warn, "Old Viv'll ever have first pick of all the men what walk the shores of St. Clement. Best you pay the lot no mind. We're far from St. Clement now, my girl, amongst our lighthouse-shoals, so don't ye concern yourself with the spectre of Old Viv. Now that you're grown, I'll tell ye true: she be nothing but a bedtime story."

The fellow squinted into the dank steam of the blocking room and stepped inside. On his head, I smile to think, was the sorriest straw hat I'd ever laid my gaze upon.

"Ahoy, I say. Where's your master, boy? I aim to buy three well-made hats from him today."

I laughed as I pushed the block into the brick chamber of the drying oven.

"Ain't no masters at Gold Brothers." I spat into the corner. "Ain't no boys, neither."

The fellow's spine grew straighter and I could see he weren't the apologizing type. No matter, gold's gold to Celie Gold and jobs were mine for choosing. Mabinty'd been gone nigh two years by then, 'twas only me what ran the place. The Gold Brothers sign—two leafed hats above two men's heads—reminded me of the space she used to take up in my life.

I filched my tobacco pouch out of my apron and began to roll a cigarillo, heading for the back door.

"Step out here in the yard," I called to him over my shoulder, "and tell me more about these hats ye seek."

§

Ye'll forgive me my delay. The workings of the rotor screeched for oiling, and a lone damned rafter pigeon had befouled the Fresnel's eye. Too, perhaps, the up and down of twelve-score stairs cost a bit of time and then some.

The Medusa transfixed me as I see it do ye now, these odd brass spider-legs dangling from the carapace. Note these weird carvings, the mother-of-pearl buttons clustered round the perimeter like bubbles on the tide-froth. Handle her gently, she's a complex contraption. Might be mistook for some fell offspring of a clockwork octopus or mechanical sea-jelly, don't ye think? Watch the spines there under the hatch, ye'll prick your finger. I promise ye they're sharp enough to puncture skin.

The Medusa was my mother's prize possession. She claimed old Mabinty'd made it, that she witnessed its assembly as a knee-high child, but it bears no maker's mark that I can see.

I presumed Celie'd ditched it on St. Clement, when she renounced the hatter's trade and took me, a babe in arms, away up here to start a new vocation, the keeping of the light. She oft made mention of the thing, told me how she used it to precisely conform hats to heads of fancy patrons.

"Naught can take the measure of a man as does Medusa," Celie often said.

Take note: the carapace settles atop the head, in exact the fashion of a hat, while the brass tentacles wrap closely round the cranium's span. The hatter lifts this oval hatch here— yes, it's cuttlebone—and there, ye see the spindles. Impaled upon them's where the conform's made, perforated on a slip of parchment.

Certainly I might show ye how it operates, if ye wish. Place her on your head, and I will fetch a scrap of paper. Never trouble yeself—the sensation's odd, but not painful. Countless other dozens have withstood the Medusa's embrace. The conforms of famous men line the walls of

Celie's strongbox, see? We may add yourn to the collection, just for fun.

§

I propped my boot on the ledge of the well in the close round back of the shop, studied the smoke curling from my nigh-gone cigarillo. I rolled around in my head how to sell this man what I needed him buying. He showed too much pride to take advice from the likes of anyone, but too much ignorance to know particulars of what to order. He'd be formidable one day, but today he were only bluff and bold.

Not a handsome man, was John Argent, I recall thinking, though perhaps he might have been, once shaven and bathed. His English jaw were cleft and stubbled, and the sun had run her fingers through his tangled hair. Had he been a planter or a scholar, I'd have called him thirty years of age, but the sea puts time on a man's face faster than landed living, so perhaps he were five or ten years younger.

"Two of rushes, one of felt, ye say?"

"Aye. The hats of rushes may be plain-fashioned, but the felt's to be the finest quality."

"I follow," I nodded. "The hats of rushes, I'll send with ye directly. The felt, if it's to be the finest and for true, I'll need to see the man who'll wear it. Send your captain by anon. I'll need his head for conformation."

John Argent's eyes darkened, taking my bait, and I saw I'd gauged him rightly.

I put kindness in my smile to reel him in, let off the steam from pressure built between us.

"Beg pardon, I misjudge. That finest hat, it's for yourself then?"

He nodded once, a curt lift of the chin. I tossed the spent cigarillo into the dirt and ground it 'neath my boot heel.

"'Tis rare a foremast jack wants the finest felt complete with conform. I should have known ye by your bearing for a man with higher sights. Come, let's introduce ye to Medusa."

§

Celie—The gunner and I are of a mind to leave Cassandra *when we see this voyage through. The captain be too fond of drink. Perhaps it's he who'll leave the ship. Perhaps it's I who'll persuade him. Time will tell. I told ye I were not the sort for writing reams, but I find ye clinging to the shape of my thoughts. It can't be healthy for a man to be distracted so. I witness well this bottle-magic ye be party to for passing letters swift between us. Perhaps ye've other secrets I've no knowledge of. I only know my mind feels part my own, but leans ever toward ye, never my Gold.*

John Argent

§

John Argent sat too-stiffly in the leather-upholstered chair centered in my conforming salon. He placed a short stack of gold ducats on the mahogany tabletop, trued them carefully with his fingers.

"That's her?" He eyed the Medusa warily. They all do at first.

"Aye, but 'tis only fun to call it 'she.' Naught but brass and wood, shell and bone. She's no more creature living than spyglass or diving bell."

Each time I used it, well I recollected all the days she labored on it, my own damn Mabinty, all the diagrams she sketched, the brass parts machined exactly to her liking and bolted gently to the carapace she'd carved. The night she came home with the cuttlebone from which she'd form the hatch. 'Twas in those days, when I were young as ye were, daughter-mine, when first from me ye learned the keeping of our shore-light, and yet I recollect them clear as yesterday. Mabinty ever tinkered with the thing, allowing me more freedom with our tradework, entrusting me with blocking and with steaming, cutting down the brims to perfect curves, while ever she passed hours with her weird-wrought second daughter, the Medusa.

As I knelt before John Argent setting the device upon his brow, I glimpsed a blue tattoo in the hollow of his throat: an anchor within the sickle's curve of a moon's crescent. A sailor's patron saint's mark, an image to recall him by.

From the small drawer beneath the table I took a piece of parchment, flensed and stretched from whaleskin: the orca, black on one side and sallow on the other. The Medusa's brass wrought arms encircled his head, gripping tightly to his temples, as I slid the parchment beneath the hinged cuttlebone.

"It is an odd sensation," he observed, "but not unpleasant."

A squeeze of the two brass anglers and the spindles pierced the parchment. I lifted the hatch and removed the perforated bit of skin, gently punched free the ragged black spot—the conform of John Argent. Like each man before him, he seemed to feel no different than mere moments ago.

Poor tar, I thought. Will ye remember me when Old Viv comes to claim ye? Come she will and no mistake. But I put that thought aside. Better him than me, work's work.

Beneath the curving carapace of the Medusa, John Argent's brassy-threaded hair hung slack in a greasy sailor's queue. A flash across my vision: that hair unbound, drifting in a seaweed cloud deep below the ocean's surface, lit beneath with phosphorescent glow...

I shook my head and laughed, lifting the Medusa and replacing it in its case.

"Share the joke, hatter."

"By the powers, I only had the strangest thought: I'd like to neaten up that queue of yourn."

I met his gaze, watched his face slowly change to something guileless and greedy. Something up next to yearning.

"Would ye, now?"

I gave him my back to look at and pinned the conform to the corkboard on the wall.

"I've work to do. Return at sunset."

I heard his footfall, felt him fill the space behind me.

"Sunset?" His hand settled on my shoulder blade. The fabric of my work shirt felt uncomfortably thin, and I shrugged roughly.

"For your hats."

Snatching his ducats from the tabletop, I crossed into the blocking room and shut the doors behind me.

§

My yearning John,

Ye guessed the Gold Brothers secret aright, after your fashion, and perhaps it sets your mind at ease for me to say it.

The Medusa came from the same source as the bottle-glamour, a peddler woman Mabinty called Old Viv. The device be naught but a bit of salesman's duff—while it takes its measure, it engenders a buyer's fealty. My hats be good enough, but what hurt's a bit of lagniappe? Be not too sore about it, John; I know ye well enough to guess the conform-spell makes only bits and portions of the fullness of your longing. Coveting's ever been your favorite sin but one, I'll wager.

Never your Celie Gold

§

What is there to say of his return at sunset?

I preferred it when they took the hats and took their leave. It weren't for me to bind my fate with theirs no more than fortune forces such a thing. But John Argent's pride drew something in me like a compass needle, and the strength of his yearning for power and fortune swirled around us like a vortex.

I settled the grey felt hat upon his brow, its brim cocked up to show his smile in the firelight. I spied a gap in the side, a tooth missing behind the incisor, hidden when his face sat stern.

"Never wore a thing so fine," he said, running a scarred forefinger along the sueded underbrim.

"That much is clear."

His smile remained. "Ye ken no sweet words, do ye, hatter?"

"Celie."

"Eh?"

"They call me Celie Gold. Been a free woman all my life and hope to die one when I go. Those be the sweetest words I hold."

I took two glasses from the sideboard, poured us draughts of spirits from a short-necked bottle.

He drank his down in one. I only swirled mine in amber eddies.

"Shall ye leave the hat on all the night, or could ye bear to put it by, and allow me smoothing of that plait of yourn?"

John Argent grinned with half his mouth. I placed a cushion on the floor below the conformation chair and indicated that he shift himself there as I sat.

"Settle back," and he complied, sliding his shoulders into the crook of my thighs. John Argent startled when I drew the dagger from my boot.

"Peace, friend. I only mean to cut the tie."

"Peace, friend." The timbre of his voice tested the phrase as if it were composed of foreign words. Then he but nearly relaxed, and I indicated with a gesture he shouldn't stand on ceremony.

"Drink straight from the bottle for all I care."

The braid lay limp in my pale palm like a bight of rope, and I curled it round the edge of my fist where the color of my skin shifts from light to dark. I unwove the queue and began to pick the tangles from his locks.

We sat in silence for a time before he spoke to break it.

"How came ye to be a hatter, gal?"

"How came ye to be a pirate?"

He laughed, a rich sound and catching, let me fight the snarls a piece longer before he spoke again.

"Sincere, what of the Gold Brothers? Kin of yourn?"

"Nay, I be one. My mother were the second. 'Twas but a ruse to bring men into the shop, no market here for ladies' hats."

"So, the other brother were your mother?"

His rhyming jest drew forth a grin.

"She'd smile as well, to hear ye say it thus, if she still walked upon the earth."

"Did illness take her?"

"Nay. She strode into the sea one night and never stepped foot out again."

"I'm sorry for your loss, Celie Gold."

I pushed his shoulders forward, swung myself out of the chair and planted my feet to either side of him.

"I don't want your pity, John Argent."

I put out my open hand to show my words weren't meant to sting. He took it and I pulled him to his feet so we stood eye-to-eye.

"It's not my pity I'm offering." He handed me the bottle and I took a swig of sweet burn.

"*Cassandra* sails tomorrow with the tide, does she not?" My voice was thick with liquor.

"She does," he nodded. "Does that trouble ye?"

"Nay, it's to your favor."

He was true to his word. He was gone upon the morning tide.

Read between these lines, my girl. There's truths ye ought to know.

§

Pardon, I don't mean to interrupt ye, but I do know one more thing that might be helpful. 'Tis no document, but a tale.

Each night, after we'd set the lighthouse beam to turning and the sun had sunk below the sea, Celie'd tell me bedtime stories as she braided my hair in the tight rows I liked best. John Argent were the hero of my favorite. The story's been tugging at my thoughts again of late, in light of all I found in Celie's strongbox. Perhaps ye'd like to hear it?

Once upon a time, there were a fearsome pirate named John Argent, who served as quartermaster aboard the ship *Cassandra*. This pirate John feared nothing, beast or man, but he had a secret weakness in his heart: his very soul was captured by a woman named Cecilia. When he were not in battle or stupefied in taverns, he thought of nothing but his darling gal.

Cecilia'd been a motherless child and fickle with her heart. The less she gave the more he yearned. On voyages, she occupied his thoughts both day and night, though truth be told he knew not why. It felt somehow unnatural: Cecilia wrote him letters of all the ways she did not care, how much she did not love him. Yearning John (for yearn he did) felt so very low, threw himself without regard into fierce battles for treasure and glory, and by and large he made a scrap of legend for himself.

One day, a day like any other, John saw a bottle bobbing on the waves. He fished it out, and inside was a letter. It said, *"My yearning John—Come to me swift. Claim what ye long for. Love, Cecilia."*

When next the *Cassandra* came into port, Yearning John stepped firstmost off the gangplank, but Cecilia were not upon the pier to welcome him with open arms. He made his way to her wee house and rushed inside, but she were nowhere to be found. Aye, but he'd been thinking with his mind. When he stopped in silence and considered what he sensed, he knew: she meant for him to meet her on the shore, a close-curved cove whose sands they'd walked a time or two.

His ship had come in with the evening tide but now the ebb were creeping off, and when he reached the cove the sands were long and strewn with wrack. He saw her then, Cecilia, the water to her knees and wading further, alone among the waves.

"Cecilia!" John called out in the ringing voice he used aboard his ship. In the quiet twilight of the ebbing tide, she couldn't fail to hear him but she did not turn nor cease her progress. He started toward her, pulling off his boots—the waves lapped nearly at her waist—but stumbled in his tracks at what he witnessed then.

The head and shoulders of a woman burst from the deep like a sleek sealion and she swam steadily toward Cecilia. The woman's sweeping arms were odd-skinned, spotted and dark-glistening like deep-sea fish. As she arced through the water, John felt a coldness in his throat. Her human shape transitioned at the waist into a smoothly bulbous sac. Below, John spied the swiveling eyes and curling tentacles of an octopus, and he recognized from tavern-talk the nature of the creature: a stauroteuth. Her bloom of tentacles beat in pulses, moving the creature ever closer to Cecilia, and her suckers phosphoresced in strange patterns, unsettling and otherworldly.

"Cecilia!" he screamed, but stopped short of weapons drawn: the stauroteuth's woman-half rose upright and enfolded his beloved in a motherly embrace.

"I tried to ever follow how ye taught me," she said to the creature, which laid a web-fingered hand upon her cheek.

And so it was John understood, Cecilia's absent mother were gone but not deceased.

A third figure rose from the waves behind them then, and in the gloaming eclipsed the embracing women's silhouettes. John gasped and forced himself to stand fast before the horror—what first appeared to be a colossal cuttlefish soon showed itself another sort of hybrid, with the armor-pincered limbs of a crustacean, human breasts and hips draped in swags of seaweed. For this creature, John knew no drunkard's name.

The leviathan cuttlewoman carved a grotesque figure against the sky, as the sea-thing's head-flesh gave way to a slender human throat. Around it hung a delicate chain of coral branchwork, from which dangled three oval pendants of a size that could fit in the palm of a man. Each appeared at first to be a cameo of sorts, outlines of women's profiles but bordered unevenly like gourds. John had seen those shapes before, on a hatter's bench. Conforms.

John Argent drew his pair of pistols, but Cecilia and the stauroteuth surged between him and the cuttlewoman.

"Ye cannot kill her, John."

"I'll see the color of her insides, mark me."

"Nay. I'm lying not: ye cannot kill her. No man can kill Old Viv."

John Argent cocked both pistols. "Step aside and watch me, gal."

"I won't. These be unknown waters, John. Gunpowder and steel might serve ye well in shipboard battles with earthly men, but they'll fail ye certain here."

The cuttlewoman whiffled, sounds like rushing water over rocks, her claws clicking like the turning of a capstan's wheel. The sea around her turned a murky black. Then, like a marching army advancing up a hill, the forms of men began rising from the waves. John watched, incredulous. Drops of salt spume clung to their chests, locks of seaweed strewn amongst their hair. Their eyes scummed over with a dull-white gleam like those of cave fish. They stopped a short piece offshore, the sea lapping at their waists. Beneath the waves, John spied an unearthly glow. He felt bile rise in his throat.

Like Cecilia's stauroteuth mother, the men too had no legs. Where their hips should have jutted, instead their skin ballooned out into the fragile glowing bells of sea-jelly caps, tentacles underhanging and drifting in the currents. The skirt-like umbrellums curled and pulsed in a strange choreography, maintaining the equilibrium of the torsos above. John knew them from rumor, legend; these were the Cnidar.

"How does this concern me?" John Argent asked Cecilia. Her smile was tinged with sadness.

"Understand: 'tis Old Viv makes the Cnidar. She began by chance, sailors washed overboard or those what once manned ships sunken in her waters, but soon she developed preferences, as a knitter gains a taste for finer yarns the more she works. Ye fit exactly to her liking, John."

"Be that so, now?"

"Aye."

"And how do ye fit to her liking?"

"I've only ever known the life to which I'm born. My mother struck a bargain with Old Viv and left no chosen part for me to play."

"Ye've ever a choice, gal."

"No, no more than ye had choice of aught to come to me. So long as Old Viv holds my conform, I be ever loyal to her. Mark, ye spy my profile as the pendant hangs to larboard."

"Damn the Medusa, I'll be no poppet cut in twain." John swung his right arm out and aimed a pistol at the stauroteuth who swam beside Cecilia.

"No!" Cecilia screamed. She leapt between the creature and his weapon, launching herself out of the path between the cuttlewoman and the pirate. John did not fire the first gun, but as Cecilia dragged the stauroteuth beneath the waves, he raised his left hand and discharged the second pistol straight into the tentacle cluster of Old Viv's face.

The cuttlewoman shrieked, an unearthly sound of doom like the hull of a ship dragged open on treacherous shoals. She surged forward in the surf, ichor streaming from beneath her whipping mouthparts. The water hindered John's agility—Old Viv pinned him to the sea floor, then hefted him aloft. The Cnidar shimmered, closing round them like some strange mockery of a bar brawl or a dogfight. Pain dropped a red scrim across his vision as he felt Old Viv's claw cut through the meat of his thigh. John bellowed, reached out and snatched Cecilia's conform from the chain around the monster's throat.

Then he saw two things in flashes: his leg, ragged and bloody, falling into the sea below; and Cecilia, pulling a dagger from somewhere beneath the waves and driving it through the cuttlewoman's slender neck. Then all went blacker than the deepest sea.

He came to days later, tucked into a bed, feverish, one-legged, but alive.

"How..?"

Cecilia hushed him. "She's dead, Old Viv is. The Cnidar tore her form to pieces before I could even pull my dagger free."

"I thought ye said no man could kill her," he gasped, his eyes rolling as the pain rushed in and wracked his broken body.

"Aye, no man could," Cecilia said. "But I be no man, John Argent."

And so it was, that Yearning John Argent lost his leg to the fell creature of the deep, the cuttlewoman Old Viv, but won the heart of his darling Cecilia. In time, John learned to get about with the help of a stick to lean upon, and he and Cecilia bought an inn called the Spy-Glass. John took up as a galley cook and Cecilia kept the bar and the books, and they never again saw skin nor shine of any creature wrong-grafted from land and sea together.

§

My yearning John—

The conform I burned before your face was my own, not yourn, which I return to ye now. Ye can't pretend to own any part of me no longer; own thyself and well may it suit ye. It almost pains me to confess my ruse. Almost. Ye know I never felt for ye sincere.

When next ye find yourself in St. Clement, don't look for me. I'll not be found. I'm done with this life—the island, Gold Brothers, all of it. May it all rot and fall into the sea.

Send the flask back if ye wish, I care not.

Always and ever, never your Celie Gold

Celie—A sentimental man might destroy your mementos, but I reckon I'll never find a better hat. Give my regards to your mother. John Argent

§

Aye, that were always how she told the story, and I should hope I know, I heard it much enough. I honest couldn't tell ye which of it is true, and which no more than tales to spook a babe at bedtime. I know what's set down in that journal, and the sheaf of letters, and ye see the Medusa with your own two eyes. I've heard it said John Argent goes about one-legged and becrutched. I'll own I've never met the man.

I know Celie dove into that sea one night, a night the tidewrack glowed upon the sand, and never swam back to shore. Sometimes, I walk the gallery round the edge of the lantern room and look far out to sea. And sometimes, I think I see her there, sleek and glistening, her legs replaced by phosphorescent skirts, the thrashing arms of a stauroteuth.

But I know that's little more than a daughter's grief, made manifest in phantom visions.

Oh, yes. What of your conform? Do ye believe these tales are true? I suppose I might keep it in a locket round my throat, damn ye to a lighthouse prison and walk into the surging sea as my mother did before me. Perhaps, as her own mother had as well.

But as I told ye at the start, this lamp-lit life suits me fine.

Robin Hood and the Eater of Worlds

Jim Mortimore

"Look to yourself. The Devil is loose!"
Message from King Philip of France to Prince John on the Ransome of Richard Lionheart, 1194

1

The merchant had been a trap.

That much was obvious now. But *obvious now* didn't fill bellies, load sacks with valves or pistons, fuelsprings or fireglasses. Didn't save an adopted father from the black lungrot. *Obvious now* put you on the backfoot, on the run. *Obvious now* got you killed, or worse. Unless–

The Wolfshead ran.

All the greywood cloaked him in winter silver.

The merchant had been lean, his daughter a prize, both worthy of respect even when taken at point of knife. Their perambulator –loaded with parts for a high temperature foundry walking the river track fast from Axedge to Hordron – was an easy target. The carriage, hydraulics violated, wheezed in bitter complaint before squatting in the greywood to take its repose, half in and half out of the fast–running Axe. There it would stay, slowly rusting until broken for spares by the other outlaws while the merchant and his daughter accompanied him to what – if they lied when questioned as to their wealth – would undoubtedly be their last meal.

A good plan and true. It had worked time and again for many years. In that respect perhaps it was too good. For neither merchant nor daughter were exactly what they seemed. In fact they were mercenaries and they walked the greywood not just with riches but also a mission.

He was their mission. Their target.

They hunted him now, running with a speed that could only mean body springs. If he could keep ahead of them until the springs unwound then he might stand a chance of escape. His springbow could plant an arrow in a sapling at three leagues. All he needed was the space to use it. Once the hunters had been dealt with he could turn to the matter of the perambulator, to acquiring the tech that might save Alun of Wrexham's life. But he'd been running for an hour now, and the hunters showed no sign of stopping, even of slowing.

The Wolfshead ran. His chest and legs burning, his mind a white glare. He understood the hunters' trap when the greywood thinned, the forest of high, dead stems opening onto a bluff. Axe Falls. From here there was only one way out – and none had ever survived the jump.

He reached the edge of the cliff, turned to face the hunters as they came out of the greywood. Their faces were lean, almost beautiful, especially the woman's. They were dressed in boiled leather and castle–forged alloy, the man shaved, the woman's hair stripped to raven wings that ran, double–ridged from forehead to the nape of her neck. They carried no scars, so successful were they at their work. Their clothes and wigs had been shed with their noble trappings. Their muscles bunched with internal clockwork. Their breath came easily. The Wolfshead, back to a high winter rainbow, retreated slowly towards the falls. He raised his springbow and knocked his last arrow. One of the dogs at least would follow him to Cromm's Great Hall. And maybe when he met Alun there his adopted father would forgive him for his failure.

The hunters advanced with measured paces, tasting the air. This was an old pattern for them, Cromm's dance and death an old friend. They nocked and drew. Bodysprings meant they could hold those bows at full tension for an hour. His own arm was already feeling the burn of holding an arrow at full draw. He could take one of them with him, not both. He cast a fast look behind him. The heel of his boot found the edge of the cliff.

The Axe fell, and roared, and fell.

The hunters advanced.

He loosed, turned, sprang from the cliff into the abyss.

He twisted. His back arched. Time slowed. Twin arrows split the sky above his face. One parted his long hair with a sigh like a lover's breath. His gaze caught on them and the perfect winter sky lost focus. The arrows were laminated alloy, jet black, the blue–umber smear at the blunted tips a bright familiar thread.

Not killing arrows, then.

The Wolfshead fell, plunging into the rainbow mist, lost in dazzling colour, the falls from which no jumper had ever returned. There was one last thought as he fell. The Wolfshead found he wanted to see his idiot brother again very badly. Just once before the Warlock of Nottingham burned his second home as he had the first, for the taxes the village could no longer pay. Then he struck the water and the shock drove every thought from his head and every scrap of breath from his body.

He sank. He was nothing. Nothing but pain and cold. Then instinct kicked in and the man kicked as well, for the surface, for life.

He broke water, sucked in great gulps of freezing air, body numb and shaking. His springbow was gone, lost in the fall. Above him rainbows danced, conjuror's flame. Above that, the hunters, gazing with confident curiosity down from the cliff.

The Wolfshead grinned and waved, let the current swirl him away.

His smile only widened when the woman nocked an arrow. No-one could make a shot at this distance, and indeed the arrow fell hopelessly short. He was still smiling when the fireglass bound to the arrowhead loosed a full charge into the water.

Lightning flashed inside Robin of Loxley's head and the world turned to glass.

2

The broken girl screamed as the world inside her head turned to glass.

The girl was sixteen summers old. Her mind had been violated deliberately and systematically every month since her seventh birthday. By any definition of the word she was insane. A broken girl with the body of an angel and nothing to fill it. Nothing except the visions which the Coven of Cromm Cruac deemed so useful.

The broken girl screamed again. Her voice carried a raw edge of pain and despair and white–hot love that would have driven any man, let alone a father, sobbing to his knees.

Tuck heard the broken girl's voice and was unmoved. It was his job to be unmoved. If not him then who else would shape her? One of the Coven's many sadists, perhaps. Certainly no–one who cared for her as he did.

Tuck, a huge man by any reckoning, turned sideways to squeeze into Marion's cell. He was dressed in dark robes, wore shaggy hair past his shoulders. His plump fingertips were stained a scarlet so dark it was almost black. The red was his mark, as much a part of him as his name. Tuck committed atrocities every day in the name of Cromm and the red fingers were symbolic of this, a celebration of the blood he shed, the minds he broke, the lives he moulded in response to his Lord Cromm's needs.

Now Tuck took a bowl of water from beneath his robes and held it to the broken girl's fluttering mouth. He muttered a quick benediction over it. "Cromm protect us, Cromm within us, Cromm bless our children and our mines, Cromm within us, Cromm protect us."

The broken girl's eyes rolled in her head. Only the whites showed. She was naked, lathered with condensation or sweat; skin like waxed parchment, just as wet and white as her eyes. Her face was a scream made flesh. The broken girl was a ghost in the darkness, a sliver of ice in the skeletal finger of light from the cell's high, narrow window.

"Trust me child," Tuck murmured. "I haven't lost a subject yet. I certainly won't begin with the one nearest my heart."

Taking a glass phial from a pocket in his robes, Tuck added three drops of poison to the bowl of water and then spat in it. Stirring the bowl with his fingertips, he waited for the right moment before carefully trickling the mixture into the girl's mouth.

The broken girl choked, then swallowed, gulping eagerly. Tuck did not waver. This was an old pattern, one that hadn't varied for almost a decade.

Her mouth closed, her voice stilled; her eyes did not.

Tuck set down the bowl.

"Tell me what you see, child," he said tenderly.

"I see an idiot…" her voice was parchment thin. Tuck closed his eyes, saw what she saw with those bone–white eyes. "… an idiot and a Knight, with heads of wolves… The Knight is–"

broken. He tends sheep and drinks too much. The idiot is broken too. He laughs too much. He's not laughing now. His brother has been lost. Lost to the hunters… lost to the shadow–giant. The idiot has his brother's weapon. All he could find at the foot of the falls. The Wolfsheads want their brother – their leader – back. Their anger is like fire, like metal in a forge. It runs molten through their minds. Their voices… smoke and bitter flame… a trap… someone laid a trap for them, and now their leader is caught. But they have a plan, smoke and flame, fire and pain, they have a plan to get him back.

"Tell me what you see, child…" Tuck's voice stole into her head, drifting through the blown glass of her mind.

The broken girl spoke again and this time her voice was thunder. The voice of a Knight, deep, with a faint metallic edge, burst from her fragile lips.

"The answer's bloody obvious isn't it? The Warlock's got Robin so we'll take something precious to him. We'll take his bloody Ward. She's the nearest thing he has to a daughter. They need her for their bloody ceremonies. We'll take the witchgirl and force a trade."

The broken girl cringed suddenly back against the cell wall. When she spoke again her voice was higher, the voice of a young man.

"I just wants him back John. He's my brother and I misses him. I'm afeared here without him. There are ghosts in the greywood, everyone knows it. Ghosts in the greywood and I wants my brother back!"

The broken girl stood suddenly, muscles cracking, body arching upward, a giant in the body of a child. The voice that came out of her was huge and dark as her shadow on the stone wall.

"Get away you idiot. The only ghosts in Sherwood are the ones the Warlock put here with his bloody mines. To hell with the ghosts! To hell with the Warlock! Tonight we travel to Biford. We take the bloody girl and get Robin back. Now who's with me?"

The broken girl's arms snapped out, fingers stretched and quivering, as if held by wires. Her mouth gaped and a torrent of voices spilled out. Five, ten, twenty, fifty. A pack of Wolves. Howling, shrieking. Blood. Blood.

Tuck touched the broken girl's brow, felt the fever there, the poison running her body and mind.

"How many, child?" His voice was gentle. "How many wolves do you see?"

She howled. She shrieked. There would be no more sense from her now, Tuck knew. All he could do was let the poison run its course and guard her in repose.

The broken girl fell, a doll and all its strings cut. She fell to the floor and lay twitching. Drool ran from the sides of her mouth. The drool was streaked with blood where she'd bitten her tongue, her lips, the inside of her cheeks. Tuck's mind whirled as he covered her with a clean blanket. A pack of Wolves. Coming here. To Biford. Tonight.

Tuck leaned over the girl, breathing hard with the exertion of moving that enormous girth. "Hear me child," His voice was a whisper. "You're perfectly safe. Nothing can reach you here in the Temple. Cromm within us, Cromm protect us." The girl's shivering began to subside. "Sleep child. Sleep and fear not wolf or evil. For none can touch you here."

And Marion of Biford, Ward of the shadow–giant otherwise known as the Warlock of Nottingham, did precisely as she was bid.

3

The dungeons were black night and icy damp, festering sores and screams wrapped in castle–forged alloy. Chained in the darkest corner, Robin lay huddled in a sleep close to death while a man dressed in blood and hate shrieked of lions and the end of the world.

"They called it the Black Crusade but in truth it weren't black, oh no, not black at all, but all the colours of madness.

The only black in that foul unholy land was whatever shrieking thread of humanity remained in our minds when that light was finally done with us."

The madman's words, prowling the dungeons like a banshee, provoked a further series of protests from other prisoners. Not from Robin.

The hunters. The fireglass–

"Where–?"

"The colours, they sucked us dry, sucked our souls like pips from fruit and left the rest to rot, oh Scarlet. The colours are in his head, every day. They're all he sees, Scarlet. *All he sees!* He fights them, praise Cromm, he fights them tooth and claw. But they're not done with him yet. They call to him, voices like leeches, sucking his soul. They are glory and terror, a treasury of madness. He knows they'll be the end of him but still he'd look on them again. He wants to go back, Scarlet. Back to the Unholy Land. Back to the colours. They call to him. *They call to him!*"

The voice shuddered and shrieked, stretching the vowels to long whispers more terrifying than any scream.

Robin groped in the darkness, found rags, torn skin, slippery with blood. "Where is this place?" He knew the answer already, spoke evenly in the hope that it would soothe some of the madness from the screamer. "Who are you?"

"The colours, *the colours!*" There was a crunch and a horrible sucking noise. "He is blood and fire, and hate, Scarlet, oh yes… He is hate made flesh… one colour that all the others may see it and leave Scarlet, leave him in the dark and never come again..."

The voice in the darkness swelled and splashed, a tide of horror.

"They Knight us, dress us in alloy and fireglass, send us to fight the Monstrosities. But you can't fight them, no, for they put their madness in you with their damned colours! They put it in him too. In the Lion, oh Scarlet and Gold. They caught him and put their colours in him, made him one of them. They want to put their colours in everyone. In all of us. *You mark what I say!* They'll put their colours in all of us and we won't be us anymore we'll be them, oh Scarlet, *them* and the Crusade will be done and they'll have won! *WE ARE DAMNED AND THE BLACK COLOURS IN THE KING WILL EAT THE WORLD!!*"

The madman's voice capered around the dungeons and a shambling host of moans and wailing followed in its wake. Robin pushed back along the metal wall as far as his chains would allow. Eventually the echo of that last terrible cry died away and silence came. But it wasn't over. Not yet. A hushed sigh, the slither of flesh against metal, then a diseased breath upon his face as, from less than a handspan away, the voice came again, cold and slow, a graveyard whisper.

"The Lion will eat the world, oh Scarlet, eat it all…"

The crunching, licking sound came again in the darkness. Robin realised it was the sound of the madman chewing and sucking at his own flesh, painting himself the colour from which he took his name, a horrifying comfort.

A moment later, something cold and hard and covered with hot slime was pressed against Robin's face. His hand raised without thought and the madman's skeletal dripping fingers closed around it. Robin could not help the disgusted noise which escaped his lips.

"This is for you. The Godstone of Yog Sothoth. All the way from the Unholy Land. All the way from blackest night itself. It was for the King, to win the war, but he'll not want it now, not now. So you have it, you keep it safe. When Scarlet fades and goes to the black, you remember, oh Scarlet, remember the colours. They call to me, oh Scarlet, *they call to me…*"

Robin felt as much as heard the weight of a body fall against the metal floor, fetched up tight by the clanking chain. A moment later warmth lapped at his legs and Robin knew it was the madman's blood, near all he had left.

Robin was still holding the object Scarlet had given him when soldiers dragged the madman's body away. They threw a bucket of water across the blood stained floor to sluice away the worst of the muck.

After the soldiers left a deep hush fell on the dungeon, a cold void filled with dark mutterings and the occasional pitiable wail.

Four days passed before the crash of metal hatches came again. Light bloomed in the dungeon. Robin shrank away from the agony of it, eyes tight shut.

Footsteps. Punches. Moans. Abuse in the voices of soldiers.

"This one. And this? This one still has meat on him." A well–fed voice. A Priest's voice. "This one too. Cromm save us, is this the best you can muster? The Temple Lords will not be pleased!"

"My lord, these dogs are all we–"

"I will hear no excuses!" the voice roared.

Footsteps rang close to Robin's head.

"And who is this? He looks healthy enough. Unchain him."

"My lord, this one is not supposed to be–"

"One more word and your name will be spoken. Just a whisper but you know what a whisper can do in the right ear. The Warlock's ear…"

"But my Lord it was the Warlock himself who–"

A sudden cry of pain. "My arm!"

"Unlock this man that I may leave this festering hole or next time it will be your tongue that will taste the Milk of Cromm."

Robin's chains fell away.

"Who are you? What do you want?"

The Priest's voice spoke soothingly. "Do not trouble yourself to speak my son. Your pain will soon be over. Cromm within us. Cromm protect us. I will take care of you. An offering for the Lord of the Moon that our Knights may emerge triumphant from the night into the day. Your lives for our Lord's victory in the Unholy Land."

The chains fell away and Robin was hauled painfully to his feet. A bowl pressed against his face.

"Drink and sleep with Cromm."

Robin spat. "Poison? If you want my death then give me a sword and fight me! Or choose your champion. I'll fight anyone!"

"I have no doubt of it my son. But this is not your death. That commodity is far too valuable to waste in the dungeons of Nottingham Castle."

Robin felt a soldier's mailed glove grasp his face, forcing his mouth open. Cold jelly splashed against his lips, his throat. There was no taste or smell. He choked, then tried to shout, to curse.

Sleep took him first.

4

Marion of Biford moaned and shook, her breath a fire in her chest. The world was glass. Fireglass, and the burning of it was a blight on her soul. Tuck moved beside her, soft hands and voice, soothing. His lips moved close to her ears. His words slithered deep into the broken maze that was her mind.

"The wolves, child. Tell me what you see."

"The Man I' the Hood is here. The Eater of Worlds to come. His heart is black and dead. But his hunger… aahhh … that is strong."

Marion shuddered, cold sweat streaming from her waxen face in the dark cell. A fireglass cast black shadows on the cold stone walls. The girl, moon–ghost in the temple night, fluttered and shook.

"The wolves from the greywood–"

walk the grounds of the Temple of Cromm, dressed in smiles, stinking of mead, cheap ale, mulled wine. They are celebrating. They have their leader back. The idiot is dancing, laughing. The knight is laughing too, sitting crosslegged in half–dead armour and still taller than any man standing.

"By the hair and teeth of my mother, Robin it's good to have you back. We thought you were food for the Warlock's dogs – or worse."

The Wolf, lounging near the Knight, nods thoughtfully. "Thank the Priest. He got us out."

"Aye he's a wily bugger and no mistake. Tuck's his name. Caught us like week old rabbits when we came for the girl."

"You John?" Robin smiles. "A week old rabbit?"

Much capered between them. "They had invisible demons, Robin. They made us go to sleep and we never even saw them! I weren't even tired!"

"It wasn't demons. Just witchsmoke, something the Priest made from tree mould."

"Well I says it was demons. The girl called her demons to make us sleep." A shadow passes over the idiot's face. "I didn't like it. Bad dreams."

"It's not demons, Much, for goodness' have a drink and cheer up. John, what does this Tuck want with us, do you know?"

"No idea. He just stopped us, locked us up, told us he'd get you out of the castle if we'd do something in return."

"And what was that?"

The knight shrugged massively. "Stop helping."

The Knight laughs and the wolf – Robin – cannot help but join in.

"And you agreed without knowing what he wanted?"

"We were half bewitched and locked up in a room with stone walls thicker than this idiot…"

"Oy!"

"... I could have knocked a hole in the wall but not before he could put us to sleep again. I didn't see we had a choice. He could have killed us you know."

Robin says nothing.

"Here. Have a drink and wipe that glum look off your face."

But Robin does not drink. Instead he lets his fingers touch the soft stubble of grass, so rare in the greywood, that grows within the temple courtyard walls. His face tilts up to the dim stars, barely visible through inky cloud. Somewhere up there, he thinks, past the smoke from the foundries and open cast mines, is the Moon. Cromm's Great Eye, gazing deep into the world, and who knew what thoughts moved in the mind behind that shining orb.

Robin stands.

"I'm going to see the–"

Marion jerked, a soft explosion of muscle. A sigh came from her lips as her body slapped against the wall. Her eyes blinked, snapped back into focus.

"–Priest. Tuck and the girl. There's something we need to talk about–"

Marion's head jerked once, twice, each movement matching a heavy knock on the wooden door.

"Wait, please."

Tuck took the robe he carried and helped Marion step into it. The material, a delicate weave, felt hot and rough against her skin after the cool, silk–smooth night air of her vision. Marion moved back from the door as the Priest pulled it open, exchanged a few hushed words with the temple novice waiting there, then reached back to take her hand and lead her from the cell.

Tuck's rooms were those of a modest man with modest desires. A hard desk, a harder bed. A small sink, cold running water. His only conceit was a large bookcase filled with books and other objects of interest.

The newest of which paced agitatedly beside the bookcase. "Why did you bring me from Nottingham?" Robin's voice was calm but direct.

"You could be helpful to me." Tuck was equally direct.

Marion moved closer to the Wolfshead and Tuck let her. Robin did not turn as she circled him, close enough to touch. And she did touch him but not with her fingers, her skin.

"The Man I' the Hood comes and his heart is black starstone."

Robin studied the girl. "Everything broken will be made whole."

Hearing the warmth in his voice a child-like smile fluttered about Marion's bloodless lips.

"Something—"

"–your father told you." Marion's smile faded.

"How did you–?"

"Your father was a blacksmith."

"And..."

"My uncle Knighted him."

"Your uncle?"

"The Warlock of Nottingham."

The warmth fell from his face even as his hand fell to the dagger tucked into his belt.

Tuck moved swiftly, soft hands raised to placate the outlaw.

Watching him, Marion saw time itself swirl around them, between them, past and future days, kaleidoscopic images of life and death. The prickling sensation grew in her body. Her breath came out in a shuddering sigh. Her limbs began to tremble.

"The boy." Her voice shrank, her body with it. She crouched suddenly, arms raised as if scooping invisible water into invisible buckets. "The boy is fetching water from the river when the soldiers come for the village tithe–"

Robin's face is white. "That's enough!"

"But the people can't pay so the giant cloaked in shadows draws an ivory handled pistol–grip springbow and shoots a steel bolt through your mother's hazel eye. The fletchings on the bolt quiver with the impact. So does your mother. The boy–"

bites back a cry. His head is filled with the look of surprise on his mother's face as she dies. As she falls the giant rewinds the pistol's fuelspring, speaking loudly as he does so. "This village and everything in it belong to the Crown. Taxes are owed! Since you can no longer supply coal or forge iron you must make payment in other ways."

The villagers shout in fear and anger.

Ignoring them, the giant signals to the carriages. Hatches swing open in each vehicle and more soldiers jump to the ground. The boy gasps, tears streaming down his cheeks. The soldiers are carrying Knights' armour.

The giant signals again. Two soldiers unchain the boy's father and drag him forward. The soldiers force the blacksmith to his knees before the giant, who sheaths his pistol and draws his longsword.

"By the power invested in me by the Crown I, Robert de Reinhardt, Warlock of Nottingham, do Knight you and induct you into the service of the King, to be his Cruacan Warrior, to serve in his army and drive the Invader back to the Unholy Land and there make an end to him in the name of Peace and Cromm."

The armour is laid out on the ground and the blacksmith is forced inside. The boy catches his father's eye as the helmet is rivetted shut. The look of mingled shame and horror is one he will never forget.

There is silence when the armour is finally sealed. The boy can clearly hear the suit powering up as it detects his father's human body within.

A deathly hush falls across the village. Water runs softly through the mill wheel. The sound is almost musical. Somewhere nearby a crow caws greedily, perhaps regarding the dead villagers, the enchanting flow of blood from their bodies. Then the Knight which had been his father sits up. The armoured form is twice the height of a man, dwarfing even the black giant at whose feet it kneels. He gestures and the Knight stands.

The giant smiles at the men and boys chained in the village square.

"We've got what we came for. Burn the rest."

The giant leads the soldiers from the village as the new Knight gestures across the square with one armoured hand. Pale flame flickers from its fingertips. Women and children fall, incinerated instantly.

The hand moves. The village burns.

Forgotten by everyone, the boy who should have died watches all he's ever loved dissolve into mountainous clouds of flame and smoke. He watches the village burn until there is nothing left but embers. Then, with the face of a giant

cloaked in shadows seared into his mind with a promise
of revenge that burns equally hot, Robin of Loxley claws
himself upright and–

5

"–I said that's *enough!*" Robin flushed, blinked back furious tears.

"Foul heart, fair wolf." Marion's words, cold blade, slipped inside him.

She leaned close, her white lips brushing his hair. Only then did he realise she was not the child she had seemed when speaking. Robin looked at the Priest. Tuck stood serenely to one side of the room, folded in shadow, blood–stained fingers steepled across his enormous belly, a half smile playing about his lips.

"The girl. A witch? Cromm's Eye?"

"She is a Seer, yes." Tuck pursed his lips, "The Milk of Cromm has made of her a lens. The Warlock inherited her as a child. In truth he had no love for her so she was given into the care of the Temple."

"Your care."

Tuck inclined his head minutely.

"You have broken her, Priest. Made a maze of her."

Tuck's eyes narrowed angrily. "And what would you or any of your Wolfsheads have made of her? A wife, a mother? For all read chattel."

"There could have been love."

A muscle in Tuck's neck twitched once, the only sign to betray his anger. But Robin noticed the girl's eyes, always in motion, lingered briefly on his own before restlessly moving on.

"Love is a cold night and no air so the stars shine like crushed coal." The girl pirouetted slowly. The robe, melting snow, dripped from her outsretched arms. "Black hearts make diamonds in the breath of the dragon."

"You see?" Robin's lips twisted in a snarl. "You have emptied her of all but madness."

"And yet she recited your childhood." Tuck's body relaxed. "A truth never told, and nine years her elder, unless I miss my mark."

Robin bit his lip, said nothing.

"Marion will know more than love. Past and future are the garden of her heart." An expression of sympathy passed across the Priest's broad face. "A garden others may walk."

Robin's hand fell from the dagger at his belt.

"There's a truth in this room." Robin felt the Priest's gaze upon him, studying him, weighing him as he might have

done some herbal concoction. "I'll have it now." Silence.
"Well?"

Marion continued her slow dervish, eyes raised to
examine the vaulted ceiling, a series of exquisite sighs
passing from her lips as if she beheld the finest paintings.
She spoke but her voice was a whisper, so low and dark
it seemed to Robin little more than the flicker of candle–
shadow in a darkened room.

Tuck licked his lips, turned to the bookcase.

"There is a plot to kill the King. Marion has seen it."

"The Wolf will kill the Lion, the Lion kill the Wolf. The
Man I' the Hood with heart of starstone will eat the world."

Robin looked from one host to the other. "The wolf and
the… do you mean me? Why would I want to kill the King?
It's the Pretender we hate. Prince John who takes our wealth
for his coffers, our loved ones for his Crusade. Him I would
kill without hesitation."

"You are naive, Robin. The Crusade is Richard's
pleasure, not John's." Tuck touched the side of the bookcase.
Pistons wheezed. The case hinged aside. Revealed was an
alcove. Robin stared curiously. Inside the alcove was an
icon. Rough wood. A naked man transfixed to a cross at
wrists and ankles.

Robin stared at Tuck. "What is it?"

"An image of Christ our Saviour."

"Who?"

Tuck swung the book case shut again.

"My life is a lie." Tuck poured water into a goblet and sipped delicately. "My rank in the Coven is Inquisitor. I have been so for twice your age, and a good one too. My task is to monitor and interrogate cults such as Christianity which might one day represent a threat to Cromm Cruac. In truth…" Tuck blew out his cheeks. "I am a great deal more than that."

"A spy for the cults you're supposed to destroy?"

"Call me a historian. The Coven has been interested in Christianity for some while. Eight hundred years ago the Great Library of Alexandria was burned by them, an act which provoked a terrible reprisal. Christianity was repressed into near–extinction while Asian and Egyptian religions flourished. Ptolemy's scrolls, surviving as a gift from Mark Anthony to Cleopatra were read, the information in them developed. Hydraulics, metallurgy, steam–power. The harnessing of lightning. What you call fireglass. All this survived its intended destruction."

"And what does it have to do with me? Why free me from Nottingham?"

Marion spoke then but her words were not the Kings English, nor any language Robin had ever heard.

"Yog–Sothoth zna vrata. Yog–Sothoth kapısıdır. Yog–Sothoth darvazadan əsas və dostudur. الماضي واحلاضر واملستقبل، كل واحد يف Yog – Sothoth."

She spoke, and her voice was deep and hollow and filled with pain.

"O köhnə yaşlı vasitəsilə qıraraq harada bilir, və onlar yenidən vasitəsilə fasilə qalacaqlar."

At the touch of those words the fireglasses guttered, the light retreating from the darkness in her voice. Dressed in shadows, Marion seemed to grow without moving, her skin darkening, her face shrouded until only her ice-bright eyes pierced the gloom that fell around her.

"Ξέρει όπου έχουν πάτησε πεδία της Γης, و جاىى مک آنها ج آ ار آنها زونه Ecce quare nemo eorum calcare."

Marion's shuddering voice fell silent at last but the room seemed colder and the light from the fireglasses never quite returned to full strength.

Tuck reached out to sooth the girl. She clutched his hand gratefully, almost desperately, pressing fat fingers to her face, her waxen cheek. For a moment Robin saw tears trembling on long lashes.

Tuck stroked Marion's hair, translating softly. "Yog–Sothoth knows the gate. Yog–Sothoth *is* the gate. Yog–Sothoth is the key and guardian of the gate. Past, present, future, all are one in Yog–Sothoth. He knows where the

Old Ones broke through of old, and where They shall break through again. He knows where They have trod Earth's fields, and where They still tread them, and why no one can behold Them as They tread."

Robin felt a blackness crawl across his body and shivered.

"These words are from the *Necronomicon*. An ancient religious text. I studied the manuscript in a secret monastery in Dunwich."

Robin frowned. "What else does this Necronomicon say?"

"On the eve of the First Millennium in the City of Al Basrah, mind–destroying Monstrosities, part man, part dragon, part rock, with faces like starfish and compound eyes "akin to suns wherein the fire of them has been extinguished by Cromm himself," were unleashed into the world from an Abyssal Void by Ibn al–Haytham, a Muslim scientist and the so–called "Father of Optics," then conducting experiments in an attempt to view other worlds. The Monstrosities are the spawn of a Behemoth named Yog–Sothoth, a being which is one with all space and time and the gateway through which other, even stranger and more violent Abyssal Gods may enter the world."

Tuck hesitated. Tiredness lined his face. Marion fluttered one hand close to his cheek, an oddly comforting gesture.

When he spoke again it was almost as if she directed his words. "The eye is the window to the soul," Tuck said softly. "When Ibn al–Haytham looked into the Abyss, the Abyss returned his gaze. It destroyed his mind, replacing it with somehing inhuman and unknowable. Something that wants to come here, to our world, to feed." He took another drink, a long gulp. "To devour this Earth as it must have devoured the worlds in its own universe. Those caught in its sight become Monstrosities with but one objective. To open more gates through which it may feed. Its name is Yog Sothoth and it is *hungry.*"

Robin shivered. His hand crept inside his shirt, withdrew holding something hard and cold, crusted with screamer's blood.

"You spoke of Yog Sothoth. So did the madman I was imprisoned with. He gave me this. He said it came from the Unholy Land. He said it came all the way from night. As if night were a place."

Robin held out the object. It looked like nothing more than a jagged piece of quartz about the size of a crossbow pistol bolt.

"He said it was called the–"

Marion sucked in a sudden breath. Her eyes rolled up until only the whites were visible. Her voice, when it came, was a storm.

"*–Godstone, he brings it, the Wolf brings it, qurd onu gətirir qara kainatın şüşə ürək the Godstone of the Necronomicon, the glass heart of the black universe the Wolf brings it he–*"

The girl's words dissolved into a senseless shriek of horror and desire. She began to shake, arms flailing, back arching, tendons standing out on her neck as if sculpted there by a master craftsman.

6

Rising with a speed Robin would never have believed had he not seen it, Tuck took a glass phial from a sleeve pocket and forced its contents into the girl's gaping mouth. She collapsed immediately, uttering a long shuddering sigh. Tuck caught her in his arms, holding her the way a child would hold a broken toy. He eased her into a chair and after a few more long breaths her eyes fluttered open. Her gaze locked on Robin's and the light there was impenetrable.

Tuck settled Marion, then leaned closer to the object which had caused her so much alarm. He reached out a hand towards it but stopped short of actual contact.

Robin studied the object closely. It was the first time he'd looked at it in any detail since it had arrived in his care. The crystal was slim, many sided and sharply pointed at each end. It was symmetrical, as if worked, polished to a high sheen. It was the colour of milk, hazed with flaws, yet something in there seemed to move, something deep and far away in the swirling colours…

Eyes narrowed, Tuck turned down the fireglasses to dim the hall even further and as the light faded Robin felt the immeasurable distance that seemed to fill the crystal retreating, shrinking away. Going back to the Night.

Tuck leaned forward, steepled his fingers in front of his face, caging it in shadow. "You were lucky to have been given this in the dark," he said eventually. He took out a square of raw silk from another of his sleeve pockets and offered it to Robin. "Put it away now. We'll need it later."

Robin wrapped the object and tucked it back into his shirt, noticing as he did so that Marion opened her eyes the moment the object was out of sight.

Tuck took wine from a shelf and poured two goblets. He handed one to Robin and both drank.

"After several hundred years Cromm Cruac emerged as the dominant European religion. Recognising the threat from the Monstrosities the Coven declared war in the Unholy Land, using the most advanced form of Ptolemy's hydraulic technology to make an army of Knights for the Crown."

Robin shuddered. *His mother dead. His father Knighted.*

Marion's eyes were fixed on Robin's. Had he thought her empty? Had he thought her broken?

"You know the rest," Tuck said, seeming to take strength from the girl's touch. "Walking siege engines, flying castles fitted with coal–fired anti–gravity drives and armed with "optic spears", weapons developed by defecting Muslim scientists and driven to war in the Unholy Land. That war…" Tuck shuddered, fell silent.

"You fought in the Crusade?"

Tuck seemed to gather his strength. "Not fought. But… that war… is a nightmare. To witness the Monstrosities without protection is to be driven insane. Insane humans that aren't immediately destroyed become Monstrosities themselves." Tuck closed his eyes for a long moment. "If your friends fall you don't dare settle for just killing them. Death isn't enough. *It isn't enough…"*

Tuck took a great gulp of wine. In hush between his words Robin found himself thinking back to the screamer in the dungeon of Nottingham Castle.

The colours. They call to me, oh Scarlet, THEY CALL TO ME.

Tuck said, "The Crusades have been going on for nearly two hundred years. Much of the Unholy Land has been consumed. Cities such as Al Basrah and Jerusalem have been transformed into mobile mountains of indescribable geometry. And here? Our green land has become a slagheap, mined for fuel to fight Cromm's endless Crusade. Sherwood is near dead, a maze of open cast pits choked by tree–sized weeds. Green parks are property of the rich, walled in by noblemen. The people of England have been enslaved to mine coal and minerals, to manufacture the weapons necessary to continue the Crusade. Any resistance is brutally repressed. Crush the people to save them." Tuck exhaled, a long sigh, filled with sadness. "A madness to equal the enemy itself. And all of it wasted. The Crusade will soon be over. For the Lion will return. But I don't think he is entirely the Lion anymore."

Marion uttered a sudden chilling groan. "The Lion will return! The Wolf will kill the Lion, the Lion kill the Wolf! *The Man I' the Hood will eat the world!"*

Tuck stood. "I must put Marion to bed but I will return. There are darker things yet to discuss."

Tuck held a hand out to the girl. Rising, she took it and followed him from the room. Robin turned up the fireglasses and the room brightened. But the darkness seemed to come back when Tuck returned a short while later.

"How's the girl?"

"Asleep. Dreaming of wolves I have no doubt."

Robin nodded. "You had something to show me?"

Tuck led Robin to the heart of the temple, a stone arch over a staircase winding down into darkness. At the bottom of the stairs was a short passage. At the end of the passage was a heavy metal hatch, braced and rivetted, with a knurled lockwheel and several levers set into its solid bulk.

Tuck glanced at Robin. "What lies beyond this door is the best kept secret in the country."

"Why show it to me then?"

"Because you must believe. And to believe you must be Witness to the Miracle of Transubstantiation." It seemed to Robin that Tuck weighed his next words very carefully. "What awaits here – I will not say rests – is the bread and wine become body and blood. But not of any god you've ever known."

"I don't understand."

"Take out the crystal." Robin did so. "Hold it before your eyes when entering the room. Whatever you do, do not look upon what lies within with your naked eyes. Do you understand?"

"I–"

"Do you understand?"

"Not really."

Tuck rolled his eyes. "Cromm preserve us from questing fools and questioning idiots." He sighed. "What lies beyond this door is a captive. Our only prisoner. A Saracen infected by one of the Monstrosities." Tuck shuddered as he spoke of the thing behind the door. "Its human body has become an inconceivable obscenity of soulless unflesh. It is hideous but you must feel no sympathy. It will speak to you with all the colours of madness but you must not heed its voice."

Tuck took balls of wax from his sleeve pockets and rolled them between his fingers until they were soft. By the time he forced them into Robin's ears they had absorbed some of the red–black hue from his fingertips. To Robin it seemed Tuck was plugging his ears will greasy clots of blood.

"Remember," the Priest continued in muffled tones, "Only look upon it through this," He indicated the crystal which had caused Marion so much consternation. "Only this, for your life."

Tuck pulled levers in sequence. Robin smelled old grease and dust, the somber damp of the deep earth. Pistons withdrew heavy bolts from the door frame. Tuck spun the knurled wheel. The door opened. With a last look at the Priest Robin held the crystal before his face, crouched down and stepped through the doorway.

There was a clash of metal and the hatch slammed shut behind him. Robin resisted the impulse to bang on the door. He looked around. He was in what felt like a large chamber. The light was dim and came from a tiny fireglass high on the wall above the door. As his eyes adjusted to the gloom he began to make out his surroundings more clearly. He stood in a cave. Stone columns swept from the uneven floor to the roof. A natural cave then, not man–made. Robin closed his eyes, adjusting to the dark, opening them quickly when a sense of uneasiness crept over him. He peered deeper into the shadows. Was that movement? Robin breathed deeply to steady his nerves. Why was he scared?

Do not look upon what lies within with your naked eyes.

The crystal.

Only look upon it through this.

The Godstone.

Only this, for your life!

Robin brought the crystal up to his eyes.

He looked. And *saw.*

And screamed

The world

7

is glass, all glass, the world is glass. And not just the world but all of time as well. He screams and his scream is glass. His mind and body are glass. There is nothing to separate him from all of time and space, everything that ever was or would or could ever be.

He is a man and his heart is fear. He is a knight and his body is war. He is a King and his mind is desire.

He is a man, and he hangs suspended in eternity in a hall of stone made glass. Fingers, granite fleshed bones of the earth, rise to crush him in a tightening fist. To force him into a space he cannot occupy, a void from which his mind recoils in utmost horror and

> *he is a Knight and he runs the field of war wreathed in steam. His armour is rose–red, lacquered with gore and engine oil, the steel castle–forged and folded until finer in quality than any eastern blade. He has a mission. It cannot fail. Clenched fists punch high, loosing optic spears that gouge chasms in the feeding Monstrosities as rank upon rank of the Lion's Knights march on the ever–shifting mountainous geometries which had once been Al Basrah, Jerusalem and*

> *he is a King and he stands in the castle–forged battlements of London Tower as it soars on invisible wings across the Unholy Land. To either side a fleet of bronze and folded steel run the sky. York, Malden, Norwich, Colchester, a hundred castles loosing fusillade afer fusillade of optic cannon fire into the dark night that is the enemy. The Unholy Land is a lightning storm. Beneath him legions of Knights and siege engines hurling fireglasses without number pound towards their deaths in the enemy's colours. Men and metal shriek and tear. Monstrosities shift and flow, erupting from the earth, from fallen Knights. Ahead the walls of Jerusalem surge and rise, Heaven's–city–that–was now a black tide of incomprehensible and ever–shifting geometry*

flooding the land, ambling across the desert to meet him, meet the Lion and consume him, meet the world and

he is a King but he is also a Knight and a man and when the end comes it is sudden and shocking. To the east, Colchester is burning, fuel gone, engines failing, adrift on the wind, a jagged bronze cloud. Nearby York, its clean edges infected with monstrous geometry, tumbles dying from the sky, splitting into three great sections as the armoury and coal–stacks blow; furnaces and cannon tumbling to the earth, engines bursting free of their moorings in sheets of flame, in roiling clouds of steam and smoke, to hurl themselves into the sky until lost in the endless blue. Men and Knights fall, clouds of tiny dots, or rise clinging to the engines. An easy escape for them, lost in the sky, their deaths clean and quick. Not so York, which, colliding with Colchester in an almighty explosion, destroys the smaller castle utterly before falling free of the mountain of smoke and smashing into the ground among a horde of Monstrosites. Purifying flames are drowned in the flood, men and machines and battlements alike consumed, only to rise again as part of the black tide. To the west, Malden and Norwich continue to fight, flinging lightning into the darkness. The King who is also a man turns at the sound of screams. Monstrosities have claimed the battlements. His mind recoils from the vision. But the Lion is no coward.

Arming his optic spear, he leaps to the breach. Inside the tower, the song of steam falters and dies. The tower tilts. Dark cliffs surge and rise, surge and rise, as Jerusalem approaches, tumbling geometries moving faster than any engine could ever drive them. Terror blooms in the King's mind. He pushes it aside, cutting his way through friend and foe alike, reaching the bridge as the first of three great explosions tear the belly from London Tower. The Lion reaches for the helm. A Monstrosity erupts from the bodies of the dead crew, bursts upon him and begins to feed. The Lion shrieks. Through the broken portholes the dark cliffs of Jerusalem loom dead ahead and rising fast. The Monstrosity grows in the King. The heart of the Lion, already stone, cracks at last. Richard I, Duke of Normandy, Aquitane and Gascony; Lord of Cypress, Count of Anjou, Maine and Nantes, Overlord of Brittany and King of England screams the name of his wife, Berengaria, a woman he has not yet learned to love and now never will, into the face of the enemy, before driving the dying Tower of London into the black heart of Jerusalem in a concussion of light which, for the space of his last human heartbeat, shines brighter than the sun.

And in the black madness that follows, the scarlet Knight snatches a tiny shard of hope, the rainbow heart of the enemy and, man and armour alike broken by the madness of war, flees into the desert.

Clutched in a fist made of stone-made-glass, the man screams. He shrieks but there is no sound. He writhes without ever moving. Past and present, time and the land, everything is inside him and there's no room for it, no room in there for him. Driven from his body the man flees, across time and space and

countless worlds, an infinity of universes
consumed by the darkness
by Yog Sothoth and

the Lion will return, he will return and his heart will be black, and his mind, and he will bring the black to his brother Prince John, to the Warlock and the Coven, and Church and Crown will raise the black tide, the Old Ones with their awful colours from the stone heart of the earth to feed, Cromm save us, to feed until man is gone, woman and child are gone, land and sky and sea are gone, until worlds and stars are gone and all of time and space, and nothing is left but void, oh Scarlet, just endless, lightless, loveless void!

8

"Robin, are you out of your *mind?*"

John's voice boomed in the Great Hall of Cromm loud enough to shake the temple walls. His armoured fist struck a table laden with food and drink. Tuck flinched as the table cracked. Much blinked and shivered, backed up to the wall between two fireglasses, watching meat and wine tumble to the floor and strugging to understand his brother's words.

"We can't do that," his voice trembled, a terrified child. "Robin, we *can't*. It's the *King.*"

Robin stood tall and straight beside the broken table. His gaze raked the circle of faces around him. There was somethng near–crazed about that gaze. A fire burned there. The same cold fire that burned in Marion. And was that white in his hair? An unearthly pallor in his waxy skin?

"I told you Much, weren't you listening? I told all of you. It's not the King. Not anymore. It's one of them. A Monstrosity. A vessel for Yog Sothoth, the Eater of Worlds. Something that willl feed on us, on the land, until there's nothing left. No heart, no soul… not even memories. Then everything – *everything* – will be forgotten. Because no–one and nothing will be left to remember it."

Robin's eyes fixed bleakly on mid air, the past or maybe the future.

"Marion was right."

His last words were simple and quiet, and no–one in the room challenged them.

"Волком úlfur olmalıdır occidere leo!"

Marion. Her voice was flat and sharp. She walked into the hall and shadows rose to cloak her.

"The Wolf will kill the Lion." Robin's gaze locked with hers.

Much frowned, scooped up a fallen apple. "Here, Robin, if you know what she said does that make you mad too?"

Robin ignored his brother.

Marion wound into the room, arms up, a slow dance.

"The Lion will rise at the circle's end." Her words were sinuous, a mirror for her body. "The travellers shall fall at the circle's end. The Wolf will kill the Lion, the Lion kill the Wolf."

Marion's body met Robin's and clung. Her lips were soft and cold and bone white. Her skin was ice but somehow she burned. Her mouth opened against his. She breathed into him. Other worlds. Other times. They filled him. *She* filled him. Filled even the tiny spaces the Monstrosity which had once been Abdul Fattah, Servant of the Opener of the Gates of Sustenance had left unviolated.

"The Man i' the Hood with heart of stone will eat the world." Her words were a whisper, pressed against his lips.

Much was frozen, his apple touching his lips, teeth bared and motionless in mid *crunch.*

John shook his head minutely at the kiss. "Travellers?" His voice was puzzled and annoyed. "Circle's end? Just for once can't you speak the King's English?"

Much waggled sticky fingers in sudden excitement. "There's travellers at Hordron," he exclaimed through a mouthfull of fruit.

John sighed. "There are probably travellers at all the inns, Much."

Much shook his head. "Not them sort of travellers, John. Stone travellers."

Light bloomed in John's eyes. "The stone circle at Hordron Heath." There was surprise in his voice. "Much, I take it all back. You're not an idiot, you're a genius."

Much pointed triumphantly at John. Wet specks of apple flew from his fingers. "Sec. See. We used to play *count–the-stones* there when I was small." He frowned, remembering, then added, "Never worked though."

Tuck's eyes flickered from Robin and Marion to the Much. "The stones walked?"

"It weren't that." Much's face fell. "I can't count higher'n five, see? They tried to teach me but… well…" Words failed him then, so Much just shook his head sadly and took another bite of apple instead.

Robin felt Marion release him, whirl away. He lifted one hand, trailed a finger across his cheek, his lips, the places their skin had met. Bare of her touch, he was ice. Cold, hard, clear as glass.

"The Prince will send men to Dover, soldiers, to meet the King. But the King won't be there, will he?" Robin looked at Marion, still whirling gently, arms raised, fingers rippling. "The Lion will rise…"

"…at Hordron Heath," they finished as one.

Robin felt the room snap back into focus. He looked quickly at John. "The hunters' carriage. Is it still in the river?"

"I sent some men to take it to camp." John's brow furrowed. "Robin," he said warningly. "What are you thinking?"

Robin grinned. Suddenly everything was clear. Clear as glass.

"When steam engines go wrong they make a *really* big bang."

Robin felt Much's gaze on him. The idiot was shaking his head, a terrified expression on his face. Not fear of Robin's plan. Fear of Robin himself.

"Much, please. This is the only way. You're my brother, surely you understand?" Much trembled but did not answer. Instead he cast a fast sideways look at John. Robin followed the look with one of his own. "John. You've seen battle. You know I'm right."

John sucked in a long breath. He looked from Robin to Much and back again. "I took a vow to follow you and I won't break it. But this isn't the same – and you know it. What's got into you Robin? Your own *brother* is terrified of you." John glared at Tuck, at Marion gyring slowly, slowly, about the broken table. "What madness has your witch put in my friend's head?"

Tuck's big head raised so his eyes met John's. And although the Knight was near twice the Priest's size and armoured too, he drew back from that gaze as if it were the ghost of his mother.

"Not madness, John." Robin's voice was soft. "Understanding."

"The King," said Tuck slowly and clearly. "Is not the man he was. He will betray this country and its people. He will betray everythig good in this world. And then he will destroy it. And there will be nothing."

Whispers squcezed out between Marion's lips as she turned slowly on one heel. The words spiralled into the hall and filled it with shadows. John's eyes half–closed in pain. Much put his hands to his ears. Droplets of apple juice clung to his fingers. He uttered a soft moan.

Then Robin spoke, and his voice was as harsh and pale as that of the broken girl. "The King must die, you all know it." His words fell in total silence. "If you do not care for this land and will not help protect it I will go alone. I will kill the King alone. The Wolf will kill the Lion."

One by one Robin looked at everyone in the room. When no–one except Marion would meet his gaze he took up his bow and quiver, turned from his friends and ran from the hall.

9

They followed as he knew they would. John from loyalty, Much from fear of being left behind. The others… it did not matter why they followed him, only that they did.

The perambulator was intact. A few hours work on the main pressure relief valve Robin had damaged and the vehicle was fuilly operational. Better than that it was fully stocked. The hunters had kept an arsenal within. Arrows, steel, fletchings, caulked jars of blue–umber paste. Curare. Fuelsprings. Spring chargers. Hydraulic pumps for bows. There were chests crammed with fully–charged fireglasses. Much, slightly entranced, picked up three and juggled them.

"Idiot. Are you trying to blow yourself up?" John plucked the deadly ordinance one by one from the air before Much could kill someone with them. "In the name of my black-hearted mother leave the flying to the birds."

Much complained about that. But John had already found something that took his fancy enough to make him laugh out loud. A pneumatic telescoping quarterstaff. How it came to be among the hunters' booty Robin could not guess. But John's delighted laugh meant it would not lay there long.

Robin could not sleep. He spent the rest of the night thinking, pacing, thinking again, mind and body as fully charged as the fireglasses. The pressure in his head was near-unbearable. He felt he must surely burst. Finally the sun rose. A bright day, clear and cold. It was time to move.

Tuck and Marion met them at midmorning on the road to Hordron, driving a pony laden with straw–padded baskets full of clay jars. Much's eyes widened when he saw them. "Witch–jars," he said. "Them's what they used to catch us Robin."

"Not quite the same." Tuck shook his head. "If any of these break near you hold your breath and run like a rabbit. Don't stop, don't look back, just run."

The sun was at its zenith as they approached Hordron. They circled, coming to the heath from the northern escarpment because no road ran there; riding the perambulator which, needing no road, negotiated the jagged slopes better than any pony would have done. Before they came within earshot of the Travellers, Robin called a halt to prepare the carriage's boiler and send a scout ahead.

All they could do then was wait.

Marion had not been able to say with any certainty when the Lion would rise but Robin felt it would be soon. Maybe even that afternoon. He spent the rest of the day apart from the others, walking the escarpment in the shadow of the sun, letting the cold winter day enter him and warm him. Everything was sharp, perfectly in focus. He watched a snow–fox at the edge of a frozen pond hunting. White on white, a ghost of the land. Something caught the fox's attention. There was a flurry of frantic movement, Cromm's dance upon the ice, then nothing. The fox was gone. The prey was gone. All that remained were three frozen drops of bright blood. Scarlet and grey. Those were England's colours now. Scarlet and grey to fight the black rainbows.

Ice cracked nearby. Robin turned. Marion was silhouetted against the sky, white on white, like the snow fox, another ghost of the land. He did not need to listen to hear her words. They came to him on wings of cold fire, slipped into his head without ever passing his ears.

The Lion is rising.

Robin nodded. "When will he come?"

Soon.

Robin took a breath.

"Speak what you will, Marion. If there's aught unsaid between us I'd have it now."

Without moving, Marion was beside him. Her face close to his. Her breath was cold, so cold it did not steam in the day as his did. Robin marvelled at that as he marvelled at all of her. How could he ever have thought she was broken? She was whole. More gloriously whole than anyone he'd ever met.

She looked at him. Into him. Knew him.

He smiled, a ghost smile.

"I am six and twenty," he said. "I walked this earth near a decade before you were born." A breath. "When I met you, I thought you a girl. A broken girl with the body of an angel and nothing to fill it. All the time it was me who was broken." He moved closer to her. "I had thought revenge would leave very little room in a man's heart for love." His voice was barely louder than a whisper. "It seems I was wrong about that too."

She came to him then. They met upon the ice near three drops of frozen blood and no breath to cloud the space between them. The sky was their only witness. Ice blue, shot with grey. To the west a cold sun hung low in the sky. To the east, a crescent moon slowly rose. Snow fell as they kissed, a few large flakes, thick and heavy. The flakes touched his skin, and hers, and warmed them.

As a promise of marriage their lovemaking was cold, as rare and beautiful as the sun glimpsed through ice. Robin did not care. The words of his father touched his mind but briefly before they were driven from him by the touch of another, the cold scent of her skin against his.

Everything broken will be made whole.

He was snow. She was ice. They melted together and a new shape was born.

10

The Travellers at Hordron were massive, easily as heavy as those of the larger henges at Avebury and Salisbury, and they sank their roots deep into the earth. The stones were arranged in a double circle, with an avenue running south-west penetrating both and leading to the center. Smaller stones lay outside the main circle, an ancient altar stone within. Above the circle, the promised snow tumbled at last from the sky. The moon was ghost, the sun a pale spectre. Cold, eerie twilight cloaked the stones.

A low mist came to the heath and movement followed. Mounted soldiers wielding pneumatic crossbows or spring–loaded longbows. Witches from the Coven of Cromm Cruac riding blood–dyed mares. And a steam–driven perambulator from which a richly dressed figure descended to the scrubby heath surrounding the stone Travellers flanking the mouth of the avenue.

Prince John had come with full retinue to meet his brother.

The carriage squatted, hissing, fuelsprings idling, boiler sweating melting snow.

The Prince came forward. His face was sharp–featured, lean, his lips thin, his eyes cold as the snow gathering at his head.

"Brother!" His voice was cold too, soft, yet somehow penetrating. "We are well met in this place!"

Snow drifted

Bone white flakes

Cold as any Seer's eyes.

The Prince took another step.

Mailed boots crunched on frost–brittle scrub.

Deathly hush. Somewhere a horse *huffed* nervously.

Half hidden by snow a figure moved within the circle where none had stood but a heartbeat before. A man in armour, not a Knight. The figure walked out of the snow and his shield and helm bore familiar arms.

A single lion *rampant*, gold on scarlet.

The Prince raised an arm in greeting.

"At last! Welcome

A single arrow parts the snow, flashing pale gold and silver, finds the eye–slit of the King's helm and buries itself there. The fletchings shiver. Snow falls from them.

home my–"

The Prince gaped, his words undone.

"What treachery is this!?" His voice was a scream.

For a heartbeat, the Lion stood transfixed, unmoving. Then, slow as any tree felled for the foundries, he toppled to the ground and lay still.

The Prince whirled. *"Who fired that arrow?"* he shrieked. *"I'll have his fucking head!"*

Nothing.

Into the silence came a single note. A thin, unwavering note that stretched sanity to breaking point. Soldiers and witches recoiled from the sound. Horses complained, some stamped nervously. The Prince whirled again. Inside the circle, beyond the snow, something moved.

"Brother…?"

Black rainbows pulsed in the circle of stones.

The Prince stepped back from the stones, the King.

The black rainbows exploded, a concussion of shadow– light. The movement was a breath. A scream of colour. That scream sucked the sun and moon from the day. Horses squealed. Soldiers cried out. Some fell from their mounts. A shockwave of hail and gravel blasted out from between the grasping stones, shredding armour and stripping flesh from anyone standing too close, driving everyone else to their knees. The Prince stumbled, safe in the blast shadow of one enormous stone.

The black rainbow pulsed again.

The Travellers *moved*.

They shivered. They blurred.

Rock shrapnel burst from them.

They stretched. They creaked and tore.

Within the circle, shadow-light bloomed. Where it touched the stones moss fell from them, powder brown, lifeless. The Travellers flexed, a double row of teeth in the yawning chasm of some unearthly churning maw. The bones of the earth, torn free from their age–old seat, arching up into a new day, a new world, a hundred tentacles muscled with ropes of granite, crawling with black rainbow light, eternally hungry, eager to feed.

The black rainbows *screamed*.

They shrieked and howled.

Armour split, the King rose, lifted on shadows. Black rainbows poured from buckled steel. Madness lived there.

The Prince uttered a wail of terror, scrambled away, fell, wrenched himself upright. Before him soldiers and seers alike writhed broken and screaming or fled the indescribable monstrosity dragging itself free of the heath, the stones, the body of his brother. The Prince ran too, only to stop suddenly as a hooded man rose before him, cloaked in snow, springbow charged, arrow nocked. Beside the hooded man, a knight, a witch, a priest, a fool.

The Prince grinned savagely. The Wolves had come to kill the Lion.

"Take them you dogs!" He shrieked. *"Kill them all!"*

11

The battle of Hordon Heath was born and died in shadow.

Arrows ran the snow, hissing breaths, shattered against stone limbs, sucked life from wolves and soldiers and seers alike. Lightning bloomed on scrub and rock, a rain of fireglasses spat flame into the gloom. Lightning flashed and died. Witch–jars burst, coughing yellow fog into the white snow. Whatever that fog touched, be it skin or armour, scrub or stone that thing burned and melted and died.

Marion, threading the blizzard, a slow and sinuous dance, witchbreath from open phials felling all it touched. John, a giant striding the pale heath, his quarterstaff felling two, four, six opponents at every swing. Much, running, sword and dagger cutting frenzied arcs through snow and soldier alike. Tuck, arms like a windmills tossing clay jars with deadly accuracy.

Monstrosities burst from every corpse. Stone tentacles, crawling with black rainbow light, arched through the snow, fanged, grasping. Wolves ran, bit, fell. Witches, scarlet bladed, followed. Soldiers slashed with swords, sought targets for arrows.

It was chaos.

Madness.

Robin of Loxley drifted through the fire–shot night, eyes cold as snow, loosing arrows with lightning speed. Confronted with the shrieking form of Prince John he had for a single heartbeat considered retreat. But there could be no retreat. The Lion must fall. And now there was chaos. It was madness and it must stop.

"Listen to me!" His voice was a storm. "The man you see is not the King. The Lion is gone, taken from us by the Monstrosities in the Unholy Land. This is their tool, their puppet and it comes to destroy us. If you value your lives, your children, your lands, then find him. Seek out the King and kill him now! THE LION MUST FALL!"

Dark rainbows exploded from the stones. Where they touched life that life fell, screaming, to writhe, to shudder and die, to rise again as black Monstrosities.

"Robin!"

Roped tentacles slilthered out of the snow. Robin turned, hurled himself away. There was no escape. The

Monstrosities arrowed in. Then the ground shook as John leaped clear over Robin's head, landed, fell to one knee, raised the quarterstaff horizontally and fired. Steam hissed. The staff telescoped out twice the length of a man to either side. Castle–forged steel struck the hungry rock to left and right and shattered it. Robin gaped, shrapnel stung. But John was already gone, leaping away, armour flashing in the fireglass blooms.

"The Lion!" his voice rumbled distantly back through the gloom. "What are you waiting for lad!"

"Much!" Robin's voice slashed through the fighting. "Now!"

Curtains of snow split as the hunters' carriage drove through the storm of men and metal. Much was at the helm, driving the perambulator on at a shrieking gallop. The machine charged along the avenue of writhing Travellers towards the circle and nothing and no–one could stop it.

Robin sprinted after his brother.

"Much! Jump you idiot!"

Robin did not see if Much managed to leap clear of the charging machine before the hard–stoked boiler uttered one last scream and exploded. Metal split, peeled back, burst apart. Molten steel splattered, a sun–bright rain, to melt hissing snow and rock alike. The explosion triggered the five hundred fully charged fireglasses Robin had carefully packed around the boiler.

A sun bloomed on Hordron Heath.

The concussion drove Robin to his knees, snow from the sky. His head rang. The world was glass. He could see *everything*.

The Lion stood, gold–ringed in a rain of molten steel, what crawled within sloughing flesh and armour as it struggled to be born.

Robin stood. Bow drawn. Arrows nocked.

Dark rainbows crawled.

Robin drew, aimed.

A long moment passed.

Finally he let the bow fall.

A giant, shadow-cloaked, rose before him. Flanked by his hunters, the Warlock of Nottingham stood, and Robin was a boy again, on his knees as the shadow giant shot a crossbow pistol bolt through his mother's eye, as he sealed his father in armour and had his new Knight destroy his home.

The shadow giant held something. A bundle of rags. No. Not rags. Alun. Alun of Wrexham. Much's father. The man who had taken Robin in, saved his life. The man to whom Robin *owed* his life.

The hunters had already drawn crossbows and taken a bead on him.

The Warlock smiled. Only his teeth and eyes were visible in the black silhouette. Behind him, the Lion burned with black fire and roped stone, bones now of another Earth, rose from the ground to challenge the storm. The Warlock held his crossbow pistol at Alun's temple. At his feet lay armour. Dented, scarred. Waiting.

The Warlock touched the armour with one black boot.

"Hear me, Wolfshead. This man is dying. I can save him. Can you?"

Robin tried to catch Alun's eyes but they were lost in the rainbow storm. Instead Robin saw the eyes of his own father, gazing at him from his own helm as it was rivetted shut. Robin couldn't save his father. He'd only been a child. He was no child now.

Robin lifted his head, bow raised and arrow knocked so fast the hunters could only blink at his speed.

The Warlock laughed. "You've forgotten to count your arrows, Wolfshead," he said. "I see only two. There are three of us."

Robin held the Warlock's black gaze for a moment.

"Nothing is forgotten," he said, unsmiing, and loosed.

The Warlock began to

Robin nocked, drew, loosed again.

turn as the hunters moved, spring driven muscles raising

Robin's second arrow struck his first arrow, splitting it cleanly in mid flight, driving through it to strike the Warlock between the eyes, bursting from the back of his head in a spray of blood as the two halves of the first arrow flew sideways into the faces of the two hunters, striking one in the left eye and one in the right.

All three fell as one.

Even before the arrows had struck, Robin had leapt, reaching the Warlock before his body hit the ground, snatching the pearl-handled crossbow pistol from the air, the Godstone from his shirt, ejecting the crossbow bolt as he fell, somersaulting over Alun of Wrexham, rolling to his feet as the Lion's armour finally split to reveal the crawling horror within, loading the Godstone and firing the pistol into the horror that was the barest tip of the face of the thing that called itself Eater of Worlds.

"Nothing is ever forgotten."

The world screamed.

The day burned.

The Lion fell.

And when Robin finally stood, deafened, half blind, it was to find himself weaponless before a ring of soldiers.

And a languidly applauding Prince John.

12

"The Crown owes you much, Loxley." The Prince's voice was soft. "But a new King has responsibilities. Duties which cannot be ignored." The Prince drew out every word, savouring his victory. "You saved the land but you murdered a King."

"Bollocks!" John's voice. "The King was dead already – you saw it!"

The Prince ignored the outcry. "You killed my brother," he said softly, and now there was venom in his voice. "No doubt you expect a reward for your heroism."

"My actions were in service of the land and the Crown," Robin said softly. "No reward is asked."

The Prince sighed. His cloak swirled about him, the white fur trimming almost lost in the drifting snow. "The Crown has always been threatened by your popularity with the people. On the other hand the Crown always needs a public enemy to punish should the need arise. Today… the Crown has many such enemies. Wolfsheads. Priests. Knights. Fools. Witches. All culpable in the sight of Cromm."

Robin said nothing.

The Wolf will kill the Lion, the Lion the Wolf.

The Prince said, "With the death of the King, the Crown has the perfect opportunity to end a well established political threat and also the life of a man who has at last outlived his usefulness."

Robin frowned. "Pardon them," he said at length. "Let them have peace. Do what you want with me but pardon my friends."

The Prince nodded. "Give me your life and I will. There will be conflict, maybe other wars. But they will not be part of them. You have my word. As King."

Robin smiled thinly. "You're not King yet."

The Prince waved a generous hand. "Details, details."

Robin considered. "I'm listening. Name your terms."

The Prince pursed his lips. "Pardons for the Wolfsheads. A hundred crowns for the Priest and the Witch to assign as they please. A new temple perhaps. Or a Christian priory." A humourless smile touched his cold eyes. "A flock, for the Knight, if he wishes."

"And Alun?"

"New lungs." The Prince's lip curled, contempt and amusement. "The crown will always need taxes."

"And honest men to pay them." Robin said bitterly.

The Prince waited. Snow fell.

Robin nodded slowly.

"I agree."

"Of course you do."

The Prince signalled to a nearby soldier.

"Give the Wolfshead his bow. One arrow only."

Robin took the bow, nocked the arrow, drew... then hesitated. He turned, his eyes seeking Marion's. They were cold, white, and all of his life waited there. One arrow. One Prince. It was a slim chance but... his eyes found Much, John, Tuck, Alun... the knot of outlaws, weaponless, surrounded by soldiers. It wasn't a slim chance. It was no chance at all.

"Do not think to play me false, Loxley." The Prince's voice, still soft, held an impatient edge. "I would not have the people's hero die with his honour besmirched."

Robin lowered his head, closed his eyes.

"Where my arrow lands, there let me lie."

Eyes still closed he raised the bow, drew, loosed.

The arrow flew silent and straight. Across the heads of soldier and outlaw, through snow and cold sunlight, passing over the bodies of the hunters, the Warlock of Nottingham, the human wreckage that had been Richard *Coer de Lion*. Straight and true, the arrow passed through the avenue of stones, and those who saw it later swore the broken Travellers moved to let it pass. And sunlight shone upon that arrow, they would say, and moonlight too, and it shone silver, as bright as any summer, and it penetrated to the very heart of the stones, the inner circle, there to vanish from this world forever.

The Prince *huffed* in surprise. "Well, Loxley, this is a fine jape. Your arrow has flown where none living may follow. How so shall we bury you thence?"

Robin turned with a thin smile touching his lips. Sun and moon painted his face pale gold and silver but his eyes lay ever in pools of shadow. He glanced at the suit of armour, the same Knight's armour the Warlock of Nottingham had used to promise Alun's life. He looked for his father's face in the open helm but saw only castle–forged steel, dented and scarred.

The Prince followed Robin's gaze and for the first time a full smile parted his lips. He took out his sword. Robin set down his bow and knelt. The Prince touched Robin's shoulders and forehead with the sword.

"By the power invested in me by the Crown I, John Lackland, Lord of Ireland and King of England, do Knight you and induct you into my service, to be my Cruacan Warrior, to serve in my army and drive the Invader back to the Unholy Land and there make an end to him in the name of Peace."

Robin rose, climbed into the armour, waited while it was sealed shut. He stood, painted pale gold and silver. The suit powered up. Fuelsprings whirred. For a moment he was still, more still than any man could be unless parted from life. Then Robin of Loxley, Knight of England, walked without a backward glance along the avenue and passed through the circle of broken stones.

And though a hundred people watched with curious, desperate, even loving eyes, none saw what happened there, for the snow took him from their sight first.

13

Everything broken will be made whole.

And that included me, Marion thought.

Robin's words had been as prescient as her own. A decade had passed since the fall of the Lion. A decade in which life and colour had slowly crept back into the greywood.

Changes. There had been many. As a forester Marion had seen the closing of the mines, the return to a more rural way of life. Many hundreds of new trees had been planted, including Oak imported from Europe. As yet there were only saplings. Time would change that. A hundred years from now the forest would be green again. Oak, Elm, Birch, Hazel; Boar, deer, rabbits, birds. She loved birds. And there would be wolves. She smiled. *Real* wolves.

The Coven of Cromm was no more, the temples thrown down and burned by King John's men, long gone to the wild, the greenwood bursting gloriously through tumbled stones to reclaim its stolen kingdom. Marion was not sorry to see them go. Christian priories bloomed among the rubble, few as yet but more every year. Tuck and the stonemasons were seeing to that.

On summer days such as this Marion found herself drawn to the sky. Blue, cloudless, a perfect glimpse of summer between verdant trees. Pollen clung to the air and bees whirred. On days like this she found her thoughts turning often to the Wolfsheads. John had returned to farming. Much joined him. The madman Scarlet's emaciated body had been brought from Nottingham Castle, by some miracle still clinging to life. The Abbess at Kirklees had personally nursed him back to health, though his mind had never recovered. Now he wandered the greenwood, accepting charity where it was offered, living off the land where it was not. Abdul Fattah, Servant of the Opener of the Gates of Sustenance, the Saracen Monstrosity, remained entombed in the cave under what was now a Christian Monastery. It could not be killed, this thing from another place and time. Marion did not think that was necessarily a bad thing. It had not been human for centuries but some part of it deserved pity. Now it simply remained, neither man or beast but simply a process, a slow petrification of all that had once been alive.

Marion lowered her eyes to the ground beneath her feet. Summer seemed to fade from it as she walked. And was that any wonder? Hordron had never recovered from the shock of its violation. The ground here was near dead. Travellers unlucky enough to be caught nearby after sundown said the ground glowed at night, faintly and with rainbow colours. All that grew on the bare rock around the blasted circle crawled only in moonlight and shunned the day. Marion had visited the place but once, a year after Robin had passed through that dread gate to whatever void was his fate. Though it was bright summer when she arrived, still there was a shadow upon the heath, a long shadow as if the light that moved there was not earthly daylight but some other world's night. The loneliness and horror she felt that first awful day lingered still, as strong as ever, and she had never returned.

Never until today.

What had drawn her back? It had been ten years to the day since Robin had left them. She had thought him forgotten. But nothing was ever forgotten.

Now Marion walked the powdery brown heath at Hordron and her cautious footsteps seemed to release the smell of burning. What wasted grass her feet trod did not recover from the touch but remained flattened, limp and oozing a thin rainbow coloured sap.

She saw other footprints pushed into the ground and followed them, coming upon familiar travellers within sight of the Hordron Stones.

"John," her voice was soft. He turned. Much was there too. And Scarlet. Many others. One enormous shape turned at her voice.

"Marion!" his voice was as big as he was, rich and warm and full of love. "Come here child. Let me look at you."

"Tuck." He was still fat but now he was older, his hair just as long but marbled with grey. She went to him and they hugged.

Closer to the Stones was an unfamiliar figure. A tall man, dressed in green. He looked to be around her own age. He carried a bow – a traditional longbow, unpowered. His face was hooded, his eyes in shadow.

Marion nudged Tuck and pointed. "Who's that?"

Tuck frowned. "Huntingdon's son, the Earl to be. Robert is the name he goes by."

"Why is he here?"

"Why are any of us. You saw the falling star?"

"No. What star?"

"It fell upon Hordon but five nights ago. Some take it for a sign. A dark omen. Surely you heard of it?"

"The news did not reach Kirklees." Tuck favoured her with a long look. She sighed. "I am considering taking vows."

Tuck nodded, slow understandng.

"What of this star?"

"It fell to ground at night." John spoke without turning. "It blasted the nearby villages with colour, dark rainbows."

Tuck nodded, adding, "People have disappeared. Some are crazed, wailing, their skin turning brown and powdery. In its crypt the Monstrosity awoke. The monks there commited suicide three nights hence. The Priory has been abandoned. Guy of Gisburn, the new Sheriff of Nottingham, ordered the place burned. That's him over there, with the soldiers. The Monstrosity is in the carriage. The one with no windows."

Marion shuddered. "He brought it here? Why?"

Tuck shook his head. "As a weapon. Perhaps a hostage."

"If Gisburn thinks that then he's a fool."

Marion felt a dark light cast shadows across her heart.

The travellers will fall at the circle's end.

As Tuck fell silent her eyes returned to the stones. They had not rested upright for years but now it seemed to her that something had pushed them even further aside, something that wanted to make room in this world for itself. As she watched there was a shuddering crash. One by one the

stones toppled and fell. No. Not fell. Because falling was
not something that fingers did. Not something that a fist did.
And the stones were a fist, she could see that now, a fist as
they had been ten years before, a fist clutching at the day as
it clawed itself out of the earth.

Light bloomed there, a dark rainbow. Marion cried out.
Tuck drew a dagger from his belt and offered it to her. The
weapon was useless against this enemy. As useless as John's
staff, Much's sword.

The hooded man who stood between Marion and the
stones nocked an arrow and sighted his bow. What could
he see? It was a question Marion did not need to ask. In the
light flooding from between the stones something moved.
A human shape but much larger. Bright armour now black
and pitted. It rose from the stones, from the clutching fist
pushing clear of the earth, stepped through the light as a man
might step through a waterfall.

Marion moaned softly.

The Wolfshead, once human, hooded now in metal and
shadows.

*The Man I' the Hood with the heart of starstone will eat
the world.*

The Monstrosity, once a man, then a Knight, uttered
words. Broken and black they split the day, clawing the light
from the sky, felling birds in flight, turning grass to rot in

a wide circle around the stones driving all but John in his armour to their knees.

Nihil praetermisi. Heç bir şey heç unutdun edir.

Marion reeled from the awful sound. *His* words.

Everything broken will be made whole.

The Knight–that–was raised the visor of its armour. Inside was a face she knew, even loved. The eyes in that face swam with dark rainbows. Other things moved there too. Crawling things that made her want to scream and clutch her face and claw out her eyes.

And then with a sucking *crack* the great stone fist came shuddering from the earth, pulling itself into daylight. Arms followed, stone-muscled, writhing. The barest tip of what lay beneath, *beyond*. The Thing that was coming. The Thing he had brought back into the world to feed.

Everything broken will be made whole.

Marion took the dagger Tuck had offered her and raised it. She did not scream. She did not panic. She did not run. After all this moment was really no surprise. No surprise at all.

The thing in the light gazed at the array of weapons raised against it.

A cyborg farmer, a mad Crusader, a faithless priest, a fool, a witch, a Saracen horror… and a hooded man whose eyes seemed somehow able to take the black rainbow light and made it white, and whole.

Robin, once of Loxley now of Night, smiled a wide and terrible smile, and all the colours of madness came forth into the world.

The Hooded Man raised his bow, sighted, loosed.

The Fourth Crusade had begun.

ABOUT THE AUTHORS

Alan K. Baker was born in Birmingham in 1964. He has published a number of non-fiction books on the paranormal and popular history, which have been translated into seven languages.

Rachel E. Pollock is a Professor of Costume for Dramatic Art at the University of North Carolina, Chapel Hill. Her creative writing has appeared in the *Harvard Summer Review, Southern Arts Journal,* and *Mason's Road*, as well as the anthologies *Steampunk, Confessions: Fact or Fiction?*, and *Knoxville Bound*. She is also the sole author of the professional weblog, La Bricoleuse: Costume Craft Artisanship (http://labricoleuse.livejournal.com/).

Alison Littlewood is a writer of dark fantasy and horror fiction. Her first novel, *A Cold Season*, is published by Jo Fletcher Books. Her short stories have appeared in magazines including *Black Static, Crimewave* and *Not One Of Us*, as well as the British Fantasy Society's *Dark*

Horizons. She also contributed to the charity anthology *Never Again* as well as *Read by Dawn Vol 3, Midnight Lullabies* and *Festive Fear 2*. Her life writing has appeared in *The Guardian*. Visit her at www.alisonlittlewood.co.uk.

Simon Bucher-Jones was born in Liverpool in 1964. He wrote two novels for Virgin's *Doctor Who* range (one, with typical good timing, after they lost the right to use the Doctor). He followed this up with two co-written novels for the BBC line, and a number of short stories. He's also written well received Cthulhu mythos horror stories, a book of self-published poetry, and once a year appears in Panto for charity. He's presently working on a novel with Jon Dennis for Obverse book's revival of Faction Paradox. He can be seen on Twitter making bad puns as @Bucherjones.

Jim Mortimore's 2009 short story *The Sun in the Bone House* was submitted for the Nebula Award. His work – including *Doctor Who, Cracker, Babylon 5, Farscape, The Tomorrow People* and *Bernice Summerfield* together with his first original novel *Skaldenland* (Obverse Books 2011) – is available on Amazon or Lulu, or direct from rocketman2012@hotmail.co.uk, where he'll happily barter books for cash, lego or vintage synthesizers.

Cavan Scott has written audio dramas, books, short stories and comics for such popular series as *Doctor Who, The Sarah Jane Adventures, Highlander, Power Rangers* and *Judge Dredd*. His new novel *Blake's 7: The Forgotten*, co-written with Mark Wright was published in 2012 by Big Finish. He is also the author of a number of non-fiction titles including *Planet Dinosaur*.

Kim Lakin-Smith is the author of *Tourniquet; Tales from the Renegade City* (Immanion Press: 2007), *Cyber Circus* (Newcon Press: 2011) and the YA novella *Queen Rat* (Murky Depths, 2012). Her dark fantasy and science fiction short stories have appeared in various magazines and anthologies including *Black Static, Interzone, Celebration, Myth-Understandings, Further Conflicts, Pandemonium: Stories of the Apocalypse, Mammoth Book of Ghost Stories By Women*, and others, with *Johnny and Emmie-Lou Get Married* shortlisted for the BSFA short story award 2009. Kim has a background in performance and is a regular guest speaker at writing workshops and conventions.

Roland Moore has written for film, TV, stage and radio. His credits include the 1950s set science fiction film, *The Survivor* (winner of the Redemptive Storyteller Award), creating and writing the award-winning BBC1 returning period drama series *Land Girls*, and a new full-cast adaptation of *The Mezzotint* (by MR James). He won the London Writers' Award for his comedy drama *Spring Chickens*. His other TV work includes writing for medical dramas, children's shows and several high-profile sketch shows on British television.

Paul Magrs lives and writes in Manchester. His most recent novels are *Enter Wildthyme* and *Brenda and Effie Forever!* (Snowbooks) and *666 Charing Cross Road* (Headline).

Juliet E. McKenna has always been fascinated by myth and history, other worlds and other peoples. After studying Classics at Oxford she worked in personnel management before combining motherhood with book-selling. Since her debut novel, *The Thief's Gamble,* was published in 1999, she has written a dozen epic fantasy novels, most recently *The Chronicles of the Lescari Revolution*, plus assorted and diverse shorter fiction. She reviews for web and print magazines, teaches creative writing and fits all this around her husband and teenage sons. Living in West Oxfordshire, she's currently working on a new fantasy trilogy *The Hadrumal Crisis*.

Adam Roberts was born two thirds of the way through the last century in London, and still lives there, or thereabouts. He is the author of a number of SF novels and stories, some of them pseudo-Victorian in style, and is also Professor of Nineteenth Century Literature and Culture at Royal Holloway, University of London. His most recent novel is called *Jack Glass* (Gollancz 2012).

Philip Palmer is the author of five 'new pulp' science fiction novels published by Orbit books: *Debatable Space, Red Claw, Version 43, Hell Ship* and *Artemis*. He is also an experienced screenwriter and radio dramatist, and his previous work ranges from historical (*The King's Coiner*) to contemporary political (*Breaking Point, Blame, Red and Blue*) to epic literary fantasy (his adaptation of Spenser's *The Faerie Queene*). For TV he's written the single film *The Many Lives of Albert Walker*, as well as TV series episodes of *Rebus, Heartbeat* and *The Bill*. His movie credits include *Arritmia*.

Bruce Taylor, aka. "Mr. Magic Realism", writes magic realism. He has nine books published. A collection (*Alembical*) with his novella, *Thirteen Miles to Paradise*, received a starred review in Publishers Weekly. *Kafka's Uncle and other Strange Tales* was nominated for the &NOW Award for Innovative Writing (SUNY, NY). Other titles are *Edward: Dancing on the Edge of Infinity, Magic of Wild Places* and (with Brian Herbert) *Stormworld*.

With Elton Elliott, he co-edited *Like Water for Quarks*, an anthology about the blending of magic realism and science fiction. Living in Seattle, he has a smashing view of Mt. Rainier. His website is: www.brucebtaylor.com.

Brian Herbert is the New York Times bestselling author of nearly 30 books, including *Man of Two Worlds* with his father Frank Herbert, and the ongoing *Dune* saga novels, including *House Atreides* and *The Butlerian Jihad*, which he co-writes with Kevin J. Anderson. In 2003 he wrote the official biography of his father titled *Dreamer of Dune* and is currently writing a new science fiction trilogy with regular collaborator Kevin J. Anderson called the *Hellhole* series.

Scott Harrison is a scriptwriter and novelist whose stage plays have been produced in both the US and UK. He has written audio plays for a number of Big Finish ranges, including *The Confessions of Dorian Gray* and *Blake's 7: The Liberator Chronicles,* and his novel *Archangel* is the second book to be published in their new Blake's 7 novel range. His comic book scripts and short stories have appeared in a variety of anthologies, including *Into The Woods: A Fairytale Anthology* and *Faction Paradox: A Romance in Twelve Parts*. As editor he has worked on a charity eBook anthology for Great Ormond Street Hospital and is range editor for the Modern Masters Of Audio series.

He lives on the edge of werewolf country with his wife and a stack of books he will never get around to reading.